CRYSTAL LAKE PUBLIC LIBRARY

SO-BFB-666

FEB   2011

WITHDRAWN

His, Unexpectedly

w7/12
w2/14

PROPERTY OF CLPL

His, Unexpectedly

SUSAN FOX

BRAVA

KENSINGTON PUBLISHING CORP.
www.kensingtonbooks.com

BRAVA BOOKS are published by

Kensington Publishing Corp.
119 West 40th Street
New York, NY 10018

Copyright © 2011 Susan Lyons

All rights reserved. No part of this book may be reproduced in any form or by any means without the prior written consent of the Publisher, excepting brief quotes used in reviews.

All Kensington titles, imprints, and distributed lines are available at special quantity discounts for bulk purchases for sales promotion, premiums, fund-raising, educational, or institutional use.

Special book excerpts or customized printings can also be created to fit specific needs. For details, write or phone the office of the Kensington Special Sales Manager: Kensington Publishing Corp., 119 West 40th Street, New York, NY 10018. Attn. Special Sales Department. Phone: 1-800-221-2647.

Brava and the B logo are Reg. U.S. Pat. & TM Off.

ISBN-13: 978-0-7582-5929-5
ISBN-10: 0-7582-5929-8

First Kensington Trade Paperback Printing: February 2011

10 9 8 7 6 5 4 3 2 1

Printed in the United States of America

Chapter 1

What a fabulously perfect June morning: a stretch of coastal California highway unfurling like silver ribbon ahead of me, the top down on my old MGB, a sun visor shielding my eyes, the ocean breeze cooling my cheeks.

Open roads meant possibilities. What was around the next curve? A sliver of white sand beach, a field of bright orange California poppies or one of grape vines, a hawk drifting high in a clear blue sky?

Or, to be practical for once, a gas station. Mellow Yellow was running on fumes.

Yeah, I'd named the butter-yellow convertible I'd bought when I was eighteen. My mom used to play the old Donovan song when my sisters and I were little, and we all sang the chorus. Little known fact about Mom: though she was now one of Canada's top legal eagles, she used to play sixties music with her kids. Given what she was like now—so f'ing serious all the time—I had trouble believing it myself.

Reality check. On the plus side, the open road. On the less plus, the end of that road, the house where I'd grown up, in Vancouver, British Columbia. I only made it back there once or twice a year. Same with my two older sisters; my family loved better at a distance. But this time we had no choice. Our baby sis was getting married.

When I arrived, it'd be same-old, same-old.

Jenna, we can't believe you're still driving that old clunker. Tell us you didn't pick up any hitchhikers along the way. That'd be my parents. Born to worry, not to mention criticize.

You certainly took your sweet time getting here. Thank heavens we weren't actually counting on you to do anything for the wedding. My two older sisters, Theresa and Kat, were know-it-alls. Not that either of them really wanted my help anyhow.

As for Merilee, I could almost hear her squeal from here. *Jenna, I knew you'd make it home for my wedding!* But there'd be relief in her voice, because she really hadn't been so sure.

Yeah, the whole gang would be at the house. Including good old Matt, Merilee's fiancé, and—surprise, surprise—a couple of additions. It seemed Tree and Kat were bringing dates to the wedding. Knowing both of them, that had to mean they were serious about these guys.

Oh man, was I dying of curiosity. Not that I wanted the same for myself. For me, single was perfect. There were too many fun, interesting, sexy men out there to settle for just one. Besides, I'd learned my lesson at seventeen. Falling in love shot my judgment all to hell. It made me stupid. And that stupidity had cost me my dearest dream.

When I caught myself stroking my barren belly, I jerked my hand back to the steering wheel and tossed my head. The past was the past. I was almost thirty now and my life was amazing. My family'd never understand me, but—I grinned smugly at the sight of a gas station ahead—the universe approved. It provided pretty much everything I needed at just about the right time.

I pulled up to a pump and got the gas flowing. Waiting, I

stretched, enjoying the sun on my skin. I took off my visor and ran my fingers through hopelessly tangled curls, then hiked my patchwork tote onto my shoulder and went inside to pay.

My wallet was stuffed with bills, mostly tips from waitressing gigs in Santa Cruz, where I'd been living for the last couple of months. That was my travel money, together with what I made from selling my used surfboard.

A quick trip to the ladies' room, a fresh application of sunscreen, a refill of my stainless steel water bottle from the tap, and I was ready to hit the road again. Unfortunately, when I turned the key in the ignition, Mellow Yellow didn't share my mood. Not a thing happened.

"Please, please," I pleaded, trying again. "Come on, don't do this to me." A woman filling up at the next pump sent me a sympathetic smile.

"The joys of owning an old car," I said, climbing out again and glancing around.

The older style station had an adjoining set of service bays, so I headed over. The doors were open, revealing an ancient truck in one bay and a modern SUV in the other, but I didn't see any sign of life. "Anyone around?" I called.

An overall-clad man—fiftyish, with a balding head and full mustache—emerged from an adjoining room. "Hey, there. Help you?"

I read the name tag on his pocket and smiled at him. "Hi, Neal, I'm Jenna. Sure hope you can. My car's dead at the pump."

"Okay, Jenna, let's have a look."

When we walked outside, he grinned. "Hey, a classic B. Nice."

"Yeah, sweet. When it starts."

After five minutes of cranking it over and peering under the hood, he raised soft brown eyes to me. " 'Fraid your alternator's shot. Gonna need a new one."

I groaned. "How long and how much?"

"Have to get one from San Francisco or farther afield. Run you a couple hundred, prob'ly, unless I find a rebuilt. Then you got two, three hours labor."

Shit, shit, shit! I'd scraped up gas money for the drive home, but fixing the car would take almost all of it, and I didn't have a credit card.

"Want me to locate the part, get you the price?"

"I'd appreciate that."

"Sure. Likely take half an hour." He tipped his cap back and scratched his forehead. "Diner down the road, Marianne's, has good coffee and home cooking."

"Thanks."

I wandered in the direction he indicated. Though I didn't have money for restaurant food, I needed a place to wait. And to ponder what to do next.

Leave the car with Neal and spend my gas money on a bus trip home? Get the car fixed and hope the universe would rain money on me? Or, option three: phone home. My parents, Tree, and Kat had all volunteered to pay for plane fare, but I was independent. If I called . . . well, that expression *No questions asked* wouldn't apply. They'd want to know how I'd screwed up this time.

Organization, planning, contingency plans—all that stuff was their shtick, not mine. And vastly overrated. I loved being a free spirit.

A Volkswagen Westfalia camper passed me and turned into a parking lot. I'd reached the diner Neal had recommended, a cute building with white paint and blue shutters. A half dozen cars and a couple of trucker rigs sat in the parking lot. The camper pulled into an empty spot on the far side, under the sparse shade of a palm tree.

The driver's door opened and a man jumped out, a magazine in one hand, then headed toward the diner. Hmm, not bad at all. Loose sage-green tank top and khaki cargo shorts, longish medium brown hair, and lots of brown skin over nicely muscled arms and legs.

My gaze sharpened with interest. I'd done a lot of surfing in Santa Cruz, when I wasn't working on a peregrine falcon survey or waitressing, and had scoped out lots of excellent bods. This one, at least from the back, was right up there. He might even top Carlos, the Mexican surfer-dude I'd hooked up with until a couple of weeks ago.

I wandered past the camper. It was pretty beat-up, covered with save-the-environment stickers, and had a British Columbia license plate.

Hmm. The universe might not have rained cash, but maybe it had sent a different solution to my dilemma. Maybe it had rained me down a ride and a sexy chauffeur.

Mark Chambers closed the door of Marianne's Diner and glanced back through the paned window. The woman he'd passed as he turned into the parking lot was walking toward the building.

Sunshine backlit her so he couldn't make out her features, but saw a dazzling halo of white-gold curls, a slim silhouette, and a long, loose skirt that was so filmy the sunshine cut straight through it, outlining her long legs. All the way to the apex, where the breeze plastered the fabric against her thighs and the sweet triangle between them.

Lust rippled though him, thickening his blood, shocking him. He didn't make a habit of lusting after strangers—usually he was so caught up in work he barely noticed women—but the picture she made was strikingly erotic. And it was . . . hmm. Months since he'd had sex, now that he came to think about it.

"Good afternoon," a voice behind him said, and he swung away from the door.

Behind the restaurant counter, a middle-aged African-American woman with short, curly hair and round cheeks smiled at him. "Take a seat wherever you like."

The place, a renovated fifties-sixties diner, was maybe half full, all the patrons seated in booths or at tables. He chose a bar stool and dropped his reading material, the latest issue of the *Journal of Experimental Marine Biology and Ecology*, on the blue Formica counter. "Thanks. Could I get a coffee and a menu?"

"You bet." She poured a mug of coffee and handed it to him along with a plastic menu. "The fruit pies are great if you're in the mood for something sweet."

For him, things fell into one of two categories: those to be taken seriously and those that weren't worth paying attention to. Food fell in the latter category.

Coffee, though . . . He lifted the mug to his lips and sniffed. Mmm. Rich, robust, not acidic.

He should have asked if the beans were fair trade, but he doubted the answer would be yes, and he needed coffee. Every man was entitled to one indulgence. Though, to be strictly accurate, as he tried to be, it was more of an addiction. Even if the stuff was poorly made, as was so often the case, he'd still drink it. Now, he savored the scent a moment longer, then lifted the mug to his lips and took a sip.

Well, now. Another sip, to confirm his first impression. "This is excellent," he told the woman approvingly. If you were going to do a job, you should do it well.

Behind his back, the diner door opened and closed. It'd be the blonde. And it would be rude to swing around and look.

"Thanks," the woman behind the counter said. "You should try the fresh strawberry pie."

"Strawberry pie?" The feminine voice from behind him was light, eager, like a kid who'd been offered a present.

A moment later, she slid onto the stool beside him, and this time he did look.

She was stunning in a totally natural way. Her face was heart-shaped, fine-boned, glowing with a golden tan and a flush of sun across her cheeks and nose. A tangled mass of white gold ringlets tumbled over her shoulders, half hiding a scattering of colorful butterflies tattooed on her upper arm and shoulder.

Then he gazed at her eyes, and oh, man. They were the dazzling mixed blue-greens of the Caribbean, and he was diving in, losing himself in their depths.

Vaguely he was aware of the diner woman saying, "So you'll have the strawberry pie, miss?"

He blinked and dragged himself back before he drowned.

The blonde's delicate tongue-tip came out and flicked naturally pink lips, and again lust slammed through him. She shook her head and said wistfully, "Just a chamomile tea, thanks. So, are you Marianne?"

"That's right, hon. This is my place. One chamomile coming up."

Chamomile tea? That jarred him out of his reverie. Might as well drink lawn clippings in hot water; it'd taste as good. Alicia, his biological mother, had been big on the stuff. And why didn't the blonde order the pie she'd sounded so enthusiastic about? Was she one of those constant dieters?

She sure didn't need to be. He'd seen her legs through that filmy flower-patterned blue skirt. Above it, her faded blue tank top revealed toned shoulders and arms. Full little breasts, unconfined by a bra.

Pink-tipped nipples. Not brown. Somehow, he knew that.

Shit, what was wrong with him?

Besides a growing erection that made him glad his cargo shorts were loose and his tank untucked. He'd been in tropical places where women walked around almost naked and not had so strong a reaction. Okay, he was a man of science. He could analyze this phenomenon logically. It was a simple combination of a bodily need that had gone too long unsatisfied and a woman who was a lovely physical specimen. Perfectly understandable, even if disconcerting.

When he returned his gaze to her face, she urged, "Have the pie." Ocean-colored eyes dancing, she added, "Maybe if I'm really, really nice to you, you'll let me have a taste." Her tongue flicked out again.

Blood rushed to his groin as he imagined that pink tongue lapping his shaft. The blonde would be appalled if she had any idea what he was thinking.

Unless . . . His friend and colleague Adrienne—whom he'd known since grad school—said women found him attractive, though he never noticed it himself. The blonde couldn't be flirting, could she? No. No possible way. She could have any man she wanted, so why would she want a science geek like him?

The diner woman put a small china teapot and a mug in front of her and she said, "Thanks, Marianne."

"I'll have the pie," he choked out.

"Sure you will," Marianne said with a knowing grin. She glanced at the blonde. "Whipped cream?"

"Is there any other way?"

He imagined the blonde painting his cock in whipped cream and licking it all off, and wanted to bury his face in his hands and groan. Since he'd first seen her, he'd been . . . bewitched. Except, there was no such thing as bewitchment in scientific reality. This was very unsettling. He rather desperately fingered the scientific journal he'd brought in with him. If he buried himself in its pages, he'd be on safe ground.

"You'd rather read than talk to me?" she teased. "My feelings are hurt."

"Uh . . ." He glanced back at her.

Her impish grin revealed perfect white teeth. "If we're going to share . . ." She paused.

He held his breath. Share? What man wouldn't want to share any damned thing with this woman?

"Pie," she finished, "I figure we should introduce ourselves." She held out a slim hand with short, unpainted nails and several unusual rings. "Jenna Fallon."

"Mark Chambers." He took her hand warily. Sure enough, when she shook firmly, he felt a sexy sensation. A cross between a glow and a tingle spread up his arm. He hurriedly let go, picked up his coffee mug, and took a sip, trying to regain his equilibrium. "You live around here, Jenna?" Likely so, since she'd been on foot.

She shook her head, curls dancing, revealing a couple of simple stud earrings in each ear, then settling. "I'm from Canada. Been living in Santa Cruz, working on a peregrine falcon survey that's run out of UC Santa Cruz."

"Great," he said with relief. She was into the environment like him. A colleague, not a woman. Well, of course she was a woman, but he was okay when he dealt with them as colleagues. He was actually okay in bed, too; sex was one of the activities that deserved to be done well, and his partners always seemed happy. It was the in-between stuff, the social part, that gave him problems.

Carefully, she poured a disgustingly weak greenish brew from the pot into her mug, sipped, and smiled. Eyes bright, she said, "It's part of a really successful conservation project. Did you know the falcons are an endangered species in California? In 1970, they only found two nesting pairs. Now, after a captive breeding program, there are over two hundred and fifty."

On firm conversational ground now, he said, "Yeah, the DDT and other pesticides almost did them in. Thank God those have been banned, and the captive breeding programs worked." He studied her. "Bet it was a challenge to track them down. They have a habit of nesting in remote areas."

When her eyes widened in surprise, he said, "I'm a marine biologist, and I've learned a fair bit about marine birds.

Oddly enough, I've been in Santa Cruz too. Working on a research project at UCSC's Long Marine Lab."

"Seriously? Isn't this wild? We never met in Santa Cruz, yet we both happen to walk into Marianne's Diner at the same moment." She grinned. "The universe is pretty amazing."

"Yes, it is." A place of science and of still-to-be understood mysteries. A place mankind seemed hell-bent on destroying. He knew people often found him rigid, but he had no patience for those who didn't give a damn about this incredible world.

Marianne refilled his coffee and put a plate in front of him. He barely glanced at it, except to note two forks, until Jenna enthused, "Now, that's a work of art."

He took another look. Flaky-looking crust, plump red strawberries suspended in glaze, a mound of whipped cream. Not bad at all.

Jenna told the other woman, "Neal at the service station sent me your way, and I'm sure glad." She picked up a fork, then gazed up at Mark with wide, expectant eyes.

How could he say no to those eyes? "Go ahead. I have a feeling I'd have trouble stopping you." He only spoke the truth, but she grinned as if he'd said something amusing.

She carved off a sizable chunk—an entire, huge berry, a portion of crust, and a hefty dollop of cream, and opened those pink lips wide to take it in. Her eyes slid shut, and she tilted her head back, humming approval as she chewed, taking forever to consume that one bite. The sounds she made and the blissful expression on her face reminded him of slow, very satisfying lovemaking.

His cock throbbed and he swallowed hard, wanting what she was having.

Finally she opened her eyes and beamed at Marianne. "Perfection." Then she frowned down at the plate and up at Mark. "Aren't you having any?"

Pie, she meant pie. "I was . . ." *Watching you get orgasmic.* "Uh, waiting for you to taste-test."

"It's delicious." She dug in her fork again. "Here."

Next thing he knew, that laden fork was in front of his lips. Startled, he opened and let her slide the hefty bite into his mouth.

"Close your eyes," she said. "Things taste better that way."

Yeah, if he kept staring at her beautiful, animated face, he wouldn't taste a thing, so he obeyed even though he felt weirdly vulnerable about shutting his eyes while she gazed so expectantly at him.

Normally, when he ate, his mind was on work not on food, but now he concentrated as he chewed. Ripe, juicy fruit, the sweetness of the glaze, a rich, buttery taste to the pastry, and unsweetened cream with a hint of vanilla. Each flavor was distinct and the way they blended together was . . . perfect.

If all food tasted this good, he'd get as addicted as he was to coffee.

He finished the bite and opened his eyes. "She's right," he told Marianne. "That's the best pie I've ever had."

"Glad you like it," the woman said, grinning as if she was enjoying a private joke, then turned to deal with new customers.

He turned to Jenna, who held her empty fork poised. "Go on," he said, "we'll share."

"Thanks." Speedily, she prepared another forkful and stuck it in her mouth.

It was as pleasurable watching her savor the food as eating it himself. All the same, he plied his own fork and matched her bite for bite as they finished the pie. When all that remained was a streak of scarlet on the plate, he said, "Not that I mind sharing, but it seems to me you were hungry enough to order a piece of your own."

"It has nothing to do with hunger," she said wryly, "and everything to do with finances."

Huh? She couldn't afford a piece of pie?

"I'll order you another piece," he said quickly. "Or a sandwich. Whatever you want."

"You're totally sweet, but I'm not starving to death. Just watching my pennies. Speaking of pennies, though . . ." She flicked her head so her pale gold curls shimmered. "Are you just out for a day's drive or are you actually heading somewhere?"

"Vancouver. The Canadian one," he added so she'd know he didn't mean the one in Washington State. He lifted his mug for another swallow of coffee.

"Yeah? As it happens, so am I."

She slanted her body to one side, raised a slim, bare arm, and cocked her thumb in classic hitchhiker body language. "Got room for one more? I'll split you on the gas."

He almost spewed coffee. "You want a ride to Vancouver? You're *hitchhiking* to Vancouver?"

She made a face. "Dude, you sound like my parents. No, I'm not *hitchhiking*. I'm asking you for a ride." A mischievous grin lit her face. "Of course if you say no, I guess I'll be forced to stick my thumb out at the side of the road. And you know, it's dangerous out there for a girl on her own. Never know what might happen. You don't want that on your conscience, do you?" Her teasing tone told him she wasn't serious.

But he was. He was always serious. And it *was* dangerous out there. Surely she wouldn't really hitchhike. "How did you get this far?"

She picked up her mug. "By car. But the alternator packed it in back at the service station, and I'm stranded."

"So, get it fixed," he started, then paused. "Oh. If your finances don't run to pie . . ."

She nodded. "Exactly."

"Put it on a charge card." He wasn't a fan of running up credit, but that had to be better than hitching or bumming a ride with a stranger like him. Not that he wasn't boringly trustworthy, but Jenna had no way of knowing it.

"No charge card," she said airily. "I don't believe in them. If I don't have the money to pay for something, I don't need it."

A good philosophy. And yet she believed in taking rides from strangers. This was one of the oddest women he'd met in a long time. Along with being the hottest and most bewitching.

"How do you know I'm not a serial killer?" he asked.

She grinned. "Serial killers don't share pie with their victims."

He frowned at her frivolity. "You just met me."

"Your camper's awfully cute." She flicked her head in the direction of the parking lot.

He had to admit the Westfalia with all its environmental stickers looked pretty innocent. All the same, "Ted Bundy wore a cast and looked like the boy next door."

She gave a long-suffering sigh. "Yeah, I'd probably have fallen victim to Ted Bundy. So, you're telling me you are a serial killer? A serial killer who reads the *Journal of Experimental Marine Biology and Ecology?*"

He snorted. "Of course not."

Her eyes twinkled. "So we're good, right?"

She was incorrigible and she'd bedazzled him. Suddenly doubting his own judgment, he asked, "How do I know *you're* not a serial killer?"

She chuckled. "Good one. Just when I was thinking you were too stuffy for words."

He was. Again, she'd misinterpreted his serious question as a joke. Or was she avoiding answering? "Are you insulting me so I won't notice you didn't answer the question."

Another chuckle. Dancing eyes. "A sense of humor, and smart too. As well as having a great bod."

Huh? Yeah, he was smart, but he didn't have a sense of humor and his body was . . . functional. And, at the moment, lustful. He glanced down, hoping his clothes camouflaged his erection. She'd been checking out his body? Or maybe she really was a criminal and this was another tactic to put him off guard.

Jenna turned to Marianne, who'd returned with the coffee pot. "Marianne, what's your opinion? Do I look like a serial killer to you?"

The older woman chuckled. "Honey, if you do that boy in, I don't think it'll be with a knife."

"Not all serial killers use knives," he pointed out. The statistical odds were against the pretty blonde being a killer, but all the same . . . "And, though most serial killers are male, there have been a few female ones." The thought crossed his mind that if he fell victim to Jenna Fallon, he well might die with a smile on his face.

Chapter 2

I grinned as Mark spoke. Marianne's sexual innuendo had whooshed straight over his head, and so had my flirting.

What was up with this guy? He wasn't gay, and he wasn't oblivious. The hefty bulge under the bottom of his loose tank top, one that wasn't a natural drape of the fabric, told me that. It also made my whole bod hum with sexual awareness and need.

The man just seemed to take everything dead seriously. Like with his current discourse on serial killers and their M.O.s.

His low, husky voice would've suited a rock singer better than a scientist, and his lean, toned body, tantalizingly revealed by the sleeveless top and shorts, was that of a natural athlete. His face was lean too, angular, masculine and arresting. His summer blue eyes were piercing, especially in contrast to his tan. Mom would've said he was months overdue on a haircut, but I liked long hair. His, the mixed brown shades of nutmeg, was casually tousled, softening the almost harsh lines of his face.

Oh yeah, Mark Chambers was hot. Yet, he didn't seem aware of it, or maybe he didn't care. Over the years, I'd

known all sorts of guys—yeah, often in the biblical sense—
and this one confused me.

But in a good way. He was intriguing. A challenge. Like,
he was obviously turned on, but he'd rather talk about falcons or serial killer statistics than flirt. And, oddly, he was
kind of sexy when he lectured in that rough voice more
suited to a concert stage than a classroom.

"Female serial killers usually kill for personal gain," he
went on, "not the thrill of killing, and their victims are people they know rather than, as with Bundy, total strangers."

"So you're safe," I joked. "You're almost a stranger. But,
hmm, you do have that cute camper, and I do need a ride.
Would it count as personal gain if I bumped you off and
stole your camper?"

"That's an awfully minor personal gain." His tone was
still serious. "Usually, it's a more significant financial or material gain." He went on to give examples.

"Hmm," I teased. "You've made a real study of this. I
think you're a serial killer groupie."

He shook his head. "I read a lot, and things stick."

An academic, like my dad and oldest sister. They'd probably get along.

Bizarre thought, that I'd be attracted to a man my family
might approve of.

As a little kid, I'd craved my parents' approval, but to get
it I'd have had to warp my natural instincts and become the
perfect daughter like my two older sisters. Nope, not happening. So I became a "take it or leave it" person: *This is
who I am. Take it or leave it.* That was the great thing about
being a grown-up. You got to decide for yourself who you
wanted to be.

As for Mark, I hoped he'd realize the universe had put us
together for a reason, and he'd take me. To Vancouver—and
who knew what sexy mischief we might get up to along the
way. Mmm, I did love possibilities.

Marianne brought us our bills, and I paid her and included a good tip. Mark dragged a battered brown leather wallet from his pocket. He, too, tipped generously, I was glad to see. I hated bad tippers.

"Fabulous pie, Marianne," I told her. "If I'm ever back this way, you bet I'm stopping in."

"Come in August. I've got peach then."

"It's a date." I blew her a kiss.

"Don't you just love her?" I asked Mark as we climbed off our stools.

He frowned. "Uh . . ."

"So, what about it? Am I thumbing, or are you going to help a girl out?" He'd left the journal with the eye-glazing title lying on the counter, so I grabbed it and handed it to him, letting our hands brush. Sexual awareness pricked my skin and tingled through me.

He glanced down, staring at his hand and the magazine as if he didn't recognize them. "Uh, thanks." Then his gaze lifted to my face and he frowned. "You wouldn't really hitchhike?"

I sighed, following him to the door. "I might get the car fixed then see how far I get on the gas money that's left. The mechanic is checking things out and doing an estimate."

"Then let's go see what he says." He opened the door.

We walked over to the camper, where he unlocked the passenger door. "Ooh, taking a risk," I teased. "Or do the stats say a female serial killer never strikes within the first mile?"

"I don't recall any statistics on—"

"Mark! Joking?"

"Oh, right. I knew that."

He so obviously hadn't. The man was pretty damned adorable. I climbed in, swiveling to look in the back as Mark got into the driver's seat. "Totally cute." It was like a tidy dollhouse. Table and bench seat, sink, mini fridge, and stove top. I guessed the seat would make into a bed.

One bed. A double. Nice and cozy for two people.

As Mark started the Westfalia and drove onto the road, I gazed appreciatively at his muscular, tanned thighs, his lean, strong shoulders and arms, the well-shaped hands on the steering wheel. Hot bod, great face. Smart, serious, intriguing. A tingly shiver of anticipation rippled through me. Would he ever loosen up enough to have fun?

He pulled into the service station.

"That's my car." I pointed to Mellow Yellow, which had been moved from the pump to a corner of the parking lot.

The corner of his mouth twitched then straightened as he parked beside it. "How old's that thing?"

"It's a 1974."

"Older than you by a fair bit."

"Yeah." This year, I'd turn thirty, which probably made me a few years younger than him. "First car I got, and we suit each other." I poked his forearm, appreciating his warm skin and the solid muscle below. "You're not exactly driving the latest in wheels yourself."

"It serves its purpose." He swung out of the camper and, in long, loose strides, headed toward the service bays.

I scrambled to catch up. The mechanic I'd spoken to earlier was pumping an SUV up on a hoist. "Hey, Neal."

"Hey, Jenna."

Mark, eyebrows raised, glanced between us, maybe wondering at our informality. I got the feeling he wasn't as much a people person as I was. Pity. Life was so limited when you hung back and didn't share it with others.

"Neal, this is Mark. A friend." Of course he was. He'd shared his pie, even if I hadn't given him much choice.

The two men nodded at each other, then I asked Neal, "How's it looking?"

He stripped off a work glove and ran a hand over his bald

head. "Found a rebuilt alternator in San Francisco. If you give the go-ahead, they'll send it out. Today's Friday, it won't get here until tomorrow. We're booked up for Saturday already. Usually take Sundays off, but if you're in a hurry I could work on your MGB then."

"You're the sweetest. What would it cost?"

"You'd be looking at around three hundred."

I grimaced. "Ouch." That'd burn through my gas money.

"Sorry," he said sympathetically.

"I hate to ask you to work Sunday, but if you did, when would the car be ready?"

"Late Sunday afternoon."

I thought it through. Assuming for the moment the universe might actually shower money . . . "Best case scenario, I'd get home Wednesday." My family'd be pissed. "The rehearsal and dinner are Friday, and the wedding's Saturday."

"You getting married next weekend?" Neal asked, at the same time Mark said, "You're getting married?"

Their stunned expressions made me laugh. "Not me. My baby sis." Definitely not me. Being tied to one man in a stifling, paternalistic institution that subjugated women and discriminated against gays? No f'ing way. But M was a traditional girl and knew what she wanted, and her fiancé Matt was a sweetie. They'd been M&M since grade two.

She'd popped the news only a week ago, calling to say she and Matt were getting married in two weeks rather than next summer. Tree, Kat, and I—known in the family as the three-pack—had said we'd help organize the wedding.

I knew no one was counting on me, but it'd be nice, for once, not to live up to their low expectations. Okay, so maybe I hadn't entirely gotten over craving family approval. So long as I could get it for being me, not warping myself into the hopelessly boring woman they wanted me to be.

If I went with Mark, the sexy guy with the one-bed camper, I'd be home by Sunday night or Monday. Just as I'd estimated when I e-mailed this morning to say I was on my way.

It was the responsible thing to do. Hey, look at that, I could be responsible.

I nodded. Yeah, that was obviously what the universe had in mind. I'd have to leave Mellow Yellow. I hadn't planned past the wedding, so clearly it was fated that I was supposed to come back to California.

And fated that I'd travel north with Mark Chambers.

While I'd been deliberating, Mark, tanned, tousled, and serious, had been grilling the mechanic, asking a bunch of logical questions. All of which Neal had good answers for. I broke in. "And now you're reminding me of my mother." A litigator, her conversations were more like cross-examinations.

"Huh?" Mark turned to me, looking puzzled.

"Never mind. Okay, here's what I've decided. I don't have enough money for repairs and gas, and I don't want to be late getting home."

To Neal, I said, "Could I leave the car here for a couple weeks? I'll give you money for the parts." I hated to abandon Mellow Yellow, but I trusted Neal just as I trusted Mark, and my instincts about people were good. At least when I wasn't in love—and I sure wasn't about to fall in love again. Not in this lifetime.

"No need to pay until the job's done." The mechanic grinned. "After all, I got your car as collateral."

"I love you to pieces." I went to hug him.

He, grinning, held his hands out to ward me off. "I'll get grease all over you. Not to mention, my wife'll hear I've been hugging some blonde, and I'll get an earful."

I laughed, then held out my hand, and he matched it with his. We shook firmly, sealing the deal.

Then I turned to Mark. "Decision time for you now. I know from all those stickers on your camper that you're into saving the ocean and the whales and all that stuff. Are you going to save one stranded Canadian?"

Expression a little shell-shocked, he muttered, "Seems I don't have much choice."

"Yes!" I squealed. "Thank you!" I flung my arms around him and squeezed tight. "Ooh, I love you, you're the best." Wow. He was hot, firm, and he smelled like the ocean. I wanted to hang on, but he wasn't hugging me back, just staring down looking as stunned as if a peregrine falcon had perched on his cock.

And Neal was touching my shoulder. "Now wait a minute. I thought you two were friends."

I released Mark, stepped back, and turned to the mechanic. "Yeah, we met at Marianne's."

He frowned at both of us. "Jenna, you can't go off with some strange guy you just met."

"That's what I told her," Mark said, sounding vindicated. He frowned slightly. "Though I wouldn't say I'm strange."

I gave the two of them an evil grin. "Of course, ten percent of serial killers are female." A statistic I totally made up.

Mark scowled. "That's not what I said."

"Serial killers?" Neal said, brows high. "What?"

"Joking." Jeesh, did no one have a sense of humor? "Okay, look, Neal can write down your license plate, Mark, and take our driver's license info. If one of us turns up dead, he'll tell the police who did it." Truth was, I'd have asked Mark for ID anyhow, to back up my gut instinct.

"Let's take a look at that ID," Neal said grudgingly.

But once he'd made a careful examination of the contents of Mark's wallet, he gave a satisfied nod. "Okay, Dr. Chambers."

"I'll go get my stuff," I said, heading toward Mellow Yellow with Mark behind me. He helped me put up the convertible top and roll up the windows, then I made sure the registration was locked in the glove compartment and collected any loose belongings.

He popped the trunk. "That's all your luggage?"

"It's all my worldly possessions, pretty much." I hauled out a backpack, leaving another pack and the small cooler for him.

"Really?" he said incredulously.

"Aside from some old clothes and stuff at my parents' place. I figure if it doesn't fit in my car then I can't need it very much."

When I said stuff like this, a lot of guys—and most women—thought I was nuts. But Mark grinned approval. "I hear you." He slung the backpack strap over one shoulder and hoisted the cooler, muscles rippling in a deliciously effortless way. "What's in this?"

"Cheese and crackers, fruit." I gestured toward the two items that remained in the trunk: a faded sleeping bag and a thin pillow. "Do I need these?" I wouldn't if he shared his bed.

"Uh . . ." He looked at me and a spark of sexual awareness zinged between us. But, as before, he didn't acknowledge it. Instead, he frowned. "Jenna, where were you planning to sleep?"

"Either in the car or on the beach. Maybe a campground."

He shook his head. "D'you have parents?"

I chuckled. "Yeah. And yeah, they'd be on my case. Which is why I generally don't tell them what I'm doing. So, should I bring this stuff?"

"No, I have it covered. The Westfalia's luxurious compared to this." Which could mean that he was anticipating cozying up in bed together—or that he had a spare sleeping bag. Of all the guys I'd ever met, he was the hardest to read. And totally intriguing.

When I gave Neal my keys, he handed me his card. "Call me or drop me an e-mail in a few days. And tell your sis, best wishes."

"Thanks." I planted a kiss on his cheek. "You're the best." Once again, the universe had provided exactly the right person at the right time.

Just as it had with Dr. Mark Chambers. The sexy scientist was in for the road trip of a lifetime. And so was I.

I followed him to his camper, admiring his butt and the stretch of his muscles as he slid open the side door. We slung my gear on the floor and I said, "Ready to hit the road?"

This time, he gave a firm nod, like he'd finally got with the program. "Let's do it."

We buckled up, and I smiled. This was intimate, the two of us side by side in this cute little house on wheels. Too bad there wasn't a bench seat rather than two big swivel seats. Even so, we were really going to get to know each other—in many senses of that phrase, I hoped—in the next couple of days.

A few minutes later, the Westfalia was on the coast road heading north.

I rolled down the window and sighed with pleasure. "I love the open road." Possibilities. Not only poppies and beaches now, but maybe smoking hot sex with a man who had the body of a surfer and the mind of a scientist. Totally tantalizing.

"Are you planning on taking the coast road all the way?" I asked.

He'd unrolled his window too. His left arm rested on the window frame and the breeze ruffled his nutmeg-colored hair. "I was. That a problem? You're in a rush, eh?"

"Not enough of a rush for I-5."

"Good. I hate freeways. Avoid them like the plague."

"Me, too. They're soul-destroying. Country roads are better."

He smiled over at me. "Always. Especially if they're by the ocean."

"You said you're a marine biologist." I tilted the seat back a notch and got comfortable. Getting to know people—especially sexy guys—was one of my favorite things in the world. "Is that because you love the ocean?"

"Yeah."

I waited. When he didn't go on, I prompted, "Tell me more. How did you come to love the ocean? Did you grow up by it?"

"No. Inland, in Oregon."

Born an American, but now he drove a camper with a British Columbia plate and had a B.C. driver's license. So many things to learn about him. Some men were in love with talking about themselves, and others needed to be drawn out. Give Mark a scientific topic, and I'd bet he could go on forever, but I was going to have to work to learn his life story.

"When did you first see the ocean?" I asked.

"When I was five."

"It's like pulling teeth," I teased. "Come on, Mark, tell me more."

"Uh, why do you want to know?"

"Because I'm interested. It's called *conversation.*"

He glanced at me quizzically, as if I were speaking a foreign language, then again focused on the road ahead.

"We're going to be in this camper for a lot of hours," I said, "so let's get to know each other. Now, think back to your first visit to the ocean and tell me about it."

My strategy worked. A moment later a smile touched his mouth. "We all went to the coast, and it was incredible. Awe-inspiring, yet I felt like I belonged there."

"Maybe in a past life you were a sailor."

"Tell me you don't believe in past lives."

"I dunno. I keep an open mind. Anything's possible, right?"

"Anything? I don't think so. Some things are too far-fetched."

"In your humble opinion," I teased. "Look out there." I gestured out the window at the ocean. "Once, the scientists of the day scoffed at the far-fetched notion that the earth was round. They used to think if you sailed too far, you'd fall of the edge."

"Hmm. You have a point."

I leaned over to squeeze his bare forearm gently. "I know you scientists hate admitting you don't know everything." But he'd conceded my point, which impressed me. I let my hand linger, savoring the warmth of his skin, the subtle flex of muscles, before I sat back in my seat. I hoped he was feeling tingles.

"True." His gaze flicked from the road ahead, down to his arm, then back again.

"And yet, that's what science is about, isn't it? Exploring the unknown."

"In large part, yes." He glanced over again, blue eyes sharp with curiosity. "You're an ornithologist?"

I snorted. I told the man I'd been surveying falcons and he assumed I was an ornithologist? "No way. My dad's the scientist in the family." As dear old Dad would be the first to say, I didn't have the brain or the discipline for it.

"What does he do?"

"He's a geneticist. Researching genetic links for cancer and trying to find a cure."

He nodded approvingly. "Impressive. And your mom?"

"A litigator. On the side of good, not evil. Mostly, she represents plaintiffs in class action suits against big corporations that are doing nasty stuff."

"Good people, your parents. How did you come to choose the environment as your field?"

My field? "Mark, I don't have a field. I'm interested in too many things to settle on one. When something intriguing comes along, I do it." I went wherever the wind, the mood, the next tempting guy or job took me.

"The falcon survey?"

"I was in Santa Cruz and someone mentioned it. It sounded good so I volunteered. I love birds, love being outside." In my own unstructured fashion I was an environmentalist. I felt an affinity for nature that was almost spiritual. Like, it healed wounds and sorrows, and in return I wanted to take care of it. But I loved people, too, so often switched between nature jobs and people jobs. I was versatile, a quick learner; I just couldn't work at anything that required special education or skills, because I didn't have any.

"Besides," I went on, "I liked working irregular hours, having time to surf." In fact, I'd gone to California because of a sexy surfer dude, Carlos. "The survey was perfect." I gave a rueful smile. "Except, of course, for the part about no pay. I supported myself by waitressing."

"Hmm." Just a sound, but one that told me he wasn't impressed. The man was so serious; he probably didn't relate to a free spirit.

I shoved breeze-blown curls off my face and, curious to know more about him, said, "You said, you *all* went to the coast. You mean your family?"

"In the broad sense of the word. I grew up on a commune."

"Ooh! Seriously?" Wide-eyed, I stared at him. "That must have been so much fun. I'm totally jealous."

His mouth twisted. "Too bad we couldn't have traded. I wanted a normal family, a conventional life." He slowed to pass three cyclists. "Which I did eventually get, with my grandparents."

"What happened to your parents?"

He picked up speed, leaving the cyclists behind. Seemed as

if he wasn't going to answer. Was I being too pushy? People usually responded to my friendly curiosity.

Slowly, he said, "There was only Alicia." His tone was cool, distanced. "I was born on the commune and paternity wasn't relevant. People thought monogamy, much less marriage, was archaic."

"Well, yeah. Look at how it originated. Political alliances, property exchanges, possession of a woman and kids. Women needing some strong guy to protect them and their babies. None of that stuff's relevant anymore."

Wryly, he said, "At least that's a logical argument."

"At least? Meaning you don't agree?"

"I agree marriage is pretty archaic. But I'm not sure most people are evolved enough to handle jealousy and unstructured relationships."

I grinned to myself. I loved unstructured relationships and didn't have a jealous bone in my body. Well, maybe toward my sisters, but not when it came to guys. Nice to know I was so highly evolved. "How did things work on the commune?"

He snorted. "Poorly. Freedom Valley wasn't exactly organized around a philosophy—except hedonism."

"There's nothing wrong with pleasure."

"Depends where it comes from."

I reflected. "Like, no one should take pleasure from hurting someone else. Or harming the environment."

He nodded strongly. "Agreed. But lack of knowledge, disregard, and the wrong priorities create as dangerous results. Take your falcons. They wouldn't have become endangered if it wasn't for pesticides. At first, no one really understood the impact of pesticides on the environment, then for a long time economic interests outweighed environmental ones. Until people realized that destroying the environment didn't make economic sense." He went on, and I listened intently.

Later, I'd ask again about life on the commune. For now,

he was talking about something interesting and, even better, the passion in his husky voice, the animation on his face, the way he gestured as he spouted off in scientist mode were pretty damned sexy.

Mark glanced over at Jenna, aware he'd switched from conversation to lecturing. Discoursing on science was effortless; discussing philosophy—like the sociological pros and cons of the institution of marriage—was interesting; but talking about himself was uncomfortable. Not because he had any deep, dark secrets, but because he so rarely did it.

Usually, he interacted with people through work. He was the team leader or the expert consultant. When the others hung out at the end of the day sharing a meal, having a few drinks, chatting, he either retreated to bury himself in work or took a seat in a back corner and kept quiet.

Let's face it, aside from his work, he was one of the most boring guys alive.

His lovers had always been colleagues and they'd mostly talked about the project they were working on.

Jenna was gazing at him with apparent interest, but probably she was only being polite. Yeah, here he was with a beautiful woman and he was boring her to tears. He should shut up now.

No, he had a better idea. They were coming into Fort Bragg, and there was a spot here that fascinated him, one she might enjoy. It would throw them off schedule, but not by a lot. "Have you ever been to Glass Beach?"

"No. What's that?"

"It used to be a dump. People heaved all kinds of garbage on it, including lots of glass. Finally the town wised up and tried to clean it up. They got the big stuff, but not all the broken glass. Waves pounded the glass, and now the beach is covered in little colored glass pebbles."

"Cool! Let's go."

Her eager response made him smile. She reminded him of a little girl who was excited about a treat, just as when she'd tackled that strawberry pie. The woman was engaging, no doubt about it, even if she wasn't the intellectual, cause-oriented type of person he usually associated with. Normally, when he drove, he liked being alone with his thoughts, but Jenna made the journey more interesting.

He turned toward the beach. No doubt about it, she'd charmed and bedazzled him. Here he was, holding out the promise of a sparkly beach as if it were a special treat to tempt her.

He parked and before he'd turned off the engine, she jumped out. He locked up, then led her down a dirt path to a cove framed by jagged rocks, where a half dozen people roamed about. Small, white-fringed waves rushed onto shore then retreated, making a low, steady whispering sound. From a distance the beach looked like normal little stones, albeit kind of glittery in the sun, but when you looked closer—

Jenna darted past him. "This is incredible!" A stiff breeze tossed her hair and swirled her skirt around her legs as she bent to scoop up a handful of pebbles.

So beautiful. His cock was hardening again and even his hands ached, wanting to touch her. She'd brushed against him a couple of times. Casually. It had taken all his willpower to shift away rather than pull her into his arms.

She'd said nice things about him, said he had a nice body, but did that mean she was flirting? His friend Adrienne told him she'd never met a man who was so oblivious to being hustled. But how was a guy supposed to know? He sure didn't want to offend Jenna, and—

She darted up to him, beaming and holding out the pebbles she'd gathered. "Mark, they're so beautiful!"

Another man would have said, "No, you're beautiful." Instead, he stared down, trying to regain his composure as he focused on her collection.

He'd visited here before, his scientist's curiosity engaged by the history and the processes that had transformed a dump into this unusual beach. Yet he'd never actually thought about the beauty of the bits of glass. Now, he studied the handful: gleaming and sparkling in the sun, pieces of sea-polished glass mingled with regular beach stones and seashells. Most were clear or white, and there were a few amber bits, some green, and one of vivid blue.

"Cup your hands," she commanded.

When he did, holding them below hers, she gradually let the pebbles trickle between her slender fingers into his cupped palms, sunlight glinting off them as they fell. "There you go. A handful of magic." She curved her own hands around his, her palms and fingers warm against the backs of his hands. "We're holding magic."

His pulse raced. Yes, the bits of glass were pretty and sparkly, but the magic was in the sparks that hummed between her hands and his.

She sighed. "I wish I could take them home. But if everyone did that, there'd be no more beach to enjoy." Her hands moved away from his. "Besides, it wouldn't be right to lock these lovely pebbles up in a glass jar. Set them free, Mark."

Rather than toss them down, he opened his fingers and let them slide through in a slow, light-catching cascade until they were a part of the beach again. The only single one he could identify was the bright blue one, as distinctive as Jenna herself.

"Let's walk," she said, kicking off her sandals.

"Careful, there's still the occasional bit of metal garbage. Don't want to cut your feet."

She gazed at him as if he was crazy. "Mark, you can't wear shoes on a beach on a sunny day."

"I can't?" He would have taken his sandals off—it was her feet he was worried about—but now he was curious to hear what she'd say. "Why not? Is that some kind of rule?"

"Are you a rule follower?" she teased.

"If the rule has a good reason behind it. Otherwise, not so much." He had no qualms about bending or breaking a rule that was senseless or harmful.

"Shoes are disrespectful to the beach," she said promptly. "They can crush seashells. This is an environmentally fragile area. You don't want to damage it."

"Okay, you've convinced me." He bent to pull off his leather sandals. Under the soles of his feet, the pebbles were a bumpy carpet holding the sun's warmth.

Jenna headed toward the edge of the water, leaving her sandals behind. He collected them, along with his own, and followed her. She splashed her toes in the ocean, gave a sigh of pleasure, then began to walk along the edge. He fell in step beside her, the soft fringes of waves rippling around his feet.

"Thanks for bringing me here," she said.

"You're welcome."

They walked in silence for a few minutes. The wind plastered his tank top against his body and ruffled his hair, reminding him he was overdue for a cut. This was rare for him, taking time out to stroll a beach. He felt vaguely guilty at not doing anything productive. On the other hand, what was wrong with simply enjoying the sun, the breeze, the sparkly beach, and, not least, the pretty woman beside him?

"You never said what happened to, uh, Alicia," she said quietly.

"She died when I was nine."

"I'm sorry." Jenna squeezed his forearm gently.

Another simple touch, yet again his body stirred. She was so appealing. Toned and tanned, her pale gold curls drifting in the breeze, the butterflies on her upper arm looking as if they were ready to lift off in flight. Tonight, he wasn't likely to get any sleep in his sleeping bag under the stars, knowing she was curled up in the bed in the camper. Unless, of course—

"How did she die?" Her question interrupted his lustful thoughts.

"She and a couple of others got their hands on some bad drugs." A stupid end to a life that had been pretty much meaningless. Maybe the saddest thing was that he hadn't known his biological mother well enough to truly love her and grieve for her.

"And you were nine with no father. Damn, Mark, that's rough." She linked her arm through his and squeezed it. "What happened then?"

Rational thought deserted him. There was something so potent about Jenna's effect on him. She did these totally innocent things, and lust surged through him. No other woman had ever got to him this way.

It had to be biological. What did attraction studies say? People were drawn to mates based on DNA, in particular the difference in their major histocompatibility complex codes.

"Mark? What happened then?"

"Then . . ." he echoed. What had they been talking about? Oh, yeah. "The leader was one of the people who died. Without a leader, Freedom Valley fell apart. The deaths brought them to the attention of the state, too. Suddenly, officials were interfering, like trying to get kids vaccinated and sent to school."

"You'd been home-schooled?"

He snorted. "You mean, taught how to plant vegetables, harvest marijuana, and read Tarot cards? There wasn't much education happening. Look, I know there were some great communes, but Freedom Valley wasn't one of them." A bunch of drifters, losers, people with no focus in life.

A golden retriever came bounding out of the water in front of them and shook madly, spraying them both. The chilly shower felt good, reminding him of how he and the other kids had run through sprinklers, naked, at the commune.

Jenna laughed, a sound as unrestrained as the dog's gyrations, and droplets of water sparkled on her cheeks. When a woman with a leash came to clip it to the dog's collar and apologize, Jenna said, "No problem. He's a sweetie."

Then, as she and Mark walked on, she said, "So the commune was dissolving and you didn't have any parents?"

It had been a long time since he'd talked about, even thought about, those days. "Kids had been cared for by all the adults. Shared around, you know?" Yeah, there'd been fun like darting through sprinklers, yet he'd longed for a conventional home and a mom who tucked him in every night. "Biological parenthood wasn't important. But when things dissolved, kids and parents got matched up. Two of us were left over."

"You went to Alicia's parents? Did you already know them?"

He shook his head. "She was completely estranged from them. They hated the life she'd chosen. But they took me in."

"Oh Mark, how hard that must have been." She squeezed his arm closer, so it brushed her unconfined breast under her thin top.

His arm tingled and his cock pulsed, distracting him. "Yeah, in the beginning. For all of us."

"Tell me about it."

He stopped walking and she did too, gazing up at him as he said, "Uh, why do you want to know all this stuff?"

A curl blew into her eyes and she flicked it back. They'd left their sunglasses in the camper and the colors and sparkle of her Caribbean eyes put the glass pebbles on the beach to shame. "Because I'm interested in you. I want to get to know you."

To get to know him as a person, not a scientist. This was the social kind of chat he usually avoided except sometimes with his old friend Adrienne. Yet there was something about Jenna, this day, this beach that made him want to open up.

He cleared his throat and they started to walk again, still arm in arm. "It was hard on my grandparents. Alicia was an only child and they didn't want me to turn out like her. They said she'd ruined her life, so they must have done something wrong. They're disciplined, well-educated people and they cracked down on me right from the start. Order, structure, rules—man, they had all of it. They said they mustn't have been strict enough with Alicia."

"Wow, that must have been hard on you. Going from a commune to an environment like that."

"At first. But after a few struggles, I saw the benefit. For the first time in my life, I knew what I was supposed to do, and what I wasn't, and that there'd be consequences. My actions brought about consequences, good or bad. It was a powerful lesson." His grandparents weren't demonstrative people, but their words—*We're disappointed in you* or *We're proud of you*—had meant everything.

She gave a throaty laugh. "We're such opposites. I've always hated structure and discipline."

"You might've liked them better if you'd experienced life on the commune." He'd gone from chaos to security, from being one of a pack of kids to being the center of attention and having people actually care about what he did. Care about him.

"I never thought of it that way. I just resented the hell out of how *organized* my whole family was. Mom and Dad with important jobs, my oldest sister Tree—"

"Tree?" he broke in, figuring he'd heard wrong.

"Theresa. She's two years older. When I was little, I couldn't pronounce her name properly. Anyhow, she's a total brainiac—" She broke off, squeezing his arm again.

"You two'd get along, though her field's sociology. Anyhow, her whole shtick was school. Then Kat, who I call Kitty-Kat, was Ms. Sociability, all wrapped up in friends and activities. They all had their roles, their *things*."

"What was your thing?"

"Same as now. Everything. Fun, exploring the world, meeting interesting people. Whatever lies around the corner."

That sounded pretty aimless to him. A person needed a goal, a purpose, something to give their life meaning and make it count.

"How did it feel," she asked, "having two parent-type figures and being the only kid?"

"Nice. Like I was . . . me. Mark. Not just one in a group. Does that make sense?"

"For sure. Individuality is important. Me and my older sisters are the three-pack, but we always had distinct personalities." A mischievous grin lit her face. "We made sure of that."

"You label them. The brainiac and Ms. Sociability. How do they label you?"

She tossed her head, curls flying, and touched a finger to the top butterfly on her arm. "When they're being polite, the free spirit. That's what my butterflies symbolize."

He winced. Alicia had used that term to describe herself. Her parents had called her willful, wanton, and irresponsible. "And when they're not being polite?" he asked tentatively.

She wrinkled her nose. "A flake. Mom says I'm a hippie who was born in the wrong decade."

A hippie. Like Alicia. He glanced away from her toward the rocky point they were approaching and reviewed his observations of Jenna. Her appearance: the untamed hair, lack of bra, floaty skirt, butterfly tattoos. Her behavior: picking up a stranger, not having money to get her car fixed, talking

about hitchhiking home. Her opinions: envying him growing up on a commune, thinking monogamy was outdated,
volunteering for the falcon survey on whim.

When he'd first met her, her beauty and openness, her
sheer unexpectedness, had distracted him. She'd mentioned
the falcon survey and he'd assumed she was a serious, committed person like him. Most people he met were, because
his life revolved around his work.

He'd been wrong. And he didn't like flakes and hippies,
people who were frivolous and had no purpose.

He heard Adrienne's voice in his head: *Don't be so judgmental. What right do you have to judge others?* Yet his
grandparents had raised him with a strong social conscience
and an aversion for frivolity.

"A falcon!" Jenna cried.

He turned to follow her pointing finger and his bare
upper arm brushed her breast, the only thing separating
flesh from flesh one thin layer of cotton. He forgot everything he'd been thinking and for a long, perfect moment
watched the falcon soar regally across the blue summer sky.

When he glanced again at Jenna, her face wore a look of
wonder, a joyous smile. Whatever their differences, the falcon touched both their hearts.

He felt a tug in his body and an urge to pull her into his
arms and spin her around. An urge that was so uncharacteristic, he turned away and began to walk, tugging her along
with him.

Hmm. Research on major histocompatibility complex
codes indicated that you were attracted to people whose
codes were very different than your parents'. It was a biological mechanism to avoid inbreeding. So, Jenna's MHC
profile must be radically different than Alicia's, even though
she had some similar personality characteristics, attributes
that normally wouldn't attract him in the least. It was puz-
zling.

Yet if it weren't for Jenna, he wouldn't be here on this beach, feeling warm pebbles under his feet, the sun on his face, the resilient curve of her breast against his arm. He wouldn't have tasted strawberry pie or been given a refreshing shower by an exuberant dog.

For the next couple of days, maybe he should lighten up. He had a pleasant trip ahead of him, much of it alongside the ocean, and a pretty woman beside him. The paper he was scheduled to present in Vancouver, at the international symposium on global change in marine social-ecological systems, was written. For once, there wasn't much he could do except enjoy life.

Grandma and Grandpa wouldn't approve.

"My grandparents," he said slowly, "Heather and Ken Chambers, they're great people." Was this actually him, volunteering personal information without being prodded? But Jenna made it easy to talk. She made him want to talk.

"Of course they are. They took you in."

He liked the warmth and certainty in her voice, even if she'd misunderstood. "I mean, they're probably a bit like your parents. They're making a difference in the world. He's a subatomic physicist and she's a neurosurgeon, though only in a consulting capacity now."

"Yikes. More brainiacs."

"Definitely. They're in their eighties, but they haven't retired. They'd hoped Alicia would be like them, but she was the opposite."

"It happens." She shrugged casually, but there was a touch of bitterness in her voice. "My parents wanted a boy brainiac, and instead they got me. Tough luck for them."

Had her parents made her feel unwanted? "Uh, I'm sure your parents, uh—"

With a quick laugh, she rescued him. "Oh sure, we all love each other. But we're not an easy match. And neither, I gather, were Alicia and her parents."

"No." From what his grandparents said, she'd been rebellious from the moment she was born, never giving them a moment's peace.

"Poor kid," Jenna said. "It must have felt like prison for her. No wonder she ran away."

Hmm. He'd always taken his grandparents' side. He, too, knew how much pain could result from Alicia's pursuit of hedonism. Yet now, for a moment, he wondered what it had been like for a vivacious, high spirited girl—one like Jenna—growing up with parents who were determined to impose rules and structure. To squash her spirit. Was it possible she felt that they'd driven her away?

"Mark?" Jenna tugged on his arm and he saw they'd reached the end of the beach. The rocks sheltered intriguing tide pools, but exploring them would mean putting their sandals back on. Besides, they needed to get back on the road. In silent agreement, they swung around, arms still linked, and began retracing their steps.

"It sounds as if you and your grandparents were a good match," she said.

He nodded. "Very much so." They'd given him structure, security, attention, approval, affection. The only thing they hadn't given, because it wasn't in their nature, was softness. Hugs at night. Laughter. Feeling disloyal, he brushed that thought away.

"Sounds like y'all got a brain or two to rub together," she drawled teasingly.

"I soaked up learning. From my parents, teachers, tutors. By my next birthday, I'd caught up the grades I missed."

"How old were you when you graduated high school?"

"Fifteen. Why?"

"Hah. Tree beat you. She was fourteen." She grinned. "Gee, I'd take you home to meet my sis, except it seems she's just hooked up with a guy. A thriller writer. It's so unlike her." She reached over with her free hand and ran her fingers lightly down his bare arm, from shoulder to elbow, then down his forearm. "Besides, maybe I'd rather keep you for myself."

"Uh . . ." He gaped at her. She was clearly the opposite of his grandparents: overly demonstrative, hugging everyone in sight, telling strangers she loved them. But this . . . This didn't seem like a casual touch. And what did she mean about keeping him for herself?

Jenna's fingers drifted up again in a caressing touch that quickened his breath and made his cock pulse. "What kind of women do you go for, Mark?"

Right now, he sure as hell went for her. But that was an aberration. He stuffed his free hand casually in his pocket, fisting it to disguise his growing erection. She'd asked a question. He'd answer it seriously, because he didn't know any other way to respond. "Women who are like me. People I meet on projects I work on."

"You don't believe in attraction of opposites?"

He considered the question. "In terms of MHC profiles, yes. But not in terms of personalities."

"MHC profiles?"

Rather than launch into another scientific lecture, he kept it simple. "Kind of like pheromones."

She nodded. "Gotcha."

A woman who was like him would never have accepted such a simple explanation. All the same, he was definitely physically attracted to Jenna. It was biology, pure and simple.

Was he crazy to think she was attracted to him, too? He wished Adrienne was around to ask.

But even if Jenna was attracted, were they going to do anything about it?

On the one hand, he was a scientist. Who was he to argue with biology? Yet, that was too pat an answer. Sex wasn't just about biology, at least not with the human species.

Often there were expectations, emotions, complications—especially on the part of the female.

It wasn't that he didn't want emotion—love, to be specific. Long-term, he did want a life partner and kids. But so far, with his lovers, no matter how intellectually and sexually compatible they'd been, his emotions had never gone beyond strong affection. Besides, he didn't have a clue how he could have a family yet still travel the world doing the work that meant everything to him.

Strolling the shoreline, he gazed out at the ocean, the constant that gave his life direction and meaning.

When he was managing an environmental project, he knew exactly how to get from point A to point Z. But in his personal life—what personal life?—he didn't have a clue.

One thing he did know was that a woman like Jenna had no place on that straight line from A to Z. So, it would be pointless to take a detour. Wouldn't it?

Chapter 3

Why did people make things so complicated? To me, life was simple. If you wanted something, or someone, you went for it. You didn't freaking analyze it to death.

I was drawn to Mark, and I knew I turned him on—even if he was acting strange about it. And who cared if we were attracted because we smelled good, or because we both had tanned, taut bodies that I figured could give each other fabulous orgasms, or because we were opposites in terms of personality?

Time to go for it.

I stopped abruptly, firming the arm that was linked through his so he jerked to a stop too. "You know what I feel like?" I turned to face him and rested both hands on his shoulders, overlapping the fabric of his tank top and spreading my fingers onto hard, sun-warmed flesh. Oh jeez, did he feel good.

His eyes crinkled at the corners and he shook his head, looking baffled. "Jenna, I have no idea."

"This."

I pushed up on the balls of my feet, feeling all those amazing multicolored bits of glass, shell, and pebbles digging gently into my skin. As I tilted my head up to his in a clear invitation, his eyes, as blue as the sky above us, widened in surprise.

Come on, Mark. You're too tall, and I can't kiss you unless you cooperate. Get with the program, dude!

His gaze sharpened with awareness, with purpose. The blue of his eyes deepened, then he tossed our sandals on the beach and caught me firmly by the waist. He lowered his head and kissed me.

My eyes closed against the dazzle of sun as his lips met mine. Tentative, for the briefest moment, then hard, fierce, demanding. Oh yes, that was more like it. I kissed him back just as hungrily.

One kiss, and somehow my whole body, my whole being, got sucked up in it the way objects get whirled up into a tornado.

Thought wasn't possible. Only heat, passion, the exploration of tongues and lips. Strawberries, coffee, the tang of ocean, the blaze of sunshine. A repetitive roaring that was either waves crashing on the beach or the pulsing of my blood.

The sun had climbed inside me, melting me into something malleable, liquid, and yearning. My body softened, slid against his, clothing brushing, the rigid thrust of his erection against my belly making me whimper.

He swallowed the sound, then tore his mouth from mine, panting for breath. "Jesus," he gasped.

I dragged my heavy lids open and at first, dazed by the sun and the kiss, couldn't focus. When I did, he was staring down at me with a stunned expression.

How many men had I kissed? I hadn't kept track. But never had I lost myself so totally in a kiss. "Mark? That was . . ." I couldn't find words to describe it.

He let go of my waist and ran a hand through his already messy hair. A touch of humor glinted in his eyes. "Unexpected?"

"Uh, yeah."

Now he grinned. "I get the feeling that should be your middle name."

I grinned back, loving not just the kiss but the way it had loosened him up. "Beats being boring."

"That kiss definitely wasn't boring."

The breeze caught my filmy skirt, whirling it around my legs. Making him glance down, and making me aware that all I wore under it was a thong, and the crotch was soaked. "There's more where that came from," I told him. If our first kiss was that mind-stunning, what would sex be like? I knew I'd find out. A kiss like that meant sex was inevitable.

His gaze tracked slowly up my body and I didn't need to look down to know that my nipples stood out like pebbles against the soft fabric of my tank.

I didn't need to look down to know he was still erect.

When his gaze finally made it back to my face, I gave him a teasingly sultry smile. "Pity there are so many people on this beach."

He shook his head slowly—not denial, more like bewilderment. "This isn't like me."

"Then you need to loosen up, dude."

A snort of laughter. "Maybe I do at that." He drew in a breath, let it out firmly. "We should get back on the road."

"Mmm. The sooner we do, the sooner we'll stop for the night," I teased.

Heat flared in his eyes. Then he blinked and bent to pick up our sandals. The man sure looked more like a surfer than a stuffy scientist. Muscular, naturally graceful in that powerful, masculine way that was incredibly appealing, tanned like he spent more time outside than in a lab.

Maybe he was the Indiana Jones type of scientist.

As we headed up the beach, I linked my arm with his again, hugging biceps to breast. "D'you ever travel any place really interesting in your work?"

"I've worked on projects in Thailand, Papua New Guinea, the Mekong Delta, Costa Rica."

"Wow. Doing what?"

"Helping underdeveloped countries with conservation and restoration projects, research, education. Setting up eco-tourism that's done right."

Oh yeah, that was kind of Indiana Jonesy. "Cool job." If I'd given in to my parents' obsessive urging that I go to university, I, too . . . Nah. Academia and discipline weren't my thing. Travel, though . . . "I've only been outside Canada and the continental U.S. twice. Mexico and Hawaii." Mexico with a girlfriend, and Hawaii with a lover. "I love living in different places, learning about different environments, meeting different kinds of people."

"Yeah. I'm not much for staying in one place, especially if it involves a classroom or lab. I like to get outside. Breathe the ocean. And I get bored if I spend too long on one project."

"I like variety, too."

We slipped back into our sandals and took the path away from the beach to the parking lot. His camper had heated up so we threw open the doors and windows. He climbed in the back and emerged with bottled water, chilled by the tiny fridge.

I drank gratefully. "All the comforts of home." Glancing inside and thinking of that incredible kiss, I gestured toward the couch. "That makes into a bed?"

"Yeah. Folds down." Voice going even huskier than usual, he added, "Into a double bed."

"Can't wait to try it," I purred, itching to get naked with him. "In fact, why wait?" I was teasing, but if he'd taken me up on it, I'd have been right there with him.

He stared at me for a long moment, his tank top not disguising the rapid rise and fall of his chest. Oh yeah, he seriously wanted me, too.

A minivan pulled into a spot across from ours. Two adults and what seemed like a dozen kids piled out, everyone talking.

Mark took a hurried step back. "We're behind schedule."

"We have a schedule?"

He slid the camper side door closed. "I figured on stopping for the night at Patrick's Point State Park near Trinidad. One of my colleagues recommended it. If we're too late, we won't get a spot."

"Do you always plan ahead?"

"Pretty much. I take it you don't?"

No, that was Tree's shtick. My big sis even had a project plan for M&M's wedding. I shook my head. "My way's more fun. Look at the things you discover. Like Glass Beach. That wasn't on your *schedule*, was it? Nor was strawberry pie, I bet. Nor me." I gave him a mischievous grin. "And look at how much fun I am."

He gave a husky laugh. "I'll give you that. Now climb in, and let's get going."

I couldn't wait to find out what he was like as a lover. He definitely had the body for sex, and he was one hell of a kisser. Surely, he wasn't pulling back; he had to realize sex was inevitable.

Once we were under way, a beep sounded from my tote bag. My cell telling me I'd missed a call. "Crap, didn't I turn that off?" I was always running down the batteries. At least on this trip I'd remembered my charger, but only because I'd gone through all my belongings, deciding what to take and what to give to friends or charity.

I opened the phone and picked up the message. It was Tree.

"Hi Jenna. You're really on the road, right? Please drive safely."

"Nag, nag, nag," I muttered. Would my family be more or less worried if they knew I was with Mark rather than driving Mellow Yellow?

Her tone shifted to conspiratorial. "Listen, there's fascinating news. Give me a call. You aren't going to believe this!"

I closed my phone and frowned at it. Just because God invented e-mail and cell phones, it didn't mean people had to jump like Pavlov's dogs when they beeped. And I sure didn't need to be nagged by my sister.

But she'd hooked my curiosity. "That was my big sis. I should phone her."

"Sure."

I dialed Tree's cell. After three rings, I heard, "Hey, Jenna, you actually called."

"Your ploy worked, damn you," I joked.

"You are on your way, right? And you've had your car maintained recently?"

"I'm on the road and even have a *schedule*." I rolled my eyes in Mark's direction. "As for my car, it seems like only a few hours ago I was talking to my mechanic." Eventually they'd find out the truth. No point in having them worry and fuss at me until I was home safely.

Mark shot me a skeptical look, which I ignored. I asked Tree, "What's this news?" I still couldn't believe my cynical, divorced professor sister had hooked up with a hottie thriller writer. Easier to believe in a parallel universe. "Is it about your Aussie super-stud?"

A snort of laughter from beside me made me cover the phone and "Sshh" Mark.

"Not this time," Tree said. "This is about Kat. You won't *believe* the guy she brought home."

"Brought home? Last I heard, her wedding date was flying out from Montreal next week."

"So we thought. But he came on the train with her. We picked them up this morning. Major shock."

I winced. Poor old Kitty-Kat. "She's brought home some real losers. What's the fatal flaw this time?"

"That's the bizarre thing," my sister said wonderingly. "Nothing. At least nothing I've been able to find."

"Oh, come on. You always think they're too dumb."

Another snort, muffled this time. I curled sideways in my seat to watch Mark at the wheel. He looked relaxed and confident, steering with one hand, the other resting on the rim of the open window. The cargo shorts and sage-green tank were casual, flattering, perfect on him.

Tree was saying, "Well, he doesn't have a Ph.D., but he does have an M.B.A. from Cambridge, which is moderately impressive."

"Oh yeah, *moderately*. So the poor shmuck didn't go to Harvard. She should obviously dump him. What does he do?"

"Nav's a photographer," Tree said. "He has his own business, and he's talented. He has an exhibit coming up at a prestigious gallery in Montreal."

"Wow. That's pretty cool. So he's bright, well educated, creative, and successful." I snapped my fingers. "Okay, got it. Another of Kat's high flyers, like the Olympic skier and the NASCAR champ. With an ego a million times bigger than his cock."

Mark laughed, and I gave him a mock scowl.

"What was that?" Tree said. "Where are you anyway? Was that the car radio? Are you driving while you're talking on the cell?"

It figured. We could only be simpatico for so long. She had to get back to being the nagging big sis. "No," I snapped, "I'm not driving while I'm talking on the cell. Jeez, Tree." I ignored her other questions. "Now, wait a minute, you said there was nothing wrong with the guy. So he's not an egomaniac?"

"Nope. He's confident but in that charming, unassuming way. You know what I mean?"

"Totally. And he treats her nice? Those larger-than-life guys of hers make her act like a second-class citizen."

"He respects her and seems to totally adore her."

"He sounds wonderful." Even I, who didn't have the slightest interest in a serious relationship, felt a twinge of envy. "There has to be a downside. He's goofy looking. Short, fat, balding?"

Mark's lips twitched, but this time he kept quiet.

"Tallish, lean and toned, masses of long, curly black hair. He's Indo-Canadian and has lovely skin, beautiful eyes. Jenna, the man's gorgeous. He's almost as good-looking as Damien."

Damien, her Aussie hottie. I glanced at Mark, thinking he'd probably give both those guys a run for their money. "There has to be a hitch. With Kat, there always is. What do Mom and Dad say?"

"They only met him this morning, briefly, at the train station. Tonight, we're all having dinner. That'll be the test. If anyone can intimidate the hell out of the guy and find a flaw, it will be them."

"Very true." And if they didn't, Kitty-Kat would do something to jinx things. My poor sister really wanted to be married and have kids, but she had the worst track record with guys. I hoped this time her luck had changed.

"Damien survived the parents. Maybe Nav will too."

No boyfriend ever survived long in my house. I figured her Aussie only had because he'd been there such a short time before heading off on a book tour.

I was the only kid who didn't give a damn what the family thought. In fact, I'd been known to bring guys home just to shock them. I glanced at Mark. He was too impressive to have shock value. My parents and Theresa would even approve of his academic credentials and career. Kat would dump on him though; she'd say his social skills were defective, and he needed to pay more attention to his grooming.

"You said his name's Nav?" I asked my sister.

"Naveen Bharani."

"And they were dating in Montreal?"

"I haven't got all the details yet. Kat's being a bit cryptic."

"Aha. A deep, dark secret. Wonder what it is?"

"Don't know, but hurry home, Jenna. You're missing out on all the fun. You even missed the fitting for the bridesmaids' dresses."

"Are they terrible?"

"Not at all. They're pretty sundresses. Yours is a lovely teal color, the closest we could get to matching your eyes."

"Really?" My sisters had actually cared enough to do that? "Nice. Thanks, Tree. So, how're M&M doing? Pre-wedding jitters?"

"Matt's the same as always. Steady and sweet. Merilee's tired from making up coursework and writing exams. Happy to see Kat and me but a little ticked off we brought guys home, as if we're trying to upstage her." She gave a fond laugh. "Good God, it's her wedding, of course she should be the center of attention. Anyhow, she's excited, maybe a little on edge. But she and Matt will be great. They've always known they belonged together."

My baby sis and her guy had been bonded—hips, brains, hearts—since they were seven. "How's her health?" Merilee'd been diagnosed with endometriosis and had surgery this spring, which was why she'd gotten behind on university work.

"She's doing well." A pause. "We should have realized there was something wrong."

"Yeah." Guilt wasn't an emotion I had much time for, but Tree was right. At least she, Kat, and Mom shared this one with me. "Thank God for Matt."

"He'd been trying for years to get her to see a doctor about her bad periods. But she listened to us, the females who said cramps were normal and told her to take ibuprofen."

At least Merilee had finally taken Matt's advice. She'd been diagnosed and had surgery.

"It's a big reason they moved the wedding to this year," Tree went on.

"I know." M&M wanted kids, and endometriosis messed up fertility. I glanced away from Mark to look out the window. We were inland now, and my gaze lit on a couple of boys on bikes. "I sure hope things work out and she gets pregnant."

"Me, too. She's always wanted to be a mom. Her and Kat. Not like me, who's open to it but not obsessed. Or you, who used to talk about having children then decided in your teens you didn't want them."

We passed the boys, and I didn't turn to watch them. A familiar pang of regret moved through me, and I hugged my free arm across my belly. "Right." Or at least so I'd made everyone think, because I hated pity. Besides, it was stupid to want what you couldn't have.

I'd never told a soul that I couldn't have children. What my family and friends had seen was a romantic seventeen-year-old who ran away with her boyfriend one summer, then came back in the fall saying I wasn't cut out to be a one-guy girl and never wanted to be tied down to a husband and family. What else could I say? That I was even worse of a screw-up than they thought I was?

Tree chuckled. "You, with kids. It boggles the mind. You're still a kid yourself."

The subtle dig pissed me off. "Best way to be," I said flippantly. "If you mean having fun, being optimistic, and seeing the best in people rather than being cynical and middle-aged."

There was a moment's silence, and I knew my jab had hit target just as hers had. What was it about me and my sisters? We were adults with different, happy lives, yet together we so often turned bitchy.

"Jenna? Come home soon. It's . . . I . . . We all miss you." Her tone was uncharacteristically tentative.

They missed me. I missed them too. No one could annoy me the way my family did, yet we shared blood, history, and love. "Me, too. I'm on my way."

"Don't pick up any hitchhikers."

If only she knew. I smiled to myself and gave her one of my flip, trademark lines. "You know me; I was born to shock."

Still, when I hung up, it was the old grief that lingered with me. Grief over the loss of the old Jenna, the one who'd been full of dreams. Grief, too, that my family always judged, that my teenage self hadn't had a safe place to confess my mistakes and share my deepest sorrows.

Usually, Mark paid more attention to the subtle messages offered by the ocean than to human communication. But this afternoon he had a bewitching woman beside him.

A woman who—maybe?—had offered him sex. Surely she'd been teasing. Flirting? No matter how carefree and impulsive she was, she wouldn't have sex with a virtual stranger. Would she?

Would he? Hell, with a woman as beautiful and bewitching as her, he'd be insane not to if she really wanted him.

At the moment, she didn't look so carefree. Despite the provocative closing line she'd shot at her sister, she was subdued, staring out the windshield with one arm across her waist as if she might have a stomach ache. It was the first time he'd seen her anything other than animated, which made him curious and concerned. "Are you all right?"

"Hmm?" She glanced over, nodded. "Fine, thanks."

"That was your older sister?" he asked. "The brainiac?"

"Uh-huh."

Earlier, she'd chattered away and drawn him into being more talkative than usual. What had happened during that phone conversation?

He scratched his head, feeling clumsy about his conversational skills. "Everything okay at home? The wedding on track?"

"Seems so."

Normally, he'd never pry. But she'd certainly asked him enough questions. "Your other sister, Kat, brought home a new guy? You're worried about her?"

"A little." After a moment, she gave a little shake, as if she was tossing off whatever had upset her. She curled her legs up on the passenger seat under the drape of that gauzy skirt and turned toward him. "Kitty-Kat's so driven to find Mr. Right that she's always falling for Mr. Wrong."

He pondered that. "I went out with a woman like that." It had been the first and only time he'd made the mistake of not discussing expectations before sleeping with a woman. "She was on my Costa Rica ecotourism project."

"She thought you were her Mr. Right?"

Embarrassed, he shrugged. "Guess she wanted me to be. We worked well together, seemed compatible. I thought—assumed—she was totally into her career, but after we got together she surprised me by saying she wanted to settle down and have kids." She'd been older than him by several years, nearing the time that it would be too late to safely have children. "She urged me to get a teaching position at a university." She'd even said she loved him, but he'd known it wasn't true. The emotion he'd seen in her eyes was desperation.

"You don't want that whole white picket fence thing, with the wife, two kids, and a dog and a cat in the yard?"

A tough question. "Yes and no. I hate the idea of being stuck in one job, one place, for years and years. And I'm no fan of the institution of marriage. Yet, I do want a life partner and kids."

"A lot of people do," she said quietly. Subdued again.

It didn't feel right for Jenna to be subdued. So he probed again. "How about you? You said you don't believe in monogamy?" Whereas he had enough of the caveman in him that he'd never share his mate with another man.

"No, I think it's unnatural."

"You've never felt so strongly about a man that you'd be jealous if he slept with another woman?"

A pause. "Once, when I was very young. But it was stupid, and I was wrong."

He glanced over, seeing her brows drawn together in a frown. He wished he wasn't driving, so he could keep watching her face as they talked. "I don't think it's stupid or wrong. I think it's . . ." He paused, reflecting. In evolutionary terms, jealousy made sense for a female. She needed to hold a man so he'd look after her and their kids. As for the male, the drive was to reproduce, so he didn't want some other guy messing with his female.

"Romantic? Dr. Chambers, the romantic?" she teased, and he was happy her mood had lightened.

"God, no. I was going to say it's hardwired into our genes." He explained his reasoning, then went on. "It's good for kids, too. I think about how I grew up. At Freedom Valley, free love was the rule. There were no stable couples, no stable families. For me as a kid that meant uncertainty. When I went to Grandma and Grandpa's, I had stability and security."

"Mom and Dad drove me nuts, but there was definitely security. Still is. Even though the three-pack's rarely home, our rooms are there waiting." A rueful note in her voice, she said, "Even if I screw up, I know I can always go home. I avoid it, though, because they nag and criticize."

"I imagine they only do it because they care about you and worry about you."

"I know. Plus, they're sure they know best."

"That goes with parental territory. Wait until you have kids of your own."

A long pause then, flatly, "Not going to."

Of course, not every woman had maternal instincts, but he could imagine Jenna splashing in the ocean with children, laughing at their antics, pointing to a peregrine falcon and teaching them to respect the environment. "Seriously?"

She flicked her head, curls flying. There was an edge to her voice when she said, "Told you I'm a free spirit. Doesn't work to have kids tying me down."

So it wasn't about maternal instinct; it was her irresponsibility. The quality that made him think of the hippies at the commune. The quality he liked least about her.

He had no right to judge, he reminded himself. As his friend Adrienne often told him, he sure as hell wasn't perfect.

Jenna rested her head against the window, hair hiding her face, and didn't say anything else. After a few minutes, he figured she'd drifted off to sleep.

A while later, needing gas, he pulled into a station at Fortuna.

She lifted her head, yawned widely, and said, "Where are we?"

"About an hour from where I planned to stop for the night. Just stopping for gas. The Westfalia's a hybrid, but it still needs fuel occasionally."

Another yawn, smaller this time, and she shook her head as if to clear it. "This is a hybrid? It's too old, isn't it?"

"Had it converted."

"That's cool." She opened the door and hopped out. "Bathroom break."

"Want something to eat or drink?" he called after her and got a head shake in response.

After filling up with fuel and water, he went inside to buy a coffee. As the woman behind the counter, a brunette roughly his own age, took his money, her fingers brushed his and she smiled brightly. "Haven't seen you before. Just passing through?"

"Yeah. Heading up to Patrick's Point for the night." His nostrils twitched at the unpleasant scent of her heavy perfume.

"Pretty place but kind of lonely." She winked, or was that a tic? "If you know what I mean."

"I'm never lonely when I'm by the ocean." He sipped the bitter coffee, so nasty after that lovely blend at Marianne's Diner.

"I'm just saying, Fortuna's a friendlier place." She gave him his change, and red painted fingernails rasped unpleasantly across his palm.

"That's nice," he said politely as he dumped the change in his shorts pocket.

When he removed his hand, Jenna was there, twining her fingers through his and making his blood heat. "Oh, I think Patrick's Point will be plenty friendly," she said, giving the older woman a grin.

The brunette shrugged. "Can't blame a girl."

Jenna chuckled. "No harm, no foul."

Baffled, and disconcertingly aroused by the clasp of her slim fingers, he let her tug him outside. "What were you two talking about?"

He opened the passenger side door, and she turned to him, freeing his hand. "Didn't you realize she was hitting on you?"

"She was?" He thought back. The woman had said the ocean was lonely and the town was friendly. That was hitting on him? No wonder he was so hopeless when it came to male-female stuff.

"Totally. I was browsing through magazines on the other side of a rack behind you and heard it all. I bet this happens to you a lot, doesn't it?" Then her laugh rang out. "No, wait, you wouldn't even know."

He ducked his head. "Adrienne says I can be pretty oblivious when women, uh, like me."

"Adrienne?"

"We went to grad school together and became friends." He met Jenna's curious gaze. "She's at the University of B.C. now, teaching and doing research. We stay in touch, and she's worked on a couple of my projects."

"I bet Adrienne's in love with Mark," she chanted in a kid's singsong voice.

"No. God no. She just, uh, we have common interests. Hit it off." She was his best friend, his only close friend.

"Oh, she's totally in love with you," she teased. "Pining after you all these years and you're too oblivious to notice."

He shook his head. "She's in love but not with me. Adrienne's lesbian, married, and pregnant."

"Man, I had that one pegged wrong, didn't I?" She winked. "Guess I just didn't see how a woman could resist you."

In a way, her teasing reminded him of Adrienne. Except there'd never been a sexual vibe between him and his friend, and there definitely was with Jenna. He was so out of his depth with her.

She couldn't really have been offering sex—as if it were nothing more significant than enjoying strawberry pie together. Could she? Yes, in fact, it was simply a physical act based on a biological urge, but it was one society had turned into something much more complicated.

Of course, Jenna didn't seem to give a damn what society thought . . .

Confused, he stuck to what he did know. "Let's get on the road, or all the camping spots will be filled."

They climbed into the camper. He put the coffee in the cup holder, then pulled back onto Highway 101, heading for Eureka.

Jenna took a drink from a steel water bottle and tilted her seat back. She slipped off her sandals and rested her bare feet against the dash.

The woman even had sexy feet, slim and brown like she'd spent a lot of time on the beach. He hadn't noticed before that she had a silver ring on one of her toes.

"We were talking about your sister, uh, is it Kat?" he remembered.

"Right. When it comes to men, she has crappy judgment and even worse luck. But she brought a new guy home and Tree's given him a tentative stamp of approval. I can't wait to meet him. If he lasts until I get home."

"They don't usually last?" Gazing at her slender feet, catching glimpses of her legs as the breeze teased her skirt, gave him a very basic male reaction. Arousal quickened his breathing and pulsed through his cock.

"Not past dinner with my parents."

Her comment brought back memories. "I can relate. When I was in university, I took a few women home. As study partners or dates. Grandma and Grandpa never approved."

"Why not?"

He took a sip of coffee and grimaced. If anything might break his addiction, this foul brew would. "Apparently, they were either not serious enough or too much like me. My grandparents believe human partnerships are similar to base pair bonds."

"Huh?"

The word *bond* made him imagine Jenna's legs, naked and wrapped around him. He cleared his throat and clarified what he'd said. "It's molecular biology. Complementary nucleotides from opposite DNA or RNA strands that are connected by hydrogen bonds make up a base pair."

"Oh yeah, that totally clarifies it."

He was so used to talking to other scientists that it was hard to remember to put things in lay terms. "The way my grandparents apply it to relationships, they say you have to be different enough, yet complementary enough, in order to fuse into a strong bond."

"Hmm," she said reflectively. "My parents are both super smart, incredibly hard workers, and share common values. But Dad's happiest in a research lab, and Mom really enjoys being with people, helping people."

"Yeah, I think that's what they mean. My grandparents have the same things in common as yours. They're wonderful, committed people. They're both really serious, not very demonstrative, and they don't have much sense of humor." He grimaced. "Guess I inherited that one."

"Ah, so that's your excuse. How are your grandparents different from each other?"

"Grandpa's super intellectual, and he's all about research. Even in his eighties, he's working at TRIUMF, one of the world's leading subatomic physics research labs at UBC. Grandma's always been hands on, a born surgeon. It's like she's at war with disease and injury and determined to win."

"You're more like her than him," she commented.

Surprised, he glanced over. "I am?"

"You're not into research labs; you're about application. And you're at war with everything that's destroying the environment."

"You're right. I never really thought about that." Much less talked about it. There was something about Jenna, her interest and openness, and something about being side by side in the camper, the road stretching ahead of them, that brought out a side of himself he'd never realized existed. One that surprised and actually kind of pleased him.

Curious about her, he asked, "Which of your parents are you most like?"

She gave a wry chuckle. "Neither. I keep expecting them to admit I was adopted."

"I was nothing like Alicia. Probably nothing like my biological father, who I'm sure was the hippie type."

They'd come out to the coast again and were entering Eureka, a small city. "Shall we pick up groceries for dinner?" he asked. "I have a portable barbecue, and it's going to be a warm night. We could eat outside."

"Perfect." She reached over to trail soft, caressing fingers down his arm. "And yes, I'm betting it'll be a very warm night."

His skin prickled with awareness, and he suppressed a shiver of arousal. "Uh . . ." Now, that was flirtation, wasn't it? She was being suggestive, hinting that they'd have sex. Would they?

He'd never slept with a woman he'd just met. Did the fact that he wanted to make him no better than all those free love freaks at Freedom Valley? On the other hand, in the few short hours since he met Jenna, he'd shared more personal stuff than with any other woman except maybe Adrienne. Was this fascinating stranger becoming a friend? And maybe soon a lover?

"Mark, there's a grocery store." She pointed, pulling him back from his thoughts. "Aren't you going to stop?"

"Yeah, right." He swung the camper into the parking lot. Again, they both climbed out, him taking a couple of cloth bags from behind the driver's seat.

As they walked toward the store, Jenna linked her arm in his. By now he was almost getting used to the casual intimacy and the way her touch made his pulse quicken and his blood heat.

"Any food preferences?" she asked. "Are you vegetarian?"

He should be, but it made meals—and travel—too complicated. "No, though when I can I eat organic food and avoid red meat. But vegetarian's good with me if that's what you want."

She shook her head. "How about fish if they have something wild?"

"Great."

Strolling through the nicely appointed store, he let her choose. A fillet of wild local salmon, a lemon, a bunch of baby carrots with frilly green tops, and a box of local strawberries. She added a loaf of crusty bread, then said, "Looks good to me. How about you?"

It had taken only a few minutes, but she'd assembled a meal that was healthy, featured local products, and would be easy to cook. "Yeah, great." No, wait. If he was going to share this meal with Jenna, perhaps beside a campfire, there was something missing. "A bottle of wine?" he suggested.

"Love it," she said promptly. "But it's not in my budget."

"My treat."

"Thanks."

They studied the selections. "I don't know a lot about wine," he confessed. "Do you?"

"Yeah, I've waitressed in some good places over the years. Tell me a price range, and I'll choose something nice."

"Uh . . . twenty dollars? Is that okay?" He knew nothing about this stuff.

"We can get a great wine for less than that." She picked out a bottle with an intriguing moon label. "I like this one. It's an unoaked chardonnay from Valley of the Moon in Sonoma. It's fresh, flavorful, kind of a green apple undernote. It'll stand up to the salmon but won't overpower it. Sound okay?"

"Yeah, sounds good." Her knowledge impressed him. He guessed that, with her bubbly, outgoing personality and her beauty, she'd made good tips. But really, waitressing? For a woman of . . . "How old are you?"

She shot him a startled look. "Where did that come from?"

"Just curious."

"You know how they say no woman's ever older than twenty-nine?"

"That doesn't make sense."

She shook her head tolerantly. "You really do live with your head in science journals, don't you? It just means women are sensitive about their age, and guys aren't supposed to ask."

"Oh. Sorry."

"No problem. I'm not your typical woman."

"That's certainly true."

The corners of her mouth twitched. "You always speak the truth, don't you? You're not into compliments; you just tell it like you see it."

"Is that bad?"

She shook her head, curls bouncing. "Refreshing. And I *am* twenty-nine, for real. But ask me again in three months, and I'll be thirty."

Four years younger than him. But it was as if they were a generation apart when it came to their approaches to life. Of course, once he'd gone to live with his grandparents, he'd never been *young,* in the sense of carefree and irresponsible like Jenna.

When they reached the checkout line, she pulled out her wallet. "I'll pay for my share of the food, and I owe you for gas."

"Put it away. We can settle up when we get to Vancouver."

"Okay. But I don't need charity. If you want to buy wine, great, because I can't afford it, and I love it. But food and gas are in my budget."

He nodded as they moved ahead. "No charity." He respected that. She took responsibility for herself, though she didn't want any other obligations tying her down. His scientist's brain kept wanting to analyze her; she was the most intriguing woman he'd met.

Now she was telling the young Latina cashier that her name—Esmeralda, according to her name tag—was beautiful. Jenna noticed people. Engaged with them. Whereas he, shy and often absorbed in his thoughts, rarely did.

When the cashier wished them a pleasant evening, he thanked her and took the bags.

Pleasant. Such a bland word. Being with Jenna was the opposite of bland. As for the evening and maybe going to bed together . . . His pulse quickened and he felt as anxious as the time, at age eighteen, he first donned scuba gear and dove under the ocean. Uncertain, a little scared, excited.

That dive had been momentous. For the first time, he'd been absorbed into the ocean that had for so long fascinated him. He'd been on intimate terms with it. The experience had been the fulfillment of a long-time passion, the beginning of a lifelong adventure.

"You going to open the door?" Jenna's voice called him back.

They'd arrived at the Westfalia. He was just standing there, staring blankly at the side door, seeing not it but that first tantalizing glimpse of the ocean depths. He shook his head, clearing it.

Quickly, he unlocked the door. As he stowed the groceries in the compact kitchen, he puzzled over why he was thinking of the dive and feeling anxious. He'd had sex before, plenty of times. Like anything else he took on, he believed in doing it well. So he'd studied female anatomy and sexual response, and with each lover he'd experimented to find out what gave her the most satisfaction. If he and Jenna did get together, he'd follow that tried-and-true course of action, and they'd both enjoy themselves.

But he was getting ahead of himself. A little flirtation wasn't an offer of sex.

It wasn't far to Patrick's Point, a state park he'd never visited before that one of his Santa Cruz colleagues had recommended. Though the visit to Jenna's mechanic and the stop at Glass Beach had put them behind schedule, it wasn't five o'clock yet. The campground wasn't full, and they'd still have two or three hours of daylight to explore the park before dinner. At the gate, he paid the camping fee to a young woman in uniform who handed him a park brochure. He passed it over to Jenna.

A few minutes later, he pulled the camper into a pleasant, open space framed by tall spruce and fir trees and containing the standard wooden picnic table and fire pit. He found the most level spot and turned off the engine.

Jenna jumped out and gazed around as he joined her. "Very pretty," she said happily. "Love the way the sunshine filters through the trees. Let's go explore."

"Great. We can take a look at the brochure and decide what to see."

She wrinkled her nose. "Or we could pick a direction and see where we end up."

"But then we might miss something we want to see."

"Or find something cool and unexpected. Come on, Mark, trust in the universe." She tossed him a grin. "I'm going to change into shorts."

She opened the side door of the Westfalia and went inside, not closing it after her.

Trying not to think about her getting changed, he sat at the picnic table, his back to the camper. He'd have scanned the brochure, but she'd taken it with her. His scientist's mind itched for information. His colleague had mentioned a reconstructed Yurok Indian village, a beach with agates, and a native plant garden.

"I could use a snack." Her voice made him turn. "How about you?"

He forgot all about Yuroks, quartz, and botany. Her legs, long and lean below faded denim cut-offs, were stunning. Every bit as fine as he'd imagined, seeing them through her filmy skirt, and then some.

"See something you like?" she teased.

He dragged his gaze from her legs to see that she was holding out the small cooler, its top hinged back so he could see the contents. A block of white cheese, a package of multi-grain crackers, and half a dozen apples. Was that all she'd planned to eat for dinner, or had she been going to buy groceries or a restaurant meal?

The sight of food made his stomach growl, a reminder that all he'd had to eat in hours was half a slice of pie. "Yeah, that'd be good." She was touchy about her finances. Proud. "If you provide the snack, dinner's on me."

Her eyes narrowed, then she nodded. "If you're sure. Bet you have a knife somewhere to cut the cheese."

"I'll show you where everything is." He rose.

"Great." She clambered back into the camper.

Very nice, curvy butt in those tight shorts. Oh yeah, he saw something he liked. As he followed her, his hands tingled with the desire to touch her, as did other portions of his anatomy.

Even when he was on his own, the space inside the West-falia was tight. With Jenna in there, too, it was almost impossible to move without bumping into each other. When he reached past her to open the drawer, his hand brushed her arm, and she took a step backward, her bottom nudging his hip.

Primal desire made him want to grab her waist and haul her against him, to grind his growing erection against her firm curves. Damn, why did this woman make him react like a caveman?

"Sorry," she murmured, turning to face him, the mischievous sparkle in her eyes belying the apology. "Not a lot of space in here." The front of her body was inches from his. "People really have to be friendly."

"Uh, yeah." He wished Adrienne was here to interpret.

"I'm friendly."

He cleared his throat. "I've noticed that." Not only with

him, but with service station staff and cashiers. But he was the one she'd kissed. That kiss had stunned him with its force.

"Did anyone ever tell you . . ." Her pink lips parted like in a kiss, and she pronounced slowly, stopping between each word, "You think too much."

In his opinion, it was virtually impossible to think too much. On the other hand . . . No, he was glad Adrienne wasn't here. He could handle this himself. He closed the small distance between them, leaned down, and touched his lips to Jenna's, abandoning thought and giving in to the experience.

The overwhelming experience. She was everything at once: lips, tongue, summery scent. Breasts, hips, little sounds deep in her throat. Too much to take in. Yet, not enough, because he wanted her naked, flesh to flesh.

Gasping for breath, he freed his mouth from hers. Somehow, their arms had got wrapped around each other; their bodies were pressed tight. His cock was rock hard, and his hands gripped her butt, though he had no memory of putting them there.

Kissing her was like . . . being hit by lightning. Except in a good way. An amazingly good way. "Jesus, Jenna, you're . . ."

Her eyes were glazed and unfocused, her lips swollen and damp. "Yeah. That was . . ."

His body throbbed with the urgent need to mate, to climax. A primitive need. But he wasn't a primitive guy. He'd never felt this kind of urgency before.

He forced himself to let go of her and step back. This whole thing was extremely odd. The theory about MHC profiles explained attraction, but he didn't recall any studies saying that the sexual spark would be a virtual inferno and well nigh irresistible. "I need to cool down." His voice came out hoarse with unslaked lust. "Let's go for that walk."

"Walk," she echoed. "Right. I was getting a snack."

"I'll wait outside." No way could he stay in here without following through on his body's urging. He clambered out of the camper, erection still painfully hard, grabbing the park brochure on the way.

Pacing slowly around the campsite, taking deep breaths, he read every word of the brochure even though his brain, usually so sharp, had trouble concentrating. Probably, little oxygen was getting to it. Most of the blood in his body had surged below his belt.

The only thought that managed to hold his attention was this: if kissing Jenna had such a potent impact, what would making love be like? Would the two of them survive it?

He had that feeling again, the same one he'd had when he was donning his scuba gear, ready to plunge into the ocean's depths for the very first time.

Chapter 4

My hand shook as I sliced cheddar with Mark's knife. What was up with those kisses?

Aside from his hard-on, which was totally impressive. And irresistible. My thong was soaked, my pussy throbbed with achy need, and if he hadn't been waiting outside I'd have applied a couple of fingers and finished myself off.

I should be pissed at him for breaking the kiss rather than letting the tidal wave sweep us both away to orgasm.

Except . . . Was it just orgasm I craved, or was there something special about the sexy scientist?

I was glad he'd gone out, giving me a little breathing space. I hadn't felt so discombobulated since I'd met Travis. At seventeen, I'd had sex with one guy before, and done a lot of fooling around with several. But Travis—he was different. Physically, it was a sudden revelation of what it meant to be a woman, sensual and sexual. Emotionally . . . Well, that was where I'd made my mistake.

That was what I got for not listening to my mom. When we girls were ten or eleven, she'd given each of us a boringly scientific talk about becoming a woman, sexuality, birth control, STDs, yada yada. I'd heard it all at school, not to mention from Tree and Kat, so I tuned her out. I tuned in again when she said you always fall a little in love with the man who awakens your sexuality, but you shouldn't make the mistake of believing that first love was a forever one.

But then, from age ten to seventeen was a lot of years, and no amount of maternal lecturing could have prepared me for Travis. He was twenty, gorgeous in a dark, moody way, and he rode a motorbike. He had that whole sexy bad boy thing going on, and sex with him was a revelation. More than that, though, he'd said he loved me, and I'd believed he thought I was special.

In my family, I'd never measured up to my two older sisters, nor to Merilee, the sweet, perfect baby. But then, with Travis, I'd believed I was the center of someone's world, and I'd made him the center of mine. And look where my stupidity got me: infected and infertile, my dreams of love and kids shattered.

Yes, there was adoption. But I couldn't think about that, or I'd begin to hope again, to dream, and the dream would be a stupid one. Let's face it, how could I look after kids when I hadn't even looked after myself? Not only that, I honestly had no desire to settle in one place, with one job— and I'd never let myself fall in love again. There were plenty of great guys in the world to have fun with and still remain heart whole and fancy free.

"Jenna? Everything okay?"

I glanced around to see one of those guys peering into the camper.

"Coming." I'd been slicing white cheddar automatically, and had cut too much. I crammed the extra into a plastic bag and put it in the fridge, then bundled cheese and crackers into a couple of paper towels. I handed one bundle to Mark and tossed him a Fuji apple, which he fielded in a neat, one-handed catch. Then I took my own snack and jumped out of the camper to join him.

My little trip down memory lane had put things in perspective. No matter how stunning his kisses were, that was only pheromones, like he'd said. Mark was just another guy to have fun with. He wouldn't get under my skin any more than any of the men I'd hung out with since Travis.

Sunshine, the scent of pine, an intriguing guy—what more could a girl possibly want? Smiling, I closed my eyes and spun in a circle. "Let's go"—I stopped, pointed, and opened my eyes—"that way."

Smart enough not to protest again, Mark fell into step. We found a well-traveled path with a carved wooden sign that told us we were heading for Sumeg Village. Hmm. We were in the woods, near the ocean. Why would there be a village? Where were my instincts taking me this time?

Munching on sharp cheddar and crackers full of grains and seeds, we hiked at a relaxed pace on a weathered chip trail framed by tall trees. From the nearby campground, the smell of roasting wieners and hamburgers drifted on the air, mingling with the green scent of the forest.

I loved being out in nature, feeling as if I were breathing it in through every pore. "We're lucky to get sunshine," I commented. "It rains a lot here."

"Yeah. How did you know that?"

"How tall the trees are, the number of plants, how dense everything is. Trees and shrubs growing on rotten logs. It reminds me of B.C., with the Sitka spruce, Douglas fir, pine, red alder, hemlock."

"You know your trees."

"I hung out with a park ranger a few years ago." Though I had no formal education past that grade twelve diploma my parents had forced me to get—imagine being grounded for an entire *year!*—I was interested in lots of things and absorbed information easily. I finished my cheese and crackers and stuffed the used paper towel in my pocket as Mark did the same.

I was about to take a bite out of my apple when we came

out into a grassy clearing with a few old, apparently unin-
habited wooden buildings. Sumeg Village, the sign said, and
a carved redwood canoe told the story. "It's Native American." There was a sense of peace and timelessness that made
me lower my voice instinctively.

"Yurok." His voice, too, was low.

"Not original?" The few wooden buildings were weathered, but didn't look ancient.

"A reconstruction built twenty years ago by local Yurok
together with park staff. A cultural, educational project."

He must have read about this when he was planning his
trip. I nodded, and moved toward a low structure made of
rough planks and large rocks. "This is odd."

"Sweat house."

"Mmm. Like a sauna." We wandered around, studying
the family homes, the canoe, and what Mark said was a
brush dance pit.

"Brush dance," I echoed. "That's a healing dance for children, isn't it?"

He gazed at me in surprise. "How did you . . . oh, let me
guess. Dated a First Nations man?"

"Yeah, and I volunteered to do grunt work on an archae-
ology dig. It was fascinating."

A family arrived, noisy and excited, and we moved away.
"Let's go this way." I pointed at random, and we started out
on another trail, walking in silence and munching the crisp,
sweet apples. The tall trunks and canopy of green branches
made the place feel like a natural cathedral. Voices chanting
or Indian drumming would have fit but not plain old chatter.

The dull roar of crashing waves suited the place perfectly
and grew louder. Soon we came out above a dramatic, rocky
coastline. Off the headlands, a rocky pillar was an irresistible beacon. Heading toward it, I said, "Looks like a sea
stack." The dramatic stacks were found along the west

coast—craggy chunks of rock cut off from the coast and eroded by waves and wind.

As we got closer, I said, "Oh look, it's still joined to the land. Let's hike over and take the trail to the top."

Mark tossed the nibbled-down core of his apple far into the ocean where frothy waves caught it. I did the same, a respectable throw but not as strong as his. Invigorated by the brisk breeze, I clasped his hand and tugged him faster along the trail, enjoying the warm strength of his hand in mine. Sensual, arousing in a nice, buzzy way, but without the disturbing full-force impact of those kisses.

The path and steps were steep, but we made our way up the rocky crag without needing to pause and catch our breath. On a viewing platform, a couple of serious looking boys peered through binoculars. Mark and I kept going up until we stood on the very top.

Wind whipped my hair wildly, the curls stinging my face. Talk about invigorating, and what a fabulous view of open ocean and the spectacular coastline to the north and south.

"You know what this is?" Mark asked, voice raised so I could hear him over the waves.

I shook my head, expecting a lecture on geology.

"Wedding Rock."

"Sorry, what did you say?"

He repeated himself. "People come here to get married."

"You're making that up." Not that he seemed the fanciful type, nor a romantic.

"Apparently it's true." He pulled something from his pocket, careful not to let it fly away in the wind, and I saw it was the folded-up park brochure.

I laughed. "You've been studying."

"Once a scientist, always a scientist. Besides, I didn't want us to get lost."

I rolled my eyes. "It's a park, not the wilderness." I

thought about what he'd said. "For people who believe in vows, this would be a good place to swear them." I tilted my head up to him. "Especially for someone like you who's into the environment, in love with the ocean."

Would he marry? He wanted a partner, kids. The conventional route would be marriage, but he'd said *life partner*, not *wife*. From what I'd seen so far, he was an interesting mix of conventional and unconventional. What kind of woman would he end up with?

An odd pain throbbed in my chest, and I rubbed at the spot. Heartburn, from eating while I was walking?

Not jealousy. I never felt possessive about the guys I slept with—and Mark and I weren't even lovers. Yet.

A gust of wind blew my hair straight back and raised goosebumps. His arm came around my shoulders slowly, almost cautiously. I leaned into him, appreciating his warmth and solidness atop this windswept, rocky column, and put my arm around his waist. He was so firm—sleek muscle over bone. "It seems like a place to kiss," I told him. "But . . ." That tornado might catch us up and hurl us right off this rock.

His body shook slightly as he chuckled. "Yeah, best play it safe."

A couple of teenage boys came scrambling up the rock to join us on top. We all said hi, then one of them smirked and said, "You dudes going to get married up here?"

I winked at him. "Married? Why ruin a good thing?"

He flushed and both boys laughed.

By unspoken agreement, Mark and I surrendered the pinnacle to them and began to climb down. When we paused on the now-deserted viewing platform, he said jokingly, "So much for teaching morality to the younger generation."

"Hah hah. Morality's about things like respect and honesty, not about rules and social institutions."

"Yeah, but how do people develop morals? They don't come out of thin air; they have to be taught." This time it was Mark who took my hand—the guy was making progress—as we headed down from the viewing platform. "And, even so, you still need laws."

"Laws, rules, they can be so restrictive."

"Yeah, some are stupid. But others have value. Like, with the environment. People—and corporations—aren't all going to do the right thing. There need to be laws to punish pollution and incentives to reward green policies. Same principle goes for personal relationships."

"Such as?"

We were retracing our steps, walking the trail we'd come in on.

"Violence," he said. "Abuse."

"Laws don't do a lot to protect people. I worked in a women's shelter. Some guys take their marriage certificate as a license to abuse their wives."

"I know, and it's awful." He shook his head. "Almost makes you believe in primitive justice, like an eye for an eye."

"It does. Except, there are problems with that, too." I enjoyed talking to Mark. For all his love of science, he understood that some issues didn't have neat scientific explanations or answers.

Okay, so he was bright, thoughtful, and a decent man, on top of being gorgeous and sexy. That didn't make him special. I'd dated other guys like that. A handful, at least. Of course, none of them had been passionate about saving the environment and had traveled to exotic locations to do it. None got into sexy lecturer mode, spoke the truth unfailingly, or so adorably missed the point of jokes or the fact that women were hitting on them.

He steered us off on a trail we hadn't explored before. I

smirked to myself, guessing he'd memorized the park map and had a destination in mind. Oh yeah, he was pretty adorable.

Fine, so maybe Dr. Mark Chambers was special. Each person was special in their own way. He was still just a guy. A guy it might be safer not to kiss . . .

"Surveying falcons," he said, "helping at an archaeological excavation, working in a women's shelter. What other things have you done, Jenna?"

"Park maintenance—that's when I met the park ranger. Art programs with autistic kids. Therapeutic riding with disabled kids. That kind of thing. I've had some of the most fascinating jobs imaginable."

"Why so many different ones?"

I shrugged. "I like variety, same as you."

"My variety's all around one theme, though. One cause that I commit to." His tone wasn't exactly approving.

No surprise, considering how like my family he was. Each to their own, fair enough. But he had no right judging me. "Personally, I don't get the value of sticking to one thing when there are so many other great ones."

For a couple of minutes, we walked in silence. Then he said, almost grudgingly, "You've picked some good causes."

I squeezed his hand. "Thanks."

"I worked with a man who had Asperger's syndrome. He was bright and did his job—statistical analysis—very efficiently."

Asperger's was a form of autism. "But he wasn't much of a team player? Not into doing the social thing at the bar after work?"

"No." He paused. "Though the same could be said for me. I've never been much for socializing."

"You're not bad once you get warmed up," I teased, nudging a gentle elbow into his ribs.

His lips curved. "You do seem to warm me up."

At the side of the path, a scattering of bits of cone—fresh, cast-off outside plates—caught my attention. "Squirrel," I said, and we both stopped to gaze upward, looking for the creature that had been eating the nuts and discarding what it didn't want. "There." I pointed just as a gray squirrel, perched on a branch with its puffy tail curled over its head, chittered and scolded us.

We shared a smile, then walked on. "Seriously," I said, "you do fine at conversation once you get going. You're more comfortable with scientific talk than personal talk, though, aren't you?"

He nodded. "It's what I'm used to. My grandparents' lives center around their work. At home, we talked mostly about work or my studies."

"And even the chats about personal stuff were scientific," I guessed.

"Uh, kind of. Why do you say that?"

"That molecular biology thing about relationships."

"Yeah, that was typical." His fingers tightened on mine for a moment. "I like talking to you. You kick me out of scientist mode. You make me think differently about things."

"Thanks. I like talking to you, too. You're interesting, thoughtful."

The trail came out above a strip of sandy beach strewn with driftwood and rocks and washed by vigorous waves. "Let's hike down," Mark said.

"Sure."

As we started down the steps that began the steep trail to the beach, he said, "This is called Agate Beach."

Glass Beach earlier and now Agate Beach. He did have a way of finding interesting places, even if it was research rather than instinct that led him to them. "Tell me about agates. All I know is that they're some kind of stone."

"They're a type of quartz, usually coming from volcanic rocks or lava."

I listened to Agates 101, delivered in that surprisingly sexy professor mode. Carlos the surfer, the last guy I'd been with, had been gorgeous and athletic, a heavyweight between the thighs but pretty lightweight between his ears. It was a treat to be with an intelligent man.

Not that Mark didn't measure up extremely well in the between-the-thighs department, from what I'd felt. I was looking forward to more intimate exposure.

When we got down to the beach, I took off my sandals and began to search for stones. Unlike on Glass Beach, the pretty agates were few and far between. It was fun hunting for them and a gleeful triumph each time I found one. Mark seemed content to follow in my meandering wake, hands in his pockets, admiring the treasures I held out to him.

"You're not searching," I complained.

"It's more fun watching you. You're like a kid, Jenna."

I'd been told that many times, sometimes with a sneer and sometimes with approval. Mark's smile put him in the latter group, thank heavens.

I stood near the water's edge, hair streaming back in the breeze, breathing in the tangy salt air, and watching the sun sink lower in the sky. Then I turned to gaze at the other great view: the hot scientist. The wind only ruffled his hair, but it whipped the loose tank top against him, plastering soft cotton against firm muscles.

"Life's there to enjoy, so why not dive in?" I'd been collecting agates with every intention of tossing them back when we finished our walk. I didn't want to steal beauty from this lovely beach. Now I divvied the stones up and held out half to him. "Bet I can skip stones better than you."

A grin touched his lips then disappeared. He dropped our two pairs of sandals, which he'd been carrying, and let me pour the stones into his hand. "How much do you want to bet?"

"How much? You have such a conventional mind. Let's

bet something more fun. Like . . . Loser has to strip off and go skinny dipping."

"Jenna! It's a public beach. And the water's freezing cold, and the waves could be dangerous."

"Oh jeesh, you're no fun. And you're a coward, Dr. Chambers. You know you're going to lose."

The quick grin reappeared. "Actually, I'm pretty sure I'm going to win."

I liked that rare touch of male arrogance. "Oh, I see. So, it's that you don't want to see me naked."

"Damn." He ran a hand through his hair then rubbed the back of his neck. "Yeah, of course I do. I'm male, aren't I?"

Oh, yeah! From those angular features to the broad shoulders and slim waist showcased by his tank top, the muscular legs in shorts, the hard thrust of cock I'd felt when we kissed. "Then get with the program. Skip away." And I sure hoped he did lose, because I wanted him naked sooner rather than later.

The woman's cockiness was appealing—so much about her was appealing—and Mark felt almost guilty about taking advantage. He'd spent a lot of hours beside oceans all over the world, monitoring measurements, supervising staff and volunteers, musing about research or papers he was working on. Rocks of all sizes had found their way into his hands, and he'd become a proficient stone-skipper.

When he won, she wouldn't really strip down, would she? Did he want her to? Clothed, she was virtually irresistible. Naked . . .

"Best out of six tries?" she suggested.

He nodded. "You go first."

"Want to size up what I've got?"

"I plan to be doing that once you lose." He wasn't flirting so much as stating the truth.

She gave an amused hoot. "Dream on, Science Guy."

From the collection in her hand, she selected a stone. She arched back, breasts pressing full and unconfined against her tank top, and sent it zipping across the dark, ruffled surface of the water. She'd timed it well, between waves, and sent it far enough out that it hit an almost-flat surface. It bounced four times, then sank.

She applauded herself vigorously. "Let's see you match that."

He studied the selection in his hand. Smooth, flattish stones skipped best, ones that had a little heft but weren't too heavy. Few of his agates met that description. For the first try, to get his arm warmed up and a feel for the water and wind, he chose one of the poorer ones. He'd save the three best for his last attempts.

He threw it low and easy, but its shape counted against it, and it only skipped three times.

Jenna booed, then threw a five, which had her jumping up and down, cheering.

The sun dipped toward the horizon, a huge golden ball that dazzled the eyes and cast stripes of light and shade over the water, adding to the challenge.

They took turns, with both of them ranging between three and five. Her scores were heading downward as she ran out of good stones. Her last throw was a two, accompanied by a disgusted, "That sucks."

Mark held his last stone to his lips and breathed on it, as gamblers did with dice. It was his best. A six should be easy. He was about to throw when she said, "Looks like it's going to be a tie."

If he threw a six, she'd lose. If he threw a five, it would be a tie. Then what?

No way were they both going to strip and dash into the water. Were they? His breath quickened and his cock twitched at the thought.

The rational thing to do if they tied—or even if he won—

was to laugh and call off the bet. If Jenna actually started to take her clothes off, what would he do?

"Mark? You going to toss the stone or throw in the towel?"

He took a breath, then let fly. Five skips. Exactly as he'd intended.

Expectantly, he faced Jenna. "Looks like it's a tie."

"Well now, didn't that work out nicely?" In the fading light, her eyes gleamed and for the first time he wondered if this had been her plan all along.

"Sun's almost down," he pointed out. "It's chilling off."

"Then we'd better hurry up." She reached for the hem of her tank top.

Tearing his gaze off her, he scanned the beach. It was almost deserted now, people no doubt heading to their campsites for dinner. The only ones left were a group at the far end, clustered around a driftwood shelter they'd been building. At that distance, in this light, he could only make out silhouettes.

When he turned back to Jenna, he gasped and froze, eyes locked on her.

She was naked from the waist up, tossing her top onto the beach.

Stunning. Sexy. Primitive, like a nature goddess, with her long, wild hair catching the last rays of sun, her slim, toned shoulders and arms, and those lovely, perfect breasts. Rose-tipped, just as he'd guessed. Shit, had he died and gone to heaven?

He sucked in air, chest heaving, cock pulsing and thickening, and took a step toward her. "Jenna." His voice came out even huskier than usual and all he could manage were those two syllables.

Her laugh rippled through the evening air, light and golden as the fingers of fading sunlight that gilded the waves. "You're falling behind." She reached over to grab the bottom of his own tank top. When she lifted it, her fingers grazed his skin in a touch he thought was deliberate.

They were going to do this. They really were.

Anticipation and lust raced through his veins, and he grabbed his top out of her hands and yanked it off. He was breathing fast, like he'd been running, and his chest pumped to get air.

Jenna smiled approval and reached for the waist of her shorts.

He mirrored her movements, undoing his own button, lowering his zipper. Under his zipper, a rising bulge pressed insistently, demanding release. He grabbed the waist of his shorts and tugged downward, and a moment later stood naked but for light cotton boxers.

Jenna . . . Holy shit. If she'd been wearing underwear, she'd skimmed it off with her shorts because, as she straightened from pulling them off, she was naked. Utterly naked.

So beautiful, the sight of her stole his breath.

She was slim, but with gentle, womanly curves and a tiny vee of dark gold curls between her thighs. He wanted to bury his face between her legs, run his fingers through those curls, then down to the softness of her inner thighs. To smell her, taste her, explore every intimate, erotic inch with his fingers, his lips, his tongue.

When he focused on her face, he saw the knowing smile of a woman who was confident of her effect.

Wordlessly, he pulled off his boxers and watched as her gaze lowered and she saw the effect she had on him. Was it his imagination, in this dim light, or did her throat ripple with a swallow?

What was she thinking? Did she, too, want to touch and taste?

At the thought of her pink lips wrapped around his shaft, he barely managed to suppress a groan.

She grabbed his hand, her fingers a little chilly. "Together. On three. One . . . two . . . three!"

Together they ran across the pebbly beach. Icy cold water nipped their toes as they splashed through the fringe of waves. Mark's erection quickly subsided as they forged ahead, up to their knees now, then their thighs. The water hit his genitals and they shriveled. Would he ever see them again? "Jesus, it's freezing!"

"Faster! If we don't keep running, we'll get too cold."

And if they kept running and submerged themselves, they'd get hypothermia. Still, he let her tug him forward until she let out a whoop and threw herself forward into a wave, taking him with her.

Shock made them let go hands, and when he submerged he saw her beside him, scooping masses of wet hair back from her face, laughing even as shivers wracked her.

Much as he loved the ocean, now was not the time to be in it. He grabbed her hand again and tugged her toward shore, moving as quickly as his rapidly numbing legs would take him.

When they cleared the ocean and reached the beach, she wrapped herself around him, a bundle of icy-cold, shivering limbs and breasts. At first, he was so chilled he barely registered the contact, but then their bodies began to heat.

Blood surged through his veins, almost painfully as he went quickly from icy to warm. Warm, at least, wherever his skin met hers.

She wriggled closer, arms tight around him, and he returned the embrace, gripping her butt. Her breasts were so soft against his pecs, and the curls of her pussy hair teased his groin. Hello, the shrinkage hadn't been permanent. His frozen cock began to fill and he eased their bodies apart slightly, to let it lift up his belly, then he closed the gap again, sandwiching his erection between them.

"God, Jenna, I want you."

Voice breathy, teasing, she said, "Well, it's about ti—"

His kiss cut off the last word and they both flung them-selves into it, mouths open, lips demanding, tongues thrust-ing and mating. Desire and need were irresistible now. Who cared if this made sense? They had to have sex.

Now.

Somehow, he had enough presence of mind to remember they were embracing naked on a public beach. He forced himself away from her, grabbed up their clothes, and looked desperately around for a private spot.

She pointed. "I think they've gone."

As best he could see, the people who'd been building a shelter had deserted the makeshift driftwood structure.

He followed Jenna as she hurried toward it, her back and tumbling hair pale in the fading light, her butt seductively curvy.

Driftwood logs and planks of assorted sizes, loosely piled together with many gaps between them, formed four sides and a roof. There was no actual entrance, only one side where the space between two logs was wider. She bent and slipped through it.

He tossed their clothing and shoes inside and climbed in after her. The structure wasn't high enough for them to stand upright, and besides, it wasn't standing he had in mind. For-tunately, the builders had picked one of the rare sandy patches on the beach, so, when he caught her around the waist and tumbled the two of them down, himself on the bottom, his back grazed rough sand rather than rocks.

Laughing softly, she shifted to her knees, straddling his thighs. "Oh yeah, Mark. I knew you had potential."

His swollen shaft rose between them and she grasped it in one hand, purring, "Mmm, nice."

His cock was harder than he remembered it ever being. Her fingers, stroking down his shaft, teasing the crown,

were more than he could take. Her rings added teasing fric-
tion. He'd explode in her hand like a kid if she kept this up.
Usually he was a good lover, one who understood foreplay
and would do his best to satisfy his woman. But this thing
with Jenna, since he'd seen her walking toward the diner a
few hours ago, was different. This was primal. "Jenna,
now," he said, trying not to beg. "I need you now."

"Yes, me too," she breathed urgently. "Right now."

Thank God.

She let go of him, shifted, and suddenly he remembered.
"Shit, no condom."

Her husky laugh sent ripples of longing through him.
"And here I thought you were the kind of guy who'd always
be prepared."

He was. Just not for sex. Not for Jenna Fallon.

She hooked her discarded shorts with one hand and
tugged them over to reach in the pocket. "You brought a
park map, Dr. Chambers. I brought . . . Ta da!" She flour-
ished a condom. "Now who's more prepared?"

"You are, and thank God." He grabbed it from her hand
and ripped the package open, blood surging through his
veins, the deep ache inside him demanding release. Still
straddling him, she eased back and somehow he got the
thing rolled onto his erect penis.

Then guilt hit him. He'd never been so selfish, so need-
driven. "Are you sure . . . ?" He tried to read her expression,
but the light was too dim.

Her amused voice, though, was certain. "Idiot, of course I
am. And yeah, I'm ready. Feel."

She caught his hand and brought it to the apex of her
thighs. Their bodies were still damp from the ocean, but this
moisture was different. Hotter, thicker, and as he caressed
her lush folds, the sultry scent of her arousal rose in the
night air, inflaming him even further.

"Now," she said. "You and me." She grasped his shaft again and rose up on her knees, lifting herself above him.

He opened her with his fingers as she guided him to her opening. Her steamy moisture bathed the head of his cock and he nudged eagerly, spreading her lips, easing into her.

Oh, she felt good, snug and steamy, the sensation so wonderful it was almost more than he could bear. The urge to thrust deep, to pound into her, rose hard inside him and he fought against it.

Instead, he held still as she lifted up and cool air brushed his damp flesh, a pleasant contrast to her heat. Hands braced on his chest, she leaned forward, hips tilting to shift the angle so that when she slid down again, she took him even deeper.

"Oh, yes, Mark," she whispered, eyes gleaming in the dusky light.

Wanting to kiss her, he tried to pull her forward but she resisted, arching back instead, straightening as she rose and fell. Wet hair straggled down to frame her lovely face, and her firm little breasts bobbed as she rode him.

Despite the chill night air, his blood was hot and thick, his cock so swollen it ached, and the need to find release coiled tight at the base of his spine. "Jenna, Jesus, this is good."

He couldn't hold back. His balls were tightening.

She whimpered and writhed against him, and he slid his hand between their bodies, found the engorged bud of her clit, and gently squeezed it.

"Oh, yes," she cried. "Yes, more."

Gasping for breath, needing to come, he squeezed again, a little harder, then his orgasm poured through his body, sweeping away everything but a sensation so intense that bliss and pain mingled together.

She cried out again, a high note of pleasure as he plunged hard and deep inside her. The internal spasms of her climax surged around him, ripples that caressed him as he thrust again, more weakly. And again, until he had nothing more to give.

His heart hammered so hard in his chest he could barely catch his breath, and his head actually ached from pressure. "My God," he got out between gasps.

She had sagged forward as if she didn't have the strength to hold herself upright. He couldn't see her face. "Jenna, are you okay?" He rested his hands on her waist, feeling the gentle swell of her hips.

Slowly, she straightened, as if the strength was returning to her body. Upright again, with him still lodged inside her, she flicked damp hair behind her shoulders. "Okay?" A smile spread in a gleam of flashing eyes and white teeth. "Oh yeah, I'm great."

"I mean, not just, uh, climaxing, but okay about this? About us doing this?" Normally, he treated the decision to have sex as a rational one, one he and his partner discussed ahead of time, comparing expectations.

"Having sex? Duh, yeah. Haven't I been chasing after you all day?" She lifted herself off him and shivered.

He was chilled too, the heat of Jenna's body gone, the fiery impact of climax fading. At least, now that he'd almost caught his breath, the headache had gone. "Well, uh, maybe. But still, it's an intimate act and I—"

"It's just sex, Mark," she said, sounding slightly annoyed. She pulled on a tiny thong, and her shorts. "It's about two people having fun. Don't go all heavy on me."

Okay, that was a pretty clear statement of how she saw things. No big surprise that unconventional Jenna would toss out all the messy complications society had attached to the act of sex and strip it down to its essence.

As she slipped the tank top over her head, he began to put on his own clothes.

Not that he wanted commitment, emotion, all of that relationship stuff, with Jenna. Their whole approach to life was too different, their lives were on opposite courses, and this short meet-in-the-middle time was only about enjoyment.

He'd had casual sex before, though he'd known the women in question for weeks or months beforehand. Tonight wasn't all that different. Maybe it just reminded him too much of the free love philosophy at Freedom Valley. Perhaps that was why he felt an achy burn in his chest.

Dressed, he and Jenna climbed out of the driftwood shelter, put their sandals on, and walked back in the direction they'd come from. A crescent moon and a few stars gave enough light to find their way, but they might have trouble when they got into the park where the trails were overhung by trees. It had been foolish staying on the beach after sunset.

But for Jenna, he wouldn't have done it. She turned him into a man he barely recognized. He threaded his fingers through hers. "When we were talking about jobs," he said tentatively, not wanting to insult her but trying to understand, "you said there are so many interesting things and you like variety. Is that how it is with men, too?"

"Sure," she said promptly. "With people in general. You like someone, so you hang out with them for a while. You're turned on by someone, you have sex with him. Easy, fun, no complications."

Yeah, that was like Alicia and the others at the commune. To Jenna, he was just one of a string of guys she'd slept with. If she'd asked some other man for a ride, she'd have had sex with him tonight.

That wasn't exactly flattering. The pain throbbed in his chest again. A residual ache from the vigorous sex? Or a twinge of primal male jealousy?

Ridiculous. Jenna wasn't his mate. As bewitching and fun as she was, he wanted a woman who was more serious about life, more committed to a worthwhile cause. She was good-hearted, but a dilettante. And then there was the true bottom line. Unevolved though it might be, when he found his mate for life, he'd want her to be faithful.

He'd want her to *want* to be faithful. To love him so deeply she had no desire to ever make love with another man. He wanted a woman he'd love the same way.

What were the chances of finding that? He wasn't even sure what love was. He and his grandparents rarely spoke the word and when they did it meant security, blood ties, affection, but not powerful emotion.

Alicia had tossed the word here and there with abandon, rather the way Jenna did. Jenna had even said it to him when she'd finally twisted his arm into giving her a ride. *I love you, you're the best.* A few minutes earlier, she'd said virtually the same thing to the mechanic.

An odd thought hit him. Maybe she had no better idea than he of the deeper emotion that could give the word so much power. The kind of emotion he knew Adrienne felt for her wife and their unborn child.

"You think sex is about fun and monogamy's archaic," he said. "So, how do you feel about love?"

Chapter 5

Love? Involuntarily, my hand twitched in Mark's. Not wanting him to know he'd strummed an old hurt, I joked, "Why're you asking? You falling in love with me, Science Guy?"

"I barely know you." His tone wasn't insulting; it was that matter-of-fact way he had of stating what he saw as truth. "I'm . . . curious."

Love was dangerous. More dangerous than the night-dark ocean that crashed on the beach behind us.

"Love's great," I said flippantly. "Look at today, all the things to love. Strawberry pie, a great mechanic, just the right man turning up to give me a ride, Glass Beach, stone-skipping and skinny-dipping and—"

"Not that kind of love," he broke in. "The serious kind."

"Well now, there's your answer. I don't *do* serious." Before he could push, I gave a dramatic—and genuine—shiver. "I'm freezing."

After the great sex, a residual chill from the cold ocean had sunk into my bones. Shorts and a tank top weren't doing much to warm me.

"It's a steep trail." Mark pointed ahead. We'd almost reached the end of the beach, and the path up the hill loomed ahead. "The climb will heat us up, then we'll hurry back to the camper and grab stuff so we can take hot showers."

"Showers in the plural?" I teased. "Shouldn't we be green and share one?" Now that would be fun. Streaming water—hot water—a naked Mark, soapy bubbles . . . Arousal stirred again. Having sex with him had been pretty amazing.

His fingers tightened around mine and I wondered if he was imagining the same thing. Dryly, he said, "Men's and women's—separate facilities?"

"You are such a coward."

"With kids using them, too?"

"Yeah, yeah, you're right. Too bad."

We paced steadily upward, toward the top of the hill, both silent now.

Yes, I wanted him again, and yet I felt an odd uncertainty. What was it about Mark? Maybe just the pheromone thing, that odd chemistry when we kissed. When we'd had sex in that driftwood shelter, I'd avoided kissing him, afraid that . . . I shook my head. Afraid of what? That we'd combust and set fire to the shelter?

I was being silly. He might be the most potent kisser I'd ever met, but he was just another guy. That was all any of them would ever be.

All the same, maybe it was safer not to kiss him again. You didn't have to kiss to have great sex.

We set out on a path, walking as quickly as we could, but the park was so dark we could barely make out the trail. Above our heads, branches rustled in the breeze. It was cool enough to raise goosebumps, and some people might have found it spooky, but I always felt at home outside. Trusting Mark's map-reading memory, I let him choose the route until we ended up back at our campsite.

Quickly, we gathered towels, soap, shampoo, and fresh clothes, and hurried to the service area where there were restrooms and showers. The campground seemed to be full, some sites overflowing with vehicles and tents. As we passed by, people moved about or sat at picnic tables, their voices relaxed and happy. Smoke rose from campfires and the scent of wood smoke and meat cooking drifted to us, making me glad we'd had a snack earlier—and that salmon didn't take long to cook. Here and there, music played, but not loud enough to annoy neighbors.

When we reached the shower building, Mark said, "They're pay, by the way. I read it in the brochure."

"Now you tell me." I hadn't brought any money. I held out my hand. "Buy me a shower?"

When he held out some coins, I took them gratefully. "Meet you back at the campsite. I might be in here for a while."

"Sure you can find your way back?"

I rolled my eyes and joked, "If I don't, I'll just have to crash with someone else."

He studied me as if he wasn't sure whether to take me seriously. "All your gear's in the Westfalia."

I winked. "Not to mention that double bed. And the bottle of wine." I opened the door to the ladies' shower. "See you soon."

"Want a coffee? I'm going to make some when I get back."

"No, thanks." I drank coffee occasionally, but was more of a tea person.

Inside, I stripped off hurriedly and stepped into a shower stall. Too bad we couldn't shower together, but all the same it was sheer bliss standing under hot running water and lathering the salt out of my hair and off my skin. Once I warmed up, I felt terrific.

What could be more invigorating than a chilly skinny dip followed by steamy hot sex? My instincts had definitely been on target when they sent me to Mark.

I toweled off vigorously until my skin tingled. Tonight, we'd have a great meal, another lovely round of sex, and tomorrow we'd be on the road again. Easy and fun. I paused. He must realize that, too, mustn't he? I hated it when guys suddenly went serious on me, and Mark had asked about love . . .

No, that was just his scientific curiosity. When he envisioned his perfect life partner, she sure wouldn't look like me. She'd be all serious and dedicated, not half as much fun and probably nowhere near as sexy.

Ooh, man, that was a little bitchy. I liked Mark. He deserved everything his heart desired. A woman who was dedicated and fun and sexy. Of course, that was what I wanted for him.

My body was cooling off again, so I quickly slipped into jeans and a long-sleeved tee and gathered my stuff. I'd forgotten to bring a comb and my hair was too tangled to finger comb.

Back at the campsite, Mark, in jeans and a denim shirt worn loose rather than tucked in, had his back to me. He was laying kindling and logs in the fire pit, absorbed in his task, and didn't notice me. A camping lantern lit the picnic table and a mug sat there, too.

Inside the camper, I found his damp towel spread over the back of one of the front seats, so did the same with my own. A French coffee press, half-filled with freshly-made coffee, sat on the counter. The cupboard above was almost empty of food items but did contain a plastic freezer bag of ground coffee. There were no tea bags.

I rubbed conditioner through my hair, then took my wide-toothed comb and went outside again. Mark stood by the fire, sipping coffee and watching as tendrils of flame licked the kindling, making it spark and crackle. He smiled at me. "I didn't hear you come back. Enjoy your shower?"

"Mmm, it felt great." I perched on the end of the picnic

table closest to the fire and gestured to his handiwork. "That's nice. I love campfires."

"I thought you might."

I began to work the comb through hair stressed by wind, sun, and salt water. He stared at me so intently, I said, "What?"

"It's a pretty picture. You combing your hair in the light of the fire and the lantern."

"Thanks." One thing I'd come to realize with this guy: he wasn't into compliments; he just said it as he saw it. I liked that.

"Hungry?" he asked.

"Starving. I could eat a . . . mmm, how about a salmon?"

"I'll get out the barbecue."

He went into the camper and a few seconds later I heard, "Shit!"

"What's wrong?" I called.

He stuck his head out, looking pissed. "I haven't used the barbecue in a while and was sure I had a full fuel container. Turns out it's an empty. Guess I saved it to recycle it and . . . Well, doesn't matter how it happened. I'll drive to the closest store and buy more."

Hah. So Mr. Organized wasn't perfect. The poor guy sounded so annoyed at himself that I said, "Or we could eat sashimi."

"No, we don't know how fresh the fish is, and salmon's particularly prone to parasites."

"Spoil sport." Still, no doubt he was right. "D'you have any tin foil?"

"Uh . . . let me look."

He disappeared then reappeared. "I do. Why?"

"Let me play in your kitchen." I tore myself away from the fire. In the doorway of the Westfalia, I said, "You be man, tend fire. Woman cook."

He chuckled. "Yeah, I definitely see you as the gender stereotype type of person."

When he jumped out of the camper and went past me, I squeezed his butt, feeling hard muscle under well-worn denim. Oh no, he wasn't the typical desk or lab scientist, not for one moment.

Inside, I ripped off a fair-sized sheet of foil and plunked the salmon in the middle, skin side down. After opening a couple of cupboard doors, I found salt and pepper and sprinkled them on, then sliced the lemon and lay the slices on top.

I found the chardonnay in the tiny fridge and a corkscrew in a drawer. This mini kitchen was so much fun. After opening the wine, I splashed maybe an ounce over the salmon, then pulled the edges of foil together and folded them together to make a seal.

I rinsed my hands, then took the neat foil bundle out to Mark. "Can you shove the fire away from one corner of the fire pit? Leave the coals and ash."

When he did, I slipped the packet into the cleared spot. "Salmon *en papillote*. Or hidden salmon, take your pick."

"Huh?"

"The French wrap food in parchment paper with herbs, spices, and a little liquid. *En papillote*. And in Greece, guerrilla fighters did the same. Meat, potatoes, veggies, all wrapped up in parchment with enough liquid to cook everything. They didn't want the smell of dinner cooking to lead their enemies to them."

"Hence *hidden*. Fascinating. How do you know all this? No, let me guess. You dated a chef?"

I chuckled. "You're getting to know me. No, it was two different guys. The French one was a chef. The Greek was a sailor whose grandmother told him the story."

"I'm almost afraid to ask. How many men have you dated?"

The judgmental tone was back in his voice. I stuck out my chin and tilted my head to look up at him. "Dated? Meaning, had sex with, or hung out with for a while, or what?"

He shifted feet, looking ill at ease. "Uh, had sex with."

"I don't notch my belt. Most places I go, there's a fun guy or two to hook up with."

"Two? Not, uh, at the same time?" He sounded almost appalled.

I raised my eyebrows. "We already established that monogamy's not my thing."

"Sorry. I'm being judgmental. It's sort of a habit."

"A bad one. Who elected you God?"

"Yeah, you're right. You just hit a sore point. Reminded me of Alicia, the commune. Believe me, it's no fun having a mother who'd rather sleep with a bunch of guys than spend time with her kid." He shook his head. "You're not her. Sorry. But I am curious. You're so different than me."

I softened. A man who could admit a mistake. "Curiosity's okay. I'll get the wine and we can talk while dinner cooks."

A few minutes later, we were settled across from each other at the picnic table, sitting at the end closest to the fire, wine glasses in front of us. The sleeves of his shirt were rolled carelessly up his forearms and enough buttons were undone at the neck to show a V of strong chest. His skin looked dark in contrast to the pale blue denim.

He lifted his wine glass. His hands were big, long-fingered, yet he wasn't clumsy. A scientist needed to have a deft touch. After dinner, I hoped to experience more of that touch myself.

"This trip's turned out to be more interesting than I expected," he said in a sort of toast.

I always expected things—especially journeys—to be interesting. And they always were. This afternoon was one I'd save in my memory bank. Clinking my glass to his, I said, "You need to raise your expectations."

I sipped the chardonnay, enjoying the green apple and kiwi notes, tarter than the sweet Fuji apple I'd eaten earlier.

"Guess I don't like being disappointed." A pause, then he said softly, as if speaking to himself, "That happened a lot when I was a little kid."

Equally quietly, I said, "But not with your grandparents, I bet."

"N-no."

"Mark? That wasn't a resounding no. I'd have thought your Grandma and Grandpa would have been totally reliable."

"Oh, they were. And once I figured out what to expect, they never once let me down."

"So why the hesitation when you answered me?"

He took a long swallow of wine. "In the beginning I hoped for something . . . Well, people can only give what they're capable of giving, right?"

If he thought I was going to let it go at that, he sure didn't know me. "What weren't they capable of giving?"

He sighed, then after a moment said, "Warmth. Hugs. At Freedom Valley there was lots of hugging, but it was indiscriminate. When I went to Grandma and Grandpa, I got all their attention, but not—" He broke off, shrugged awkwardly. "I don't even know what I'm trying to say."

"You didn't feel loved?"

He took a long breath. "I know they loved me but they aren't emotional, demonstrative people. Even with each other, they connect intellectually. I've rarely even seen them kiss each other."

I nodded. "I get what you're saying. My parents are a bit more demonstrative with us and each other. They're not really cuddly people, though."

"But you know they love you."

"Yeah, though with me it's more the *I love you, but* kind of love."

"How do you mean?"

"Like, *Jenna, we love you, but we really wish you'd get a real job.* You know. We love you, but you don't measure up to our standards."

He nodded, but a flicker of expression made me accuse, "You agree with them. You're just like them."

His lips pressed together, then finally opened. "Yes and no. You have a right to live your own life, and it seems to me you're not hurting anyone, and you're helping a lot of people. Not to mention peregrine falcons."

He said it dead seriously, so I held back the chuckle that rose to my lips. "So far so good. Now give me the *but*."

"Your choices are unusual ones. Your parents probably think you'd be safer if you lived a more conventional life."

"But not happier. They should care if I'm happy."

"Yeah, but maybe they can't relate to what makes you happy. Maybe you're too different from them."

"Which is exactly why I used to think I was adopted."

"Look at my grandparents and Alicia. Kids aren't necessarily like their parents. It makes it hard on everyone."

"I should've been Alicia's kid, and you should've got my parents. Everyone would have been happy." Before he could protest, I waved my hand. "I know, I know. If Alicia'd been my mom, I'd have lost her when I was just a kid, then got stuck with your grandparents and that would so not have worked out."

I rose. "I think dinner's almost cooked. I'll get the rest of the food."

In the camper's mini kitchen, I rinsed the carrots and strawberries, gathered up plates, cutlery, and the loaf of French bread, then went back out. Mark had retrieved the packet of salmon from the fire, then stacked on a couple more logs which were starting to blaze. He'd also topped off our wine glasses. I realized he hadn't commented on the chardonnay. Maybe he didn't like my selection but was too polite to say so.

Together we spread out the food and helped ourselves. Before digging in, I studied my plate in the light of the lantern, appreciating the deep pinky-orange of the fish, the bright orange of the carrots, the vivid red of the strawberries, all so dramatic beside the crusty bread, and set off by the cream of simple stoneware plates.

Meanwhile, Mark had taken a couple of bites of salmon.

"How does it taste?" I asked.

"Uh . . ." He took another bite, chewing more slowly this time. "It's good," he said with surprise.

"You doubted me."

"Just never cooked anything this way." He gave a short laugh. "Actually, I avoid cooking. Mostly I grab a sandwich or eat a handful of crackers and some cheese. Food's not a big deal in my life."

"Mark, *everything* should be a big deal. You should be in the moment. If you're eating, really eat. Enjoy the colors, textures, scent, flavor."

A reflective look crossed his face. "You made me do that with the strawberry pie."

"And?"

"It was one of the best things I've ever eaten."

"It was truly fabulous pie, but you've probably eaten tons of other great things." I leaned forward, elbows on the table. "God, Mark, you've lived in Thailand, China, other places that must have terrific food. And you missed it because you weren't paying attention. I bet you missed their music too, and the clothing and jewelry and art and—" I threw my arms up to the night sky. "Everything. You missed everything but the ocean. Am I right?"

"The ocean—my job—that's what matters."

"And the people. And you. You matter. You can save the ocean and still have fun doing it."

His expression told me the idea had never crossed his mind, and now that I'd planted it there, it wasn't resting easily. Fine. When a seed opened in spring, it sent out shoots and roots and disturbed the ground around it until, ultimately, it popped its head out into the sunshine and grew into something beautiful. Maybe, inside Mark's genius brain, the same thing would happen.

Turning my attention back to dinner, I forked up a mouthful of salmon. Mmm, the combination of lemon juice, wine, salt, and pepper was classic, and the fish was moist and flaky.

"How do you like the wine?" I asked Mark.

His lips curved wryly, and he made a show of lifting his glass, sipping, and rolling the wine in his mouth before swallowing. "Really good. Like there's some fruit in it."

"Duh, it's made from grapes," I teased. Then, relenting, "Green apples, right? More tart than the apples we were eating earlier?"

"Uh . . ."

Right. He probably hadn't even noticed he was eating an apple, much less how it tasted.

I munched a carrot, then broke off a piece of bread and teamed it with another bite of salmon. Every single bite could be a different taste sensation.

It was like men. Each was unique. Most had some great qualities, the majority had a few disappointing ones, and a few were total losers.

I studied him curiously, noting that he was eating more slowly now, as if he was paying attention. "I get the impression you're shocked by the idea that I'd sleep with two guys at the same time? I mean—" I quickly amended, "not *mé-*

nage à trois, I'm not into that. But, you know, not monogamy."

His brows had risen at "ménage à trois," then settled again. "Shocked?" He tested the word. "No, it takes a lot to shock me. Just puzzled, I guess. But wait, what's wrong with ménage?"

Well, how about that? I'd really misjudged the guy. "You're into ménage? Seriously?"

"God, no."

Mark had never had this kind of conversation about sex with anyone, male or female. It was totally fascinating. From a scientific standpoint, of course. At Freedom Valley, any and every sexual practice had existed. For him personally, as an adult, he was completely into one man, one woman, but he had no problem with the idea of sex that was purely casual and not aiming toward a future. If he hadn't been, he'd still be a virgin.

"I'm just saying," he explained, "that everybody has their own boundaries. It's kind of fascinating. Like you, you'll date two men at the same time, so what have you got against ménage?"

"It's not a moral objection," she answered promptly. "But I like to concentrate on one person, one thing, at a time."

Just as she'd said earlier, about living in the moment, he mused, chewing a mouthful of salmon and tasting the tang of lemon, the zing of salt, the sharpness of pepper. He had to admit, he'd enjoyed the food and wine since she'd made him slow down and taste them. And he enjoyed Jenna. All the moments with Jenna, whether they were exploring the beach, discussing their philosophies of life, or having incredible sex.

She was so lovely with golden light flickering over her face and highlights gleaming in her hair, her expression intent as she studied him over the rim of her wine glass.

Right now, she was intent on him. Totally focused. Next week, maybe tomorrow, she'd be equally intent on another man. Yes, that hurt his ego. But also, he couldn't relate to it. If Jenna was his lover, no way would he want another one.

Another reason they'd never be more than a temporary thing. He'd want fidelity, and that'd be like trying to harness a butterfly.

"How long does it take you to switch?" he asked. "Like, do you need a couple of days between, or will you sleep with one man in the afternoon and another at night, or—"

"Mark." She held up her hands, stopping him, shaking her head so her curls tossed. "Why all these questions?"

"Just trying to understand."

She shook her head again, laughing. "Sorry, I'm not a scientific equation. I don't have any rules, it's what feels good at the time." Her brows drew together and she studied him. "Okay, my turn. You normally only sleep with someone when you're in a committed relationship?"

"Uh . . . I'm not sure I've ever been in a committed relationship." He'd dated one woman for a year in graduate school, but they'd agreed from the start that they had no future. She knew she'd return home to India and marry a man her parents approved of. They'd enjoyed each other's company, had good sex, but neither had harbored romantic feelings. In a way, that was like what Jenna did with her numerous guys, except she leaped into sex way more quickly than he did. "But I don't sleep with a woman until we get to know each other."

"Best way to get to know each other is sex."

"Not necessarily."

"You're advocating conversation? I thought you'd never been a big talker."

"I hadn't." He frowned and rubbed his forehead. At least not until today. "Damn, you get me confused."

"It's my goal in life."

He had to smile at that. "I guess by talk, I meant talking about mutual interests. Scientific interests."

"And how do you get to know someone that way?"

You got to know them as a scientist, but not as a person.

"Don't you find," she went on, "that once people are sexually intimate, they talk more? Share more? That's when you really get to know them."

Disgruntled, he said, "Have you been taking lessons from your mother, the litigator? You're pretty good at cross-examination."

"Hah, I'm the intellectual lightweight in the family."

He reflected on everything she'd said and shook his head. "I don't think so." Maybe she was a career lightweight in that she didn't want to settle into one occupation, but . . . "You're definitely not stupid."

Her eyes flashed wide, and a pleased expression crossed her face. Then her lips quirked. "Why, Dr. Chambers, you sure know how to flatter a girl."

He winced. "Sorry, that was clumsy. I mean, I think you're smart and thoughtful."

She waved a hand. "Actually, it was okay the first time around. It's one of the nicest things anyone's ever said to me."

He snorted. "I don't believe that for a moment. I can't imagine you don't get showered with far more poetic compliments than I'd ever dream up. You're probably the most beautiful woman I've ever seen, you're fun to be around, and you challenge me to think."

Her lips shaped a soft curve, and her eyes glowed as she leaned across the table and touched his forearm. "You get points for sincerity."

He'd rolled up his shirtsleeves when he was tending the fire, and not rolled them down again, so her hand rested on bare skin. "What do these points win me?" He wasn't sure if she was talking about sex or if this was another of her crazy games, like the stone-skipping.

"Anything you want." A seductive smile flashed. "Tell me, Mark, what do you most want from me?"

He wanted her to be someone different. To have that same intellectual curiosity, perceptiveness, and sense of fun, but to be a woman who committed to one cause and one man. Because then, she'd be a woman he could let himself care for.

Now, where had that thought come from?

"Wow," she teased, "you're really putting a lot of thought into it. Okay, maybe you don't have to settle for just one thing. How about we do *everything*?" She breathed that last word meaningfully, then seductively ran her tongue around her lips.

Everything? He suspected, when it came to sex, she knew things he'd never even heard of. "You'd probably kill me," he said honestly.

A bright laugh bubbled out of her. "Just like Marianne said. But what'd be the fun in that?"

Marianne? The woman in the diner? He scanned his memory. They'd been discussing serial killers and Marianne had said something to Jenna like, *If you do that boy in, it won't be with a knife.*

He squeezed his eyes shut. Now he got it. Sexual innuendo. And he'd taken her literally and gone off on a lecture about female serial killers. He really was hopeless.

What on earth was sparkly, sexy Jenna doing with a stodgy guy like him? Well, getting a ride to Vancouver. And offering him sex.

He frowned at her bright face. "This isn't your way of paying me for the ride, is it?"

Her face scrunched up in puzzlement, then she said, "Sex? You mean, am I trading sex for a ride? Jesus, Mark." She shook her head, seeming more amused than angry. "Give us both a bit more credit."

"But I don't really get why you're attracted to me," he confessed.

She raised her eyes heavenward, then down again. Then she extracted herself from the picnic table seat and came around to his side of the table. She shoved their now empty plates down the table, together with the leftovers, the bottle of wine, and their glasses.

Having cleared a space in front of him, she climbed up on the bench seat then carefully maneuvered so she sat on the table facing him, one foot on the bench on either side of his hips. Old jeans hugged her thighs and the spread of her legs made it impossible not to gaze at her crotch.

Inevitably, his breathing quickened and his blood surged. A couple of hours ago, he'd been inside her. Now, what was she doing? "Jenna?"

"You don't get why I'm attracted? How can a scientist be so unobservant?"

He wasn't used to being teased, and normally it disconcerted him and made him feel inadequate. When she did it, though, it was kind of fun and flattering. "I don't know," he confessed. "I'm great at observing the ocean. Not so good with people."

"Then let me enlighten you." She leaned forward, the neck of her loose, long-sleeved T-shirt gaping so he could see her soft, firm breasts, the skin several shades lighter where she'd worn a bikini top.

Under his fly, his cock filled with blood. He forced his gaze away from her breasts and up to her face.

To see a grin. "You may be some fancy marine biologist, but you're such a guy."

"It's hardwired." Show a straight guy a woman's breasts, and he was going to look. Especially when they were as pretty as Jenna's.

"Well, it's not just guys who look. First thing I noticed about you? Well, you're sitting on it."

His butt? She'd ogled his butt? Nah, she had to be kidding.

"But then," she said, "I sat beside you and looked at your face. It's a very angular, masculine face." In a soft caress, she drifted the fingertips of one hand across his forehead out to his temple, down the side of his face, then in along his cheekbone.

Sensation rippled through him. Like shivers, but warm, thick, sexual ones.

She traced the line of his nose. "Nose like a hawk."

"Hawks have beaks. Curved beaks." What was she getting at?

"I stand corrected." Humor laced her voice. "You don't have a curved beak, you have a big, straight nose that's almost arrogant. But I don't think it's in you to be arrogant."

Occasionally, he'd been accused of arrogance by workers on his project teams. He'd told Adrienne, and she said they were wrong; he was confident, judgmental, and oblivious. Like that was any better.

Still, he was what he was. Same as with Jenna. At their ages, neither of them was likely to change.

"Mmm, and these lips," she murmured. With a single fingernail, she traced the outside line of his upper lip.

Jesus, that must be an erogenous zone, one he'd never known about before. The sensation was intense, almost as much as if she'd been touching his cock, which was now painfully hard.

She traced the bottom line.

He'd never thought much about lips before, or kissing. Kisses were just something you did with a woman you were seeing. Not a single one stood out in his mind. Not until today.

"Very sensual lips," she said approvingly, teasing the crease between them with her fingertip.

He opened, intending to suck her finger into his mouth, but she pulled it away, laughing. "Oh no, I'm not finished with the inventory yet. But to finish, I need to get a little closer."

Suddenly she slid forward, shifting her weight from the picnic table until she was sitting on his lap, wedged with her back against the table and her crotch pressed tight against his groin. Against the erection behind his fly.

Heat surged through him, and even more when she wriggled her crotch against it and said, "Oh yeah, that's one very big reason. Then there's your broad shoulders and lean, strong muscles. Narrow hips, great legs, sexy arms. I definitely noticed those. You're too covered up now, but I can fix that." She leaned away from him enough that she could reach between them and start unbuttoning his shirt. "You are definitely worth looking at."

Though his body urged him to grab her and get on with it, his brain hadn't entirely shut down, and he was curious. When he'd first seen Jenna—not knowing a single thing about her—he'd felt lust. Seemed it has been the same for her, too. "So the initial attraction between us was physical. From a biology standpoint, that makes sense," he mused. "The female goes for the strong male protector; the male chooses the healthy woman who'll bear lots of kids."

Her eyes widened and her fingers stilled, one or two buttons from the bottom. "Then your *biology* made a bad choice, didn't it?" The edge to her voice said that for once she wasn't teasing.

"Sorry, I just meant in the larger sense, the biological imperative. Not, uh, you and me. I mean, of course I don't think we—"

Awkwardly, she climbed off his lap, not meeting his gaze.

He caught her hand. "Jenna, wait. I know you're independent, you don't want a protector, and I know you don't want to have kids."

She tugged her hand free and stared at him. Her face was shadowed so he couldn't see her expression. "Right on all counts. So much for biology." She turned her back and walked over to the fire.

He'd ruined the mood, pissed her off with his scientific musings. What an idiot. He rose, went to stand beside her. "I'm sorry I upset you. I didn't mean to." Though, as he studied her profile in the dancing firelight, she didn't look mad so much as sad. "Like I told you before, I'm kind of clueless when it comes to women."

She took a deep breath, loud enough he could hear over the soft crackle of the dying fire, then let it out again. "I overreacted. You were just being you, the science guy." Hands clasped behind her back, she stared into the fire. Withdrawn. Much the way she'd looked after she'd talked to her sister and when they'd been talking about whether they wanted kids.

Kids. It seemed there was something about that topic that touched a nerve with her. Did people give her flack for not wanting children? If he'd had any confidence in his ability to reassure her, he'd have tried, but more likely he'd only make matters worse. "Apology accepted then?" he asked, daring to brush a few golden curls behind her ear.

She turned to him, a smile touching her lips. "Yeah. And I'm sorry for overreacting. And spoiling the mood. Let me make it up to you." Now there was a twinkle in her eye.

"Uh . . . How?"

"Add some more wood to the fire while I tidy up the dishes, then I'll show you." Purposefully, she moved toward the picnic table.

He got the fire blazing again, then glanced around to see that Jenna had cleared everything off the table but the lantern and their glasses of wine. From inside the camper came the sound of running water.

He retrieved his glass and went to stand by the fire again. Remembering her advice, he took a sip of wine and let it rest in his mouth then slide slowly down his throat, tasting the complexity of the flavor. Gazing at the fire, he appreciated all the shades of yellow and orange in the flames, the scent of smoke on the cool night air, the brush of warmth against his bare chest between the open sides of his shirt. From a nearby campsite, a quick burst of laughter sounded.

If he'd been here alone, he'd have hiked the entire park this afternoon, map in hand, until the light faded. He'd perhaps not have bothered to make a fire—or, if he did, he'd have forgotten to keep adding wood. He'd have eaten a ready-made sandwich, picked up at a gas station, and read the *Journal of Experimental Marine Biology and Ecology*.

"Mark?"

Her voice made him swing around, to see her walking toward him. She'd changed from her jeans to the long, filmy skirt she'd been wearing earlier.

"Come sit down again," she said, eyes dancing and tone seductive, taking his hand and pulling him toward the table.

She indicated the end of one bench and he sank down obediently, legs toward the fire rather than tucked under the table. When he put down his wine glass, he saw a condom lying on the table. Just the sight of it made his body tighten.

Sex here? Outside again? Was that why she'd traded her jeans for a skirt? Though their campsite was secluded, it was by no means private. Did risk of discovery turn her on?

Did it turn him on? He'd never thought about that before, but there was no denying the thrill of excitement that coursed through him, and the pressure as his cock expanded behind his fly.

Jenna had a sip of wine then sat down on his lap again, facing him. "Now, where were we? Oh yeah, buttons."

She undid the bottom two shirt buttons, finishing the job she'd started earlier. Her fingertips grazed his bulging fly, and he knew it was no accident. Then they drifted over his body, brushing his ribs, pecs, wandering through the scattering of hair, tweaking a nipple. Stirring him with each soft touch, sending pulses of arousal through his blood.

He should take her inside, convert the couch to a bed, make love to her slowly, the way she deserved. Yet those deft, sensual fingers wove a spell that held him there, unable to move or even speak.

By the time she unfastened the button at the waist of his jeans, he was rigid with need, aching for her touch.

She shifted her butt back, closer to his knees, and drew down the zipper.

He tensed, holding his breath.

She reached inside, slid her hand through the slit in his boxers, and wrapped her fingers around his shaft. Firm, warm pressure encircled his swollen flesh, and he let out a groan of pleasure.

Gently she tugged his penis free of his clothing, then to his surprise she took her hand away and simply stared.

He looked down, past her golden-curled bent head, to see his naked cock standing full and upright, not fazed one bit by the chill night air. His first impulse was to cover up, but he fought it down, not wanting to seem naïve. "Jesus, Jenna, I feel . . ."

"Exposed?"

"Yeah."

"Mmm. Exposed and so sexy. What a beautiful cock you have, Mark."

Beautiful? She had to be kidding. Breasts were beautiful. Penises were . . . functional.

"It makes me want to—" She clambered off his lap. "Pull down your jeans and boxers."

Then she was grabbing something—a towel? a sweater?— placing it on the ground, and kneeling in front of him.

Stunned, aching with need, he shoved down his clothes.

She dipped her head, then took him in her mouth.

"Oh, God." Erotic pleasure shot through him, so intense he had to fight the urge to pump, and pump again, hard and fast until he found release. Instead, as she'd taught him, he focused on the moment and gave it his full attention.

Her tongue, agile and insistent, licked down and around his shaft, then up to swirl around the crown, then down again. Her lips circled him, moving up and down, full and firm and damp. Her fingers teased and stroked the root of his shaft, tangling in his pubic hair, toying with his sac. A hundred individual sensations tingled through him, making him swell impossibly harder.

He watched her bent head, curls gleaming and dancing as she worked him. Unable to speak, he ran a hand through her hair in wordless thanks and encouragement.

She shifted position, drawing back so her head no longer blocked his view. Now he could see his shaft disappearing between her lips as she sucked him in.

Rarely had a woman gone down on him, and never had he watched. It was unbearably sexy, and he had to fight against the building, nearly irresistible need to thrust hard and come in her mouth.

At that moment, she released him, and the cool air hit his naked, overheated flesh, a welcome relief. But now she was tonguing him, not taking him into her mouth but licking around him, hot, wet strokes on night-cooled skin, each a flame that stoked the fire inside. Watching her pink tongue dart across his most intimate flesh was damned erotic.

Holding onto an iota of sanity, he remembered she'd brought a condom. She'd planned for intercourse. Wanted intercourse. And, blissful as this felt, he wanted to bury himself inside her.

Unable to tear his gaze away from her, he groped the surface of the table for the condom package, then grabbed it and managed to find his voice. "Here," he croaked as he thrust it toward her.

She glanced up and teasingly ran her tongue around her lips. "Are you sure?"

From somewhere he found another word and grunted, "Together."

Dimly, he was aware he should be caressing her breasts, sucking her nipples, stroking her inner thighs, exploring her intimate folds with his tongue, stimulating her clitoris— doing all the things a woman wanted and needed. But his body was in control, desperate to merge with hers.

When her fingers stroked the condom down his shaft, he gripped the rough wood of the bench to stop himself from thrusting.

Jenna rose lithely, hiked up her skirt, and straddled him. Oh God, she was naked under that skirt, and the bare flesh she pressed against the base of his shaft was wet with arousal.

He was going to reach under the folds of fabric that draped their laps, to stroke her slick, heated pussy, but she was ahead of him.

She put her own hand down to grip his shaft, to guide him, and a moment later he slid inside her, smooth, hard, and deep.

"Oh, yeah," she sighed, eyes closing. She opened them again, smiling. "That's damn good."

Good was an understatement. He thrust a hand through her hair to grip the back of her head and tug her toward him for a kiss.

She resisted for a moment. "Mark, I'm not sure that's a good—"

His lips cut off the rest of it.

Sweet, salty, musky, she tasted of sex as he feasted on her

mouth. She gave a soft, almost desperate moan, then answered back as hungrily, and he was swept under by a tide of passion.

His tongue plunged into her mouth, his cock thrust hard into her core, and she sucked and writhed and made needy, panting sounds that brought out the animal in him. Everything in the world disappeared but for their bodies merging in a pulsing, glittering spiral of sensation that consumed and satisfied at the same time, until it ended in an explosion that wrenched a groan of pure joy from him then cast him free, drained and exhausted.

Vaguely, he was aware they'd stopped kissing. That his bare butt sat on a hard wooden bench. That his limp arms circled Jenna, who'd folded inward against his heaving chest, and his chin rested atop her head. Heavily.

What the hell had just happened?

Well, sex, yeah. But more than that. Sex was a physical act. Usually he was aware of everything that was happening, conscious of looking after his partner, but this . . . it had swept him away. There wasn't any scientific explanation he was aware of.

Everyone in the campground could have been watching, and he'd never have noticed.

As the hammering of his heart slowed, he forced words from his dry throat. "Are you all right?"

Chapter 6

Was I all right?

My first instinct was to say no. I was shattered in a million pieces. But those pieces still tingled with pleasure, and before I'd shattered I had felt the most amazing sensations.

"Yeah," I murmured, almost surprised to find my voice worked. The sex, the orgasm, had been so powerful it seemed as if all my body parts had been shaken up and re-arranged. I'd never experienced anything like this. The closest I'd ever come was when I was seventeen and fell for Travis.

A disconcerting thought.

With Travis, I'd been an inexperienced girl, just coming to life sexually. I'd mistaken orgasms and vows of love for the real thing.

With Mark . . . I shook my head against his naked chest, so warm and strong under my cheek. I'd had a dozen years of sex since Travis. Loads of lovers, many of them pretty talented. Stunning climaxes that made me scream, multiple orgasms that kept me peaking until I couldn't take it any longer. But nothing so . . . profound. Was it because we'd kissed? Something very strange happened whenever we kissed.

What was freaking going on? I summoned enough strength to raise my hands to his chest and push myself away so I could look at him. "There's a scientific explanation for this, right?"

Light from the fire reflected off his face, illuminating his puzzled expression. "Uh, well, MHC codes . . . Pheromones are . . ." He shook his head. "No, not that I know of."

I scowled at him. "You're supposed to be able to come up with a scientific lecture on any given subject."

Humor softened his mouth. "Sorry. Sex isn't my field."

"You are so wrong." I blew out a breath. "Maybe you don't know all the science, but when it comes to application, man are you something." And I would firmly believe there was a scientific explanation for the way I felt because . . . because there had to be.

He shook his head and said in that husky rock-singer voice, "Actually, I'm a pretty good lover, but—"

"I'll say."

"I mean, I know the right things to do, but with you, I forget all that stuff and something comes over me and . . ." Another head shake. "All my good intentions go out the window, and I turn into some kind of animal."

"You sexy beast," I teased.

He smiled back. "Glad it works for you." Then he touched my cheek, stroked tendrils of hair back, and caressed the shell of my ear. "Next time, I promise there'll be foreplay."

"Sounds good to me." Particularly if it kept his lips off mine. I had an adventurous spirit, but instinct—survival instinct—told me kissing Mark was dangerous.

I maneuvered myself off his lap, leaving him to deal with the condom while I adjusted my skirt. "I'm going to use the facilities."

"Me too. I'll walk with you."

We gathered toothbrushes and a few other necessities

then, arms snugly around each other, strolled through the campground. Most people had turned in for the night, but at a few sites people still clustered around the fire or picnic table. "Wonder if any of them are fooling around?" I murmured.

"I'll never think of campgrounds in the same way again."

We went our separate ways when we reached the facilities. Inside the ladies room, I got talking to an older woman from New England who said that when she and her husband retired the previous year, they'd bought a motor home and were driving all over the country.

"Wherever the whim takes you?" I asked, spreading toothpaste on my brush.

She nodded. "After decades of alarm clocks and office buildings, we're enjoying being gypsies. And we figure we deserve it."

"Of course you do." I didn't say that a person shouldn't have to slave away for years and years at some dull job to *deserve* freedom. Hadn't she read her country's constitution? "Have an awesome trip."

"You too. Night."

I returned her good night, then brushed my teeth and went outside to meet Mark. Yes, the first day of the trip had definitely been awesome. And we hadn't even made it to that double bed.

We strolled back to the camper and he said, "It's such a small space inside. Why don't you stay by the fire while I set up the bed?"

"Okay." For a few minutes, I watched the dying flames and wished we'd thought to buy marshmallows, then he called softly, "All ready."

Inside, the bed covered much of the space. He'd made it up with a couple of sheets and pillows and an unzipped sleeping bag tossed on top like a duvet. "Much more comfortable than sleeping in my car," I said appreciatively. I tossed him a wink. "Not to mention, the company's pretty good."

"I didn't pull the curtains. Is that okay? I like seeing the morning sun."

"Me, too." Quickly, I skimmed off my long-sleeved tee and bra, then my skirt, and slipped between the sheets, shivering a little. In mid June, the nights were still on the cool side.

Mark stripped unselfconsciously, and without the shivers. Such a perfect male body, and he didn't seem to have a clue how attractive he was.

He clicked off the ceiling light, and the world went black. The bed shifted, then he slid in beside me, knees bumping me.

Again I shivered, then turned on my side and snuggled my butt against him. "Brrr, it's chilly. Spoon me."

He shifted position then tugged me into the curve of his body. His front warmed my back, and his arm crossed my body holding me close. His knees brushed the back of mine, and his toes tickled the soles of my feet, making me giggle.

For a few minutes, he just held me as my body warmed. It was peaceful and cozy—but against my bottom, his cock twitched and grew, and my sex throbbed and moistened in response. No, we wouldn't be going to sleep any time soon.

He pulled back to nuzzle through my curls and blow warm air across the back of my neck. Next came licks and gentle nips, teasing and sensual. His hand stroked my arm where it crossed my waist, then smoothed the curve of my hip, down then up again, and back down.

I murmured approval.

His hand drifted up to cup my breast, caress it, and squeeze the nipple gently, sending warm tingles straight to my pussy. "Nice, Mark. More."

"I promised you foreplay, and this time nothing's going to distract me."

"Nothing?" I wriggled my butt against his growing cock.

"Stop it. D'you *want* me to be distracted?"

"When you put it that way . . . No, I want foreplay."

His warmth pulled away from my body and before I could grumble a protest, firm hands rolled me onto my back. When he leaned over me, my eyes had adjusted to the dim light but still I could barely make out his shape.

He tugged the sheet down to expose my torso. "Let me know if you get cold." His hand molded my breast, plumping it up, and he licked around my areola. Around and around, his hot tongue, then cool air, then his tongue again, gathering arousal and centering it. Then his tongue flicked back and forth across my nipple.

When he finally sucked my nipple into his mouth, I gasped with pleasure. "Not cold. Definitely not cold." His mouth was hot, and the sexy way he teased my flesh with tongue and lips warmed me inside and out.

When he'd finished lavishing attention on one breast, I expected him to move to the other, but instead his lips cruised upward, over the upper curve of my breast, my chest, my collar bone. His tongue played in the hollow at the base of my throat, then he pressed nibbling kisses into the tender flesh of my neck.

One strummed a particularly sensitive spot, a spot linked directly with my sex, and I let out a surprised "oh."

He lingered there, sucking the flesh while my hips rose involuntarily, muscles tightening with anticipation and need. If his touch was this arousing on my neck, what would it be like when he finally made his way between my legs?

From my neck, he went to my other breast, seeming in no hurry despite the thick erection that brushed my leg. I lay back, glorying in every delicious sensation, sensitive, achy, craving release but happy for this to go on forever.

He sure knew his way around a woman's body. Hard to believe this was the same man who said he lacked social skills. I remembered something one boyfriend, a software designer, had told me: *Geeks try harder*. It seemed science guys did, too.

Mark dropped kisses down the lower curve of my breast, along my waist and out to the flare of my hip, then back in to my tummy. Whenever I sighed or twitched with pleasure, he took his time, licking, sucking, and teasing.

By the time he made it to my bikini-trimmed bush, my hips writhed with need. The coil of arousal inside me had wound so tightly, my breath came out in soft pants, and I was desperate for release. I spread my legs and begged, "Please, I can't wait. Make me come."

He held my hips up and dipped between my legs where by now I was soaking wet, and with quick, firm strokes lapped my juice.

"Oh, God, yes."

His tongue flicked across my clit, and I whimpered. Then he settled there, teasing that swollen nub into his mouth and sucking gently.

Every nerve ending in that sensitive bundle fired at the same time, and orgasm rocked me, making me cry out.

Still holding me to his mouth, he eased off, releasing my clit and going back to licking me, at first in gentle, barely there touches. Then, more firmly, and as one climax faded away I felt another begin to build.

"Oh, Mark," I moaned, fisting the sheet below me as I pressed myself against his face.

His tongue probed me, a finger slid inside, then another finger joined it and he pumped them into me, circling, exploring. The pad of his finger brushed my G-spot and I gasped.

He tapped it again, and his mouth was back on my clit. Pleasure surged through me from both spots, sparking another explosion.

My body was still quivering in release when his fingers

slid out of me, and only moments later he was sheathed and thrusting into me, hard.

His body rose above mine and I grabbed onto his shoulders, then his butt, as he drove into me relentlessly.

Arousal gathered in me again as I tightened my internal muscles to alternately grip and release his shaft.

"Jenna," he muttered, the first word he'd spoken since he'd begun to explore my body.

His head lowered, then his lips took mine before I could think whether this was wise. Before I could stop him.

Once our mouths fused, no way could I pull away, I had to kiss him back. Gasping for breath, we kissed, licked, and I tasted myself on him.

I tasted me, him, sex, something dark and sweet and intense. Powerful.

Some shred of sanity told me it was dangerous, I needed to pull away. But I wasn't me anymore; I didn't have control over my body. I was part of something bigger, something all-consuming, as if Mark and I weren't two separate beings but an *us* that fused in a world of passion and pleasure to form something entirely new.

Mouths still glued together, I heard his primal shout inside my head, felt his orgasm as if it was my own. Except, it *was* mine. I, too, was bursting apart in stunning waves of pleasure.

Shuddering, we clung to each other, mouths falling apart as we sucked in air in great, wrenching breaths. Feeling boneless, my legs and arms flopped against the bed. Mark collapsed down on me, barely managing to take some of his weight on his arms.

As the after tremors rippled away, I began to feel panicky. Imprisoned. By his weight, his body, and whatever it was that had happened between us. When he shifted off me to deal with the condom, I quickly rolled onto my side, my back to him, as far to one side of the bed as I could get.

He lay down again and touched my shoulder. "Jenna?"

"That was great. Now I want to go to sleep."

"Are you all right?"

"Stop asking me that," I snapped. "Of course I'm all right. It's sex, just sex. I like sex."

There was a heavy silence, as if he were debating whether to say something more. Then he sighed, took his hand off my shoulder, and rolled so his back was to me.

I lay in the dark, tense, knowing sleep was a long way off. But that was all right, because I needed to figure this thing out. That in itself was weird. Normally, I wasn't the least bit analytical. I took life as it came and enjoyed it. But Dr. Mark Chambers threw me off balance.

Bottom line: sex with Mark was incredible. The best I'd ever had. Why should that scare me? Yeah, it rocked my world, and I lost myself in it in a way that had never happened before, but afterwards I was me again. I should be thrilled to bits to have hooked up with him and be having such amazing sex. And beyond that, he was smart, interesting, and a good man. It was fun to rattle his scientific cage, fun to tease him away from being so conservative and rulebound.

So, why was I shaken?

Oh man, did this have something to do with turning thirty soon? Was I getting all middle-aged, analyzing stuff to death and getting wary about new experiences?

Not good, Jenna. Definitely not good.

Oh for God's sake, I was obsessing. I should do what I always did: live in the moment and do what felt right at the time. If the thought of kissing Mark bothered me, for whatever crazy reason, then I wouldn't do it. But if I did feel like it, then I'd go for it. Simple, just the way I liked things.

Resolved, I breathed deeply, inhaling cool air scented with the tang of green trees and ocean, and let myself drift toward sleep.

*   *   *

When he was a kid, Mark had developed the knack of sleeping whenever and wherever he needed to. Getting a good night's sleep was no surprise. Waking with his arms wrapped around a warm female body, a morning erection nudging her soft butt, was much more rare.

As for yesterday, rare wasn't the word. *Unique, special, incredible* were the more appropriate terms. At least for him. She'd classified it as "just sex."

Jenna was more experienced and presumably knew what she was talking about, but as far as he was concerned, the evidence pointed in a different direction. He'd had *just sex* in the past. He'd had good sex, even great sex. With him and Jenna, it was a whole different category of experience. What he didn't know was what it meant, or why she wanted to deny it.

Maybe he could slip away and call Adrienne, get some female advice.

He studied the quality of the light slanting through the windows of the Westfalia. Around six o'clock, he figured. Too early to phone on a Saturday morning. Besides, if he got up, he'd likely wake Jenna.

This was the first time he'd seen her utterly still. Awake, she was animated, full of life. Stimulating to be around, yet he'd felt an ease with her that was unusual for him. Now, curled around her relaxed body, he realized how small she was, and felt almost protective.

A ridiculous sentiment. She'd be the first to tell him she could look after herself.

She stirred, sighed, then he felt her body tense as if she'd woken and was getting her bearings.

"Morning," he whispered against a tangle of soft curls.

"Mmm. Is it morning already?" She wiggled her butt against his swollen penis. "Someone's up, I see."

"You can ignore that." He didn't want to push her just because he'd woken up erect.

"What if I don't want to ignore it?" Another wiggle. Delicious pressure.

He pumped once. "Won't hear me complain." His arm had been lying across hers, and now he moved to cup a soft breast and squeeze her nipple gently, feeling it tighten under his touch.

She curled her body tighter and reached down between her legs to find and grip him. He tilted his hips, helping her as she guided him until his shaft was lodged against her pussy, where her flesh was growing damp.

He slid back and forth slowly as more moisture slipped from her body, coating his cock and making it slick. Pressing a kiss into her bare shoulder, he squeezed her nipple harder. "Want to roll over?"

"No, let's do it like this. Feels so good." She tapped his shaft gently, a motion like drumming her fingers on a table, sending pulses of arousal through him. "Got a condom?"

"Right here." He'd put the box by the bed last night and now eased away briefly to find one and sheath himself. Then he slid back between her legs as she tilted her hips, changing the angle so that this time he could slip inside the welcoming heat of her channel.

He groaned with pleasure at the same time she said, "Oh, yeah."

Pumping slowly in and out, he played with her breast then stroked down her flat belly and cupped her mound.

She thrust back against him, matching his timing then speeding it a little.

This felt great, but something was missing. They hadn't kissed, and he couldn't see her face. This morning, she'd yet to even say his name. He kissed her shoulder again, the only part of her his lips could reach, wanting to make this more

personal. Wishing that, as she gave soft whimpers of pleasure, she'd call his name.

He'd never been one for talking during sex. But now he
murmured, "Jenna, this feels great. Sure you don't want to
roll over?"

Her head shook. "Like this. I want it like this."

It. An impersonal word. Damn, he shouldn't have asked
her, he should have just taken charge and rolled her onto her
back so he could kiss her. But now that he'd asked, he felt
bound to respect her wishes.

Huh. He was being analytical, the way he normally was
during sex. Rather than swept away, like he'd been yesterday. The sexual pleasure was intense, but he didn't feel that
same sense of merging and getting lost.

Maybe it had been a fluke. Or maybe it only happened
when they kissed.

Maybe, despite the intimacy of this act, she was shutting
him out.

All the same, his body was fully engaged, a climax building. He rubbed his finger lightly over her clit, and she
bucked. Her moan of pleasure urged him to keep doing it.

When he heard her gasp, and her body clutched, he let go,
pumping his own release deep inside her.

After, he held her until their breathing slowed, then eased
out of her. He rested his hand on her hip and tugged lightly.
"Give me a good morning kiss."

Her body jerked. Then, "Morning breath," she said
lightly, scrambling out of bed and tossing him a quick, superficial smile. "I need to brush my teeth, shower." As she
spoke, she threw on clothes haphazardly, moving awkwardly in the cramped space.

He could have reached out and grabbed her, but held
back. Though he was no expert at reading female behavior,
her signals pretty clearly said she wanted space.

She was dressed in a flash, then grabbed her tote bag, said, "See you in a bit," and was gone.

He frowned at the door she'd flicked shut behind her, then got up, pulled on a pair of boxers, and found his cell. Too bad if it was early. He needed help.

First, he put water on to boil for coffee, then he dialed.

Adrienne picked up after the third ring. "Mark? It's seven on Saturday."

"Sorry, were you in bed? I need to talk to you."

"No, we're up. Just deciding what to do for breakfast." Indulgently, she said, "Okay, let me guess. You were reading some obscure journal, stayed up all night, and discovered some fascinating connection between . . . No, I can't even guess."

"No, it's not that. It's, uh, a woman."

"Oh, yeah? Do tell." He heard her say, *sotto voce,* "He's met a woman."

"Say hi to Laura," he said belatedly. "And how are you feeling anyway? Are you over the morning sickness?"

"Yeah, thank God. I'm feeling terrific. Now tell me about this woman."

Using his free hand, he got the coffee opened and spooned some into the French press. "Her name's Jenna. She's bright, beautiful, fun."

"You wouldn't be calling if there wasn't a problem."

"The sex is weird."

A pause. Then, cautiously, "Weird? As in kinky? I'm not sure I want to hear this. Innocent ears and all."

A hoot told him Laura disagreed.

"No, not kinky." Then he thought of having sex on the beach in the log shelter, and Jenna going down on him in the campsite. "Well, maybe a little kinky, but that's not the problem."

The rich aroma of brewing coffee made him impatient.

"The more, uh, personal it gets—like, if we kiss—it's like . . . Well, it's great, really intense, but uh . . ." He was analytical; he could find a way of describing this. "It's like being struck by lightning. No, more like a tornado effect. I get whirled up in the funnel, and we're both carried away. I have no control and can't even think. Does that make any sense?"

She let out a low whistle. "My buddy Mark's finally fallen in love."

He almost dropped the mug he was taking from the cupboard. "Love?" No, that was impossible. He'd just met Jenna, and they were such different people.

"Was she working at Long Marine Lab with you? She's a marine biologist, too?"

"No, she's . . . Wait a minute." He depressed the plunger in the press, poured carefully into the mug, and took that first, delicious sip. "She's not a scientist. I guess right now she doesn't have a job at all. She was volunteering on a pere-grine falcon survey"—he wouldn't mention waitressing—"and now she's taking a break for her sister's wedding. After that I've no idea what she intends to do." In all likelihood, nor did Jenna.

"Really? She doesn't exactly sound like your type."

"No, she isn't, actually." He sat on the side of the bed.

"Okay, um . . . She isn't your type but you have this in-credible sex. Hmm. How long have you known her?"

"I met her yesterday."

"*Yesterday*?!" Her voice was so loud he jerked the phone away from his ear, almost spilling his coffee.

"Yeah. I'm driving back to Vancouver for the symposium and met her in a diner. She needed a ride, so I gave her one."

"She's a *hitchhiker*?"

"Not exactly."

"Good God, Mark, what are you thinking?"

"I, uh . . . Jenna has a way about her."

"So I gather." She was quiet for a long moment, and he

drank coffee, waiting. Finally, she said, "She seduced you. So what does she want from you?"

He'd like to think he'd had a hand in the seduction, but maybe that was wishful male thinking. "Just a ride. Her car broke down, and she needs to get home. She's insistent about paying her share of the gas and food." He shrugged. "What else could she want? It's not like I'm some rich guy with a fancy car and expensive clothes."

"No, you're sure not." Another long pause. "Tell me more about her. Not the sex part," she added quickly. "Do you like her?"

"In a lot of ways. She's easy to talk to."

A snort. "Mark, your idea of conversation is talking science. She isn't a scientist so let me just take a wild guess and say she's faking interest."

He had lectured more than once. She'd seemed attentive. Besides . . . "We talk about other things than science."

"As in, she talks and your eyes glaze over, though you pretend to listen?"

"My eyes do not glaze over," he snapped. "I'm interested in other things than science."

She gave a soft chuckle. "Okay, it's true. Maybe just not as interested."

"Anyhow, I don't just listen. Jenna makes me talk."

"Aha! She's trying to pry information out of you, like how much you make?"

"Not that kind of talk." Man, Adrienne really was cynical about Jenna. "More about personal stuff. The commune, Alicia, what it was like being raised by my grandparents."

"Alicia?"

"My biological mother."

After a long pause, she said, "I don't think you ever told me her name. Because you *don't* talk about this stuff, not even with me, your best friend. What did this woman do to you?"

Bewitched me. "She's interested in me."

"So am I, damn it."

"Sorry. But you and I have other things to talk about. We're colleagues. And when I've dated, they've always been colleagues, too."

"True."

"Anyhow, Jenna asks questions and makes it easy to answer. We're sitting there in the camper, side by side, the road ahead of us. It feels almost natural to talk to her."

When she didn't say anything for a long time, he said, "Adrienne? Still there?"

"You know, that's as special as the merging together sex. Somehow this Jenna, in one day, broke through a barrier no other woman's managed to disturb. Maybe you really are in love," she said in a marveling tone.

Feeling an odd throb in his heart, he frowned into his now-empty mug. It would be completely illogical to fall in love—with a woman like Jenna especially, who wasn't even a scientist much less a marine biologist—in a single day. "I was wondering if it could have to do with MHC codes."

"That could explain immediate attraction and good sex," she mused. "Are you in an endorphin haze, seeing only her good qualities and thinking she's perfect?"

"No, she's not perfect. She's a drifter. For her, life's about having fun."

Another whistle. "That's so not you. Okay, no rosy haze, and she sure doesn't sound like the right match for you."

"No." How ridiculous to feel a pang of sadness. He rose and poured the rest of the coffee before it got bitter from sitting on the grounds. "She keeps saying it's just sex, and sometimes I think she's avoiding kissing me. But when we do kiss, I feel like she's right there with me. That it's as powerful for her as it is for me."

"Hmm. Don't some prostitutes avoid kissing? Because they find it more intimate than sex?"

"Jenna is not a prostitute!" Of course, he didn't know that for a fact, but every instinct told him that high-spirited, carefree Jenna treated sex as a fun act to share, not a source of income. "Jesus, Adrienne."

"Sorry, I didn't mean it that way. Just that, if she doesn't want to kiss, might she be resisting intimacy? Intimacy's kind of like commitment, and from what you said, she's not big into commitment."

"She's not. She doesn't believe in monogamy."

"Hmm. Maybe she's never been in love, so she's never felt the desire for monogamy. Or maybe love scares her."

"Why would it scare her?"

"There could be a hundred reasons. What does love symbolize to her?"

"Uh . . ." How was he expected to know that?

Out the window, movement caught his eye. Jenna, returning.

"Have to go now," he said. "See you in Vancouver." Then he closed the phone. Man, this love stuff was complicated.

When the door opened, he was rinsing his mug. "I made extra coffee," he said casually.

"Thanks." She stood outside, watching him almost warily. This morning she wore the same shorts as yesterday and a green tee. "Are you going to shower?"

"Yeah, right now." Used to the small amount of space inside the camper, he efficiently dressed, grabbed a few things, then jumped out. Leaving the bed down.

Deep in thought, he walked to the facilities and went through his morning routine by rote. Could Jenna be afraid of love? Could she be falling for him, and resisting? Could he be falling for her? How on earth did a person know these things?

If Adrienne was anywhere near right, what would he do about it? Jenna wasn't his kind of woman any more than he was her kind of man.

A scientist theorized, experimented, observed, recorded, and analyzed, he reflected as he walked back to the campsite. Typically, it was best to examine one theory at a time, but he had two, and they interrelated. His, that Jenna was avoiding kissing him, and Adrienne's, that Jenna was scared of love.

A scientist designed experiments and tested hypotheses, he observed and analyzed.

For example, Jenna had twice avoided morning kisses, had fled the camper quickly after sex, and had avoided sharing space with him when she returned from her shower. Now, as he walked into the campsite, he saw she'd set plates, mugs, and food on the picnic table. When he glanced inside the camper, he noted that she'd stripped the bed and folded it back into couch form, indicating she wasn't interested in another round of sex.

She was at the sink and, before he could climb in, she gave him a bright smile and thrust the box of strawberries toward him. "Want to put these on the table? I've laid out bread and cheese, and made a fresh carafe of coffee."

"Sure." He took the berries but didn't move away as she climbed out, carafe in her hand. "Good morning again," he said quietly, then leaned toward her with the obvious intention of giving her a quick kiss.

She turned her head so his lips brushed her cheek rather than her mouth, but she did squeeze his butt in passing.

No kiss, and she no longer had the excuse of morning breath, yet she had no problem with the casual, sexy intimacy of a butt-grab. Yes, she was treating this as "just sex." But why? Because to her that was truly all it was, or because she was avoiding something more meaningful?

"I bet you have a schedule for today," she said breezily. "Want to tell me about it?"

He followed her to the table. She'd set the plates across from each other as they'd been last night at dinner, and automatically he took the seat opposite her. While she poured coffee, he sliced chunks of crusty bread.

Often, he skipped breakfast, settling for two or three cups of coffee. Now he bit into a strawberry, plump and sweet as the lips Jenna didn't seem to want him kissing.

"Today's schedule?" she prompted.

"I figured on driving the Oregon coast then across the border into Washington. There's a park on the Long Beach Peninsula."

"Sounds good. Then it'll be no problem getting back to Vancouver tomorrow."

"I do need to make a stop somewhere there's internet."

"Another person who's ruled by technology." She rolled her eyes.

He shrugged. "I've got things in the works. Plans for an upcoming project, research I'm supervising." Responsibilities. A concept she didn't seem big on.

And that raised the question, why was he testing theories about kissing and love? The two of them were such opposites. Wouldn't it be smarter to simply enjoy her company and the great sex?

Chapter 7

As Mark drove slowly down the main street of Crescent City, a small California town close to the Oregon border, I peered at storefronts in search of an internet café. "There, on the right."

He found a parking spot and retrieved a battered black laptop case from the back. Figuring I might as well check in with my family—they'd be totally stunned to have me make contact two days in a row—I went along with him to the café.

Inside, he ordered a coffee and said to me, "Chamomile tea?"

"I'd love one. Thanks."

"Don't know how you can drink the stuff. It tastes like lawn clippings."

I grinned at him. "Gee, I've never tasted lawn clippings. Thanks for sharing your personal experience."

His lips curved. "Okay, you got me. It tastes the way I'm guessing lawn clippings would taste."

We took our drinks to adjoining work stations. He moved the existing computer aside and plugged his laptop into a network cable. Catching my questioning look, he said, "My portable office. There are files on here I may need to refer to."

I nodded, then logged on to my own e-mail and found messages from Merilee, my young friend Anna, and a couple of casual friends. I'd deal with the casual stuff first.

I clicked on a message from the Greek sailor, Milos. We'd kept in touch off and on for a couple of years now. This past winter he'd returned to Crete because his father was ill, and Milos had to help run the family's small inn. He wrote:

> To my surprise, I'm more of a businessman than I thought. But now that my mother has me back home here, she says I must think of marriage. You should come visit before she succeeds in finding a bride for me.

Crete. How I'd love to. I typed back:

> Can I hitchhike there? LOL. Or stow away on a freighter? If you hear of any cheap—really, really cheap—flights, let me know <g>.

If I did manage to go, we'd probably be lovers again. He'd been a good one. The sex had been . . . a lot like sex with Mark this morning. Very satisfying, but not explosive and consuming the way it was when Mark and I gazed into each other's eyes and kissed.

I glanced over to see my lover, his gaze intent as he read an e-mail, the cardboard coffee cup poised near his mouth. Why was sex different with him? If I avoided kissing him, maybe I'd never find out. It'd be safer that way. I wouldn't feel that all-consuming force that swept me up, that made me lose myself.

That rocked my world like a million fireworks bursting all at once.

I'd always liked fireworks . . .

I grabbed my tea and took a hefty swallow, then opened the next e-mail. Elizabeth, a university student from England who'd worked at the art therapy program when I was there, had now finished her graduate degree and was organizing a similar program in her home town in Yorkshire. As with the sailor, we'd remained e-mail pals. Now she caught me up on her news, saying they were almost ready to get going, and she needed staff. She offered me a job if I wanted to come work for her.

Kids, art, England, not to mention working with—no, for—a friend. Sounded pretty good to me, except for that same pesky problem about airfare.

Milos and Elizabeth had both been fun to hang out with. Now, he had roots and family responsibilities, and she was building a program that would benefit hundreds of children over the years. I'd bet their families were proud.

I shoved down a twinge of envy. Yeah, if I did stuff like that, my family might be proud, too. But the paths that were right for Milos and Elizabeth were too straight and narrow for me. I ran a finger across the cloud of butterflies on my shoulder.

After sending a quick reply to Elizabeth, I opened a message from fourteen-year-old Anna, a very special person in my life. She'd taken therapeutic riding lessons when she was six, after losing both legs in a horrendous car crash that killed her parents. The kid had had more guts than any adult I'd ever met. Over the years, I'd worked with lots of children and adults, but Anna and I had formed a real connection. When her aunt took her away to her new home, a small town in northern Alberta, Anna had cried. I'd told her she could e-mail me and she had.

Her father's much older sister, an unmarried woman, seemed well-intentioned, but she didn't really get kids. I sure wasn't any kind of role model for a child, but at least Anna could share her thoughts and dreams with me and know I'd always be on her side.

For eight years, through e-mails, I'd watched her grow up. She'd turned fourteen in January, a tough age for a girl who walked on prosthetic limbs and feared no boy would ever be interested in her. For the past two months, she'd been crushing on a boy who barely noticed her. She wrote:

You know how you said I should think about when I first started riding? About how I wanted to ride but I was scared, but I'd never get what I wanted if I just kept staring at the horses like a sissy? So, anyhow, guess what???
Lawrence is, like, SO bad at math. And I get straight A's. So I said I'd help him study for the final exam, if he wanted.
And he looks at me like he doesn't even know me. Yeah, right, only been sitting across from him for almost 10 months!!! And he says, "You're kidding, right?"

I winced. Poor Anna. What an asshole the boy was.

So I say, "Just trying to help. Because I'm so much SMARTER than you!!!!"

I laughed out loud. "That's my girl," I murmured.

And he just goes, "Whatever," and stomps away. But I'm okay, Jenna. Honest ;-) Like you said, if someone's a jerk to me, that's their loss. He'll probably flunk math, and I'll get an A.
Anyhow, it's almost summer, and this year I get to assist at riding camp!!! I can't wait until I'm grown up and can run my own camp!
XXXXOOOXXX
PS – J + A = grrrrlpower! [that's math!]

Grrrrlpower. Yeah. I loved seeing Anna becoming more self-confident. I wrote back:

You did great, Anna. Lots of guts, sweetie. As for Lawrence, yeah, he lost the opportunity to get to know a wonderful girl. Not to mention, he's probably going to be a high school dropout and end up working in McDonald's all his life!!! Can you say, LOSER? LOL.

When I was Anna's age, I was pretty and popular. All the boys wanted to date me, and I had lots of girlfriends too. My problem had been schoolwork. Following after genius Theresa and very bright Kat had been tough, because I just wasn't as smart as them. The more my parents and teachers told me to apply myself, the less I wanted to. I always hated being told what to do.

I'd found, though, that once I was out of school and living my own life, I really liked learning about things that interested me.

Anna, though, was a perfect student, smart and motivated. For years now, she'd known what she wanted to do when she grew up. Having that goal made her happy, helped her self-confidence, and gave her a sense of purpose. Who knew, one day I might be working for her. She'd probably do as well in her field as Mark did in his.

Beside me, he stood up and asked, "Want a refill?"

"No, thanks. I'm good."

He strolled across the room to get more coffee and I watched, thinking how great he looked in shorts. When he turned and gazed my way, I gave him a sexy wink then refocused on the screen.

I finished off my e-mail to Anna, then opened the last one, from Merilee. My baby sis, who a week from now would be walking down the grassy aisle in VanDusen Gardens.

Hey, Jenna. Theresa said she talked to you and you're on the road, so maybe you won't check e-mail but I hope you do.

It's crazy in the house with almost everyone home now, and Theresa and Kat all wrapped up with their new guys. Well, that's not fair, they're definitely working on the wedding but they're . . . I think they're both in love. Seriously!!!

With Theresa, it's not like how she was with Jeffrey-the-jerk. Not that I really remember him. I was too young when they were married. But I've heard ALL the stories, and I know he was a pretentious jerk who totally used her.

Damien seems cool. Confident and successful but not at all pretentious, and he and Theresa are talking about being partners writing some book. He seems really crazy about her, and she's on the phone with him every night while he's on this book tour. (Phone sex!!!) And did I mention, he's really hot? Well, I guess that thing about being one of Australia's 10 sexiest bachelors kinda tells you that, right?

As for Kat, she hooked a total hottie too, with a Brit accent to die for. Nav totally adores her—it's so obvious every time he looks at her—and the passion between them sizzles. He's an awesome photographer, and guess what, as his gift to M & me, he's going to do the wedding photos!! Very cool, and a big relief because all the photographers Theresa tried were booked for next Saturday.

Next Saturday. I'm getting married next Saturday. Can you believe it? Now that it's so close, I'm kind of in shock. Good shock, of course <g>. I mean, this is Matt. I've loved him since forever. And every bride has some pre-wedding jitters, right?

Anyhow, I can't wait to see you, sis.

(Tell me you won't be bringing home some incredibly sexy guy you've fallen madly in love with, okay??? Two's enough!!! LOL. I know, I know. You're never getting serious about any guy. You're having too much fun sampling the smorgasbord <g>.)

Hugs and more hugs,

M

I frowned at the screen, thinking there was something just a little off about M's e-mail.

Pre-wedding jitters? Merilee? I'd never have expected that. And was it my imagination, or did she sound the tiniest bit envious of Tree and Kitty-Kat? She'd barely mentioned Matt, and usually he showed up in every second sentence; he was that firmly embedded in her life. And she didn't want me to bring home an incredibly sexy lover.

I shot a glance at the man beside me, absorbed in a technical looking document on screen. No, of course I wouldn't take Mark home—even though he'd fit better in my family than I did.

I stared back at the screen. What could I say to Merilee? She couldn't be asking for advice. No one but Anna ever asked me for advice. Yet, I sensed she needed . . . something. Reassurance? About what? I sure wasn't the one to be giving relationship advice to a woman who believed in happily ever after. Slowly, I began to type.

> Hey, M, thanks for the update. Now I don't feel quite so out of it, and I'm sure curious to get home and see all this with my very own eyes. I'm still halfway convinced it's not the real Tree, but some Aussie impostor <g>. And it's hard to believe Kitty-Kat has finally found herself one of the good guys.

Beside me, Mark typed rapidly, peering intently at the screen. Yeah, good guys did exist. Why shouldn't my annoyingly fabulous sisters have found themselves a couple? As for M, her Matt had been born into the good guy label.

> Of course, you got the original good guy. Give Matt an extra-big hug for me. You know I love him to pieces. He's the nicest person in our family <g>. Well, he's the nicest to ME, anyhow. And to you, too, which is almost as important. LOL. I think he might actually be good enough for my baby sis.

I did adore her boyfriend, though he was almost too perfect. A guy should have a few flaws, a rough edge here and there, a little unpredictability, to keep life exciting.

Science guy Mark was exciting, a strange mix of conservative traits like having a schedule, and the unconventional, like basing his life out of a laptop computer and little Westfalia camper and traveling all over the world. He had passion too, for the ocean and his mission to protect it. He really was kind of Indiana Jonesy with his strong sense of mission, but Mark's work was far more important than retrieving a few dusty artifacts.

He was a lot sexier than Indy, too.

He nudged me with his leg, the touch of his bare knee against mine sending a quiver of awareness through me. "How's it going, Jenna? Almost done?"

"Yeah. Just one more sec." Quickly, I typed,

Relax and enjoy life, M. I know Tree has a meticulously organized wedding plan, and she and Kat'll make sure everything gets done. As soon as I'm home I'll help however I can, even if it's just to take you out for gelato and keep you sane <g>.
XOXO, Jenna.

I logged off e-mail as Mark shut down his computer, then we headed back to the camper, both carrying our drink cups.

"Any ocean-type crises?" I asked as he pulled back onto the road.

"No crises. Just a couple of things to do on my next project."

"What's the next one? Is it in Vancouver, and that's why you're heading back?"

He shook his head. "No, I'm going to Vancouver to attend an international symposium on global change in marine social-ecological systems."

Now there was a sentence with a bunch of big words. I sorted them all out in my head. "You mean things like the effect of global warming, pollution, overfishing, introduction of non-native species?"

"Yeah, exactly. I'm presenting a paper on the current status of rehabilitation of the maritime environment after the tsunami in Thailand."

"A project you worked on?"

"Uh-huh."

Oh yes, rebuilding after a tsunami was way more significant than hunting artifacts. I'd just bet his grandparents were very proud of Mark.

"You're staying with your grandparents? I guess it'll be good to see them."

"Yes, though it won't be for long. I'm off to Indonesia on Thursday. I've organized a team to go to several locations to help the locals repair and rebuild coral reefs."

"Wow. Another great project. And what a cool place to visit." I sighed. "Today in e-mail I got invitations to go to Crete and to Yorkshire, both of which I'd love to do, but no way can I afford the airfare."

He shot me a sideways glance, eyes narrowed. An edge to his voice, he said, "Let me guess, the Greek sailor and some English guy you dated at some point."

Let me guess: he didn't approve. He really did belong in my family. Evenly, I said, "Mark, I never lead guys on. I'm always honest, and we almost always part friends. What's the big deal?"

His frown turned from disapproval to puzzlement. "Uh, I'm not sure. Sorry."

I nodded, glad he'd seen my point. "Yes, the Greek's the guy I mentioned before. The person in England is a woman I worked with once, who's setting up an art therapy program for autistic kids."

"Good for her."

"Yeah, isn't it cool?" I gazed out at the view. The road had turned inland, and I missed the ocean vistas. I drank some chamomile tea, tepid now but just as tasty as when it was hot. Lawn clippings. Honestly. He really could be judg-mental.

"Any other interesting e-mail?" he asked. "I heard you say, 'That's my girl.' Your youngest sister?"

"No, a friend." The thought of Anna made me smile. I told Mark a bit about her, and her triumph over Lawrence. "I'm so proud of her."

"She sounds like a great kid. How long have you known her?"

"Eight years. She was just a little girl, and now she's a young woman."

"You've been e-mailing all that time? Do you ever see her?"

I shook my head. "The therapeutic riding program was in the Kootenays. Kids came from all over. She lives in a small town in northern Alberta. So no, I haven't seen her since then but we e-mail every week or so." In fact, Anna was the main reason I checked e-mail.

"Sounds like you're pretty close."

I nodded, gave a quick grin. "We get along better than my sisters and I do."

"Maybe because you're not her sister; you're more of a mentor."

"A mentor? Me?" I was hardly typical mentor material. "No, just a good friend."

"Hmm." After a moment, he said, "Any news from your family?"

"Seems everyone back home's in love." I wrinkled my nose. "It's like there's an epidemic."

"Epidemic refers to a disease."

"Yes, Science Guy, I know that."

He laughed. Then, tentatively, "I asked you before how you felt about love, and you said you don't do serious. So does that mean you don't believe in love at all?"

"Like I said, our species isn't designed to be monogamous. So what's the point?"

"You mean, you think your sisters' relationships are doomed? And what about your parents? From what you said, they're happy together. My grandparents too, and they've been married fifty years."

"Okay, I guess for some people—really conventional ones—it works. My parents, your grandparents. Maybe it will for my sisters, at least for a while." M&M had been together for almost fifteen years now . . . "Maybe if both people want it badly enough, they can commit to fidelity, to the long term." When I'd been young, I'd believed in that ideal. Then I'd realized I was being naïve. I'd formed a new philosophy of life, and it hadn't let me down.

"It's a waste, though, don't you think?" I went on. "There's so much else in life to experience. It'd be like . . . Okay, blue's my favorite color. But do I want to spend the rest of my life only wearing blue?" Or being with Milos, or Carlos, or any other of the men I'd hooked up with? If I'd stuck with one of them, I wouldn't be with Mark now.

"People are more complex and interesting than colors."

"There are a lot of shades of blue," I countered.

His lips twisted in a quick smile. "Have you ever been in love, Jenna?"

I'd created a monster. When I met him, I had to poke and prod to get him to talk. Now he was interrogating me, reminding me of my mom again.

"Once I thought I was," I said lightly. "My bad."

"What happened?"

"I gave fidelity a try. He didn't."

"I'm sorry. I can see how that would make you cynical."

"Not cynical. Realistic."

"Hmm. How old were you?"

"Seventeen. Why?"

"A high school boyfriend?"

"What is this, twenty questions?"

"No, it's called *conversation*."

I chuckled as he deliberately echoed the words I'd tossed at him yesterday. "Touché." I'd tell him the basics. "Okay. I was in grade eleven when I met Travis. He was twenty, a dropout. Sexy, exciting. In June, some of his friends were hanging out in Kelowna, and he asked me to go along. The idea was, we'd goof off, go to the beach, party. My parents would never have let me go, so I kinda ran away from home. I did tell them I was okay, and I sent a couple postcards from other towns because I didn't want them to worry or send the cops after me."

"Like they wouldn't worry. Jesus, Jenna, you were seventeen."

"Seventeen and rebellious. At home, it was rules, criticism, curfews." I stared out the windshield. "I loved Travis. He said he loved me. I had crazy, romantic illusions about love."

"You had romantic illusions about the wrong guy. Not about love. You said he cheated on you. Seems to me, if one person loves another, they have no desire to have sex with anyone else."

"Oh, come on, don't be so conventional. Having sex doesn't make you blind. You see other people, you're attracted, why wouldn't you have sex with them? Why tie yourself down."

"Is that Travis speaking, or you?"

"It's me! I've always . . ." Shit. "Okay, maybe he said stuff like that, but he was right."

"He was twenty. Ruled by his little head not his big one."

"Oh, thanks," I snapped, "now you're saying I'm immature because I'll date more than one guy at the same time."

"I'm saying, if you met a man you loved, you wouldn't want to date anyone else."

"So now you're the big expert on love?" I taunted. "Have you ever even been in love?"

He turned his head, sent me an assessing look, then stared back at the road. "Maybe not. But I'd like to think that, while love doesn't turn you blind to other people, you wouldn't follow through on any attraction you felt. Because you have something better, and deeper, with the person you're in love with. You want to build something with them, and if you keep getting distracted by other people, that's not going to happen. It'll only ever be superficial."

I knew he was using *you* in the general sense, not meaning me, personally. Still, his phrasing reminded me that I'd once dreamed of finding that kind of love.

But that was long ago, and I was no longer that girl. Quietly, I said, "Maybe that works for some people. Maybe it will for you. But me, I like variety. I like to experience lots of people and things."

"But never truly invest in any of them."

"Maybe I don't have a lot to invest," I retorted, stung into repeating one of the criticisms I'd heard from my family.

"I think you do."

The certainty in his voice touched me, but also annoyed me. "Mark, you sound like my family. Don't you get that I don't want to be like everyone else, with traditional goals and a boring, conventional life?"

Mark frowned as he watched the road ahead. They'd come out by the ocean again, so the view was great, but the Smart Car in front of him was poking along way below the speed limit. The Westfalia didn't have a lot of get up and go, but if he could find an opportunity to pass, he'd take it.

He wished he had as clear an idea of where to take this conversation. Jenna was an adult and seemed perfectly happy being footloose and fancy free. Yeah, he guessed he did get that. He just didn't particularly like it.

Yeah, he had feelings for Jenna. Or at least he could. But not if she continued to live life the way she was doing, flitting here and there without ever committing to anyone or anything. She had a right to be that way, but it wasn't a lifestyle he respected. And he sure as hell couldn't love a woman who needed to screw other guys.

Was there any hope she'd change?

A flicker of motion in the rearview mirror caught his attention and then—"Shit!" A black sports car flashed by on the left, going way too fast, a guy with spiky black hair driving, no passengers. Rather than tucking in ahead of the Westfalia, it blew on by the Smart Car too, cutting sharply in front of it with a squeal of tires to avoid an oncoming SUV.

Automatically, Mark braked even before the Smart Car's brake lights came on and it jerked almost to a stop.

Checking the rear view to make sure no one else was coming, he accelerated again and passed the small car.

"Jeez." Jenna, who'd been holding her cardboard tea container, rubbed a splash of spilled tea from her thigh. "That guy's insane. He's going to cause an accident."

"We should report him before he does. I didn't catch his plate number, did you?"

"It happened too fast." Hurriedly, she drained the last of her tea and set the empty cup on the floor, then rustled around in her big bag and came out with her cell. "Oops, it's dead. It's an old one and the batteries run down quickly."

"Use mine." His was plugged into the battery charger on the dash.

"Where are we?" she asked as she opened the phone. "On the 101, but . . ."

"Almost to the Oregon border."

She made the call, describing the vehicle and their location, then closed the phone. "They ought to take his license away and—"

A horrendous sound—squealing, crashing, crunching—shattered the peaceful morning. "Goddamn!" A flood of adrenaline had him pushing the gas pedal to the floor on this straight stretch.

"Oh my God, Mark. That sounded bad!"

He crested a slight hill, slowed to take a corner, then cursed again at the sight before him. His brain took in the whole picture at once, and he realized what had happened.

The speeder had tried to pass again, an old red Toyota in this case. But an oncoming pickup truck had been too close, or approaching too fast. When the black sports car cut in front of the Toyota, the speeding driver miscalculated or maybe skidded, and smashed into the driver's side of the Toyota. Then the truck smashed into the speeder's car, almost squashing the sports car between the truck and the Toyota. The three vehicles blocked the entire road in a huge mess of mangled metal.

Mark jerked the Westfalia off onto the shoulder. "Call 911!" The moment the camper came to a stop, he was out and running, taking inventory as he approached the scene.

A gray-haired woman emerged from the passenger side of the Toyota, legs wobbly, clutching the door frame for support. The driver of the truck was pinned by an airbag. Mark couldn't even see the drivers of the Toyota and the sports car, the two vehicles were so mangled.

As he ran up, the woman, still clinging to the door, tears pouring down her face, screamed, "My husband's in there. Help him!"

"I will." He took her by the shoulder, noticing glazed eyes, blood on her cheek and arm, but nothing that looked life-threatening. "You sit down and I'll do what I can. We've called 911."

He eased her away from the door then bent and peered inside. Shit, what a mess. The driver's side of the car was crumpled inward, the window shattered and glass all over the place. The driver was squashed in by the side of the car, slumped forward with his head on the steering wheel, seat belt done up. No airbags in this older model vehicle.

Probably a concussion, maybe spinal injury. He shouldn't be moved.

The smell of gas hung in the air, indicating a fuel tank had ruptured. Cars didn't actually burst into flames after accidents, did they? No, gas wouldn't burn without an ignition source. Of course, if batteries were ruptured . . .

Damn it, where were the paramedics?

Mark climbed in the passenger side and held his fingers to the man's neck. Damn again. His pulse was fast, indicating more serious injuries than were apparent.

"How is he?" the woman cried desperately behind him. "Can you get him out?"

"Best not to move him." He leaned over for a better look. "Oh, fuck!" The guy's left forearm, pinned between his body and the door, was spurting blood. Bright red blood. An arterial bleed. He could bleed out before help came.

Mark ripped off his T-shirt and wadded it up. Still no sirens.

"What are you doing?" the wife yelled. "What's wrong?"

The only way to get to the arm and apply pressure was to shift the man back, away from the steering wheel. Risking further neck injury. But better that than bleeding out. Now if only the fuel didn't ignite, and the car didn't burst into flames.

As gently as he could, he shifted the man—elderly, white-haired, with minor facial lacerations but no other major bleeding—back so his head rested on the padded headrest.

"He's bleeding," he called to the guy's wife. "He cut his arm. You should get back, move away from the car." He didn't want to mention the risk of fire for fear of panicking her even more.

"Help him!"

Yeah, that was the general idea. He leaned across the man and held the bundled shirt against the wound, applying as much pressure as he could in this awkward position. Best as he could figure, the man must have instinctively flung up his arms as the car hurtled toward him, then the window shattered and a piece of glass sliced the artery that ran down his forearm.

"Hang on," he whispered. "Help will be here soon." Crap, if this man died right in front of him . . . No, he couldn't think about that, he just had to keep applying pressure.

The wife was sobbing, screaming, not heeding his order to move back. He sympathized, but her shrill voice only ramped up the tension. He wondered how the other accident victims had fared, but there was nothing he could do to help them. Nor to shut out the smell of fresh blood and gas fumes.

What were the odds of a fire with three smashed vehicles, leaks and spills, overheated brakes, and people milling around?

"Mark," Jenna said from behind him, and a hand gripped his bare calf. "What's happening? Someone says there's a fuel leak; the cars might explode."

He swallowed hard. "Can't let go." He didn't turn or let up the pressure. "He's got an arterial bleed. Make sure no one smokes out there. And keep away, Jenna. Keep everyone away, just in case."

"Shit." He heard her draw a noisy breath, then, "Yeah, okay. Can I help? I have your first aid kit."

She'd found the first aid kit he kept under the sink? "Just towels, I need towels." His tee was already drenched in bright blood.

A couple of minutes later, she was back, thrusting several towels at him. As he swapped a towel for the soaked tee, Jenna said, "The truck driver's out and walking around, dazed but okay. The driver of the sports car is wedged in there, unconscious. No one can get to him. 911 says there's a fire truck and ambulances on the way."

"Thanks." The status report steadied him.

He heard her say to the wife, "Mark's doing everything that can be done for your husband. Come with me, you need to sit down over here. Let me look after those cuts. And we should call your family."

The wife's sobs faded, and he blessed Jenna for tending to her. Seemed his travel companion was good in a crisis.

A siren sounded, growing louder. How long had it been?

Maybe less than five minutes, but it felt like forever. Long enough for a man to live or die. He only hoped the one he was huddled over would survive.

The bleeding was slowing. Mark hoped that was a good thing, and not a sign he'd expired. He couldn't take the guy's pulse because he needed both hands to press on the towel.

The siren screamed closer, whooped, died.

Seconds later, a male paramedic leaned into the passenger side, trying to see past Mark. "What you got here?"

"Arterial bleed in his left forearm. I've applied pressure and it's slowed a lot. I had to move him, his head was on the steering wheel and I couldn't get to his arm."

"Okay, keep applying pressure but shift over so I can check his pulse."

Awkwardly, Mark moved, feeling glass slice a bare knee, and let the paramedic reach through to assess the man's condition. "His pulse was fast when I took it."

The man felt his neck, then his wrist. "Still is. But you're doing the right thing." He shifted backward. "Are you okay? Were you involved in the accident?"

"No, I drove up just after. I'm fine."

"Can you hang in a few minutes longer? We're first on the scene and need to assess the others. There's another ambulance and a fire truck on the way. Someone'll take over in a couple minutes."

"Sure."

When the paramedic left, Mark shifted back to his original position, feeling glass grind under his knee. "Not much longer," he said to the unconscious man as he settled in to wait.

More sirens, urgent voices outside, then the same paramedic was back. "I'll take it from here. Hang on while I slide in."

Awkwardly, they juggled positions in the cramped space, and did a quick, clumsy exchange. Then Mark backed out and slowly straightened and sucked in a deep breath. The air was foul with the scent of fuel, but it sure felt good to stretch and feel the sun on his bare shoulders. He hadn't realized how cramped and claustrophobic he'd been.

A second paramedic joined the first as Mark turned away from the car. The driver's wife sat on the grassy verge, face white as she stared at him questioningly. Jenna was beside her, one arm around her shoulders, her face pale too. "Mark?" She gave the woman a quick hug, then came to him.

Softly, she said, "You're covered in blood. His wife's upset enough; she doesn't need to see that." Grabbing a towel he hadn't realized he was holding, she quickly swabbed his hands.

"Yeah." He glanced down at the blood and swallowed against a surge of nausea.

After the initial shock of the accident, he'd acted instinctively and adrenaline had pumped through his veins. Now, relief and reaction set in, draining him. Glancing around, he reassured himself that the emergency workers had everything under control. Then on wobbly legs, he went over to sit by the woman.

Jenna came to sit on her other side. "The paramedic said Mr. Watkins is holding his own," she said.

He nodded, and said to the wife, "The bleeding is under control, and he's in good hands. He's a strong guy, your husband." He wanted to promise that the older man would be all right, but he wasn't positive and couldn't lie to her. "How are you doing?" He noted small bandages on half a dozen cuts and scrapes.

"I'm pretty shaken." Her voice was hoarse. "It all happened so sudden, that car coming out of nowhere."

Something stung his knee and he realized Jenna had opened his first aid kit and was dabbing antiseptic on his glass cuts. "We called their son and daughter," Jenna said. "The ambulance is going to take Mrs. Watkins and her husband to the closest hospital, and her son, who lives in the area, will meet them there."

She'd just finished bandaging his knees when a female paramedic walked over. "Hey, are you trying to do me out of a job?" she joked. "First Mrs. Watkins and now him?"

Jenna grinned back. "I figured you had enough on your hands."

"Are you all right, sir?" the paramedic asked.

"Yeah, just a couple of little cuts." He glanced down at his hands, where the remains of Mr. Watkins's blood had dried. "I need to wash up, get a fresh shirt."

"You go ahead," she told him. "I'll stay with Mrs. Watkins." She smiled at the older woman as if they were friends. Mark assumed she'd been over earlier to assess her condition.

"Police will need you to make a report, though," the paramedic said. She turned her back to Mrs. Watkins and lowered her voice to a murmur. "My colleague Tom says you saved her husband's life. Good job."

"I'm just glad I was here."

As he headed toward the camper, still feeling a little unsteady, Jenna caught up and slipped her hand into his, seeming not to care about the blood. He squeezed her fingers and asked, "How bad is it? I don't know what happened to anyone but Mr. and Mrs. Watkins."

"The truck driver was stunned by the airbag. He came to and got out the passenger side, even though some of us told him he probably shouldn't move." Her hand tightened on his. "He said he could smell fuel, he was afraid everything was going to go up in flames."

"I could smell it, too. Kept telling myself it wouldn't ignite if nothing sparked it." He paused beside the camper. "How about the asshole who caused all this?" Much as the guy deserved whatever he'd got, Mark didn't want him to be dead.

"I don't know." She shivered. "No one could get to him. I think they'll need the jaws of life to get him out."

As they climbed into the back of the camper, a departing ambulance whooped behind them.

Jenna stowed the first aid kit under the sink.

"I'm glad you found that."

"I figured you'd have one," she said, collapsing onto the couch, face still pale, arms wrapped around herself.

He realized that she, too, had been running on adrenaline, doing her best to help the accident victims, and now the shock and reaction were setting in. He wanted to hug her, but first he needed to get rid of the blood and bits of broken glass that stuck to him.

Moving slowly, feeling much older than his years, he ran hot water, soaped his hands, and scrubbed them together. He took a washcloth and cleaned his forearms and his torso, wiping away dried blood and sweat and carefully picking out tiny shards of glass, which he put in the garbage.

As he toweled off, Jenna rose and washed her hands thoroughly, then dried them on the towel he'd used.

Then she wrapped her arms around him, and rested her

cheek against his bare chest. "I was scared, Mark," she said softly, a tremor in her voice. "You were inside that car and the truck driver kept saying the whole thing could go up any minute."

He rested his chin on her soft curls, hating that she'd been upset. Yet it warmed him to know she'd worried about him. "I'm sorry. There wasn't any other way. I couldn't move the guy. I had to keep pressure on his arm."

"I couldn't do anything," she whispered. "I felt so powerless. All I could do was try to calm Mrs. Watkins, when really I was just as worried as she was."

"You helped her, just like I helped her husband."

She eased away so she could gaze up at him. "You saved his life."

It was the truth. And perhaps the reason his legs still felt shaky. If he and Jenna had been even a few minutes later, or if the car had been so badly crushed he couldn't get inside, an old woman would have become a widow today.

A shiver rippled through him. No, it didn't bear thinking about.

Jenna gazed at him steadily, blue-green eyes glowing, then rose up until her mouth was an inch from his. "You did good today, Dr. Chambers." Her lips brushed his.

He grabbed onto her, holding tight to her warm, firm body, and let her lips banish everything else in the world. Gently they caressed each other's mouths, tasting and savoring, and something seeped into him—like sunshine, warm and healing, almost glowing as it spread through his body. The essence of Jenna's sweet soul, pouring into him and making everything else go away.

This wasn't like their previous kisses, it wasn't about passion and sex, but it was just as profound. Maybe more so.

He was so lost in the kiss it took him a while to realize someone was knocking on the door frame. Finally, he pulled back from Jenna, noticing that her cheeks were no longer so pale, and glanced past her to see a female cop with a smirk on her face. "Sorry, folks. Need to get your statements."

"Come on in," he offered. "We can sit down and you can use the table."

As she climbed in, her gaze fixed on his chest.

Jenna gave a soft, amused chuckle, and he quickly found a fresh shirt and pulled it on.

Giving statements only took a few minutes as he and Jenna hadn't seen the accident. Jenna asked about the driver of the sports car and the officer said that emergency workers had managed to free him, but he was in critical condition.

"We'll have the vehicles towed pretty quickly," she went on, "and open the road to alternating one-way traffic while we clear the rest of the mess. You can be on your way soon."

"Thanks," Mark said as she left, raising his voice to be heard over the whoop of another ambulance siren.

When she'd gone, Jenna, sitting beside him, nudged him with her shoulder. "So much for that schedule of yours." Then she rose and took bottles of fruit juice from the fridge. "Grapefruit or orange?"

"Orange. Thanks." Was it knowledge or instinct that made her realize they both probably had low blood sugar right now? He opened the bottle and took a long swallow. "How are you doing?"

"Fine. Once I realized there wasn't much I could do for anyone, I just hung out with Mrs. Watkins."

"Thanks for calming her down. Her screaming was driving me crazy."

"She was terrified."

"I know. I was kind of terrified myself. Kept thinking that old man could die right in front of me."

"He didn't." She stared into his eyes. "He's going to be all right."

He took a deep breath. "I hope so."

"Believe it," she said firmly. "I do." A smile touched her lips. "D'you know, they've been married forty-five years? And have two kids and five grandchildren?"

Yeah, Jenna had "hung out" with the older woman. Meaning, she'd got her to sit down, bandaged her cuts, and kept her from panicking by talking about her family. "And you say you don't have much to invest in people or projects."

"Huh?"

He shook his head, lacking the energy to explain right now. Or to point out Mr. and Mrs. Watkins were one of those couples who'd found a lifelong love.

For the moment, all he wanted was to sit here, her bare thigh warm against his.

Chapter 8

When the police gave us the go-ahead to get back on the road, I said to Mark, "Want me to drive?" After what he'd been through, he could probably use a rest.

In truth, I felt shaky myself from the shock of the accident, then the terror at seeing Mark inside that car while gas spilled onto the pavement and that idiot truck driver kept saying everything could go up in flames.

So I was relieved when Mark said, "No, thanks. Driving's relaxing for me. At least when no one's causing an accident."

"Fingers crossed." I climbed into the passenger side and let the soft seat cradle my nerve-jangly body as the cops directed vehicles around the accident site. The truck had been towed away, but the sight of the mangled sports car and old Toyota made me shudder.

Mark was alive, I reminded myself. And so was Mr. Watkins, thanks to my brave lover.

He glanced over, then touched my leg, a brief, affectionate graze. "It's good to be alive."

"It is."

"Want to find some music?"

"Sure." I turned on the radio and cruised through channels, rejecting rock and a couple of talk shows, pausing for a moment on country, then moving on to an oldies station that was playing "California Dreaming." Another song my mom used to play when I was a kid. "This okay?"

"Good music for a drive by the ocean."

Good music to calm jangled nerves, too. "When I heard this as a kid, I asked Mom where California was. She told me, and I announced that I was going there one day." I laughed softly. "It's another *I must be adopted* thing. I'm the only person in my family who has the travel bug."

"Doesn't one of your sisters live in Montreal?"

"Yes, Kat, and Tree's in Sydney, Australia. We all needed to get away from home, spread our wings as adults. But they're settled, happy where they are now."

"You never see yourself doing that?"

"I'm not the nest-building sort. There are so many great places to see."

"Yeah, and worthwhile things to do."

The next song was "Good Vibrations," another old classic I heard every now and then.

When the Beach Boys sang the chorus, Mark said, "This song makes me think of you."

So I gave him good vibrations, did I? Hard to argue with that. "Exci-ta-tion," I sang along, exaggerating the word.

He chuckled. "Yeah, that for sure. But also the colorful clothes, the sunlight in your hair. That's like when I first saw you. And then there's what happens when I look into your eyes."

"Happens?" I knew my eyes were a pretty color, but didn't get what he meant.

He glanced over. "It's like going into the ocean. The reflection and refraction of light; every shade of green and blue, sparkles of sunlight, secret shadows. I'm drawn in, like there's so much to explore, and I may just want to swim around in there forever."

"Wow," I breathed. What a great compliment. And coming from Mark, I knew it was sincere.

He was watching the road now, but the corners of his lips twitched. Maybe he wasn't used to me being unable to find words. It would have sounded cheesy to compliment him on his eyes, but the truth was, they were pretty amazing too. Like the purest, bluest, most vivid sky.

As for gazing into them . . . That was a little scary. Like with his kisses, there was something a little too powerful, too irresistible.

The radio drew my attention, one of those old girl group songs. The lead singer was asking how she'd know if her guy loved her. And the answer was, *It's in his kiss.*

Bizarre that this song would come on right when I was thinking about kissing Mark. I should flip the freaking dial until I found "What's Love Got To Do With It?"

Disgruntled, I folded my arms across my chest and tried to tune out the stupid song.

Mark reached over and turned off the radio.

I sent him a silent thank you.

"Before the accident . . ." he said.

It seemed so long ago. "Yeah?"

"We were talking about love."

Oh, right. And debating the merits of variety versus monogamy. Oddly, this seemed to be one of Science Guy's favorite topics.

"This guy Travis . . ." he said.

I tossed my head. "Look, I was stupid. I don't want to talk about it anymore."

"You were seventeen. Everyone's allowed a mistake."

Not that mistake.

"You loved him."

I shrugged. "I thought so."

"You didn't want to be with anyone else. You were into fidelity."

"I was a foolish romantic."

"Tell me the story."

"I told you. A silly girl runs away from home with a bad boy on a motorbike; he cheats on her and dumps her for another girl; she goes back home sadder but wiser."

"No, tell me the long version."

I hugged my arms tighter. I'd never told anyone. Not a soul. "Let it go, Mark. I did, long ago."

"We're on the road with nothing else to do but talk. I want to get to know you."

Why did he keep turning my own words back on me? Still, it was kind of sweet that he was interested. Was that why I felt an odd compulsion to finally share the story?

"Hey," he said, "I told you about my mistake with the woman who thought I was Mr. Right. You tell me about yours."

"Oh, mine was a whole chain of mistakes."

"Give yourself a break."

How could I? Not when I lived with an ache deep inside that no exciting place, man, or job had ever managed to erase?

"Jenna?" Mark said softly.

Was it his persistence or my own need that finally got through? Deliberately, I unfolded my arms, then flicked my hair back, reached for my water bottle, and took a long swallow. "We went to Kelowna on his motorbike. His friends were renting half of a rundown duplex. The place was pretty bad, but I thought everything was so cool. The others were a few years older than me and it was fun having no rules. Doing whatever we wanted, whenever we wanted to."

I paused. "Though it wasn't so fun when no one ever cleaned the bathroom, and when they spent half their time stoned out of their minds."

"You did drugs, too?" His tone was neutral.

"I wanted to fit in so I tried a couple of things. But I like experiencing life, and the drugs warped things. The others accepted me anyhow. They were pretty live and let live." In fact, Travis's friends had been nicer than he was. "Travis had said he loved me, but then I got sick and he dumped me."

"Sick?"

I drank more water and stared out the window, not at Mark, torn between telling and not telling.

He touched my leg. "Jenna?"

I looked at him just as he glanced at me, and I saw the concern in his eyes before he turned back to the road. I took a deep breath. "Believing him, falling for him, that was my first mistake. Number two: he didn't want to use condoms. Said he loved me, we were exclusive. I was on the pill, I trusted him." I swallowed against old pain and said flatly, "He gave me gonorrhea."

"Jesus. I'm sorry."

I could leave it there. Except now, after so many years of silence, something inside wouldn't let me. "I didn't realize it, just knew I didn't feel so great. Kind of like I had the flu. My stomach hurt, I . . . well, I won't go into all the gross symptoms. But as it got worse, I didn't feel like sex, or going to the beach, or going out drinking. I just lay on the bed feeling crappy."

"You didn't see a doctor?"

"Chain of mistakes, remember? No, I was afraid a doctor would call my parents. I thought it was the flu, and I'd get over it. But Travis . . . he said I was no fun to be with. He'd been sleeping with another girl, and they were going to take his bike and ride to Alberta."

"The shit."

"Yeah. I said, 'But you told me you loved me,' and he said, 'Fuck, that's just something guys say so they can nail a girl.' Anyhow, after he left I felt worse and worse but even then I didn't see a doctor. I was such a freaking idiot. Finally, the kids I was staying with took me to emergency."

"And the hospital called your parents."

I shook my head. "I refused to give their contact info. I gave the hospital my Kelowna address and said one of the girls there was my next of kin."

"A rough thing to go through alone," he said sympathetically. "I guess they gave you antibiotics?"

I could say yes, and it wouldn't be a lie.

He touched my folded arms, and I realized that, without being aware of it, I'd wrapped them tightly around my belly again.

"There's more, isn't there, Jenna?"

This was why I'd never told the story. Because it wasn't just about Travis, the loss of my first love, my stupid mistakes. It was about what those mistakes had cost me in the end.

I closed my eyes against the soul-deep pain. Slowly, I said, "Yeah. By then I had a really bad PID—pelvic inflammatory disease—and an abscess that had ruptured. They had to operate to drain it. And . . ."

He squeezed lightly. "And?"

I'd never said these words to anyone. They sat like heavy, nasty weights inside me, more painful than that damned abscess. Maybe if I spoke them, I'd dilute their power. "Such bad scarring that I can never have children."

His hand jerked. "Damn."

"Didn't see that one coming?" I said bitterly. "Nor did I."

"I'm so, so sorry."

I glanced at him, saw the sincerity in his eyes, felt tears rise. "I was too," I admitted. Then I forced down the tears and shrugged, "But hey, look at my lifestyle. Kids would have tied me down anyhow." It was the truth—I'd created a wonderful life that didn't include children—yet that didn't banish the pain.

He signaled a left turn, then steered across the road and into a scenic pullout above a rather wild stretch of beach. A sign said Cape Sebastian.

"Mark?"

"Get out."

When I didn't move, he unbuckled his seat belt, got out the driver's side, and came around to open my door. He even reached across me to unbuckle my belt, a feat made difficult by my still-crossed arms. Taking me firmly by my right upper arm, he tugged until I climbed out of the camper.

"What?" A stiff breeze blew my hair across my face. I didn't pull the strands away, let them sting my eyes so this time the welling tears did fall.

He pulled me close, tucking my head against his chest and wrapping his arms around me. "Don't brush it off, Jenna. It mattered. It hurt. You're allowed to hurt."

"Crying over spilled milk," I murmured against the soft warmth of his tee, letting the fabric absorb my tears and feeling comforted by his strong arms around me.

"Is that what your parents told you?" he asked, voice harsh.

I shook my head against his chest, raised my arms to encircle his waist and sniffed back the tears. "No, but it was one of my mother's sayings, so I figured it would fit this situation. Mom's very practical."

"But what did she actually say when you told her?"

"I didn't. I didn't tell my family."

His arms tightened. "My God, why not?"

"Because . . ." I sighed, remembering back. I'd been so damaged, so messed up, and I hadn't wanted to be that way. I'd wanted to reinvent myself, to forget the old dreams and start fresh, to not even acknowledge the old Jenna. "Because I'd screwed up again."

I pulled back in the circle of his arms, keeping my own

around his waist, and stared up at him. His eyes were bluer, fiercer, than the bright sky behind. "I ran away, fell for the wrong guy, didn't have safe sex, didn't have the sense to get medical attention when I should. I didn't need a lecture. And," I narrowed my eyes warningly, "I didn't need pity."

He stroked my cheek gently. "How about caring? How about love? Did you need those?"

The bright sun, the breeze . . . again my eyes teared up. "I knew my family loved me."

"You said that before. That it's an *I love you, but* kind of thing. Like, *I love you, but you should have known better than to run off with that boy?*"

"Yeah, like that." And they'd have been right.

"I love you, and I'm sorry for what happened to you. That's what they should have said."

Those words, the kind of words I didn't remember ever hearing from my parents or my sisters made the tears spill. I buried my face against his chest and said, trying for a jokey tone, "That might've been nice."

Mark stared down at her white-gold curls, blazing in the sun, and felt an ache in his chest around the region of his heart. He wanted to reach back into the past and change things, to fix it all up so Jenna hadn't been hurt.

Impossible, fanciful, not like him at all.

In his adult life, the only woman he'd ever told "I love you" was his grandmother, and the words, while genuine, had felt awkward. But a minute ago, they'd flowed off his tongue. He'd been talking about what Jenna's family should have said to her, and yet . . . The words had felt right.

He couldn't really be falling for Jenna, could he?

Examine the hypothesis. Why couldn't he? At first, he'd bought into the image she presented, of a free-spirited drifter who wouldn't commit to anyone or anything. One who didn't want kids. Now he knew better. She'd committed to being there for an amputee child for the last eight years. She'd loved a boy who had betrayed her.

Her mom had told her not to cry over spilled milk, and Jenna had decided to just stop drinking milk. To pretend to herself that she didn't want love, didn't want children.

Or at least, that was his current working theory.

If he and Jenna did fall in love, they could have kids if they wanted them. There were so many children in the world who needed parents.

He gazed over her shoulder at a vista of deep blue ocean studded with craggy rocks, white-capped waves foaming their way to shore. Was he getting ahead of himself or what? It had been a hell of an unsettling morning. Time to take a breath, literally and figuratively.

He could see Jenna felt vulnerable after sharing such personal, sensitive information. She didn't want pity and was trying to joke, so he accepted the tone she wanted to set, and said, "Parents. We sure don't get to pick them, do we?"

A soft laugh. "Nor they us." A moment later, she lifted her head to gaze at him. "Thanks, Mark. Thanks for being here for me."

The word *always* stuck in his throat. It wanted to fly out, but he couldn't make that promise. Who knew what would happen between them over the next couple of days of this journey? Instead, he said, "My pleasure." Gazing into her damp-lashed eyes, eyes so much brighter and more beautiful than the dark ocean below them, he had that same sense of diving in and getting lost. Very happily lost.

"And now we're really behind schedule," she said. A statement of fact—yes, they were a good three hours behind—but he was learning to read her. The twinkle in her eyes said she was teasing.

"Guess I'll have to learn to adapt." He glanced down at

the strip of sandy, wave-swept beach below. "D'you want to go down to the beach for a walk?"

She eased out of his arms and gazed at the view, blond curls whipping around in the breeze. "Yes, but no. I really do need to be in Vancouver tomorrow night."

And then what would happen to the two of them? "Me too. Shouldn't be a problem." Yesterday, her car had broken down. Today, they'd been held up by an accident. Surely there'd be no other major delays.

They walked to the camper and she said, "It's lunchtime and I'm hungry. Want to eat while we drive?"

"Sure."

She popped into the back to assemble a snack, and soon they were on the road again. An easy road, a lovely one that mostly hugged the ocean's edge and offered stunning vistas, bright orange California poppies, very few towns, and the scent of ocean air coming through the open windows. Companionably they munched on bread and cheese, crackers, carrots, and finished up with a couple of rosy apples.

"I wish we had a slice of Marianne's pie," Jenna said. "That was the best."

"Too bad we didn't think to bring some with us."

"Planning's not my strong suit."

"What is?" He had his own ideas, but wanted to hear hers.

"Having fun. Living in the moment."

"Helping people. Abused women, disabled kids, autistic kids, a girl with no legs who doesn't have a mom or dad, an old woman after a car accident. Helping falcons, doing park maintenance. I'm sure there's more."

"I've had a few other jobs, done other volunteer work here and there. But it's just . . . you know. I'm passing through. I'm one of many pairs of hands."

"Your mom's just one lawyer, your sister's just one sociologist."

A quick laugh. "And here I thought they'd like you."

"Well, am I right?"

She shook her head. "You haven't met them. Yeah, everyone in my family kind of pisses me off—except M, most of the time, because she's too sweet to piss anyone off—but I'm actually proud of them."

"Tell me more about them." He'd been getting a picture of her parents, seeing them as not unlike his grandma and grandpa. People who expected their child to be studious and structured. For him, that had worked perfectly because it fit his natural personality. But Jenna would have been a kid like Alicia. Outgoing and fun. When his grandparents had seen those qualities in Alicia, they'd tried to squash them, and she'd rebelled.

"Ah," she said, "more *conversation*, to make the miles fly by."

"Someone told me it was a good idea." The longer he knew Jenna, the more interested he was in her. Besides, he had theories to check out. Was her footloose behavior her own rebellion? If her parents had understood her better, might they have fostered her particular talents rather than tried to squash them? Might they have helped her realize and achieve her true value instead of telling her she had little to invest?

She took a long swallow of water, tilted her seat back a notch, and put bare feet up on the dashboard. "Okay, starting with my folks."

He glanced appreciatively at her long, tanned legs. Toned, shapely legs that made him think of naked limbs twining together, of her wrapping those legs around his hips as he pumped into her. Then he tore his gaze away and concentrated on the road and her words.

"Dad graduated from Harvard and came to UBC to get his doctorate, studying under a top geneticist. Mom was doing pre-law when they met. They were both serious, disciplined, smart as blazes." She flicked him a grin. "A lot like you. They got married the summer before she started law school. They had the whole plan worked out."

"I'm sure they did." Yes, they were exactly as he'd theorized.

She gave a mischievous giggle. "It didn't include kids, not until they were both established in their fields. But nature had its own ideas. Mom was on the pill, but she got pregnant in second year law."

"Your sister Theresa? They didn't consider abortion?"

"I'd bet they did, not that they'd tell us. Instead, they reworked the whole plan. Mom thought one parent should stay home for the first year, and Dad, well . . . Typical absent-minded prof, you wouldn't want him looking after a baby. They wanted two kids, a boy and a girl, and quickly, so Mom could get back to her career."

"Makes sense. Except, all of you are girls, right?"

"Nature foiled them again. Still wanting a boy, they gave it one more shot. Along came me. A big disappointment."

"I'm sure you weren't." Yet, in some ways she likely had been: a butterfly born into a family of worker bees. They wouldn't have known what to do with her, except try to shape her into their image.

She snorted. "Yeah, right."

He could only imagine how tough it had been for her, and realized that not only was he coming to understand Jenna but to have more sympathy for Alicia. Parents and kids; maybe it was always a tough relationship. If he had children, he wanted to do better.

"Anyhow, then Mom went back to law school. You said she's just one lawyer? Nope, she's become one of the best class action lawyers in the country."

"Hmm. Tough parents to live up to."

"Not a problem for Tree, the genius kid. Went to Harvard and the New School for Social Research in New York, got a

Ph.D. in sociology. She specializes in indigenous people. By the time she was twenty-two she was teaching in the native studies program at the University of Saskatchewan."

He whistled. Another tough act to follow.

"But, poor Tree, though she had an off-the-chart IQ, her experience with boys was zero. She fell for a senior prof, got married, and the asshole ripped off her research."

"Shit."

"It put her off men."

Interesting that Theresa's response to betrayal was avoidance, and Jenna had gone in the opposite direction: the more, the merrier, so long as she never fell in love. Coping mechanisms in both cases, neither of them particularly healthy. In his humble opinion. What the hell did he know about relationships anyhow?

"She's been in Sydney for a long time now," she was saying. "A tenured prof. She gives papers at all those international symposiums, same as you."

"Specializing in Aboriginal Australians?"

"Yeah. And Torres Strait Islanders."

"Aboriginal people have a tough go, no matter what country you're in. I've seen that wherever I've traveled."

"Tree'd enjoy talking to you." There was a hint of something negative—jealousy?—in her tone.

"I'd enjoy talking to her too," he said cautiously.

"You smart folks talk the same language."

She was subtly putting herself down, the way she'd done a time or two before. Echoing her parents' opinions, he'd bet.

"Intellectuals tend to talk the same language," he corrected, "though to a large extent the language is specific to each discipline. I'm sure you've seen that with your dad and your sister. Both academics, but in very different fields."

"True. I guess everyone in the family has learned some of each other's language over the years."

"Like you."

"Me?" she scoffed. "I'm sure no academic intellectual."

When he'd first met her, she'd been so effervescent and confident, but now he realized there were cracks in that bubbly exterior. Vulnerabilities. They made her even more appealing. "Maybe not, but most people would just say Aborigines and be done with it."

"Tree'd kill me." She shrugged. "Yeah, I've picked up some of the lingo. And I don't want to be an intellectual. They can be awfully dull."

"Sorry, I lecture too much," he said guiltily.

She chuckled and when he glanced over, her eyes were twinkling. "Actually, you're pretty interesting. I may not be into academic stuff, but I do like to learn."

Suddenly, she pointed out the window. "Hey, have you ever gone there?"

He glanced at a roadside sign announcing an upcoming tourist attraction called Prehistoric Gardens. "Sounds hokey."

"Yeah, totally, and it's a hoot. *Educational,* too," she taunted. "Too bad we don't have time to stop."

Prehistoric Gardens? Seriously? Still, if she liked the place . . . "We made up time by not stopping for a lunch break, and traffic's light. Besides, it's good to stretch every now and then."

Her face lit. "Really?"

It occurred to him that he'd do pretty much anything to put that sparkle in her eyes. "Why not?" He turned off the highway and followed the signs.

They were in rain forest now, a small valley sheltered by hills, and had left the sun behind them. When he pulled into the parking lot at Prehistoric Gardens, the blanket of pale gray clouds suited the almost jungle atmosphere.

They climbed out and Jenna slipped her hand into his. "Thanks, Mark. This'll be fun. It'll bring out the kid in you."

Was there a kid in him? His grandparents had taken him to museums and science centers but not to places like Disneyland. As for the action figures and video games other kids played with, he'd been raised to believe they were a waste of time. Play was a waste of time.

And now here he was, going into a hokey Jurassic Park kind of tourist spot where garishly painted models of prehistoric creatures lurked amid jungle foliage.

"Look at the baby Triceratops," Jenna cried, tugging him over to see admittedly cute little creatures supposedly emerging from broken egg shells.

"They look a bit like an Australian frilled lizard, though much stockier," he said.

A little boy, maybe four years old, came running up, yelling, "Look, look!" The kid miscalculated his stop time and was about to crash into Mark's legs, so he bent and quickly caught the boy by his shoulders, steadying him. "Hey, there, big guy, you trying to knock me over?"

"Dinosaurs?" the kid said uncertainly, pointing past Mark, then looking up at Jenna.

In the boy's family, Mom must be the font of all wisdom.

Jenna smiled back. "They're baby dinosaurs. Aren't they cute? They're called Triceratops."

"They came out of eggs! Like baby chickens."

"They did." She plunked down on the ground beside him. "But they won't be able to fly like the chickens will." She glanced around. "Where are your parents?"

"Mommy!" the kid yelled at the top of his lungs. Then, to Jenna, "I don't know."

"They probably heard you," she said dryly. "They'll be here soon. Here, let me read you what it says about this baby Triceratops."

Mark stood, charmed by the pair as Jenna paraphrased the information on the descriptive sign, and the boy listened intently. She might say she didn't want kids, but she was a natural. Had she considered adoption?

For a moment, he pictured family outings like this: him, Jenna, and a couple of children. Kids from Asia or Africa, their dark skin a contrast to her bright blond hair. He'd always figured he wanted kids, but for the first time yearning tugged at his heart.

A frazzled looking woman and man rushed up, then stopped, smiling when they realized their son was all right.

Jenna rose and dusted off her butt, chatting to the parents and the boy in her friendly way. When the family headed off to another exhibit, Mark took her hand. "Okay, what next?"

They followed a path lined with wooden fencing, and studied the Stegosaurus. A monster with a huge body and tiny head, it had hard, spiky protrusions sticking out of his spine. "Look, racing stripes," Jenna joked, pointing to the almost fluorescent blue and yellow stripes decorating his side.

On they went. "Bradysaurus looks kind of friendly and curious," Mark said, "as if he'd like a pat on the head. And even if he decides to attack me, I'll outrun him." The sign said the creature's name meant "slow lizard."

"They all look pretty slow to me," she said. "They're built like elephants."

"Once an elephant gets going, it can run twenty-five miles an hour."

She nudged her elbow into his side. "I stand corrected, Science Guy."

They toured the whole park, and he forgot to worry about their schedule. He was learning something and having fun. Jenna was easy company, and it was nice seeing families with kids having a good time together on a Saturday afternoon. Again, he felt that tug of longing. Was there a possibility he and Jenna might one day be like them?

"I never did this kind of thing with my grandparents," he

said as they gazed up at the Brachiosaurus, as tall as many of the trees.

"I did. Gran used to take all us girls out on Sundays. 'Expotitions,' we called them, like in *Winnie-the-Pooh*. Parks, the beach, Science World, the aquarium, movies, something fun and different each time." She'd been grinning, but the smile faded to wistfulness. "She'd have loved it here."

"Has she passed away now?" They moved on to another dinosaur, a winged Pteranodon.

"No. But she has Alzheimer's. She's in a care facility and most of the time she's pretty out of it. It's so sad to see her like that."

"It must be. I'm lucky; my grandparents are as sharp as ever." He shook his head. "I think the worst thing they could imagine would be an Alzheimer's diagnosis."

"Gran coped well when she was diagnosed. She was brave, kept her sense of humor. Granddad had died quite a while before, so he didn't have to see her slipping."

"Your mom's parents or your dad's?" he asked as they wandered down the path.

"Mom's. Dad's were in Maryland. They passed away quite a few years ago. We didn't see a lot of them."

"Tough on your mom, watching her mother like that. Tough on all of you."

"Yeah. But here's what I think." She pulled him into a jungly alcove off the path and stepped in front of him. Looking up at him, she held his gaze. "I think Gran's going to come out of it for Merilee's wedding. I think she has enough . . . *whatever* still left inside her, she's going to see M&M get married."

Her expression was challenging, like she was daring him to disagree. She had to know there was no scientific reason to believe it would happen.

"I'm an optimist," she said, almost defiantly. "The universe has a way of providing what's right at the time."

There was no science behind that theory. And yet, the universe had sent him into Marianne's Diner and sent Jenna in on his heels. The universe had put them on the highway this morning at just the right time to save Mr. Watkins's life. Slowly, he said, "I guess sometimes it does. I hope you're right about your gran. She sounds like quite the woman."

Her smile dazzled him. "She is." Then she rose up and planted a kiss on his lips.

She probably meant it as a quick thank-you. But, still reeling from that smile, emotions a little crazy after all that had happened today, he grabbed her head in both hands and held her there. He kissed her back, with everything that was in him. The shock of the accident, the fear that Mr. Watkins would die, the relief when the paramedic took over. The uncertainty of his feelings for Jenna, and hers for him. The fun of carefree play in a kids' park with a pretty girl on a summer afternoon. Jenna. All of it with Jenna.

Something leaped between them, mouth to mouth, body to body—that force, that fire, that thing that swept him up and away.

He'd had a theory about kissing her, and now he hadn't the slightest memory what it was.

In some fuzzy distant space, he was aware of voices, people approaching. He tore his lips from hers and, panting with the strength of whatever had just happened, got out, "I need you. I want to make love with you."

The sun hid behind clouds, yet her whole face was lit up, as if from some internal source of illumination. "Yes," she breathed.

Chapter 9

Five minutes later, Mark and I were in the camper, curtains pulled and bed down. Staring into each other's eyes without speaking a word, we yanked off our clothes. I'd never felt such an urgent need to be with a man.

To have sex with a man who made my body explode, melt, tingle, catch fire, dissolve, all somehow at the same time. A man who got me to share secrets I'd never told another soul. A man whose eyes, whose lips, reached inside me to places I hadn't even known existed. Places that had never been touched before.

Places I couldn't think about now, because we were naked and he was tumbling me to the bed.

Mark. His urgent lips, hard body, demanding hands, jutting cock so hot it almost seared my hand when I gripped it.

Me. Grabbing, stroking, needing to touch every inch of him I could reach. My nipples painfully taut as he licked and sucked them. My pussy pulsing with the desperate need to grip him and ride him to climax.

Us. Mouths fusing again, bodies flying, merging. Driving hard, fast. Him deep, deep in my core, stroking my womb, making me feel as if I were going to come apart. Making me feel . . . "Oh God, Mark!" Behind closed lids the world turned to fire as our bodies shattered together.

Bliss, as waves of orgasm pounded through me, cresting and breaking.

"Jenna. God, Jenna." His voice, hoarse, breaking too.

Finally, finally, the blaze behind my lids cooled, the waves inside me eased to ripples. Gentle. Soothing. I could try to breathe again.

His weight was on me, his head buried in the curve between my neck and shoulder. His chest heaved against mine.

One of my hands rested on his shoulder, the other on the curve of his butt. I couldn't move them, not even to caress him.

La petite mort, the little death. The French chef had told me that's how the French referred to orgasm. I'd never got it before. To me, sex was about life, not death. But today, I felt half dead—and yet, somehow reborn.

Mark struggled to lift his weight off me, then flopped on the bed at my side. "What the hell was that?"

"Uh, good sex?" I ventured.

He turned his head and stared at me, brows raised. "No. That was not just good sex. That was something else."

He reached down, then shock crossed his face. "Damn, no condom."

I jerked upright, rediscovering muscles that a moment ago had been soft as honey. "Shit! Shit, shit, shit. I *never* forget." Never, since Travis.

"Me either." He shook his head. "Jenna, I'm clean, I swear. Before this, I hadn't even had sex in five or six months. And I always use condoms."

"Me, too." Not the *no sex in six months* part. For me, it hadn't been much more than six days. But condoms, yes, always. Wryly, I said, "And we know I won't get pregnant."

The sympathy in his eyes made me turn away. He guessed the truth, that I'd once dreamed of having children.

Spilled milk. No tears.

If I could have had kids, there'd be no better daddy genes than Mark's. Smart, brave, sensitive, handsome, conscientious. After what he'd gone through as a boy, he'd try extra hard to be a wonderful parent.

And he would have kids one day. He'd find the right woman, a brilliant scientist, an environmentalist like him. They'd share life as partners—both work and family.

Things that I didn't want, I reminded myself, as a slow sadness seeped through me. More of that little death thing, I figured. Postcoital melancholy. It was unlike me, but then this had been an extraordinary day.

I rolled away from Mark. "We should get back on the highway."

His semen was sticky between my legs, dripping down my thighs. Unfamiliar. A reminder of how irresponsible we'd been. I washed quickly and pulled my clothes on as he lay back, watching.

When I was finished, I went outside to give him the space to get dressed.

And to give myself space. This journey back to Vancouver was turning into a bit of a wild ride. Too disconcertingly wild for even me.

As soon as we were under way, I said, "I'm going to take a nap." Inside the confines of the seatbelt, I twisted sideways, bare feet up on the seat, and rested my forehead against the passenger side window.

He squeezed my ankle. "Have a good one."

He was nice. So damned nice. In fact, he was close to perfect. For some other woman. A woman who wanted a serious guy.

Unfair, a voice whispered in my head. Yes, he was serious about the environment and his work, but he could be tempted to come out and play. He *needed* to be tempted. His grandparents had almost destroyed his sense of fun. Sometimes he even seemed to feel guilty about simply enjoying himself. If he hooked up with a woman who was like him, would the two of them ever play? Would they encourage their kids to play?

The hum of the tires, the warmth of the window against my cheek, the comfort of the big swivel seat all combined like a narcotic, and I found myself drifting off to sleep.

I woke when Mark pulled into a gas station. Yawning, I stretched and checked my watch, finding I'd slept for more than an hour. While he began to pump gas, I climbed out. "Where are we?"

"Coos Bay."

"Sorry I slept so long. Time for a bathroom break. Want me to get you a coffee?" He was obviously addicted.

"Thanks."

A quick glance around showed me a coffee shop across the street. Surely, they'd make better coffee than service station sludge, and they'd likely have interesting herbal tea, too.

I headed over, ordered our drinks, and made use of the facilities. When I came back to the camper, Mark emerged from the station.

I handed him a cardboard coffee cup. "Here, free trade beans."

"Really?"

"From the coffee shop across the street."

"Good idea. I'll have to remember to check around in future, not just settle for service station brew." He took a sip, then smiled. "Oh, yeah. Thanks, Jenna." He glanced at my cup. "That's not chamomile."

"Rooibos. Red sticks rather than lawn clippings."

He winced, and I laughed.

Back in the camper, as he pulled away, I asked, "Are we making up any lost time?"

"Not much. We can stick to the coast road through most

of Oregon, but since we both need to get to Vancouver Sunday night, we'll have to take the I-5 through Washington."

"Gack. That's nasty."

"There's a state park called Cape Lookout just southwest of Tillamook, which is an hour or so from Portland. I've never stayed there, only seen signs for it."

"Sure."

He glanced over. "I was thinking maybe you'd rather find a nice B&B, something like that? My treat."

"Huh? How come?"

"The accident. Stressful day. It'd be more comfortable for you."

I smiled and shook my head gently. "You're sweet, but I'm not that kind of girl. Camping suits me just fine, especially if there's a beach. And a real toilet and shower."

"I'm pretty sure they have all that." He glanced at the clock on the dash. "It's mid afternoon now, and we've got about four hours on the road to get to Cape Lookout. It'll make for a longish day today, but we'd get to Vancouver at a reasonable time tomorrow. Or we could stop somewhere else in an hour or so, but that'll make a really long drive tomorrow. It's up to you."

"Why don't we just drive and see how we feel?"

"Could, but if we're going to get to a campground late on a Saturday in summer, we may not get in. If we know we want to stay at Cape Lookout, we should phone and reserve."

He really needed to loosen up. Half the fun of life was when the unexpected happened. "If we're meant to stay there, it'll work out. If not, we'll find someplace else."

"The universe will provide?"

"You got it. Speaking of which . . ." I opened the bag I'd brought from the coffee shop. "Look what it provided when I got coffee." The lemon bars had been irresistible.

"Thanks." He glanced over as I held out a bright yellow

bar topped with powdered sugar. "Looks a little messy, though."

"Here." I held it to his mouth so he could take a bite.

While he was chewing, I nibbled on the same bar myself. Mmm, I loved the bright, sunny tang of lemon.

For the next miles, we didn't talk much, just took alternate nibbles until both bars were done. With the tip of one finger, I brushed sugar from his bottom lip. Such a warm, sensual lip.

He ducked his head, tried to nip my finger, but I jerked away in time, laughing.

"Tell me about some of the projects you've worked on," I suggested.

With a little more urging, he complied, and I listened with interest. He really had done some amazing things.

As we talked, I noticed him rotating his shoulders, wincing a little. "Are you okay?"

"Just kinked my neck and shoulders a little, stretching over to reach Mr. Watkins's arm."

"I'll give you a massage when we stop for the night." After that last round of sex, I wasn't sure I wanted to risk kissing the man again, but having him face down on the bed, his tanned, muscular body spread out in front of me, didn't sound bad at all. "For now, why don't you let me drive? I'm a good driver, honest. Tell me you're not one of those cavemen who refuses to sit in the passenger seat."

"If I were, I sure couldn't confess to it now, could I?" He gave a lazy smile. "Yeah, that would be nice."

He pulled over at the next opportunity, and we got out and stretched, then switched sides. I adjusted the driver's seat and mirrors, pulled out, and drove cautiously as I got the feel of a vehicle so much bigger than Mellow Yellow. Once I was confident I said, "Your turn to nap if you want."

"I wouldn't mind. Wake me if you need anything." He tilted the seat and stretched. A few minutes later, his soft, slow breaths told me he'd drifted off. Apparently, caffeine had no effect on him.

I always enjoyed driving, and this was pleasant, with Mark dozing comfortably beside me, a whole miniature house traveling with us.

Casually, I noticed signs go by. Dunes City, Florence. Back out to the coast and more lovely ocean views. Heceta Head, where there was a lighthouse. Yachats, a cute town tucked between the mountains and the ocean.

When we reached Newport, I needed a pee break, so pulled into a gas station. I hopped out to buy him some gas, then realized I didn't know what type the hybrid camper took. As I was deliberating, the passenger door opened and Mark emerged, yawning and running his hand through his hair, tousling it.

For a moment, I had an image of what an adorable little boy he must have been. And what gorgeous babies he'd make. I felt a pang at the thought of Mark and some other woman realizing a dream that was impossible for me.

"Hey, there," he said, dropping a kiss on the top of my head and reaching out to stab one of the buttons on the pump.

"Hey, yourself."

When he glanced around, I said, "Newport."

"Great. Only another hour or so to Cape Lookout."

From the gas station we drove to a grocery store where, once again, the universe provided beautifully for us with skewers of pink prawns fresh from the ocean, mushrooms, chunks of onion, and green and red peppers. A display of fresh local raspberries lured me. Then Mark asked me to pick wine, and I went for an Oregon pinot gris.

"I always thought it was a waste of time to fuss over food," he said.

"This was no more fuss than picking up cheese and crackers or getting a made-up sandwich, and it'll taste so yummy."

His upper lip twitched like he was hiding a grin. "I always thought it was a waste of time to actually taste food."

I bumped his shoulder. "Learn something new every day. It's a waste of time to do something and not enjoy the experience."

"Good point."

"Should we pick up something for breakfast?"

We agreed on bran muffins, and our shopping was done.

Back at the camper, I hung onto the raspberries while he stowed the other groceries in the back. I claimed the driver's seat again, popped a berry into my mouth, and handed him the box. "These cry out to be eaten."

The strawberries we'd finished at breakfast had been sweet and luscious, but the darker, richer tang of raspberries was as delicious in its own way. As we headed north on the highway, Mark shared out the berries one by one until the box was empty.

The casual sensuality was pure pleasure: the brush of his fingers against my lips, then the complex flavors bursting on my tongue.

We drove mostly in silence, with occasional comments about scenery, towns, or attractions we passed. Then I asked him to tell me about the paper he'd be presenting at the symposium in Vancouver, and listened, impressed. He'd achieved so much at such a young age.

It was kind of humbling to be around that kind of person—even though he didn't seem to have an ounce of ego, only that powerful drive and commitment. And a tendency to judge others who didn't share the same single-minded passion.

We'd reached Cape Lookout State Park, and I drove up to the gate and gave the attendant—a boy of about seventeen with acne and thick glasses—a smile. "Hi there. We're looking for a camping spot for the night."

He flushed. "I'm sorry, but we're full up."

Well, shit. Yes, the universe would find us another great spot for the night, but it had been a long, tiring day.

I was about to ask him for suggestions when Mark leaned over and said to the boy, "How about a reservation for Chambers?"

"Oh, you have a reservation." He flushed brighter. "Let me look."

"We do?" I stared at Mark. "When did you do that?"

"Last time we stopped. I was getting tired, and I figured maybe your universe could use a little help."

So much for the fun of the unexpected, but I was tired, too, and ready to settle down for the night.

Mark paid the boy, who told us our campsite number and how to find it. "It's a nice one," he said. "Right by the beach. You'll like it." By now he was almost as red as the raspberries we'd been eating.

I thanked him and drove in the direction he'd indicated. "Poor kid. Could he be any more shy?"

"I'm sure it's worse with pretty girls like you."

"I'm old enough to be . . . well, definitely his much older sister."

"You're hot. You'll always be hot, Jenna."

So would he. His build, active life, and facial bone structure would ensure that.

Since we'd had sex, I'd been doing my best to keep things casual. But tonight we'd again be sharing the bed in the camper. That idea was both irresistibly compelling and kind of scary.

This wasn't like me, fussing over what would happen in the future. What had happened to my live-in-the-moment philosophy?

I had left the window down and now took a deep breath and tuned into my surroundings. "Listen to the waves." To our left was a sand dune, and the ocean must be just beyond it. Smallish campsites dotted the road to our right, all of them occupied until we got to the one Mark had reserved. It wouldn't offer much privacy, but if we left the camper windows open, we'd hear the ocean all night long.

I pulled in, turned off the ignition, and sighed with tiredness and relief. "It's good to be here."

He had the sense to not say, *I told you so.* Or maybe the thought didn't even occur to him. Mark didn't strike me as the kind of person who wasted time trying to "one up" others.

Slowly, we both got out of the camper and stretched. Then he held out his hand. "The beach."

In perfect agreement, I took his hand. "Bet we won't need sandals. All we have to do is cross the road, hike over the dune, and we'll be on a sandy beach."

"You've been here before?"

"No, but trust me." I kicked off my sandals.

He bent to pull off his, too, then we left both pairs lying there and headed across the narrow road to the dune.

Warm sand scrunched under my soles and between my toes, and I beamed up at Mark.

He smiled back. "Yeah."

When we stood at the top of the dune, I saw I'd been right about the beach: lovely sand with two or three dozen people scattered across its length, framed by the rugged wildness of the Pacific Northwest. "We grow great beaches up north," I said. "Definitely not as civilized as the ones in California."

"Not as swimmable, either."

"True."

"There's no such thing as a bad beach," he said with certainty. "I can't count the number I've seen in my life, and they're all incredible."

"I envy you. I could spend my life exploring beaches." Of course, for him it was less about exploring as about studying, healing, saving the beaches, the ocean, and the wildlife.

His hand tightened on mine. "You could do what I do."

"Yeah, right, *Dr.* Chambers."

"You don't need a Ph.D. to work on an environmental project," he said. "You just have to be intelligent, learn quickly, and care about what you're doing. There are jobs for all sorts of people. You know that. Look at the falcon survey."

I was only listening with half an ear because the ocean called to me. I tugged my hand free of his. "I need to put my feet in the water. Race you."

Before he could react, I sprinted down the dune, going as fast as I could in sand that dragged and shifted around my feet. Then I was on firmer packed beach sand, running toward the fringe of waves that sent white lace foaming across the shore.

Quickly Mark took off after her. The pure physical actions—struggling through soft sand, feeling the muscles of his legs pumping, throwing his whole body into the race—were exactly what he needed right now.

He caught up with Jenna and they hit the water together, both breathless and laughing.

They slowed, then stopped when they were knee deep. The sprint, the laughter, the chilly water, the sight of the ocean stretching away, and the lovely woman beside him—suddenly nothing existed but pure exhilaration. When he grinned at Jenna, her bright smile flashed in return.

"Wanna skinny dip?" she asked, mischief in her amazing eyes.

"Ha ha." Given the number of people on the beach, he was pretty sure this time she was teasing. As if to punctuate that thought, a little dark-haired girl and a black poodle raced past them into the water. "Let's walk."

They reached for each other's hands and strolled, ankle deep.

"I wonder how Mr. and Mrs. Watkins are?" He voiced the thought that had been on his mind for the last hours.

She squeezed his hand. "They're doing great. I'm sure of it."

She'd also been sure they'd get a campsite. He grinned to himself. And so they had.

They didn't talk after that, not anything more than pointing out a hawk, laughing as spotted sandpipers dared the waves in their hunt for insects, exchanging hellos with others wandering the beach.

The ocean was where he belonged. Mark had been aware of that at some instinctive level ever since his first visit as a kid. It healed him, de-stressed him, energized him.

Since the accident, he'd been stressed, that elderly man always in the back of his mind. The ache in his shoulders was a constant reminder. He'd also wondered what was going on with Jenna, who'd been in a strange mood. He wasn't sure if that was due to the accident, her emotional revelation, or the intense lovemaking. Now, he felt his shoulders begin to relax and let the worries drift away on the ocean breeze.

Jenna, lifting her face to the early evening sky, seemed to feel equally at home, at ease.

He felt a surge of affection, of rightness. Was this love?

He could imagine them doing this—strolling beaches at the end of the day—in different countries around the world after a long day spent on a worthwhile project.

Hmm. If you combined his knowledge and expertise with her creativity and skill with people, they could make a great team.

"I'm getting hungry," she commented.

"Me, too. But it'll be sunset before long, and I hate to miss it."

"We could bring the barbecue down to the beach."

"Not sure they allow that."

"Then let's cook the skewers and bring them down."

"Good idea."

Walking faster now, they headed back, arguing amicably

about where they needed to cut up to cross the dune. They overshot by a little, and walked the top of the dune until they were across from their campsite.

Mark got out the barbecue and hooked up the new canister of propane while Jenna brought the prawn and vegetable skewers and a couple of plates. When he'd got the food cooking, she put the opened bottle of wine on the picnic table. While he didn't know Oregon state law, drinking from an open wine bottle on the beach might get them in trouble. "We shouldn't—" he began.

From behind her back, she produced an empty water bottle. Pouring from the wine bottle into it, she said, "Okay?"

"Works for me."

The prawns and veggies cooked in a few minutes. Soon he and Jenna, still wearing shorts, were trooping back across the road carrying food, the bottle filled with wine, and an old tan-colored rug.

Other people were scattered along the beach, considerately spread out, some on towels or blankets, some sitting on logs, others in folding camp chairs.

He and Jenna claimed a washed-up log and spread the rug, only a few shades darker than the sand. They sat with their backs against the log, plates on their laps, and began to eat.

"A table with the best view in the house," she said with satisfaction.

He unscrewed the cap from the bottle, offered her a drink, then took a swallow himself. Dry wine, fresh on the tongue and hinting of fruit. Then he picked up a prawn. They'd shoved all the food off the skewers onto two plates, and not bothered to bring forks.

He popped the prawn into his mouth, holding onto the tail and biting it off. Firm, succulent flesh, tasting of the ocean. A mushroom next, earthy and musky. A chunk of tender-crisp green pepper, sweet and crunchy. Purple onion . . . He closed his eyes, savoring its gentle bite.

He opened his eyes to see Jenna gazing at him. "What?" he asked.

"You're really tasting the food."

"It's good. Delicious."

She gave a satisfied smile. "It is. Now, I wonder what kind of performance the sun's going to put on to entertain us?"

"Nothing too dramatic, since there aren't clouds or pollution." They always made for the most spectacular sunsets.

"Gold, I'm thinking. Rather than red or orange."

"Redder to start, then gold when the sun nears the horizon."

She reached for the plastic bottle and took a sip. "Let me guess, there's a scientific reason."

"Different wavelengths for different colors. For example, blue's short and yellow is long. As the sun sinks, it's the longer wavelengths that are still visible."

"Too bad. I like to think it's magic."

He gazed at her, the dying sun deepening the gold of her hair and darkening her tanned skin. "It is magic. Just because there's a scientific explanation doesn't mean, uh . . ." He hunted for words.

"That the experience is any less magical," she finished. "Like, there's a reason those sandpipers dart around the way they do, a reason for the colors in the ocean, a reason the falcons nest in the most out-of-the-way spots. But when you see them, you're touched by magic."

He nodded. When he looked at her, he was touched by magic.

Shielding her eyes, she pointed toward the sun. "You win, no surprise."

Red tones were seeping into the blue of the sky. Watching, he picked up another prawn and paired it with a piece of red pepper. That was another thing Jenna had taught him: you could make each bite a different experience.

He'd never give up planning. But once the planning had

paid off, she had a good point about living in the moment and truly enjoying it.

As the sun dipped lower, it painted strokes of orange and gold to join the red. He and Jenna finished the food and put their plates aside. When he stretched over for the plastic bottle, he winced at a twinge in his shoulder.

"I promised you a massage," she said, swinging gracefully to her feet.

A moment later she was sitting on the log behind him, one leg on either side of him. She rested her hands on his shoulders for a minute or two, and he felt their heat soak through his tee shirt. Then she dug in with her thumbs and fingers and began to work his aching muscles.

He sighed with mingled pain and pleasure. "Thanks. Now, how about a story as well?"

"A story? What kind of story?"

"You told me about your parents and older sisters. How about the sister who's getting married?"

"Merilee. Well, after the three-pack, Mom and Dad figured they were done having kids. But then, can you believe it, eight years after me they had another birth control screwup— after which, by the way, they fixed things so it'd never happen again. Anyhow, when M was born, we all had some adjusting to do, but luckily she was an undemanding kid."

"She must be young to be getting married."

"Twenty-one. But she and Matt have been together since they were seven. It's always been inevitable."

The red and orange were fading, the sky more of a golden dazzle now. "Sounds like she's the opposite of you."

"Oh, yeah. She's old-fashioned. She always played house with her dollies." Her strong hands deftly worked out the knots in his shoulders.

"What did you play?"

"I took my dollies into the garden, and we had adventures."

He smiled at that picture, and imagined her doing the same with kids of her own. No, she wasn't conventional like her sister. Nor was he. "Is Merilee going to stay home and raise kids?"

"She does want children." Her hands stilled for a moment and sadness touched her voice. "But she may be out of luck too, poor kid. She has endometriosis, and it'll be hard for her to get pregnant. They're going to try, though."

"They could adopt." *And so could you.*

"Yeah, but they've always had this thing, this really tight bond—M&M, we call them—and they really want to create their own babies."

"I guess that's hardwired," he reflected. "The biological imperative to pass on our DNA."

"I suppose." She leaned forward, took the wine bottle, and had a swallow.

"Doesn't mean it's the only path, though. There are so many kids in the world who need parents."

"There are. And M&M would be great ones." She held the bottle out to him.

"So would you."

Her hand jerked, and she almost dropped the bottle before he got a grip on it. "Me? Yeah, for the fun times. But children need stability, responsible parents. That's not my shtick."

What the hell was so wrong with responsibility? With responsibility that was full-time and long-term, not just bitten off in little chunks here and there?

"Anyhow," she said, putting her hands back on his shoulders then beginning to work his neck muscles, "M's getting a teaching degree and plans to teach elementary school, and Matt's going to be a high school teacher."

"How about Kat? She's the one you said had bad luck with men, right?"

"Yes. She's the opposite of Tree. Smart too, but really

people-focused, socially skilled, always the center of what's going on. She wants marriage and kids but has crappy judgment when it comes to men."

The sun hovered at the horizon line, sinking lower as he watched.

"Sun's almost gone," she said.

"My neck and shoulders feel much better. Thanks. Come sit beside me and watch."

She did, and together they watched as the glowing ball slipped out of sight. Up and down the beach, people began to pack up but he knew the sunset would continue and there'd be lovely twilight colors. He knew the scientific explanation, but if Jenna wanted to know, she'd ask.

"What kind of work does Kat do?"

"She's the PR director at a boutique luxury hotel in Montreal."

"Really?"

"Yeah." A wry note in her voice, she said, "She makes sure rich folks have all the luxuries they figure they're entitled to." Then, quickly she added, "Kat's a good person."

"I'm sure she is." He might not think her job had a lot of social value, but if Jenna said her sister was a good person, he believed her.

"And you said both your older sisters, the ones who'd had bad experiences with men, had recently fallen in love?"

"Uh-huh. Like, in the last . . . How long ago was it Merilee announced the wedding? Eight or nine days?"

"You're kidding." Startled, he glanced away from the sky, a deep red-orange at the horizon line, merging into rich purples and indigo higher up.

"No, it's bizarre. It's like there's something in the air." Then she chuckled. "Pretty rarified air, to stretch from Vancouver to Montreal and Sydney."

And maybe even to the California coastal highway.

That rarified air theory wasn't such a bad one. He

brushed his finger over one of the butterflies on her shoulder. "A butterfly flutters its wings in Brazil . . ." Would she understand what he meant?

She tilted her head to look up at him. "Chaos theory?"

Yeah, she got the reference. "This one isn't even a stretch, like the butterfly flapping its wings in Brazil and causing a tornado in Texas. Here, a young woman in Vancouver decides to get married, and that decision sends her far-distant sisters on trajectories they hadn't contemplated. Trajectories that intersect with those of men they'd never otherwise have met."

"I suppose."

"And with the wedding coming up, love's on the sisters' minds and who knows, maybe they're giving off stronger pheromones and are more sensitive to men's pheromones."

Her brows lifted, and she said dryly, "I'll be sure to explain that to Tree and Kitty-Kat."

Or you could take me home with you, and I'll do it myself. Jenna didn't seem to have a clue that he was including her and him among the parties affected by Merilee's wingflutter.

The sky was growing darker and the wine was finished. Almost everyone else had left the beach now, and the air was cooling. He tugged Jenna tighter against him.

Since they'd made love earlier, she'd been keeping things light. On a public beach, with other people around, that had been fine with him. Now, though, mellow with food and wine, he hoped for more.

He caressed her shoulder. Jenna saw those tattooed butterflies as a symbol of her carefree approach to life. But now, to him, they symbolized other things about her. Had she thought about the important work those lovely insects did, pollinating the flowers they fluttered between? Or about how strong they were, to survive long, rugged migrations?

Her head nestled against his shoulder, cheek warm against

his skin, curls tickling as the breeze flicked them against him. She yawned then moved away, stretched, graceful and cat-like, and eased down to lie on the rug. Staring up at the sky, she said, "Come lie down, Mark. There's an almost full moon and the North Star. Soon we'll see more and more stars."

He shifted down to lie beside her and gazed up. There was nothing like a clear night sky over the ocean. "Too bad we can't sleep on the beach."

"Ooh, I'd like that. We could bring out the sleeping bag and pillows."

"And a park ranger would roust us. The joys of being in a supposedly civilized country."

"You've slept on the beach a lot?"

"Often, yeah."

"You're right that it's hard to do here. You need to be on private property or find a really secluded place."

He hated to think that she'd slept on beaches with other men, even though he'd done the same with a couple of lovers. Yeah, he was completely unevolved and jealous.

Though stars now brightened the night sky, he turned away from them, rose on one elbow, and gazed down at Jenna. In the dusk, her body and clothing almost merged with the rug. He couldn't see her expression, but her eyes gleamed. He leaned over to brush a kiss against her fore-head. More than that, he didn't dare do on this public beach.

But he was hungry for her. Eager to shower away the stress of the day and do the totally conventional thing of climbing into a double bed with her. Somehow, he knew that with Jenna, even the conventional would be something spe-cial.

"I think it's time for bed," he told her.

Chapter 10

I'd let myself live in the moment for the last couple of hours and enjoyed the wonderful evening and Mark's easy company. Now, a thrill of anticipation raced across my skin.

Bed. Together. Each time, it was a different, amazing experience. What would happen between us tonight?

He rose, tall and strong as he held out a hand to me.

I took it and let him pull me to my feet. For a moment I stood in front of him, our bodies almost touching. Neither of us moved, and I could barely see his face, but between us was a certain tension, a current of energy that was almost palpable.

"Let's go," he said, voice even huskier than usual.

Quickly we gathered our things and headed back to the camper. There, he said, "I could really use a shower. The accident . . ." He shrugged.

"Go ahead. I'll tidy up here."

"Thanks." He dropped a kiss on my cheek and left me in the camper.

As I tidied up and readied the bed, I imagined him under a hot, hard spray, washing away the memories of an old man's blood soaking his hands.

Such an amazing day. Mark had risked his life to save

someone else's, then he'd been my playmate at Prehistoric Gardens, a mind-blowing lover, an easy companion as we watched the sun set. He was . . . so much. So much more than any other guy I'd hooked up with.

But I couldn't let him be. The things he wanted were ones I didn't. There was no future for us. When I'd fallen in love with Travis, I'd lost my judgment and ended up heartbroken and irreversibly damaged. Love wasn't an emotion I could handle.

I opened a couple of windows, not just for fresh air but so we could hear the surf, and didn't pull the curtains.

One night and one day. I sat on the end of the bed. That was all Mark and I had left. Though the idea gave me a pang of sadness, I also felt relieved. I could keep my heart safe for that short period of time and still reap the benefits of his company.

He stepped into the camper, closing the door behind him. He wore shorts and a shirt unbuttoned down the front despite the chill in the June air. His hair was damp and uncombed and he smelled deliciously of something masculine and vaguely oceany.

My gaze tracked his exposed skin—tanned, lightly haired, lean and sexy. All the way down to the low-slung waistband of his loose shorts. Oh yes, with Mark there were lots of benefits.

He came to stand in front of me and leaned down to capture both my hands. He drew me to my feet. "Jenna." In the soft, dim light, the sky-blue of his eyes was deeper, more like the mysterious depths of the ocean.

Breath catching nervously, I waited. With another man, it would have been simple. I'd have initiated the action, leaped playfully at him, and tumbled him to the bed. But with Mark, nothing was normal. My physical reactions, my emotional ones, were off kilter.

He seemed uncertain, too, just holding my hands and gazing down at me. Then he lowered his head and I tensed, unsure if I wanted to kiss him. Not knowing what would happen when our lips touched.

He dropped a quick kiss on my nose, surprising a smile out of me. He smiled back, then reached for the hem of my tee, and slowly tugged it over my head.

I was braless under it, and my nipples immediately perked under his appreciative gaze. They tightened further when he undid my shorts and shoved them down my hips.

I let them slide, stepped out of them, and waited to see if he'd strip off my thong.

He didn't. "Get into bed. The air's cool."

Maybe it was, but I didn't feel it when his heated gaze caressed my bare skin. Still, I obeyed, sliding between the sheets and watching as he took off his shirt and shorts. When he was down to just lean muscles and a pair of blue boxers, the front distended by a hard-on, I gave a seductive smile and crooked my finger, beckoning him closer. "You know you're a hottie, right, Dr. Chambers?"

"I don't even know what a hottie is," he said, sitting on the edge of the bed beside me.

"How can you be totally oblivious to everything but science?" I ran my fingers up and down his firm thigh.

He touched the back of my hand. "I'm not oblivious to that."

"Thank God."

Gently he tugged my hand up to his mouth and feathered a kiss across the palm, his soft lips stirring arousal. He put my hand back down on his thigh, then stroked up my arm in a light caress, all the way up to my shoulder. "Not oblivious."

He leaned over to drop light kisses on my butterflies, moving my hair aside. Then he twined a long curl around his finger. "Nope, not oblivious." He tugged it back to reveal my ear, caught the lobe between his teeth and nipped lightly, darting an erotic spark down to my sex. When he followed up with a kiss, I sighed with pleasure. These kisses, I could definitely handle.

"Well, I'm definitely not oblivious to this." I drifted my hand over the front of his boxers, feeling the thrust of his cock underneath.

Wanting to kiss him there, to free him from thin cotton and take him into my mouth, I started to sit up.

He caught my shoulders and held me down. "Oh, no, it's not going to be fast and hard this time."

"I could change your mind if I tried," I teased, liking the idea of being in control.

"You could." His eyes danced. "But we'll both have more fun if you don't."

Hmm. As I'd already learned, the man gave great foreplay. "An excellent point, Dr. Chambers." I relaxed, waiting to see what he'd do next.

Mark leaned down, mouth approaching mine, and automatically I tensed, still uncertain about kissing him. Maybe he read that uncertainty in my eyes, or maybe he hadn't intended to kiss my lips anyhow, because he instead pecked my cheek. Then my forehead, my eyebrows, my other cheek. Quick, soft kisses.

"Mmm, nice."

More kisses brushed my chin, then his lips found the sensitive spots on my neck and his lips and tongue firmed, speaking erotic messages that made my body hum with need.

I answered him with soft moans of pleasure. And watched him, his lean body golden-brown, muscles shifting each time he moved.

He didn't speak, just murmured sounds of approval, arousal, low enough I could still hear the hushed roar of the ocean.

He made his way across the upper plane of my chest, then eased the sheet down to kiss my breast, making me gasp when he laved my areola then sucked my nipple. I ran my fingers through his hair and held on for the ride as he inched the sheet down bit by bit and followed up with sensual kisses, sucks, and nibbles—across my ribs, my navel, my belly—each one sending tingles to my sex, fueling my desire.

By the time he reached my pussy, I was squirming with the delicious ache of focused arousal, the need to come.

When he lapped my clit, I exploded.

He eased back a little but didn't stop, licking my sex, thrusting his fingers in and out, tonguing and sucking my clit, until my climaxes came in waves, one starting before the last one had ended.

"Oh God, Mark," I gasped, eyes squeezed shut, lost in a world of blissful sensation. Oh yeah, he had an advanced degree in foreplay.

Somehow, he must have eased his boxers off, because now he slid into me, his shaft so much thicker than his fingers, so blunt and primitive and single-minded as he drove deep.

So deep, I gasped.

Then his lips captured mine, and this time I had no thought of holding back. When our mouths fused, I felt a shift. Before, I'd been in my body, totally aware of each delicious sexual sensation he created. Now, somehow, it was different. It wasn't me, it was us.

Our mouths spoke a secret language, one of caring, of belonging, of merging. I was vaguely aware our arms were stretched above our heads, fingers interwoven as our bodies twined and melded. As tenderness and passion fused together in an erotic dance, our mouths caught and cherished soft cries and moans.

Whatever this was, it wasn't like any kind of sex I'd had before. Orgasm caught me, tumbled me, rolled me, then sucked me under until another wave rocked me.

Mark's hoarse shout rang in my ears and echoed in some

deep place where words no longer existed, just sensations and emotions.

Then, finally, the wave released us and tossed us, still clinging together, gently to shore.

We lay gasping, both emptied and filled in ways I'd never imagined. When I opened my eyes, he was staring at me, an expression of wonder on his face, but he didn't say anything.

Nor did I. There weren't words for what had just happened.

As our breath finally slowed, he rolled off me, taking me with him so we lay side by side. The surf sang a lullaby through the open windows as Mark turned off the light and pulled up the sheet and sleeping bag.

I knew I should worry about what this was between us and where it was going, but I was too tired, too satiated.

A kiss whispered light as butterfly wings across my forehead, and I was asleep.

Mark woke as dawn light filtered into the camper. For a moment, he lay with his eyes closed, feeling the soft warmth of Jenna next to him and listening to the ocean and the chirps and trills of awakening birds. What a perfect way to start the day.

He opened his eyes, and the morning got even better. Jenna was sleeping, turned on her side toward him, face peaceful and innocent. His leg lay over hers and her arm curved across his waist. Even in sleep, they'd subconsciously wanted to stay connected.

Making love with her last night had been . . . There were no words. He'd never experienced anything like it. He knew she felt it, too. She'd had lots of other lovers, so her expression of wonder and amazement last night had told him the two of them, together, were special.

His heart—even his mind—told him his friend Adrienne was right, and he was definitely falling in love. He had little experience with deep emotions, but what else could the incredible lovemaking mean? Pheromones or major histocompatibility complex codes couldn't explain so profound a connection, one that went far beyond merely physical. He and Jenna weren't perfectly compatible, but his grandparents spoke about base pairs and how a strong bond required being both complementary and different.

He was sure Adrienne was right, too, about Jenna being scared of love. When she'd been a vulnerable teen, she'd been hurt by that boy, Travis. She'd walled off her heart so she'd never be hurt again. Now, Mark had to convince her that he would never, ever hurt her, and then they could explore what their future might hold. She had to see it was time to change her life—to let herself love and be loved, to find focus and meaning, to stop drifting.

She stirred, sighed, and her soft brown eyelashes fluttered as her eyes gradually opened. She focused on him, a smile curved her lips, and a sparkle lit her blue-green eyes.

Those eyes. She carried the ocean in her eyes. If he were a romantic, that would be the only sign he'd need.

"Good morning," she said sleepily.

"It is." And perhaps so could all the rest of their mornings be. Suddenly, the future was clear. Once her sister's wedding was over, she could come with him to Indonesia. They'd work together, sleep on the beach, make love on the sand. Make love in the tropical ocean. Could anything be more incredible than loving Jenna as the ocean surrounded them?

"You look . . ." She studied him, still smiling.

"What?"

"Happy. Contented. Almost smug."

"All of those." Should he tell her he was falling for her? He wasn't sure she was ready to hear that. Nor, to be honest, that he knew how to say those words. For now, he'd kiss her, and let his body speak for him.

He touched his lips to hers and she answered the kiss, this

time without tensing, without hesitation. Again he had the sense of their two mouths becoming one, like a pulsing heart that sent blood rushing through veins, told legs and arms to twine, made bodies shift, press, interlock until their flesh had no boundaries. Until they were merged in passion, bliss, and love.

They climbed, drifted, murmured, whispered into each other's mouths, climbed again, moaned. The swell of pleasure became a wave, building higher and higher, cresting. Then it broke and spilled, and they rode it together, tumbling as it tossed them, crying out in exultation. Finally, it glided them to shore in gentle ripples.

After, still caught in the spell, they didn't say a word, just clung for long minutes, bodies locked together.

Outside, the ocean sang, a siren's call to come walk the morning beach. Regretting that they needed to get on the road, Mark said, "If we want to get to Vancouver at a reasonable time . . ."

She sighed and muttered, face half-buried against his chest, "Right now, I never want to get back. Wouldn't it be nice if we could just stay here? Go for a walk on the beach, have a lazy breakfast, have sex again . . ."

"Make love," he corrected.

Her muscles tensed. Then she lifted her head and stared at him, eyes wide and vulnerable. "Yes."

It was little more than a breath, but it was perhaps the most important syllable he'd ever heard in his life.

Then she blinked, and when she opened her eyes again, she didn't meet his gaze. Quickly, awkwardly, she untangled her body from his. "I need a shower and so do you. Then a quick breakfast, and you're right, we have to get on the road."

She was pulling away again. He debated trying to stop her, but knew they'd be driving for hours. They'd done some good talking in the front seats of the Westfalia. Somehow, it seemed easier for both him and Jenna to open up when the highway was unspooling beneath the camper's tires.

She pulled clothes on and gathered her stuff. When she opened the camper door, he said, "I'm going to make coffee. Want some?"

"Sure, thanks."

When she'd gone, he climbed out of bed and began to make coffee, using his French press and the pre-ground beans he'd brought with him. As he did, he wondered how Mr. Watkins and his wife were doing. He should have found out what hospital the old man was being taken to.

Once the coffee was made, he poured himself a mug and headed for the shower.

He returned to find Jenna at the picnic table, sipping from a mug. She wore a white shirt, the sleeves rolled up her forearms, over a long skirt in shades of yellow and blue. On the table lay the muffin bag and a couple of napkins.

She smiled as he approached. "We have time for breakfast on the beach, right?"

"Sure. Just let me dump my stuff in the camper and get more coffee."

A few minutes later, food and mugs in hand, they crested the dune and gazed out at the ocean. It was calm, the morning almost windless, which was rare for the coast. An elderly couple strode briskly along the hard-packed sand near the water's edge, and down the beach a couple of kids had started a sandcastle.

He and Jenna sat on a log and opened the muffin bag. Coffee and a bran muffin made a satisfying combination, especially when accented by the tang of ocean air and the easy company of the pretty woman beside him.

As the morning sun gathered heat, Jenna took off her shirt, revealing a yellow camisole-style top with lace trim at the top edge. Her bright hair, lightly tanned skin, and top were all golden, and he had the unusually whimsical thought that she'd brought sunshine into his life. Sunshine and play, which she'd shown him were good things. Would she be equally willing to understand that life should be lived with purpose and commitment?

Her voice broke into his thoughts. "Tonight we'll both be with our families."

"You're looking forward to seeing yours?" He wasn't entirely sure, from the things she'd said. He'd heard definite affection but also ambivalence.

She flashed a quick smile. "Oh, yeah. But it'll be same-old, same-old."

"How do you mean? That *I love you, but* stuff?"

"Yeah, and saying I'm a flake. They're all so superior, you know?"

His mother had been a flake. Irresponsible and, let's face it, useless. She'd chosen the self-indulgence of free love, drugs, and fun and games on the commune. Though he did think Jenna ought to get more focused and serious, she was really nothing like Alicia.

He rolled the last mouthful of coffee in his mouth and said slowly, "Seems to me you've done as much good in the world as any of your sisters."

"Me?" She turned wide, surprised eyes on him.

"Yeah." He touched one of her tattoos. "Like a butterfly."

She shook her head, squinting in confusion. "Huh? You mean, because I'm pretty?"

He chuckled. "Well, there is that. But I meant something more concrete. Wherever the butterfly touches down, it pollinates a flower. You fly off, touch down, and help damaged kids, abused women, endangered species."

He was about to go on, to point out how much more good she could do if she focused her energy on one field, when she said, "Mark, that's the nicest thing anyone's ever said to me." The glow in her eyes was warm, surprised.

"Really?"

"My parents and sisters keep saying I should go back to school and *learn something useful*. But you're saying I already am useful."

"Yeah, and if your family doesn't see that, they don't know you very well." They should acknowledge the contribution she made to the world, then encourage her to pick a discipline and go back to school.

"Thanks," she said softly, reaching for his hand and squeezing it.

The shared moment was so sweet that instinct told him this wasn't the time to push the merits of further education.

Three kids came pelting down the dune, racing toward the ocean, followed more slowly by their laughing parents. "Time to hit the road," Mark said regretfully.

They walked back to the camper, pausing on the top of the dune for one last gaze at the view. Their route would take them inland from here, to Tillamook and Portland. Then, to make it to Vancouver by the end of the day, they'd have to drive the I-5.

A few minutes later, they left the campsite with Mark at the wheel, a third cup of coffee in the cup holder.

"Hope the idiots stay off the road today," he said. "And I sure wish I knew how Mr. Watkins is. You didn't ask what hospital they were taking him to, did you?"

"Sorry. But how many could there be in that area?"

He gestured toward his phone. "Want to try and find it?"

She nodded and took the phone. "What d'you figure was the closest town?"

"Try Brookings."

A few minutes later, she was talking to someone at a hospital. "No, I'm not a relative," she said. "Does his wife happen to be there?" Hand covering the phone, she said to Mark, "They won't give out details unless you're a relative."

Then, back into the phone, "His son? Perfect, I'd love to talk to him."

After a pause of a minute or two, she spoke to Mr. Watkins's son, explaining who she and Mark were, and asking about his parents. Listening, she smiled and nodded at Mark. A few moments later, she said, "Thanks so much. Give our best to both of them."

She closed the phone. "The son says they're all eternally in your debt. Mr. Watkins is doing well. His arm's fine. He has whiplash, and he'll need physio for a while, but he should make a full recovery."

"Thank God."

"Thank God you were there." She stretched her seatbelt so she could lean over and kiss his shoulder. "You're a good man in a crisis, Doctor, even if you're not a real doctor."

He reached up to caress her cheek, then put his hand back on the wheel. "You're not so bad yourself. How's Mrs. Watkins?"

"Exhausted and suffering from shock, but fine. Once she knew her husband was going to be okay, they sent her home with her daughter-in-law." Jenna settled back in her seat, curling up with her floaty skirt around her legs, looking like she was getting comfy for hours on the road.

"I need to check e-mail," he said. "We'll find some place in the next town."

"Okay."

"Are your parents expecting you at any particular time? Like for dinner?"

She chuckled. "No, they know schedules aren't my thing. Mom'll be in Ottawa, anyway."

"Ottawa?"

"She's presenting an appeal to the Supreme Court of Canada tomorrow. She's been busy preparing, and M's been making up schoolwork and exams she missed when she was sick, which is why the three-pack got nominated to organize the wedding."

"And Merilee and Matt only decided just over a week ago that they were getting married?"

"They were planning to do it next summer after they graduate. But they don't want to hold off on trying for kids. Then Matt got an offer of a last-minute deal on a Mexican Riviera cruise, and everything came together." She grinned. "An impulsive decision, gotta love it! But it's really out of character for M, who's been planning her wedding since she was seven."

"I guess there's a lot to do to put a wedding together."

"Ask Tree, she's the one with the project plan. But yeah, they've done invites, picked out dresses, Kat's guy is doing the photos. They've booked the place, and they're working on finding a caterer."

"A church wedding?"

"No, I told Tree it had to be VanDusen Gardens."

When he shook his head, she said, "I'm sure you've driven past it, you just weren't paying attention. It's on Oak Street. A lovely, naturally landscaped botanical garden. It was one of our Sunday *Winnie-the-Pooh* 'expotition' places with Gran, and a favorite of M's."

"I hope your grandmother's well enough to go."

"Me, too." Then she tossed her curls. "She will be. And there'll be sunshine, even though Tree's obsessed about renting tents, just in case."

"Uh, having the reservation at Cape Lookout Park didn't hurt. Sometimes a contingency plan comes in handy."

"You sound *exactly* like my sister." Her tone said she was rolling her eyes.

"I take that as a compliment." When they got to her place, would she ask him in? He was curious to meet her family, but it could be pretty awkward. How would she introduce him? He remembered that line she'd tossed off when she was on the phone to her sister: *I was born to shock.* He could definitely see parents being shocked at his and Jenna's relationship.

"It's going to be bizarre," she mused, "being involved with this wedding stuff when it's not what I believe in. But I guess it's right for M&M. They've sure always thought so." She tossed him a sideways glance. "How about you? When you talked about the future, you used the term *partner*, not wife, and you agreed marriage is archaic."

"Yeah, I'm not big into the institution. I do believe in commitment, though. I want to find a life mate, to commit to each other and to monogamy, to plan our lives together, to raise a family." Might Jenna be that person? If she weren't, what were the chances he'd ever find such a powerful connection with another woman?

"Glad to hear you're not *totally* conventional," she teased.

He saw a sign for an upcoming town. "Hopefully there will be internet here."

"You don't know? That little detail isn't on your immaculately planned schedule?" she teased.

"I can be flexible," he defended himself.

She chuckled. "I've seen evidence of that, Dr. Chambers, but mostly in bed. As for today's schedule, when are you due back in Vancouver? Are your grandparents expecting you for dinner?"

"No. Believe it or not, I left it loose. The symposium starts tomorrow, so they know I'll arrive sometime today. Wouldn't hurt to call and give them an update, though."

"How long is the symposium?"

"Two days. I have Wednesday to tidy up some odds and ends here, then on Thursday I'm flying to Bali to round up the team for the Indonesia project." Leaving Vancouver and leaving Jenna. Unless his morning fantasy really came true.

In the fresh light of morning, the path ahead had seemed so clear.

"Lucky you. At my house, we'll be going crazy with final preparations for the wedding. Me and my sisters do much better separate than apart." She made a pleading puppy dog face. "Guess you couldn't squeeze me in your suitcase?"

"No." He took a breath. Examined his mind, his heart. How could they find out if this was love if they lived half the world apart? "But I could get you a ticket of your own."

She stilled, then tilted her head. "What do you mean?"

"The team will be in Indonesia for six months, maybe longer. You could join us. But," he warned, "everyone has to commit to the project. If you get bored, you can't bail." What was he doing, talking about the project, when really he wanted so much more from her?

Maybe it was a test. He was approaching Jenna the way cautious people went into the ocean. A step at a time, then a pause to see how they felt. He didn't need to lay his feelings out there to be stomped on; he wanted to see signs she was feeling the same way. That she was ready to grow up and commit: to one cause and one man.

If she was, then he wanted to be with her, to explore the . . . magic between them. Because that's what it was, he realized. Pure magic, with no scientific explanation.

"But . . ." She shook her head and, sounding puzzled, said, "I don't get it. I'm not a scientist. What would I do?"

"You could assist other team members with things like measurements, recording data, liaising with the local people. You're good with people."

"I am," she murmured, excitement threading through her voice. "And the falcon survey was all about recording data."

They'd reached the town, and he looked for a café that had internet. "It wouldn't pay much. Living expenses and a little spending money." His project team was already complete and the budget was lean, but he'd happily sacrifice most of his own meager salary. Some of the jobs he worked on, like the one at the UCSC Long Marine Lab, paid decently; others were slave wages. He didn't need a lot to live on, and it all worked out fine.

"I so don't care about the money," she said. "I'm just . . ." She shook her head again, gave a nervous laugh. "Wow. That's an incredible offer, Mark. I can't, uh, get my head around it. We need to talk more—"

"Yeah," he broke in, seeing an internet café and a parking spot. "We will when we're back on the road."

"Right. Okay." She unbuckled her belt. "I'm . . . wow." She leaned over and planted a big kiss on his cheek, and he didn't have a clue what she was thinking, aside from being stunned.

As they climbed out of the camper, he reflected that he'd never in his adult life done something so spontaneous and . . . okay, rash. It was rash. Had he done the right thing? Why hadn't he thought things through and come up with a plan, the way he always did, rather than just blurting it out?

He'd stepped so far out of his comfort zone, he almost wished he could call back the invitation. Needing a bit of time alone, he said, "You go on in. I should call my grandparents."

"Okay." She wiggled her fingers in a "see you" wave and headed into the café.

He dialed his grandparents' number and, after the second ring, heard his grandmother's voice, still brisk in her eighties. "Mark, I wondered when we'd hear from you. Where are you?"

"In Oregon, north of Tillamook. Seven or eight hours from Vancouver, depending on the border."

"Will you be home for dinner?"

"Maybe, but don't count on it. You and Granddad go ahead. Save me some leftovers. This trip hasn't gone according to plan so far, and who knows what today will be like."

"You've had problems?"

Should he tell her about Jenna? His feelings were so big, so special, he was bursting to share them, yet he rarely discussed emotions with his grandparents. And these emotions were so confusing, his future with Jenna so uncertain. Undecided, he said, "There was a big accident yesterday that shut down the road for a couple of hours."

"You weren't involved?" she asked quickly.

"No, it was just ahead of me."

"Good. This wouldn't have happened if you'd flown."

His grandparents always wanted him to fly because it was more efficient. They supported his choice of marine biology as a career, but didn't understand his love affair with the ocean. "You're right," he agreed. "But I've had a nice drive despite that."

"You're presenting a paper at an important symposium. Isn't that what you should be working on, not enjoying the scenery?" Oh yes, he'd learned his "all work, no play" philosophy from her and his grandfather.

"The paper's written. I'm ready to go." Maybe that was why he liked driving—it was about the only time in his life when he didn't work. Much as he loved his career, a little downtime wasn't a crime. He used to feel guilty, but Jenna had made him think differently.

As his grandmother told him about an operation she'd consulted on, he listened with half an ear, wondering how she and Grandpa would react if he took Jenna to meet them. In his opinion, he and Jenna could well form a solid pair bond according to his grandparents' theory that each partner had to be both sufficiently different and sufficiently complementary. Yet he feared they'd look at her and see Alicia all over again.

Yes, Jenna was like his mother in a superficial way, but she made a contribution to society and was more responsible—even if she didn't acknowledge responsibility as a virtue. She'd devoted more attention to a girl she met at riding camp than Alicia had ever given him. But Jenna's philosophies of life would clash with those of his grandparents.

Best not to tell his grandmother about her yet. If Jenna didn't really care for him, if she didn't want to commit, then their relationship was going nowhere anyway. The thought made him feel hollow and chilled inside.

No, he'd be optimistic. Things would work out with him and Jenna, and his grandparents would look past her charming eccentricities and see her true worth. If they didn't . . . Since they'd taken him in, he'd never gone against them on anything important. Their pride in him had been the strongest motivator in his life, except for the ocean itself.

Grandma concluded her story and said, "Try to get home for dinner. You'll be busy with the symposium for the next two days, which leaves only Wednesday before you're off to Indonesia."

In grandparent-speak, this meant they'd missed him and wanted to spend some time with him. "I'll try my best, Grandma. Even if I don't make it for dinner, I'll be early enough so we can talk for a couple of hours before bed."

They'd talk about work. His and theirs. It was virtually all they ever discussed, and until now he'd never realized how limiting that was.

He closed his cell and took his laptop to the café, where he paused in the doorway. Jenna sat staring at a computer screen, seeming totally absorbed.

When he'd discovered marine biology, he'd felt the thrill of having a purpose in life. With Jenna, he felt a similar thrill. If they could work out their differences, they could live amazing lives together. But they sure did have differences; otherwise, he'd have told his grandma about her.

He walked toward Jenna and took the seat beside her. She jerked and shot him an uncertain look. He forced a smile. It was going to be an interesting conversation when they got back on the road.

When he opened his in-box and scanned the new messages, one from Adrienne, sent last night, caught his eye. It didn't qualify as urgent, yet he opened it first.

Well? Is the sex still "weird"? LOL.

He shook his head ruefully. Yeah, he really had used that term, hadn't he? But then, there was no perfect word to describe what happened when he and Jenna kissed and made love.

Seriously, how's it going with Jenna? Have you figured out if she's scared of love? And why? How about you? Are you falling, falling, fallen?? And when do I meet her?

Quickly, he tilted his computer to make sure Jenna, sitting beside him, couldn't see the screen. He typed back,

OK, bad choice of words. Let's try "amazing." Falling? Yeah, seems so, at least for me. Her . . . Not so sure. Trying to figure her out.
We're really different people, but there's a connection.
I asked her to go to Indonesia.

He stared at the last sentence, then deleted it. No, that wasn't for e-mail. Adrienne would be at the symposium, too, and they'd find private moments to talk. By then, he'd have a much better idea where things stood between him and Jenna.

Shit, by then they might be planning a future together, or they might have decided to never see each other again. Hard to believe that when he'd left Santa Cruz, his life had been stress free.

He darted a glance at Jenna, who was staring at an open e-mail. Yeah, life had been stress free, but far less interesting. Then he forced himself to pay attention to his own e-mail, most of it relating to Indonesia. A project he'd been so excited about, that would now feel a little empty if Jenna didn't join him.

Chapter 11

I'd clicked open an e-mail from my young friend Anna but found myself staring unseeingly at the screen, unable to think about anything but the incredible offer Mark had made: to go to Indonesia for six months and be part of his team. To live in an exotic paradise and work hard on an interesting project.

To see Mark every day.

I forced myself not to glance over, not to try to see what he was typing away on.

Mark, the man who, in two days, had made me feel things I'd never believed possible. Physically and emotionally.

But I didn't want emotional involvement. No freaking way. It was dangerous; it screwed up my judgment.

Maybe that wasn't what he meant, though. He'd invited me to be a member of his team. Did he mean, I'd work for him but we wouldn't have sex? Or would we? It was hard to imagine being with him and not wanting to leap him.

I realized my foot was jiggling with nervous tension. We needed to talk, and until then there was no point fussing. Determinedly, I read Anna's message and sent off a reply.

Next I read an e-mail from Kat. Mostly, she raved about how incredible Nav was, then she said,

And Theresa's locked up in her room every night having phone sex with Damien. Honestly, Jenna, it's like some other person's inhabited her body. You heard they had sex on Waikiki Beach, right?

"No way!" The words burst out of me. Quickly I glanced around, mouthing "sorry" to Mark and the others within earshot. Indonesia displaced in my mind, at least temporarily, I typed a reply.

You're kidding, right??? Parallel universe, for sure! 10 days ago I was telling Tree she needed to dust off her hoo-ha and get back in the game, but she's never listened to me before. LOL. Seriously, they just necked or something, right? Or had sex in a hotel room overlooking the beach?

Should I tell Kitty-Kat that I'd had some excellent action on the beach myself, with a very hot marine biologist? Yeah, I had fun shocking my family, but I'd be in for plenty enough flack when I showed up without Mellow Yellow. Best to leave Mark out of it, at least for now. Instead, I finished with:

Can't wait to hear the full story. And meet Nav. Can't believe the 'rents haven't found his fatal flaw yet, but I'm up to the challenge <g>.
I'm still ON SCHEDULE to be home tonight. See y'all then.
Hugs.

I glanced at Mark and saw he was focused on a spreadsheet. Yeah, he'd get along with my sister Tree.
Next, I sent a quick e-mail to my mom.

Mom, knock 'em dead at the SCC <g>.

I knew it was a super big deal for a lawyer to present an appeal to the Supreme Court of Canada, even though she'd done it half a dozen times before. I also knew that, if there was any possible way her side could win, my smart, determined mom would make it happen.

I'd barely sent the message when an e-mail pinged into my box from her.

Where are you?

I sat forward, typing quickly:

Tillamook. You?

She said:

Airport. I'll call you.
My cell battery is dead.
Jenna, a cell phone is useless unless you keep it charged.

I groaned. In fact, I was quite happy not to talk to her, especially with Mark here beside me, staring intently at his laptop screen. Taking flack from her was easier by e-mail than over the phone.

How's your car? (she asked.)

Mellow Yellow's feeling mellow, and so am I.

I was sure my car was, now that it was being ministered to by Neal. As for me, mellow wasn't the right word. More like excited and totally confused.

I remembered that thing Mom had told me all those years ago, about falling a little in love with the man who awakens your sexuality, but not making the mistake of believing that love was a forever one. I'd made exactly that mistake when I was seventeen. Since then, I'd had lots of great sex with guys I really liked, but my heart had never been threatened.

Now, with Mark, the sex was on a whole different dimension. I felt . . . I had no idea what I felt.

I took my hands off the keyboard and dropped them to my lap. Glancing down, I saw his leg only inches from mine. Bare, tanned skin below khaki shorts tempted me to move my knee over and nudge his.

I wove my fingers together to keep from reaching out to touch him. I couldn't be falling in love. I wouldn't let myself. My life was perfect as it was.

My mother's next e-mail arrived.

Don't get so mellow you fail to pay attention to traffic.

I rolled my eyes and returned my hands to the keyboard.

I'm fine and I'm a careful driver.

Then, more slowly, I typed:

Mom, d'you remember when I was eleven or so, and you were giving me THE SEX TALK, you said something about falling for the first guy who awakens your sexuality?

I clicked SEND then jerked my hand away from the mouse, wishing I could pull the message back. Her response came.

Tell me you didn't pick up a hitchhiker.

I groaned.

This is NOT about a hitchhiker. Forget it!!!!

She said:

That surfer? The Mexican one? Good God, Jenna, a surf bum?

No, a freaking marine biologist. Take that, Mom. But I wasn't ready to share my personal life, especially with my mother.

No, not Carlos. It's a hypothetical. Like you use in law all the time.

She was always doing that at the dinner table. Saying, "Let me give you a hypothetical," then setting out some fact pattern and seeing how we all responded.

Hypotheticals don't arise out of the blue. But all right, yes, I remember. I believe I said that most girls fall a bit in love with the person who awakens their sexuality. It's natural, but it doesn't mean they're the right one for you, or that you'll love them long-term.

Mark had awakened a different side to my sexuality. So maybe it was natural I was feeling weird, gooshy emotions. That didn't mean they'd last. And, of course, I didn't want them to. No way was I letting a guy mess up my life again. Or, rather, letting me mess up my life because of my feelings for some guy.

I read my mom's words again. When I was a girl, her comment hadn't meant much to me, but now that I really thought about it, what did it say about her and Dad? I knew she loved him. He was her "right one," wasn't he? But if he was, then he hadn't been her first love? I was dying to know, but no way could I ask her. Instead, I typed:

You really believe there's one "right one"? How the heck do you know when you find them?

It took her longer than usual to answer.

I thought you didn't believe in love. Or want it.

Oops. I should never have started this with my mom. She saw way too much.

I stared at those words on the screen. Believe in love? Well, I honestly did think Mom and Dad loved each other, and so did M&M. As for wanting it . . . After Travis, I'd decided it was easier to not want love than to risk losing my judgment, being stupid, not looking after myself. Getting hurt. I'd told myself there were lots of great guys and no reason to be with just one.

Did I really believe that? Mark had asked if that was really me speaking, or if I was echoing Travis. I had thought the philosophy was mine. I'd lived by it and had a great time.

But now . . . Was I starting to want something else? To want one person in the world I could truly connect with, who'd love me just the way I was?

Slowly, I typed:

Maybe I don't know what I believe anymore.

I stared at those words for a while, too, not clicking SEND. Fewer than ten simple words, yet cold sweat had broken out on my skin.

Another e-mail from my mom popped up.

Sorry, my flight's loading. Have to go. TBC when I get home. Drive safely. Love you.

Then she was gone, and I was still staring at unsent words. And realizing I'd opened up a "to be continued" conversation I didn't really want to have with my mom.

"Jenna?" Mark's voice broke in, making me jump. "Almost done?"

Oh God, I'd been so absorbed I didn't have a clue if he'd been watching me, maybe reading my screen. Quickly, I closed the message, not saving it. I rubbed my hands briskly over my arms, banishing the chill, the unease. "Yeah, I'm just finished."

As we left the internet café and climbed into the Westfalia, I asked, "Did you get in touch with your grandparents?"

"Yeah." He glanced at me, blue sky eyes troubled.

Maybe he'd mentioned me. Hah, that would have been interesting. Some demon made me say, "Mention me?"

His brows pulled together. "No." A pause while he stowed his laptop in the back, then, when we were both seated up front, "Should I have?"

"Why would you?" I said breezily, propping my feet up on the dashboard.

"Did you, uh, e-mail your family about me?" he asked cautiously.

"Why would I?"

"Right." Another pause as he started the camper and pulled away. "If you did come to Indonesia, they might want to meet me."

You think? "Why? It's my life. They've never met any of my other *bosses*." I was being snippy, but couldn't seem to stop myself. "If I went, you wouldn't introduce me to your grandparents, would you?" I didn't look at him, just stared out the window as if the roadside stores were fascinating.

"Uh . . . I don't know."

"They'd disapprove, wouldn't they? They'd think I was a *flake*"—deliberately, I used my family's word—"like Alicia." No, I had no place in Mark's life long-term, so of course I wouldn't be so stupid as to fall for him.

"Uh . . ."

I huffed out air and groused, "And my damn family might actually *approve* of you."

"You say that like it's a sin."

A thread of humor in his voice made me glance his way. He'd stopped at a light and was staring at me, brows cocked, an amused curl to his lips.

I was in a snit for no good reason, and he wasn't playing along. That defused my ill humor as if by magic. I sighed, and gave him a rueful sigh. "Yeah, a deadly sin. Mind you," I mused teasingly, "I live to shock, and bringing home a guy they approve of would be the biggest shock ever."

The light turned green and he drove on. "Glad to oblige."

But he didn't say he'd introduce me to his grandparents. And why would he? Though he might use fancy words like *making love*, we both knew our relationship was just about sex.

Again I wondered how that would work out if I went to Indonesia. The idea of going to places like Bali was so exciting, and the work sounded fascinating. But this situation was different than jobs and volunteer positions I'd signed on for in the past. Mark wanted a six-month commitment. Could I give that? And, just as important, what about him and me? Did he figure we'd be lovers there, or would I just work for him?

Man, I really was approaching thirty! I used to make decisions impulsively, but now I wanted more information. "Tell me more about Indonesia and your project."

Mark being Mark, he didn't start with the people stuff, he went straight to the science. "Coral reefs are suffering, partly because global warming is raising ocean temperatures and that harms coral." He expanded on that topic in sexy scientist mode.

"So your project is about fighting the effects of global warming?"

"Global warming is the huge issue, but there are other

things destroying coral, too. Bad fishing practices, tourists collecting souvenirs, and divers simply being careless."

"Those things can be changed more easily than dealing with global warming."

"That's right," he said as we crossed the bridge over the Columbia River, taking us into Washington. "Education is a big part of the project. First, in helping the local people understand that even though catching exotic tropical fish to sell on the international market and encouraging tourism have immediate financial payoffs, the current practices are destroying the resources that are their foundation."

"Then you teach them the correct ways?"

"Yes. For fishing, it's usually a return to more traditional practices. Fishing nets rather than cyanide, for example."

I gaped at him. "Cyanide? Oh my God, they use cyanide?"

"In some places, yes. It stuns the fish and makes them easier to catch. But the survival rate is lower, and it destroys the coral that the fish need to survive."

"I bet it does." I reflected. "And with tourism, you teach them about ecotourism, and I suppose try to get laws enacted so that tourists can't collect coral?"

"Yes. We also teach the locals how to treat and replant coral, to rebuild the reefs." He elaborated on what was involved.

"You help them build a sustainable economy that protects rather than destroys the environment," I said.

"Exactly." He gave me a big smile, then went on. "Members of our team help them with the economic aspects, too. Members of a community may set up their own fish export business or ecotourism business."

His enthusiasm was infectious, and I felt an increasingly strong urge to be part of the wonderful things he and his team would be doing. The six-month commitment wasn't a big deal; with work this absorbing, the time would fly by.

But what about him and me? Did he figure we'd stop sleeping together if we were in a work relationship?

I wouldn't be a colleague like the other scientists on the team, I'd be some kind of assistant. Maybe he'd hook up with another marine biologist. Maybe I'd hook up with a hot Balinese guy.

My stomach felt a little queasy. Probably because it had been hours since breakfast. I pointed toward one of the exits for Olympia. "I could use a pee break and some lunch. We're pretty low on crackers and cheese, so maybe we could pick up sandwiches to go?"

"Good idea." He took an exit and we found a sandwich shop where we got veggie wraps and giant chocolate chip cookies.

I insisted on paying my share. "We need to settle up for gas, too."

"Jenna, I was driving anyway. Doesn't cost anything extra to have you along. Put the money toward a wedding gift for your sister."

I smiled ruefully, and let my pride take the small hit. "Thanks. If she weren't doing this on such short notice, I'd have had a chance to save for something."

When we were back on the I-5 heading toward Tacoma, we munched on our wraps. My stomach felt a little better, but my thoughts were in a turmoil. Mark was different than any man I'd ever known, so smart and committed and . . . pretty freaking amazing. What would it mean for us if I went to Indonesia?

When we finished eating, he started giving me examples of projects similar to his Indonesian one. And, as we drove north through Washington, he also went into more detail about the work he and his team planned to do.

I listened, interested, but increasingly antsy. Science Guy was talking about everything but what kind of relationship he envisioned between us. I was almost scared to ask, because I didn't know what I wanted. It sounded as if he saw us being just friends, and that would be easier in a lot of ways. I usually had no trouble at all being friends with guys I'd slept with. But could I work with Mark and not want to be lovers?

The miles passed, Seattle flashed by in a maze of exits and overpasses, we made steady progress toward the border. And still he talked about the project.

"We also hope for benefits beyond the environmental and economic ones," he said. "Often there's a spillover into other aspects of society when the economy improves and when people learn to respect the environment."

"That'd be great," I said absently. Yeah, it would, but I couldn't take this any longer. I needed to know. "Mark, what about you and me? You're the project leader, right?"

He nodded.

"So, I'd work for you. And we'd . . . what? Be friends? Lovers?"

"Friends? You thought . . . Oh, man. That's not what I meant, Jenna. Lovers, of course."

A surge of warmth rippled through me. He wanted me to go to Indonesia as his lover. "You think the rest of your team would be okay with that?"

"Yeah, sure. There's one married couple on this team and likely some other folks will get together. And yes, I'm the team leader, but it's mostly a coordination role. I'm not great at working with people. I hire competent professionals, each has their own role and tasks, and we work together cooperatively."

He slowed as we reached the border. "Not much of a lineup. Good. Can you grab my passport from the glove compartment?"

I did, and found my own in my tote bag as the dozen or so cars ahead of us passed quickly through the checkpoint. I glanced at the clock on the dash and saw it was half past six.

My family'd be organizing dinner and I'd arrive in time for leftovers.

We reached the Customs booth, and Mark handed our passports to the official. We answered the routine questions and were waved through.

"What were we talking about?" Mark said, handing me his passport to stow away. "Oh, right, about relationships. On projects like this, it's not practical to say people can't get together."

"Yeah, I bet."

He shrugged. "It's all pretty loose. But, I don't want . . ." His voice trailed off.

"What?"

He cleared his throat and, not looking at me, said, "I don't want you sleeping with anyone else."

"What?" I should have seen that coming. Mark believed in monogamy. I didn't and had always hated it when a guy tried to tie me down. "Hey," I protested, "you said I'd have to commit to six months on the project, you didn't say I'd have to commit to six months of exclusivity with you."

"Does that sound so terrible?" he shot back.

"I . . . Oh come on, we barely know each other. Yeah, there's a . . . chemistry thing happening, but a week from now it could completely fizzle." I twisted sideways so I could watch his profile as he drove. "Mark, this invitation doesn't seem like you. You're not the impulsive type."

A grin twitched the corner of his mouth. "Not up until now."

"You've been planning this project for a while, getting funding, coordinating with the Indonesian communities, putting a team together." No doubt he had a project plan, like Theresa.

"Yeah."

"And you've known me two days. So, why?"

He sent an almost exasperated glance in my direction. "Because you're special."

"Special?" I echoed, feeling that same gooshy warm sensation I'd felt when he'd said I was like a butterfly that did good in the world.

"I'm doing this wrong, aren't I?" he said. "Adrienne says I don't have a romantic bone in my body."

Romantic? My pulse raced. Dr. Mark Chambers was feeling romantic? The idea of romance was . . . scary. Exciting. And just what was he freaking doing?

After casting a quick glance in the camper's mirrors, he flicked on his signal and swung off onto the side of the highway.

"You can't park here."

"Just for a minute." He turned off the engine, unbuckled his seatbelt, and swung toward me, expression earnest. "Jenna, I've only known you two days, but I feel things for you that I've never felt before."

Oh, my. Traffic whooshed by and the Westfalia rocked slightly whenever a big commercial truck whipped past. I felt even less stable, like I was walking down the shifting sands of a dune in pitch darkness. "I, uh . . . Mark, we've only known each other two days."

"I just said that," he pointed out.

"Oh. Yeah. Uh . . ."

"You feel something, too. It's not one-sided."

I swallowed. Yes, I felt something, but it was strange and scary and confusing, and what good could come of admitting it? "What makes you say that?" My voice came out nervously high-pitched.

He answered calmly. "Sometimes you avoid kissing me because you're scared of what happens when we kiss. When we kiss and make love, you look dazed and overcome, which is just how I feel. You tell me things you've never told anyone."

About the operation, my infertility. Not only that, but he'd seen into my heart and realized the truth: that much as I might try to fool myself, I'd never stopped wanting to have children.

"Do you want me to go on?" he asked, tenderness in his blue eyes.

I shook my head. I should say something, but words were all jumbled in my brain.

He reached over and captured my hand. Expression bemused, he said, "I have no experience with love. I don't know how it's supposed to feel. Am I falling in love with you? How do I know?"

Oh God, I'd just e-mailed my mother asking how you knew if you'd found the right one.

Cold sweat broke out on my skin, and I realized my tummy was queasy again. I shook my head vigorously. "I thought I was in love once. It wrecked my judgment, and I ended up getting hurt. I don't want to be in love again. I don't trust myself when I'm in love."

"You're scared. Scared you'll get another jerk like Travis."

"He told me he loved me," I said softly. "He lied, and I believed him, and I didn't take care of myself."

"I'll never lie to you. And I'll help you take care of you."

Another gooshy surge of warmth hit my heart. It almost conquered the chills and nervous tummy. Mark was a straightforward man. Things that came across as compliments or jokes were just him being honest about what he thought. Softly, I admitted, "I believe you."

"We can take things slowly."

"Slowly?" I yelped. "Going to Indonesia with you for six months isn't exactly slow."

His brows drew together. "Maybe not, but that's where I'm going. What were you planning to do next? Go back to the falcon survey?"

"I don't know, I don't *do* plans." I waved a hand a little wildly. "Get my car, then see where the open road takes me. There are so many possibilities." Though at the moment, not a single one came to mind. I took a deep breath and forced myself to think. "I could drive to see Anna in Alberta, go to Greece and visit Milos, go to England and work with Elizabeth."

His eyes narrowed when I said *Milos*. He was jealous. But in truth, Milos, the guy I'd once found so sexy, didn't tempt me. Had Mark ruined me for other men?

"Using what for money?" he asked.

"I don't know!"

He sighed, then stared levelly into my eyes. "I'm asking you to give up all the other possibilities and choose—"

Behind us, a siren whooped, cutting him off, and we both jumped. A moment later, a stocky, middle-aged cop stood beside Mark's window. "Car trouble, folks?" he asked.

Mark shook his head. "No, I just needed to say something to her that I couldn't while I was driving."

The man wasn't even capable of a white lie.

The cop's lips quirked then straightened as he said, "Let's see your license and registration. And next time, wait for an exit."

"Sorry," Mark said, fishing his wallet out of his pocket. "Jenna, would you get the registration out of the glove compartment?"

After the officer checked the paperwork, he waved us back onto the highway.

"Tell me what you're thinking," Mark said.

"I don't know. Yes, the idea of going to Indonesia is really tempting." If he was just a casual guy, like Milos or surfer-dude Carlos, the decision would have been easy. Go and have fun, for as long as it lasted. But things with Mark were anything but casual.

"Not just Indonesia," he said firmly. "Us."

Stalling, I asked, "Is there an us? Maybe it's just, you know, really strong lust that'll—"

"Jenna," he stopped me. "You know there's an us. Question is, what do we do about it?"

Part of me wanted to say, *Run like hell.* But Mark, who never lied, had said he thought I was special. He saw who I was, the real person, and he valued me.

Tentatively, I said, "Maybe we could go to Indonesia and see how things go?" I'd never planned ahead for six months, but now I kind of wanted to.

"That's what I have in mind. But if you come, I want to know you're at least open to the idea that we could make it work. Long-term."

Long-term? "I don't do long-term," I replied, panic rising.

"You haven't. Doesn't mean you can't."

I shook my head. "Mark, this is too much, too fast. I can't . . . You scare me, talking this way."

He gave a rueful chuckle. "I kind of scare myself, too." Then he reached over to touch my hand. "Okay, how about this? Let's take a step back. We can both think it over and we'll get together, uh, how about tomorrow night? There's a symposium dinner I need to attend, and you'll want to have dinner with your family, but maybe we could meet after?"

More than twenty-four hours from now. I sighed with relief. "I can handle that. I'll have to make sure there's no wedding stuff happening, though."

He put his hand back on the wheel as we approached the George Massey Tunnel, and we were both silent as we drove through. Driving under the Fraser River always spooked me. I smiled a little, thinking that if I said so, Mark would explain all about the engineering of tunnels. I'd come to know him pretty well. And yet, there were so many things I didn't know.

When we emerged into the light of early evening, I said,

"You may have schedules and project plans, but it seems to me, you really don't think long-term either. Not much past the next project."

"Guess that's true."

"Yet, you say that eventually you want a partner and kids. How would they fit into your life?" And how could he have used the words *long-term* with me, when what he really wanted was someone so different?

"Uh, I guess I haven't worked that out."

I nodded, easily able to relate to that. "My parents always ask me where I see myself in five years, ten years." I gestured out the window. "And I say, 'On the road, having fun.' "

He frowned. "That's a little superficial."

Annoyed, I shot back, "Welcome to my world."

"If you weren't trying so hard to shock them, maybe you'd say something honest, like 'working on an interesting, worthwhile project.' "

"Like that'd make them any happier."

"Jenna—"

I waved a hand, silencing him. "Mark, I tried it. Okay, yeah, I take perverse pleasure in shocking them. The few times I was totally honest about my life, they criticized. I'm never going to be the kind of person they accept, much less respect, so why try? Why care?" As with my infertility, it was crazy to yearn for something you couldn't have. "No parent-child relationship's perfect, right? I've got love and a safe place to run if I totally mess up. That's good enough."

"Guess you're right about it never being perfect. We should learn from our parents' mistakes, though. Like, if you had kids, you'd give them acceptance and respect as well as love, wouldn't you?"

I sucked in a breath, feeling as if he'd slapped me. "You know I can't have kids."

"Of course you can," he said sharply. "I'm sorry about the surgery, sorry you can't bear children. But you know there are children all over the world who need good parents. If you don't want kids, that's one thing, but don't say you can't have them."

Adoption. I had never let myself consider it because it was a stupid dream, one that couldn't work for me. "It's not true to say I don't want them," I admitted slowly. "I love children. But they don't fit my life. Tree says I'm still a kid myself."

"You can be responsible when you want to. It's a choice."

Miffed, I said, "Stop lecturing me. Look, yes, I love children, but I'm not like my sisters. All that home and hearth, white picket fence stuff gives me hives."

Almost grudgingly, he said, "Me, too." A pause. "I remember you saying you were the one who took your dolls on adventures."

I nodded, remembering many happy afternoons in the rambling garden of our family home.

A moment later, he snapped his fingers and said excitedly, "Hey, that's it. That's what I want to do."

"Excuse me? You want to take your dollies on adventures, Dr. Chambers?"

"My kids." He glanced over. "There's no law that a family has to live behind a white picket fence. We can live wherever we want. Home schooling for the kids, with home being a bunch of different places in the world. What an incredible education it'd be."

"God, yes. I wish *I'd* grown up like that." He'd said *we*. Did he mean it in the general sense, or more personally? He'd said he wanted me to be open to the possibility of long-term . . .

He was going on. "Stability for the kids, because they'd have two parents who love them. But variety and stimulation, too. And they'd learn that a person's actions matter in this world."

My parents had tried to teach us that too, but they were

so damned impressive they made me feel inadequate. To them, spending a few months helping autistic kids or counting falcons was frivolous. You had to get university degrees and pursue a serious career. Mark was the only person who'd seen true value in the things I'd done. That butterfly analogy, about me doing good in the world, had blown me away.

And then I thought about his other butterfly comment. "Chaos theory," I murmured, feeling dazed.

"Yeah." He shot me a bright smile. "A young woman named Merilee flutters her wings—announces her engagement—which sets her three older sisters on journeys they wouldn't otherwise have made. Their trajectories intersect with those of three men. Pheromones are rich in the air and . . ."

"And what?" What were we talking about here? My thoughts, my emotions, were in a mad whirl.

He shrugged and made a comic face. "Everyone lives happily ever after?"

I gave a nervous laugh. *Ever after?* "And you said you weren't a romantic."

I sure wasn't, not since I was seventeen. But yet . . . "Chaos theory," I whispered. Tree was so cynical about men that she never dated. Kitty-Kat had the worst taste and luck in the world when it came to guys. A week ago, if anyone had asked me to bet on the odds of them finding love, I'd have said the possibility was almost as remote for them as for me.

Merilee had always smirked that the one thing she had over the rest of us was being lucky in love. Had she somehow managed to share that luck?

I raised my hands, fingers spread, and pressed them against my face. Oh God, was I really falling in love, for the second time in my life? Did I dare let it happen?

* * *

As he steered the Westfalia over the Oak Street Bridge, Mark inwardly cursed the Sunday evening traffic that demanded his attention.

When he darted a quick glance at Jenna, she looked like she was in shock, fingers taut with tension as they pressed hard against her face. "Jenna? You okay?"

Through spread fingers, she gazed at him. "I don't know. I never expected this. Never expected you. My life was great, just the way it was."

One side of his mouth kinked up. "I know what you mean."

"Yeah?"

"Mine was great, but you've shown me it could be better. Hell, you've got me tasting food."

She chuckled as if he'd told a joke.

"You've shown me it's okay to relax and enjoy life. To live in the moment." He reflected on all the things he'd done, or done differently, since he'd met her. "That it can be fun to act on impulse, to pick a path at random." He paused. "At least so long as you have a map in your pocket in case you get lost."

Another chuckle.

"Not to mention," he added, "making love with you is incredible."

She nodded, and slowly lowered her hands. Then she jerked and pointed out the windshield. "You need to take a left at the next light. Sorry, I wasn't paying attention."

He checked traffic, then pulled into the left lane, signaling for the turn. "We both need to think more about this. We'll carry on this conversation tomorrow night."

"Indonesia," she murmured. "We'll talk about Indonesia."

"You know we're talking about more than just that. That idea of a family, traveling around—"

"Whoa!" She held up her hands in a *stop* gesture. "What happened to taking this slowly?"

He gave a rueful chuckle. "Okay, sorry if I came on like a steamroller. I'm just excited." Excited and joyful, his body charged with adrenaline. For the first time, he had a clear vision of a perfect future that combined three kinds of love: work, partner, and children. Partner, meaning Jenna.

And Jenna, the woman he'd feared couldn't commit to anything or anyone, seemed to be seriously considering it.

Before he got ahead of himself, he had to clarify something. He took a breath. "Okay, let me take a step back. All that stuff you said about hating monogamy and fidelity, that was because you'd been hurt by someone you loved. Right? If you and I really do fall in love, tell me you won't want to sleep with other men. I couldn't handle that."

She stuck a thumb between her lips and worried it with her teeth. Talking around it, she said slowly, "I can't imagine wanting to be with another guy. And if I think of you with another woman . . ." She removed her thumb and glared at him. "Shit, I've never been jealous before, but yeah, it'd piss me off."

"Good." He felt like a caveman claiming his mate, and he sure as hell wouldn't apologize for it. "And I'd never do it."

"It's a right turn up here, then a left in two blocks. We're almost there."

He followed her directions. They were in an older, expensive part of town with large, attractive homes and beautifully landscaped yards. "Tomorrow night. We'll talk more."

"Yeah, we definitely need to." She gave a quick laugh and shook her head. "Oh God, I'm usually the impulsive one. I hear of something fun and off I go."

"This is different," he said with certainty. For both of them, it would be a major change. A major commitment.

Major. Really major. His grandparents would say he was

insane. The thought doused the bright flame of excitement within him.

Was he? He glanced over, to see Jenna frowning. Yes, a day apart would be good. Since they'd met, they'd barely left each other's company. He'd thought from the start that she'd bedazzled him. Maybe, in some odd way, he'd done the same to her. MHC codes?

"Right at the next corner," she said. Then, "Your grand-parents will be waiting for you."

"Yes." He made an instantaneous decision. He wouldn't tell them about Jenna, not until he and she decided what they were going to do. "And your family for you."

"I don't think it would be a good idea to invite you in."

A quick pain stabbed him. Ridiculous, when he wasn't even going to tell his grandparents about her.

Were these bad signs? Or just common sense?

"Up on the right," she said. "Pull over here."

The house he parked in front of was one of the smaller ones on the street, too small for a family with four daughters. Her parents must have downsized when the eldest girls left home.

Jenna unbuckled her seatbelt, opened the passenger door, and hopped out.

He got out and walked around to open the side door of the camper, then climbed in to collect her bags. He handed them down to her, then hefted her small cooler and climbed out with it. "I'll help you carry things in."

"It's okay. Better not. I didn't tell them about my car, or getting a ride."

Would she even tell them about him? How had excited optimism so quickly turned to doubt?

He glanced at the house. From behind curtained windows, warm lights glowed, but the front door hadn't opened. Realizing that the cooler in his arms was a solid rectangular barrier between them, he put it down. "How about I call you tomorrow morning to see if getting together in the evening works?"

"Great. Call my cell." She scrabbled in her tote bag and came out with a pen and a cash register tape, and scribbled her number.

"You'll plug it in?"

"I promise." For a long moment, she gazed up at him, then her lips kinked into a rather wry smile. "Well, Mark, I have to say, it's been a *trip*."

"It sure has." He glanced at the house. The door didn't open; the curtains didn't twitch.

He tugged her into his arms, needing to restore the connection between them. "The best trip of my life, Jenna."

"Oh, Mark. For me, too." She tipped her head up and he touched his lips to hers. He didn't risk open mouths or tongues, just a brief press of lips. A gesture of hope.

Chapter 12

I watched the Westfalia drive away, with Mark's hand waving out the open driver's side window. The best trip of my life, and now it was over.

But he'd left me with the offer of another and, beyond that, amazing possibilities.

He wanted fidelity. A six-month commitment. He offered the chance at love. A future, even. Children. My mind, my heart, couldn't take it all in.

I blew out air, sucked it in again, and squared my shoulders. First, I needed to face my family.

Though I wasn't one for keeping careful track of time, I did know it had been months since I was last home and over a year since my sisters and I had been here at the same time.

I hefted a couple of backpacks and trudged past Mr. and Mrs. Wilkerson's bungalow, then the Abbott family's pretentious colonial, to the driveway of the big, rambling home I'd grown up in. No way had I wanted Mark to drive me to the door and risk the family rushing out and wanting to meet him. Not until I was ready. Not until he and I had decided what we were going to do.

What we shared felt strong in some ways, but fragile, too. Fragile, because I'd never cared so much for a man before and because this one was stirring up dreams I'd tried to bury more than a decade ago. What in freaking hell was I going to do?

Walking up the drive, I noted that the garden was perfectly manicured. The reception was going to be held here, and no doubt the gardening service had been putting in overtime. Too bad. I liked the yard a little overgrown and wild. So had my dollies.

Maybe, with Mark, I could play those games for real.

Or maybe, if I dared to dream, my heart would be shattered a second time. How could I trust my judgment when my heart got in the way?

The doors to the two-car garage were closed and Merilee's old Toyota and Matt's aging Hyundai were parked by the house.

Quietly, I placed my bags on the front porch, then went back to get the cooler and the rest of my stuff, debating what I should do. It was Sunday night. Likely they were in the dining room having dinner. If I knocked, someone would answer the door and see I didn't have my car. That conversation would happen eventually, but I'd rather put it off.

I never carried a door key. A long, long time ago, after I'd forgotten the house key for the umpteenth time, my parents had given up and taken to hiding one in a knot-hole of the old horse chestnut tree in the backyard. The one where I'd spent many afternoons curled up in a fork reading, watching squirrels, and mostly dreaming. Of California and Greece, of surfing and riding horses, of every adventure imaginable—often with a handsome guy at my side, and three adorable kids.

Maybe I'd climb up there now. Spend a little quiet time before going inside and stepping back into my role as the flaky daughter. If I climbed up to my dreaming spot, I could think about Indonesia and maybe even love. Tempting, but scary too.

But now that I was here, I felt an urge to see my family. Whatever our issues, there was a strong bond.

Sometimes I thought that Tree, Kat, and I were yo-yos. We'd fly out and away, do our tricks and spins, but there was an enduring thread connecting us to this house and our parents. It always pulled us back eventually.

I decided to sneak around back to retrieve the key, quietly unlock the front door, and get my gear inside before anyone heard me. Who said I never thought ahead or made plans?

Leaving my belongings on the porch, I headed for the backyard, and was surprised to hear voices. I slowed, then cautiously peeked around the corner of the house.

My family sat around the metal patio table. They'd eaten out there, I could see from the empty plates shoved to the middle of the table. Maybe Dad had barbecued. He was the stereotypical absent-minded professor and had trouble even showing up on time for meals, but when he put his mind to it, he could make a mean marinated steak and terrific maple-glazed salmon.

I hung back, taking in the picture, feeling a tug in my heart: love, together with a longing to be part of that scene, just as it was in this moment.

They looked so relaxed for once, so comfortable with each other as they sat back in their chairs, many of them bare-legged in shorts. Was the easy, casual mood due to Mom being in Ottawa? She was always the most demanding, the quickest to interrogate and find fault.

And yet, I felt a childish wish to feel Mom's arms go around me in a hug. Yes, a moment later she'd be nagging me about something, but I wanted that embrace.

I did a quick inventory. Merilee, my baby sis, looked tired. Her honey-blonde hair was pulled back from a face that was too pale, but she was smiling as she listened to a gorgeous stranger who had to be Kat's guy. Wow. Tree hadn't exaggerated. This man Nav was definitely hot, with long, curly black hair, cinnamon skin set off by a black tee, and striking features. Best of all was the warmth on his face, the sparkle in his eyes, a quality of genuineness about him that was so unlike the occasional other guys Kitty-Kat had brought home before.

Well, maybe best of all was the way their fingers interwove atop the table, and the affection in my sister's eyes as she listened to him and Merilee. Kat, in contrast to Merilee, was bursting with vitality, from her mass of reddish-brown curls to the animation on her face. I crossed my fingers that this time she'd be lucky.

Matt, as usual, had his arm around M's shoulders. He had squeaky-clean, wholesome good looks, and every time I saw him, he looked older—in a good way. A real man now, not the boy who'd grown up as almost one of the family.

Next, I focused on Tree, the older sister who'd alternated between looking after me, bossing me around, and ignoring me. She sure looked different. Her brown hair was still short and simple, her face free of make-up as always, but she had a light tan and wore a pretty green sleeveless blouse that was more feminine than her usual style. Even more than the superficial stuff, though, there was an indefinable something, a confidence and . . . sexiness. I grinned. Oh yeah, the thriller writer was good for my big sis.

Finally, my gaze rested on Dad, who was talking intently to Tree. For a prof, he looked pretty darned good, more due to great genes than to any effort to look after himself. His shoulders weren't stooped, he was still slim, and though his hair was silvering, he still had lots of it. His eyes, behind the glasses he'd always worn, were sharp.

In fact, when I stepped out from my hiding place and walked toward them, he was the first to see me. "Jenna! You're home." He rose quickly and came toward me.

"Jenna!" Merilee squealed, leaping up and running past him to hug me first. "You're here, you're really here!" She grabbed me tight and squeezed, and I hugged her back, for the moment purely happy to be home.

She passed me to Dad for a quick, sincere hug. Kat was next, her embrace warm as always. "Hey, Kitty-Kat," I whispered in her ear, "very, very hot guy."

Tree was next and her hug was tighter than usual. "You look fabulous, Sis," I told her.

"You look the same as always. You never age a day." Tonight it actually came across as a compliment, not a subtle dig that it was time I grew up.

Next came Matt. I stretched up to kiss his cheek. "Cool, I finally get a brother."

He chuckled and squeezed my hands. "Good to see you, Jenna. I know how much it means to M, having all of you here."

Kat grabbed her guy's hand and brought him to stand in front of me. "And this is Nav."

He held out his hand. "Naveen Bharani. Pleased to meet you, Jenna."

I put my hand in his and we shook firmly. "I must say, you do live up to all the hype."

Humor sparkled in those dark-lashed, chocolate eyes. "My reputation precedes me?"

"I bet you've heard a thing or two about me," I said wryly.

The twinkle grew. "Only good things."

"Okay, Kat, toss him out. This one's a liar."

We all laughed, then Tree said, "Have you eaten? There's leftovers—barbecued honey garlic chicken and potato salad—in the fridge. We haven't had dessert yet, but Kat made chocolate mousse."

"Sounds great. You guys go ahead with dessert and I'll catch up."

As Kat and Nav began to clear the table, I hurried to the front of the house and brought in my luggage, dumping it at the foot of the stairs, then I made quick use of the powder room and went out to the kitchen.

Quickly, I served myself, then headed out to the patio where the others were digging into bowls of mousse garnished with whipped cream and raspberries. Fresh raspberries, like the ones Mark and I had shared.

Dad was seated at the head of the table with Tree and M&M on his left. On his right, where Kat had been seated, there was now an empty chair shoved between her and Dad, and someone had poured me a glass of white wine.

As I sat down, Dad smiled at me. "How was the drive? It's a long trip."

"Yeah, but it was fine. And it's good to be home." Despite my mixed feelings about my family, those words were the truth. Sometimes, when we were picking at each other, I lost track of how much we really loved each other.

"I was almost expecting you to show up with a man in tow," Dad said.

My fork clanked against my plate. "What? What do you mean?" Had something in my voice or my e-mails given me away?

"Theresa did, with Damien, who'd been on the same flight. Then Kat did, with Nav, who'd come out on the train with her. I was starting to see a pattern."

Chaos theory. Trying to act casual, I rolled my eyes. "For the last time, I did not pick up a hitchhiker."

"We never know what to expect from you," Tree said dryly. "You're always saying you live to shock. You can't have it both ways."

"Seems like you've been doing a little shocking of your own," I challenged her. "That is, if rumors about Waikiki Beach are true."

Color rose to her cheeks. Oh my gosh, was it true she'd had sex on the beach?

I thought of being with Mark on that beach after sunset

and, for a moment, let my mind drift to pictures of sex on various beaches all over the world.

Dad was frowning. "What rumors?"

Much as we sisters might tease and criticize each other, we kept each other's deepest secrets. So, tongue in cheek, I said, "I hear your workaholic, intellectual daughter actually took time out to *stroll* the beach. Right, Tree?"

Her lips twitched. "I confess to strolling. Blame Damien. He even got me into a bikini."

And out of it too, I was sure. "Can't wait to meet him." I leveled her with a gaze that said, *And hear all the deets from you*, then turned to Kat. "Has Nav got you doing anything uncharacteristic?"

Her eyes gleamed above a spoonful of whipped-cream topped mousse. "He's taught me a thing or two. Indian men are extremely well educated."

Nav choked back a laugh as Kat leaned over and whispered, "Kama Sutra" in my ear.

"Oh, yeah?" I stared at the pair, curiosity peaked. And here I thought I was the adventuresome one.

Seeing Merilee and Tree hide giggles, I felt a rush of jealousy. My sisters had been together sharing secrets, and I felt left out. If I told them about Mark, would they tell me I didn't deserve him or include me in that girlish, gossipy warmth?

I refilled my wine glass. "Okay, now to the important stuff. Catch me up on what's happening with the wedding, and what I can do to help. I'm all yours." And I resolved not to worry about Mark and the future until I was alone in my room.

Predictably, Tree began, laying everything out logically as Merilee and Kat chipped in. I let them talk, and settled in to enjoy the chicken and potato salad.

As it started to get dark, Kat turned on the patio lights then came out with chocolate mousse for me.

"Thanks." I savored the rich, creamy dessert: dark chocolate with a hint of coffee, perfectly accented by vanilla-flavored whipped cream and ripe raspberries. My lips tingled at the memory of Mark gently pressing berries to my lips.

Dad stood up. "I'll leave you to it. I have some work to do."

"I'm surprised he lasted this long," Kat whispered. "Wedding talk isn't exactly his thing."

"Night, Dad," I said as he headed toward the kitchen, and the others chorused their good nights, too.

In the doorway, he turned and smiled. "It's good to have all my girls back home." Then he went inside.

I shook my head. "Good to have us home, but he'd rather work."

"Yes, but I think he and Mom really do like having us here," Tree mused. "That's why they keep our rooms."

"They miss you when you're gone," Merilee put in, almost grudgingly. "They're always saying how empty the house feels." She wrinkled her nose. "Like I don't count."

"You count with me," Matt promptly said.

Surprisingly, the look she shot him was almost annoyed. "I know that, but it's not the same."

"Let's face it," Theresa said briskly, "if any of us needs whole-hearted parental approval, we were born into the wrong family."

But . . . I was the one our parents always dumped on. Tree, Kat, and M were the good girls. I was about to question her when Dad came back to the patio.

A puzzled expression on his face, he said, "I know I'm notorious for losing cars, but Jenna, I can't find your MGB."

I winced. "Why are you looking for it?"

"I wanted to make sure you'd put the top up. They're forecasting showers tonight."

"My car's fine." I glanced around the table. I could possibly snow Dad—he could walk past his own car in a parking lot and not recognize it—but the truth would come out eventually. Resignedly, I said, "It's back in California getting a new alternator."

Tree's brows went up. "I talked to you. You said you were driving."

"I was. My plans changed."

"You ended up taking the bus?" Kat asked. "You hate the bus as much as I hate flying."

"I do."

"You should have called," Dad said. "We'd have bought you a plane ticket."

"I know. Everyone offered, but I'm not helpless. Just because I choose not to do the nine to five grind like you folks, that doesn't mean I can't get myself home for M&M's wedding."

"I don't like to think of you on the bus," my father said.

"Dad, I'm a big girl, and I can look after myself."

"I'm surprised you didn't meet some guy on the bus," M teased.

"No way."

I could have sworn not a muscle in my face twitched, but Kat's gaze sharpened. "You did! You did meet someone."

"Okay, okay, I didn't take the bus. I got a ride with a friend who was driving from Santa Cruz to Vancouver."

"A male friend," Kat said. "So where is he?"

"With his grandparents. They live here."

"Is he a *special* friend?" Merilee teased.

"With Jenna, aren't they always?" Tree joined in.

"They aren't," I snapped. I had male friends as well as lovers. It wasn't like I leaped into bed with every man who came within ten feet. Just the really hot, sweet ones like Mark.

Tension hung in the air, and we all kept quiet until Dad said, "The important thing is that you made it home safely. You all made it home safely. Now, I'm going to work."

We held the silence until he was gone. I took the last bite

of mousse and tried to enjoy it, wondering if I could follow Dad and escape to my room. What Mark and I shared was special, but so fragile and uncertain. Much as I'd have loved to join in the *sex on the beach* and *Kama Sutra* girl talk, I was afraid to subject our relationship to sisterly scrutiny.

When Dad was out of earshot, Tree said, "Matt, Nav, go find something to do. We need some sister time."

Oh-oh. Why did I think this wasn't about more wedding plans?

Nav glanced at Kat for confirmation, and she said, "Yes, please."

He rose. "I really should work on my photo exhibit. Is that okay with you, Matt?"

"Sure. I have some things to do at home, so I'll head back. If you don't mind, M?" He squeezed her hand.

"Sure, M," she said. "We'll talk tomorrow." They shared a quick kiss, then Matt stood up.

"Night, all," Nav said. He leaned down and he and Kat exchanged a slow, sultry kiss. He murmured something in her ear and she smiled up at him, brown eyes dancing.

Nav walked toward the kitchen, and Matt headed across the lawn toward the front of the house. When they were out of sight, Tree, sitting across from me, leaned forward and stared at me. "Your story doesn't ring true, Jenna."

I groaned. It seemed sisterly scrutiny was on the menu, whether I liked it or not.

"You're the one who's always trying to shock us," she went on.

"That's true," Kat said. "But this time, you're downplaying it. Normally, you'd be telling us about this super-hot surfer or whatever, and what a great road trip you had. Like, camping on the beach and skinny-dipping, stuff like that."

Thankfully, I'd picked up my coffee cup and could bury my quick grin against its rim.

"So," Tree said, "that means you're hiding something."

I glanced at Merilee, sitting beside Tree. "Well?"

She put up her hands. "They're the smart ones. I'm just listening."

And they'd never let up. I could tell them some of the fun stuff and maintain my wild and crazy image without letting them in on the really significant stuff. The temptation to talk about Mark was irresistible. I put my elbows on the table and leaned forward. "Okay, yeah, there was skinny dipping."

"Wait, wait, wait!" Kat leaped to her feet, holding up both hands in a *stop* gesture. "We need more wine." She hurried toward the kitchen.

"It's cooling off out here," M said. "Maybe we should go inside."

"Let's stay out," I said. Given my choice I almost always choose outdoors over in. "Do Mom and Dad still keep spare blankets?"

"Yeah, I'll get them," she said, following Kat.

I gazed across at Tree. "Guess we'd better keep our lips zipped until they get back."

Our sisters returned in a scramble, Merilee with four lightweight blankets and Kat with a bottle of pinot grigio and a corkscrew. A few minutes later we'd all settled ourselves comfortably, blankets around shoulders or across laps, fresh glasses of wine in front of us. This time Merilee sat beside me, and Kat beside Tree.

"Go on," Kat urged me. "You left off at the skinny dipping."

"That came just before the sex on the beach."

"I knew it!" Kat said. "Hah, Theresa, you and Damien weren't the only ones."

Theresa's brows pulled together. "What beach?" she said, sounding miffed.

I chuckled. "Yeah, yeah, your beach is better than mine. Mine was just a little one at a campground." Then her words sank in and I stared at her, wide-eyed. "Seriously? You had sex on Waikiki Beach?"

"And went skinny dipping," she said smugly.

An imp made me say, "In the middle of the day, like we did?"

"You didn't!" She gaped. "Good God, Jenna."

I laughed again, and tucked my bare feet up under me. It was so easy to wind my sisters up. "No, we didn't. It was after sunset and everyone had left the beach. How about you?"

"Late night, and I think we were the only ones on the beach."

"You didn't get arrested?"

"God, no." She pressed a hand to her forehead. "Don't tell me you did?"

I chuckled. "Just teasing."

"Bitch." Her face softened and I wondered how I'd ever thought of her as the plain sister. "It's so . . . primal," she marveled, "making love outside with just the moon and stars watching."

I didn't say that Mark and I had been in a makeshift shelter and hadn't seen the sky. In fact, I hadn't seen much of anything, I'd been so caught up in the act. "Yeah, the sex is pretty incredible."

"Oh, yes."

Kat cleared her throat. "Hey, M, I don't know about you but I'm feeling a distinct need to grab my guy and go find a beach. Hmm," she said mischievously, "I wonder what Kama Sutra position Nav would recommend for beach sex?"

"Damien doesn't need the Kama Sutra," Tree said. "Believe me, he knows all the right moves. Speaking of which . . ." She reached over to tap my hand, which was resting on the table. "Mile high club. I'm officially a member."

"We set off the emergency alarm in the shower on the train," Kat said competitively, tossing her thick auburn curls.

Okay, I was pretty impressed with both my sisters. Still, I

fought back with, "I went down on him at a picnic table in our campsite." What I didn't say was that when Mark and I kissed and made love, my world rocked on its foundations.

Realizing that Merilee was awfully quiet, I turned to her. "Don't be shy, M. What's the wildest thing you and Matt have done?"

"Wild?" she echoed, toying with her wine glass. "We're not exactly the wild types."

"Oh, come on," I said. "I know you and M have been in love forever, but good God, girl, you two need to loosen up and go a little crazy."

"If I can do it, you can," Tree put in.

"Get in touch with your secret bad girl," Kat urged with a grin.

Merilee flicked her head in denial. An edge in her voice, she said, "Stop giving me advice about my love life. Remember, I'm the one who's getting married. The one who found the love of her life at age seven."

"That's the problem," I teased. "Tree and Kitty-Kat and I are in the first throes of lust, and you're, like, in a middle-aged marriage."

"Throes of love," Tree corrected, and Kat nodded vigorously.

I gulped, wondering what, exactly, I was really in the throes of, but managed to wave a casual hand. "Whatever."

"Speaking of what people *ought* to do," M said, scowling at me and pulling the blanket tighter around her shoulders, "maybe you ought to give love a chance. You loosen up, Jenna, and let yourself fall, for once in your life."

Kat whistled approval. "You tell her, Sis."

We hadn't turned on the outside lights and the patio was illuminated only by the moon and light from the kitchen windows. The wine and the reunion had mellowed us, my sisters' features were indistinct, and the darkness and blankets lent intimacy.

It relaxed me enough to say, "Kitty-Kat, Tree, I'm surprised by the two of you. Kat, you keep falling for guys and
they turn out to be losers, yet you get back up and try
again." Admittedly, her mistakes had never cost her as badly
as mine had, but still . . . "How do you have the . . . I don't
know if it's naïveté or guts to do that?"

"Because I believe in love," she said promptly. "I made
mistakes and had to learn the hard way, but I've finally got it
right. With Nav."

Was she even stupider than me, or braver? Whichever, I
really wanted things to work out for her. I leaned over to
squeeze her forearm. "I hope so."

I turned to my oldest sister. "And you, Theresa. After Jeffrey you were so cynical." For the first time, I realized how
much we had in common. "You loved him, and he betrayed
you." His betrayal had cost her something important, too—
it had set her career back, and career had been all-important
to her. "How could you open yourself up to trusting and
loving again? I thought you'd figured you didn't need a
man?"

"I don't," she said immediately. "With Damien, it's not
about need, it's about love. And he's trustworthy, he isn't
like Jeffrey. He respects me."

"Respect is good," I said softly. Mark respected me; he
told me I was a good person.

"Says the woman who's all about disrespect," Kat joked.
What did she mean? "Am I?"

"Sure. You disrespect authority, rules, convention, tradi-
tion."

"You got that right. I hate being stifled. Life's supposed to
be fun."

"Everyone hates being stifled," Tree said. "But I disagree
about the rest. Life's supposed to have meaning. Pleasure,
yes, and love if you're lucky. But meaning, too. That's the
thing you've never understood."

I should have known all this sisterly warmth was too good to last. Of course the criticisms had to start.

I was about to snap back at Tree when Kat spoke firmly. "Theresa, not tonight. It's the first time we've been together in ages."

"You're all strong-willed," Merilee said. "Of course you butt heads."

"Don't put it all on us," I said. "You squabble just as much as the rest of us."

"If I didn't, I'd be left out completely," she said bitterly. "You're the three-pack and I'm the mistake."

"You're the nicest of all of us, M," Kat said.

"That's for sure," I said. "And you're not a mistake. Just because you weren't planned, that doesn't mean you're a mistake. I'm the mistake. They wanted a boy and got me."

"Same with me," Kat said. "One girl, one boy. Oh, oops, another girl. I messed up their perfect plan."

"No, that was me," Tree said. "When Mom got pregnant, I screwed up their whole life plan."

A laugh spluttered out of me. "Oh Jeez, girls, listen to us. I mean, I know we're competitive, but honestly. We're playing 'who's the biggest mistake'? How pathetic is that?"

Kat let out a snort and began to laugh, and Tree and M joined in.

When we finally calmed down, the air seemed cleansed and free of tension. Kat poured more wine and I took M's hand, where it rested on her blanket-draped lap, and laced my fingers through hers. "The big day's just around the corner. My baby sister's getting married. I've heard all the details, but how are you doing? Are you crazy excited?"

She squeezed my hand. "Sometimes, like when we were picking out dresses on Friday. But sometimes . . . I don't know. Being sick, then the surgery, recuperating, so much schoolwork to make up . . ." The wistful tone in her voice wasn't at all like Merilee.

"When you're on that honeymoon cruise, you'll get plenty of R&R. Ocean air, delicious food, great sex. You'll get your energy back."

"I'm sure." Her face was pale in the dim light, with shadowed hollows around her eyes. "This just isn't how I imagined it."

"You built up such huge dreams," Kat said softly, affectionately, "it's hard for reality to live up to them. Especially when we're pulling this together on such short notice."

"Merilee." Tree leaned forward, elbows on the table, to peer at her. "You know you don't have to do this. You can always go back to the original plan and get married next year. Then you'd have time to get healthy, and months and months to do everything exactly the way you want. I know we're really inexperienced makeshift wedding planners and—"

"No, no," M said quickly, shaking her head so vigorously that the loose scrunchie holding her ponytail slid free and her blonde curls tumbled around her face. "You're wonderful. Everything you're planning is wonderful." She turned to me. "Having the wedding at VanDusen is exactly right, Jenna." Next she gazed across at Kat. "Having Nav take the photos is so much better than having some impersonal stranger. And those cute e-vites you made are perfect, Kat."

She switched her gaze to Tree. "The flowers, the cake, having the reception here in the garden, that incredible dress that fit like it was designed for me, it's all wonderful." She swallowed. "And besides, so much work has gone into it, and the cruise is booked, it's not like we could call it off now."

"M?" I said, seriously beginning to worry something was wrong.

"Of course you could," Tree said, leaning forward to better see M's face. "Merilee, if you have any doubts, if you don't feel well enough or you'd rather wait until next year, of course you can call it off."

"No!" M shook her head, curls tossing. "No, I don't have any doubts. I love Matt. We belong together." She grabbed her wine glass and took a long swallow, draining it. "Give me a break, every bride's entitled to a few jitters. Now, let's talk about something else." She turned to me. "Jenna, tell us more about this latest guy of yours."

Jitters. Yeah, that had to be it. No girl had ever been more confidently in love than Merilee with Matt.

After a moment's silence, Kat said, "Yeah, Jenna, let's hear about him."

"What does he do?" Tree asked.

That was one of the first questions she, as well as Mom and Dad, always asked.

I knew she—they all—expected me to say something like, "he's a surfer" or "he plays in a band" or "he's a rodeo rider." I delighted in saying, "*Dr.* Mark Chambers is a marine biologist."

"A scientist?" Tree said disbelievingly, as Kat said, "You have to be kidding."

Yeah, there they went. Like no scientist could possibly be interested in their dumb sister. "He's in Vancouver to attend a symposium on global changes in marine social-ecological systems. He's presenting a paper on rehabilitation of the marine environment after the tsunami in Thailand." After rattling off all those long words, I took a welcome breath.

"Do you even know what all that means?" Tree asked, reaching for the wine bottle.

I stuck out my tongue. I did, more or less. "Mark loves the ocean, and he'll spend his life trying to save it. It, and the creatures that live in and around it. He's very committed."

As Tree topped up our glasses, Kat said, "Very cool. But more to the point, what's he like? Cute, sexy, nice?"

"More handsome than cute. Lean muscles, angular features, sky blue eyes. Definitely sexy. And nice. Doesn't have much sense of humor but he's totally honest." I grinned.

"Sometimes things he says in dead seriousness come out really funny."

In the dim light, I saw my sisters exchange glances.

"What?" I demanded.

"You sound, uh, affectionate," Kat said.

Oops. Playing dumb, I said, "Huh? Because I said he's unintentionally funny?"

"Tell us more," M said.

I shouldn't, or they'd pick up on how I felt. But the compulsion to talk about Mark was irresistible. "He likes schedules and plans, but he's not obsessive. He's brave." I shivered, remembering the accident, and snuggled into my blanket. "He actually saved a man's life."

"He did? And he told you about it?" Kat sounded skeptical. "Sounds like the egotistical kind of guy I used to date."

"No, he's definitely not. And he didn't tell me, I was there."

"You were *there*?" Her voice rose.

"What do you mean?" Merilee demanded, and Tree said, "Jenna, what happened?"

I told them about the car accident, and Mark saving Mr. Watkins.

"Wow," Merilee said solemnly when I finished.

"Yeah. I was scared shitless."

"He sounds like quite the guy," Kat said.

I nodded. He was definitely quite a guy, and he really, really liked me. My sisters were no doubt thinking he was too good for me, but he'd asked me to go to Indonesia. Not just as a lover, but because he thought I could be useful.

Tentatively, I said, "He's going to Indonesia for his next project. His team will work with local people to repair and rebuild coral reefs and get new methods in place to protect them, plus get some sustainable economies going."

"Working *with* the native people, not imposing Western

ideas on them?" Tree asked. My sociologist sister hated it when Westerners disrespected aboriginal people.

"That's right," I assured her.

"Sounds worthwhile," she said.

I took a breath. Should I or shouldn't I? I let the breath out slowly then said, in a rush, "He asked me to come work on the project."

"He did?" Tree said. "What on earth for? You don't know anything about marine biology."

Kat nudged her arm. "He wants her to keep him warm on those long, cold winter nights. No, wait," she grinned, "it's the tropics, and summer. But you get my drift."

"Jenna," M said, "how could you afford the flight? You couldn't even fly home from California."

"The flight would be paid for." I'd told Mark that there was no point trying to win my family's respect. But now I found I didn't want to play the same old role of the wild child. I put my wine glass down and stiffened my spine. "No, Kat, I wouldn't be a sex toy, I'd be working. Hard, knowing Mark. And no, Tree, I don't have any specific training but I'm interested, I learn quickly, and I'm good with people."

There was a long silence, then my oldest sister said slowly, "Okay, those things are all true."

Wow. That was almost a real compliment. Before I got too excited, I waited. And sure enough . . .

"But," she went on, "how long is this project?"

"Six months."

"Right." She exchanged glances with Kat.

Kat said, "Jenna, have you ever stuck with one thing for six months? You get bored, or some other fun opportunity comes along, or you meet some guy who wants you to go somewhere with him."

"Besides," Tree said, "being involved with your boss is a bad idea in so many ways. Something I learned from sad experience."

"He's not a schmuck like Jeffrey," I said. "And we've talked about this. He's more of a team leader than a boss, and he says people on his projects do get involved with each other and it's okay so long as it doesn't get in the way of the work." I added more wine to my glass, and everyone else's as well. We'd almost finished the new bottle.

Merilee said, "Mark sounds great, and the idea of Indonesia is so much fun. But think it through. Putting work first? For six months?"

"Why would you stick with this one," Tree said bluntly, "when you've never stuck with any other job?"

"Because . . ." In the past, I'd have tossed out some flip comment and blown off the conversation. Or I could speak partial truth and say the environment was important to me.

Tonight, maybe because of the emotions of the past days, the hugs and sense of bonding earlier, or simply too much wine, I wanted to be honest. What was the worst that would happen? They'd tell me I was crazy. Like I hadn't heard that before.

"Because of Mark," I said quietly, steadily. "I feel differently about him than any other man I've met."

They all started to talk at once and I spoke over them. "Wait, let me finish. He feels it too. There's something special between us. Other guys have liked me because I'm pretty and fun to be with, but Mark takes me seriously. He accepts who I am, likes who I am, and thinks I'm . . ." I smiled, remembering what he'd said, and slipped my hand under the blanket to touch my tattoos. "He said I'm a butterfly, and when I alight I do good, useful things. I make the world a better place."

The three of them were silent for a moment and I waited, heart racing with the hope that, for once, they wouldn't put me down. That they'd see me the way Mark did.

Merilee spoke first. "I like this guy."

I reached over to give her a clumsy blanket-wrapped hug. "So do I, M."

"He's right," Kat said slowly. "I don't know all the things you've worked on, but that horses thing was therapy for kids, right? And the counting falcons . . . they're an endangered species?"

"And you worked with autistic children," Merilee said. "I remember when I was in junior high, you talked about that and it helped me decide I wanted to be a teacher."

"Seriously?" I'd actually had a positive influence on my little sister? That made me feel incredibly good.

"Those are worthwhile things," Tree said.

Warmth coursed through me, but I knew this was too good to be true.

"But don't you think—" she started.

Kat, her gaze on my face, cut her off. "No, Theresa. Leave it there."

Across the table from them, I could barely see their faces but I knew some silent message was being exchanged.

After a moment, Tree said, "Yes, Jenna, they're worthwhile things. Good for you."

I swallowed. "Thank you. All of you." I'd trusted them with the truth and they'd come through for me. I let the warm glow touch my heart, and hugged the feelings to me.

Kat smiled at me. "Jenna, it's great that you've found a man who values you for who you are." Then she shoved her chair back and rose. "And on that note, I think it's time for bed, or my own man's going to think I've deserted him."

We all stood, blanket-draped, and began to clear the table.

"You should invite Mark for dinner tomorrow," Tree said.

Tonight had been surprisingly good, but I wasn't ready to subject Mark—and our tentative new relationship—to the family dinner test. "He's tied up at the symposium." And after that, he and I needed privacy to talk.

We trailed inside and tidied up quickly, then headed upstairs. In the hallway of the second floor, we had a group hug.

"Don't tell Dad about Indonesia, okay?" I said. "Mark and I are still talking about it. I don't want to say anything more until we decide."

They all agreed, then we wished each other good night and headed off to our rooms.

I went into my old bedroom and glanced around at the things that had been there so long I rarely ever noticed them: the crystal hummingbird mobile in the window, a couple of not awful oil paintings of flowers that I'd done, and posters of tropical beaches with families playing.

As a teen, I'd dreamed of going to California, and beyond to places like Indonesia. I'd dreamed of meeting a wonderful man, falling in love, and having babies.

After Travis, I'd stopped dreaming. I'd lived day to day, trusting the universe rather than any man.

The universe had brought me Mark. And Mark had, tantalizingly, painted images of all those old dreams brought to life. If he'd left it at inviting me on a six-month project, that would have been scary enough, but then he'd talked about the future. Long-term.

I didn't *do* long-term. Was I capable of doing long-term? Did I want to?

Did I dare believe him, trust him, give in to the amazing feelings that so confused me? Did I dare let myself dream again?

Before, when I'd loved, it had made me stupid. I'd let myself get hurt; I'd let my dreams be destroyed. How could I take that risk again?

Sighing, unsettled, I slipped into bed and turned out the light. Was there any hope I'd sleep?

A thought occurred to me, and I leaped out of bed again to plug in my cell phone so I wouldn't miss Mark's call.

Chapter 13

Monday morning, before leaving for the symposium, Mark called Jenna from the privacy of his room. Nerves quickened his breath as he listened to her cell ring.

Had she told her family about Indonesia? How would they have reacted? If they'd tried to talk her out of it, they might well have pushed her into deciding to go out of sheer perverseness. But he wanted her to made her decision for the right reasons.

Yesterday, he'd figured it was good for both of them to spend time apart, to step back and think carefully. For him, that time had only made him miss her, and feel more determined that she should come to Indonesia. What effect had it had on Jenna?

Finally, her voice sounded in his ear, breathless. "Mark?"

"Good morning, Jenna. Did I wake you?"

"No, I was in the shower when the phone rang."

He imagined her naked in a steam-filled bathroom and had the predictable reaction. "Now that's just mean."

She laughed softly. "I'm only telling the truth, the way you always do."

He smiled, liking how well she knew him and relieved

that her affectionate, teasing tone suggested she wasn't pulling back. "I miss you. Does tonight still work?"

"I miss you too. I'll make it work. What time?"

"Nine? Can you suggest a coffee shop or bar?"

"Nope. It has to be the beach. How about Spanish Banks?"

"That would be great." She wouldn't break up with him on a beach, he was almost sure of that. "Want me to pick you up?"

"No, I'll meet you there."

Did that mean she hadn't told her family about him? Or that she had and still didn't want to introduce him?

Was he being too analytical? It was so much easier to analyze nature than human beings.

They agreed on which parking lot to meet in, and she said, "Can't wait to see you."

"Me either." He'd have chatted more, asked her about her reunion with her family, but the symposium would be starting soon. "I have to go."

"Good luck with your paper, not that you'll need it."

Things were going to be okay. He could feel it.

Whistling, he hurried downstairs to say a quick goodbye to his grandparents, then climbed into the Westfalia.

Last night and over an early breakfast, he'd been struck by how huge the difference was between his grandparents and Jenna. Here they were, well into their eighties, and all they did was work. Admittedly, they were devoted to their careers and doing valuable work, but he wondered if they'd tasted the free trade coffee he'd brewed or if they'd ever even walked on a beach, much less made love on one. He couldn't remember the last time he'd heard either of them laugh.

Laughing was good. Tasting was good. Beaches and lovemaking were very, very good. Maybe tonight . . . No, Spanish Banks was too public. But the camper had curtains and a bed.

He forced the thought away and concentrated on the points he wanted to make when he presented his paper later in the morning.

At lunchtime, a couple of colleagues walked with Mark into the large hotel dining room that had been set up for the symposium attendees. They complimented him on his presentation and asked thought-provoking questions, but he answered with half a mind, searching the room for Adrienne. He'd seen her in passing a couple of times and now hoped for a few semi-private moments to talk to her.

Whatever he'd been doing this morning, even when he was behind the podium, Jenna had been in the back of his mind. Because of her, he'd broken his rather dry presentation with a few anecdotal stories about interactions between project staff and local Thai people, and had noted when faces in the audience lightened and lips curved.

He was the same guy as always, yet he wasn't. In some fundamental way, his world had shifted and him along with it.

Adrienne hurried up from behind him and caught his arm. "Mark! Hey there, stranger."

She hugged him, and he hugged her back, startled by the seven-month baby bulge that came between them.

"Come sit with me," she ordered.

"Please excuse me," he said to his colleagues and let her steer him to an unoccupied table on the far side of the room.

Once they'd sat down, he said, "You sure look different."

"The baby or the hair?"

"Both." She'd always worn her vivid red hair long, sometimes loose and sometimes tied back. Now it was short and spiky, calling attention to her expressive face. "The haircut suits you. Uh, the baby, too."

Her jade eyes sparkled from behind her glasses. "With a baby coming, I'm simplifying. Short hair's less work. But enough about me. How are things going with Jenna?"

"I think, uh, good. I mean, it's hard to tell right now but, yeah, good." He gulped some ice water. "I asked her to go to Indonesia."

"Mark! Okay, Mister, who are you and what did you do with my best friend?" she teased. "After months of budgeting and applying for funding, after reviewing dozens of applications and picking the best-matched team, you act on total impulse and invite Jenna along? Oh yeah, you're in love."

"This isn't just me wanting my, uh, girlfriend there. She'd be a real asset."

"Even better. So, she's not so different as you thought she was? When we talked on the phone—"

Adrienne broke off as a group of people took the chairs around them. Under her breath, she said, "Later. Maybe a drink after the dinner?"

"Can't. I'm meeting her."

"You can't evade me forever." She gave him a mock-scowl.

He grinned. "Not trying to. We'll find some time."

One of the newcomers asked him a question about his paper, and he refocused his attention. Soon, the whole group at the table was absorbed into a stimulating conversation.

Lunch was served: overcooked chicken in unidentifiable sauce. He smiled to himself, thinking of Jenna. Sometimes it was better not to taste your food.

Many hours later, Mark headed out to Spanish Banks, eager to see Jenna but nervous, too. So much depended on tonight's conversation. A whole future, in fact. She'd sounded great on the phone this morning, but she'd had a day to consider.

Driving along by the beach parking lots, he noted absently that even this late in the evening a number of people were out and about: strolling, cycling, rollerblading, walking dogs.

When he pulled into the last lot, he glanced around, not knowing what kind of car she'd be driving and wondering if she was there. When she didn't emerge from any of the parked ones, he reminded himself that a woman who didn't believe in schedules wasn't likely to be on time. Jenna wouldn't stand him up.

A classy black Mercedes sedan sped into the lot and parked beside the camper and he saw Jenna in the driver's seat.

He grinned widely, and she smiled back, and he knew everything was okay between them. Warmth flooded through him, centering in his heart.

She climbed out and he feasted on the sight of her: a flashing smile, her curly hair bright under the artificial lights in the parking lot, and those slim, tempting curves in a long-sleeved green tee over jeans. Eagerly, he caught her up in a hug and she squeezed back, lifting her face to his without a moment's hesitation.

He kissed her and a strong, warm current flowed between them. Love. Surely nothing else could feel like this. Before it could catch them up and carry them away and they ripped off each other's clothes in the parking lot, he regretfully eased his lips from hers.

She grinned up at him. "Coward."

"You know it." Hands resting happily on the upper curves of her butt, pelvis nudging hers as his cock—which didn't discriminate between public and private places—grew, he tilted his head toward the Mercedes. "Whose car?"

"Mom's. Lawyers have an image thing." Eyes twinkling, she wrinkled her nose. "No one else is allowed to drive it, but Dad and Merilee needed their cars, and Mom is in Ottawa tonight, so I stole it." Her arms circled him loosely. She dug her hands into the back pockets of his pants, and wriggled her hips suggestively against him. "Speaking of image, you clean up pretty well, Dr. Chambers. I wouldn't have recognized you but for the Westfalia."

Because he'd been presenting today, he'd worn tailored black pants, a long-sleeved blue cotton shirt, and a tie. He'd loosened the knot of the tie as he'd hurried to his car, but not taken the time to pull it off.

Jenna's fingers tugged at the knot, then she pulled the tie off. Draping it around her own neck, she went to work on the top button of his shirt.

He caught her hands in his. "Hey, are you planning on stripping me in public?"

"What, no skinny dipping tonight?"

About to point out that there were too many people around, he realized she might well be teasing. "Is that a joke?"

Her mouth crinkled. "Hey, you're catching on. Yeah, shocking people a little is fun. Getting arrested, not so much."

"Then should I ask why you're stripping me?"

"Maybe because you're overdressed for the beach." She ran the tip of her tongue around her lips suggestively. "Or maybe . . ."

He squeezed her captured hands, arousal mounting. "Oh yeah, I like that thought." He nudged his erection against her. "We could pull the curtains."

"Now you're talking."

He opened the camper door and they jumped inside. Hurriedly, they readied things—curtains drawn, bed down—then they tumbled eagerly onto the bed, hands tugging urgently at each other's clothing.

Murmuring, laughing, they managed to strip each other naked, then he lay her back on the bed and rose above her.

He hadn't turned on the light because it would seep through the curtains and might make a patrolling cop curious. As a result, he could barely see Jenna, and that was a real pity.

Still, when he lowered his body atop hers, he felt the familiar smooth, soft curves and sank into her as if he were coming home. The thought struck him that if they traveled the world together, they'd always be home because they'd have each other.

Surely, Jenna agreed. His feelings were so powerful, this connection between them so right, she had to feel the same. If she didn't, she wouldn't be here now, like this, spreading for him, gripping his shaft eagerly.

"I missed you," she murmured.

"Me, too."

The tip of his cock met slick heat, firm yet yielding flesh, then he was sliding inside her. He eased in slowly, inch by inch, feeling her open to him and grip him like a plush velvet glove.

A very steamy one, pulsing erotically around him, gripping and releasing, urging him to match the rhythm.

Slowly, he began to pump, drawing out each stroke so he slid almost all the way out, then back, in, deep, keeping the rhythm, deeper, as far as he could reach into her core.

She moaned, arched, threw her head back on the pillow. His lips took her exposed neck in gentle nibbles, concentrating on the spots he knew were especially arousing for her.

It was dark in here and he could barely see her, yet that made him even more attuned to each sensation.

He wouldn't kiss her lips. Not yet. If he did, he'd be swept up, swept away, and right now he wanted to be aware of every silky bit of skin he teased to arousal. Aware of each shiver, each soft gasp she gave. Of the sweet, slightly musky scent that rose from her skin.

Aware of her hands stroking his back, digging into mus-

cles, teasing the base of his spine, flirting with the crease between his butt cheeks.

She'd told him to live in the moment, to pay attention and
appreciate, and that was exactly what he was doing.

"So good, Jenna," he murmured against the pulse point at
the base of her throat, feeling the quick throbbing vibration
against his lips.

"On the weekend," he said, "I had a theory."

A giggle rippled through her. "A theory?"

"That you were scared of kissing me."

"Maybe you should test that theory, Science Guy."

"Maybe I should." He knew she expected him to go for
her mouth, but he fooled her by easing out of her and sliding
down a little so he could kiss the upper curve of a breast.

"Mmm, that's not so scary. You can do more of that. Try
an inch or two lower."

Obediently he headed for her nipple, teasing it with soft
kisses then tugging it gently into his mouth until she writhed
under him.

He did the same to her other nipple, then made his way
slowly down her body, drifting kisses across her soft skin.
Eventually he reached the tender skin of her inner thighs,
damp with her arousal. When she spread her legs in invitation, he raised his head to tease, "Not scared yet?"

"Scared I may die of sexual frustration," she said
breathily.

She wasn't the only one. His cock was so hard it ached.

"Can't have that." He swiped his tongue across her sex,
back and forth in broad strokes as she pressed needily
against him, body taut with aroused anticipation. When he
sucked her clit into his mouth, she gasped, tensed, and when
he flicked his tongue gently back and forth across it, she
broke with a cry of pleasure.

When the tremors faded, he slid up the bed again, hungry
for her mouth, desperate to be inside her again.

Her legs came up, hooking around his lower back, spreading her even wider, and he plunged eagerly into her. "God, Jenna, you're incredible."

As he tilted his head down toward hers, she whispered, "I love making love with you."

Making love. Hearing her say the words sent a thrill through him, a thrill of arousal and emotion. "Me, too."

"Kiss me," she said. "Kiss me, Mark, and carry me away."

"Oh, yeah." He brushed his lips across her chin. "First, tell me, was I right? Were you avoiding kissing me?"

"I was afraid of what happened."

"And now?" He poised his mouth just over hers, feeling the warm brush of her breath coming from between her parted lips.

"Maybe I still am." Her hands came up to curve against the sides of his face. "But I can't resist."

"Me, either."

She tugged him down that last inch. He touched his lips to hers and slipped his tongue into her mouth, finding hers waiting for him.

And then they flew on a magical journey of sensuality and emotion, and he knew he'd been right in trusting the instinct that had first attracted him to her. She was his mate, his partner, his love. She was as important to him as his first love, the ocean, and he had to make her part of his life.

It had taken him a lot of years to figure out what love was, and now he knew. There could be no other word for the emotion that filled his heart.

After, they held each other close until their breathing slowed. Should he ask her now about Indonesia? No, better to do it outside where the ocean could add its own subtle brand of persuasion.

"There's a beach out there," he said. "Want to walk and talk?"

"Sounds great. I've been running around doing errands all

day." She slipped off the bed and hunted for the clothes they'd flung aside earlier.

He'd brought jeans and put them on rather than his dress pants, then gathered up a light windbreaker. "It could get chilly. Do you want this?"

"You keep it. I have a sweatshirt in the car."

A few minutes later, they were walking barefoot toward the beach. Her fingers twined through his, warm and firm. When they stepped onto the sand, large grains scrunched under his feet. "Every beach in the world had its own unique composition, its distinctive texture. Color, too, though tonight it's too dark to really tell."

"I believe you, Science Guy. And its own magic."

"I believe you, Magic Girl."

In one direction, the lights of downtown glowed like thousands of fireflies against the night sky. By unspoken agreement, they turned in the other darker and less civilized direction. He sucked in a deep lungful of fresh ocean air.

"How's the symposium?" she asked, skirting a chunk of driftwood. "Did you knock 'em dead with your paper, Dr. Chambers?"

Was she interested, polite, or avoiding the subject of Indonesia? "It went over pretty well, yeah. I tried not to be too lecturish."

"You're kind of sexy when you lecture."

"Seriously? No, you're joking again."

She chuckled. "Actually, this time I'm not."

"Uh, okay. I guess that's good. Anyhow, the symposium's definitely worthwhile. There's some great research being done, worthwhile projects going on all over the world."

"And positive energy? All you folks getting together to save our friend?" She gestured toward the dark ocean beside them, breathing softly against the shore.

"Yeah. Lots of good energy." He wouldn't have put it that way before, but her description fit.

Knowing she'd been a little stressed about going home, he asked, "How about you? Is the family reunion going well?"

"Better than usual. I don't know why, but my sisters and I are getting along better. God knows, maybe we're actually growing up. Or maybe it's because it's the first time we've all worked together on something, and we want things to be wonderful for M&M." She broke off to exchange quiet good evenings with an older couple strolling in the opposite direction.

"How's it all coming with the wedding?"

"Great, and Tree wouldn't have it any other way. This afternoon she took me with her to make a final decision between two caterers. Can you believe it, she actually went with my judgment?"

She didn't wait for an answer. "Then I tried on my bridesmaid's dress, and it fits perfectly and it's really pretty. You know how horrendous they can sometimes be."

"Uh . . ."

She snorted. "What am I saying? You don't have a clue, do you? It's a girl thing."

"Okay." One thing he did know was that he wished he could see her in the dress. He wished he could be her date for the wedding. Not that he was a fan of weddings, but he knew there was something symbolic about being with a woman when someone close to her was tying the knot.

Of course, he couldn't be there, though. By Saturday, he'd be in Denpasar, Bali. Enough chitchat. He had to know where things stood. He gripped her hand more tightly. "Did you think more about Indonesia? Did you talk to your family?"

Her shoulder brushed his. "I mentioned it to my sisters."

"And?"

"They think you sound pretty cool."

"Me? Cool? Oh, come on."

She chuckled. "Trust me on this. You're cool, and you're doing something important."

He released her hand and slipped his arm around her. "I thought about it, too, and Jenna, I want to do it with you. Bali and everything we talked about. A future together, if things work out. What do you say?"

She put her arm around his waist, hooked a finger in a belt loop. "I'm so tempted. It'd be like"—she paused for a long moment—"a dream come true."

He let out his breath in a whoosh of relief. "Really? I'm glad. I thought your dream was, you know, going wherever the next whim took you." He hoped she wouldn't be insulted, but he didn't know how else to phrase it.

She shook her head. "That was a way of life. A happy, rewarding one, but not a dream. I'd given up on dreams."

"That's sad. Because of Travis?"

"No. Because of me. Maybe I thought I didn't deserve them. Maybe I didn't trust myself with another dream."

"And now you do?"

"I guess . . . I could be getting there."

They stopped walking and he turned to face her, resting his hands on her shoulders. "What are the dreams you gave up on?" he asked.

Her lips trembled, and she looked vulnerable in the moonlight. "Children. Love. But not the conventional way."

Dollies in the garden, not sitting around the tea table. "Adventures in interesting places."

She nodded, eyes wide as they searched his.

"Me, too," he said, feeling that warm sense of certainty again. "We're really so alike."

"I guess in the important ways we are," she said on a note of surprise. "But Mark, its scary to let myself dream again."

He touched his forehead to hers. "I'm not Travis. You can trust me. I won't hurt you. I don't know for sure where this relationship is going, but it feels so good. Like it's . . . as inevitable as the ebb and flow of the tides."

She nodded slowly. "It's felt that way from the beginning, when the universe sent us both into Marianne's Diner."

"Then trust in it. Trust in us."

He wanted her agreement, a tenderly passionate kiss to seal the deal.

Instead, he got, "Oh, God." She huffed out a sigh, then caught his hand in hers and began to walk again, tugging him along with her, the sand cool underfoot. "This has to be hard for you, too. Forging ahead on trust, with no project plan."

Okay, she wasn't sure yet. "Yeah, kind of. But someone's been teaching me to be more impulsive. You're a good influence."

"Huh. That's not something people usually say about me. Though Merilee did last night . . ." She cleared her throat. "Mark, I really like what's happening between us, but I don't want you inviting me to Indonesia just because we're, uh, maybe getting together. I want to know I'd be useful."

Maybe it wasn't her feelings for him she was uncertain about. Had her family been undermining her self-confidence again? He nodded strongly. "You'll be an asset to the team."

"Everyone else will be so much better qualified."

"You learn quickly. In Indonesia, that'll be enough." Thinking ahead, though . . . "But yeah, it'd be a good idea to take some courses whenever you get an opportunity." The more she learned, the more deeply she'd get involved, the more contribution she'd make, and the better she'd feel about herself.

"What kind of courses? You mean, I could study in Indonesia?"

She was that eager to get started? Thrilled, he squeezed her hand. "Maybe. Two of the team members are Indonesian and they'd have some suggestions. But I was thinking more of later on, once you have a better idea which direction you want to go in." She could register at a university and do distance ed. Almost anywhere their work took them, there'd be some kind of internet connection.

"Direction?"

"You know, the ocean itself, marine mammals, fish, economic aspects. This time, you can assist here and there, but you may decide you want to specialize."

"Specialize?"

Was he lecturing again? She was repeating his words as if he wasn't making sense. "Though, come to think of it, working with people is probably going to be where you fit best. You have a knack with people. So, maybe the educational and community liaison areas would be best for you. Are you good at picking up languages?"

Dryly, she said, "I can say *Voulez-vous couchez avec moi?* in ten different languages."

"Huh?"

"Joke. Mark, what are you talking about? This is a six month project. How many courses can I take, how much specializing can I do in that time period?"

"Sorry, I wasn't being clear. I meant after. After Indonesia. You've been jumping all over the place, doing good things but in an unfocused way, and without much training. Once you focus on one cause, you can get the training you need, and you'll be so much more effective."

She didn't respond, but her steps slowed, then stopped. She slid her hand free of his and faced him. "Let me get this straight," she said, face tilted up to him in the moonlight. "You want me to commit to one cause. Your cause."

Wasn't that what he'd been saying ever since he asked her to consider a future together? "Yeah. Then we can work together."

"Oh," she said flatly. "I should take on your cause so we can work together."

She sounded as if she had a problem, but he didn't understand what it was. "You're already an environmentalist. And you like helping people, and that's usually part of the projects too. This'll be perfect for you."

"Hmm. Perfect for me. Once I get all educated and focused and serious. In other words, it's time I grew up?" The words were spoken slowly with an almost deadly calm. Her tone was a warning of sorts, except he still didn't understand her problem.

Cautiously, he said, "Well, yeah."

"Shit." The word exploded out of her. "I'm not good enough for you."

"No!" He gripped her shoulders. "That's not what I said. You're great. Just a little, uh . . ."

He said, "unfocused" as she said "immature?"

"You're not immature, exactly. Just, uh . . ." How could he phrase it tactfully?

"A butterfly? I thought you liked butterflies."

"I do, but I'd rather not live with one."

"Oh, I don't see any danger of that," she spat out, wrenching herself from his grip. "If you got your hands on a butterfly, you'd net it and clip its wings."

She thought he wanted to do that? Angry himself now, he said, "God, Jenna, I don't want to tie you down and clip your wings. Just help you make your life count for more."

He could almost see steam pouring out of her ears, but he stumbled on. "You have so much to offer, and you're not making the most of it."

"Is that my duty? To make the most of my potential?"

"Uh . . . Why wouldn't you want to?"

"Because this is *me*." She flung her arms wide, eyes blazing brighter than the stars. "This is my potential. Some people actually like me the way I am. Just not my family, or you."

"I do like you. Jesus, didn't I tell you I was falling for

you?" He dragged a hand through his hair in frustration. "Damn, Jenna, I'm not perfect. I can be rigid. I'm not great with people. I suck at conversation." He snorted bitterly. "Which I'm proving right now. But hell, you've made me see I can change. Why won't you do the same?"

"Oh, big change, now you taste food. If you've changed because of me, it's to make your life *broader*." She planted her fists on her hips and glared. "You want to make mine narrow, to tie me down."

"No." He tried to explain. "To focus you."

"Same diff. You're just like my freaking parents. I'm not good enough for you unless I'm exactly the way you want me to be."

"Of course you're good enough. All I want is—" He broke off, not knowing how to finish that sentence.

"A woman your grandparents would approve of?"

It wouldn't hurt.

She gripped her head, shook it, and made an *aarrugghh* sound like a volcano about to erupt. "I was so freaking wrong about you!"

Bitterly, he said, "I guess I was wrong about you, too. You care more about flitting around having fun than making the world a better place."

"Yeah, exactly." She tossed her head. "Jesus, you're just like your grandparents were with your mom."

"Huh? You're not like Alicia. I'm not like them. What the hell are you talking about?" He was so damned confused. How had things blown up this way? Where had he and Jenna gone wrong? "I don't get it. I asked you to think about a future together, and it seemed to me you were doing that. You talked about a dream come true. I thought we were on the same track. What did you think I meant?"

"That we'd—" Her eyes were wide in the moonlight. She shook her head vigorously. "Shit, I don't know. Spend six months in Indonesia then, if things worked out with us, we'd . . . I don't know, go where the wind took us. Follow our dreams. I don't know!" She turned and stalked away from him, back in the direction of the parking lot.

Trying to figure out what she was talking about, he headed after her. "You know the ocean is my life's work. You didn't seriously think I'd . . . go to England and teach autistic kids?"

"I don't know what I thought," she said angrily. "I hadn't got that far ahead. I don't plan, Mark, you know that, and it turns out you're trying to *schedule* my entire freaking life!"

"You don't have the guts to commit to anything and see it through." As always, he spoke what he believed, but the moment the words left his mouth, he knew they'd piss her off.

Sure enough . . . "Oh, I'm deeply committed to walking away from you and never speaking to you again."

She strode as fast as a person could walk in the soft sand and he kept pace. Where before he'd felt a current of warm energy between them, now he felt spiky tension.

The thing was, he didn't want a woman who couldn't commit. Jenna had bedazzled him, and he'd stopped being rational. She'd never hidden who she was; he just hadn't wanted to see it.

She stopped dead and glared at him again. "Don't walk with me!"

"Jesus. Fine. Go." He stayed put as she again stalked off. And he'd thought he was falling in love with this woman. She was a child, and she'd never grow up.

I drove home furious with Mark and myself. How could I have been so stupid as to let myself dream? To think about love and kids? Bitter tears stung my eyes, but I refused to let them fall. Mark didn't want *me*; he wanted to manipulate me into being someone who fit his life.

And I'd been stupid. This was all my own damn fault.

Again. Just like with Travis, I'd fallen for a guy, and it had shot my judgment all to hell. If I'd been thinking rather than caught up in some romantic dream, I'd have realized that, of course, for him, the future meant his work. His projects. His choices. With me trailing along behind. Wings clipped, tethered, rather than flying free.

Stupid, stupid, stupid. How many times was I going to let a man—no, my own stupidity—kill my dreams?

When I drove up the driveway, eyes aching with the need to cry, I saw Merilee's and Matt's cars. When I pushed the control to open the garage door, Dad's car was there too. It was late, and I hoped everyone had gone to bed because the last thing I felt like was talking.

Unfortunately, when I walked into the kitchen, Mom, Dad, and Tree were at the kitchen table with mugs, a teapot that smelled of Lady Grey, and a plate of Digestive biscuits.

For a moment, surprise cut through the pain. "Mom? You're not supposed to be home until tomorrow."

"I finished early and changed my flight." She rose, trim in a tailored, navy skirt suit and white blouse though her stockinged feet were shoeless, and gave me a hug. "It's good to see you, Jenna."

For a moment I wanted to cling there and be comforted. But that wasn't how things worked with her. Every ounce of comfort was accompanied by a liberal splash of interrogation, criticism, or advice.

Sure enough, she said, "I hope you brought my car back safely."

I pushed out of her arms and glared at Tree who said, "I didn't tell her."

Mom said with a trace of humor, "I'm a mother. I have eyes in the back of my head. You girls should know that."

"Dad?" I glanced at him.

"I came back and your mother's car was gone. I didn't know you'd borrowed it."

How had absent-minded Dad suddenly started noticing cars that weren't there? And how prosaic this car conversation felt, when I was dying inside. All the same, if I concentrated on it, I could hold my feelings inside.

"Sorry, I know I shouldn't have borrowed it, but I needed to go out, and everyone else was using theirs."

"Out? To see this new man of yours?"

Again, I glared at Tree. She wrinkled her nose. "Okay, I told her that one."

"As if I hadn't figured it out myself," Mom said briskly, getting another mug from the cupboard and pouring tea for me. "Your e-mails weren't exactly subtle. Sit, Jenna."

I wanted to go to bed and cry in peace, but it was hard to say no to my mother. Indecisively, I hovered by the table and picked up the mug.

"Is it true?" she asked. "This man's a marine biologist, and you're thinking of going off to Indonesia with him? How long have you known him? And why don't you look happier about it?"

"No." The word came out heavily, and Tree shot me a startled gaze. "No, it's not going to happen." I put the mug down, tea untasted. "It was all a mistake." I fought to hold back tears as I made for the door.

"Jenna?" Mom called.

"A stupid mistake." I didn't turn around. "It's over, and I don't want to talk about it."

I hurried up the stairs, seeking the sanctuary of my room before I let the tears fall. I was almost there when quick footsteps sounded behind me. "Jenna?" Tree said quietly.

When I opened the door to my room, she came in behind me, flipped on the light, and closed the door. "Are you okay?"

"Sure, of course," I snapped, blinking against moisture. "He's just another guy."

She gazed into my eyes, concern on her face. "He isn't. You made that clear last night."

Vibrating with pain and the need to cry, I said, "I was wrong, okay?"

"Maybe wrong to trust him." She touched my shoulder tentatively. Theresa had never been the demonstrative type. "But, Jenna, you care for him. He's different. And now he's hurt you."

Shit. Shit, shit, shit. Heartbroken, I couldn't come up with a flip response or hold back the tears any longer.

"Oh, Jenna." She put her arms around me. "I'm sorry."

Cautiously, I rested my head on her shoulder, a place it had rarely been. It felt surprisingly natural, and I slid my arms around her waist and snuggled closer. "Thanks." I heaved a deep sigh, sniffled and, trying to convince both of us, forced out, "I'll get over it."

"He's a jerk."

"You can say that again."

"Want to talk about it?"

If I did, she'd take Mark's side. My whole family thought exactly the same as him: that I needed to grow up. Why couldn't anyone love me for exactly who I was? "No. But thanks." Slowly I lifted my head and tried to curve my tear-damp lips. "Thanks for the hug."

"Any time. And if you can't sleep and change your mind about wanting to talk, come wake me up."

She rubbed my shoulder in a comforting gesture, then left me alone.

I looked around my bedroom. Travel posters with happy families on tropical beaches. Dreams. Childish dreams.

Never again.

I darted over to the nearest wall, grabbed the corner of a poster, and ripped. Tears raining down, I tore every single poster off every wall.

That was what I should have done when I was seventeen. Then, I'd thought I'd let the old dreams go, but I never really had. They'd lingered on the walls of my old room, lingered in the corners of my heart just waiting for Mark to reawaken them.

Never again. Never again would I let a man make me vulnerable. Make me hope.

A strange, cold peace filled me.

Everyone had wanted me to grow up. Well, I'd finally done it. In my own way.

When I woke, feeling tired and drained, it was later than usual. But life went on. I was a new woman. A battered but stronger, smarter one.

Thank heavens for the wedding. I'd tell Tree to keep me as busy as she possibly could.

I showered and dressed in old clothes from my Vancouver closet: white capris and a sleeveless blue shirt. Then I headed downstairs. This morning was not a time for chamomile tea. I needed coffee. Serious coffee. The kind Mark brewed in his French press.

Would I ever drink coffee again without thinking of him?

I stepped through the kitchen doorway into the sunny room and stopped in surprise. At this hour, I'd have expected Mom and Dad to be off to work, but Mom was still there. Along with my three sisters. No Matt and no Nav.

The women had clearly broken off in the middle of conversation when they saw me and now, from seats around the kitchen table, they all stared at me.

"Yes, it's over with Mark and yes, I'm fine. Subject closed. Sorry I'm late." I went to the coffeemaker, paused, then decided the need for a megadose of caffeine overcame any stupid associations with Mark. As I poured myself a mug, I said, "What's on the agenda for today? Mom, did Tree rope you in, too?"

"Not exactly," she said. "Get some food and come sit down."

Our family was casual about breakfasts. Usually, no one cooked. So it was no surprise to see a litter of bagels, whole grain bread, cereal boxes, and fruit on the counter. Nothing appealed to me.

Damn, I wasn't going to let Mark kill my appetite. Or, if he did, I wasn't about to let my family know. I swung the fridge door open and peered inside, searching for something to tempt me. Aha. I reached into the back and pulled out a plastic container with leftover chocolate mousse.

I opened it, stuck a spoon into it, and came to the table, taking a seat beside Tree, across from Kat and Merilee. Mom, of course, was at one end.

"For breakfast?" Tree said.

"Let her be," Mom said.

"Wish I'd seen it first." Kat darted her coffee spoon across the table toward my mousse.

I curved my arms protectively around it. "Well, you didn't."

Merilee laughed softly, and we all joined in. How about that? I could laugh.

Then Mom cleared her throat. "Jenna, about this man—"

No, please no. "It's over," I said flatly. "I'm not running off to Indonesia. Forget about it. Now, let's get going on whatever we're supposed to be doing this morning."

"This is what we're supposed to be doing," she said, looking . . . softer, somehow, and less certain than usual. "We, uh, we're here for you."

Here for me? As in . . . "You stayed home from the office because . . ."

"Because you care for this man. You thought he was different, special. And he hurt you. We want to help."

"We do," Kat said, reaching over again, this time to rest her hand on mine.

I glanced around the table, and they all nodded. My mom, my sisters.

Tears burned the backs of my eyes. I forced them back. "Thanks. That's really nice. But, I'm okay."

Mom leaned forward, the lawyer and the mother in her both knowing how to command attention. "This is the only time you've ever said you cared for a man. Always, since that time you ran away with that boy in high school, you've said you're not a one-man girl, that you want to sample all the fish in the sea."

Did she have to use an ocean analogy? "A smorgasbord." I tried to smile. "Still sounds good to me."

"But it hurts," Tree said. "You cared for him, and he hurt you. When that happened to me, with Jeffrey, you all took my side and helped me through it."

It had been one of the rare times when our entire family came together and agreed on something. But that had been so clear-cut. Her new husband had betrayed Tree by appropriating her research. Of course we took her side.

"We've all been hurt by men," Mom said. Then, with a quick smile, "Except Merilee, who had the good sense to choose Matt and hang onto him."

My brain was slow this morning, so it took a moment for my mother's words to sink in. "You've been hurt by a guy? Not Dad?" I asked, horrified.

She smiled quickly, genuinely. "No, of course not."

"Mom?" Kat said, and all of us stared at our mother.

"The first," I breathed.

"What first?" Merilee sounded lost.

"Her first love," I answered, seeing the truth on our mother's face. "The one who ended up not being the real one."

Tree said, sounding snappish, "Why didn't I know about this?"

"None of you did," Mom said briskly, "because it wasn't relevant."

"But Jenna knew," Merilee said, a whine in her voice.

"Only by e-mail a couple of days ago," Mom said, "and because it became relevant."

"You have to tell us," Kat urged her. "This is family history. We should know."

"Does Dad know?" Tree asked.

"Of course." When Mom rose and headed over to the coffeemaker, I realized for the first time that, below her softly tailored ivory blouse, she was in jeans rather than her usual suit skirt or pants. She brought the pot over and refilled all our mugs, then rejoined us.

"It's not a big deal," she said. "Your basic story of foolish first love. My first year sociology professor had a teaching assistant whom I was attracted to. He and I got involved. It would have been unwise even if he'd been sincere, but he wasn't. I thought he'd singled me out from all those first years, that I was particularly bright, pretty, special." She shook her head impatiently. "All those ridiculous things we tell ourselves when our heads are in the clouds, and we're seeing what we want to see."

Yes. That's how it had been with Mark.

"That's exactly how it was with Jeffrey," Tree said.

Kat nodded. "That's how it was for me, with so many of those egotistical jerks I dated. Why didn't you tell us this before, Mom?"

Mom glanced at Theresa. "Your romance with Jeffrey happened so quickly; I only met him at the registry office wedding. I didn't know there was anything wrong until he betrayed you." Then she turned to Kat. "As for you, I've said over and over that you were making poor choices. You didn't want to listen."

"It's hard to listen when you're being criticized," I said,

understanding that Kat and I had more in common than I'd realized.

Kat shot me a surprised glance. "Yes, it is. And Mom, you never said you'd made the same mistake. If you had, I might have paid more attention."

Our mother, normally so vigorous and competent, looked uncertain again. "Perhaps I should have." She gazed from Kat to Tree. "Perhaps I should have told you, too. Maybe I could have helped you get over your bitterness so you could give other men a chance. Like I did with your dad."

Tree nodded. "It was hard to give Damien a chance. But I'm so glad I did."

"I'm glad you did too, dear," Mom said. "And Kat, I'm glad you finally found a man who realizes how special you are." Gaze encompassing me and Merilee now, she went on. "It's not such a bad thing to make a mistake. Not if you learn from it, so you'll know and appreciate the real thing when it comes along."

Kat and Tree nodded, but Merilee just looked troubled. It must be hard for her to identify with this conversation.

Tree nudged my shoulder with hers. "Do better than I did. Mark was your first, like Jeffrey was mine. Don't let him mess you up for years and years."

Did I want to tell them the truth after all this time? This felt so rare and special, all the women in the family gathered around the kitchen table sharing confidences. Sharing mistakes, which wasn't something Mom and Tree, in particular, often did.

Slowly, I said, "No, Mark was my second. Travis was my first."

"Travis?" Merilee asked. "Who's Travis?"

Tree and Kat shook their heads, but Mom said, "The boy you ran away with. The one with the motorbike. Your dad and I wondered how serious you were about him. Whether you were in love or just rebellious and looking for fun. When you came back—"

"You blew it all off," Kat said. "I remember now. You said you'd had a fun summer hanging around the beach in the Okanagan, but Travis was a loser and it was time to find another guy."

"Or guys," Mom said. "That was when you decided you didn't want to tie yourself down with one boy." She captured my hand and gripped it warmly. "What happened, Jenna?"

I took a deep breath, then let it out and told them the simple version. "He cheated on me. I loved him and he told me he loved me, but he was cheating on me and he ran off with some other girl." I gave a wry half-smile. "Like you said, Mom, just your basic old stupid first love." Except, of course, it had been much more. It had cost me so much.

For a moment, I was tempted to tell them the rest of it, about the PID, the surgery, my inability to have children. But this closeness, this sharing of confidences was so new, I wasn't ready to trust it. Trust didn't always work out well for me.

"Anyhow," I said with a shrug, "I figured, you can enjoy men without setting yourself up for all that pain. And I definitely have." It had been easy. No man had tempted me into loving him, not until Mark. That's how it would be again, once I got over him.

"Enjoy," Kat repeated. "But it's a whole different thing when you love each other." Her chestnut brown eyes searched mine. "You know that. That's what you felt with Mark."

I shrugged again, unable to deny it, or the ache in my heart that made my eyes damp.

"What did he do?" Mom asked. "Can I take him to court and kick his butt?"

She startled a laugh out of me and my sisters. "Sadly, no. But thanks for the thought."

"Come on, Jenna," Merilee said, blue eyes warm. "We want to help."

"We're not your old bitchy sisters," Kat said, her own eyes twinkling. "We're the new, improved version."

I sensed truth in that. Enough that I'd take a chance with them. "I thought he loved me for who I was."

Kat nodded. "He said those nice things, like about you being a butterfly."

"And that was a compliment?" Mom asked.

"Butterflies pollinate flowers," Tree explained. "He was making an analogy. Jenna flits from project to project, but whenever she lands she does good in the world."

"That's rather nice," Mom said slowly, then leveled her steady gaze on me. "And it's also pretty accurate. A fact we don't give you enough credit for."

"Uh, thanks."

"But that sounds as if he does love you for who you are," Merilee said. "I'm lost."

"I thought the same thing. But it turns out, he wants more than a butterfly." I shook my head, frustrated and hurt all over again. "He comes across as kind of unconventional— he's not big on marriage, doesn't want to settle in one place—but what he really wants is a woman who'll do exactly what he wants. Someone who sticks to one cause—his cause, of course—and who studies and specializes and devotes her life to it the way he does."

Silence greeted me. So I said, "I know, I know, you think the same way. He said I should grow up, just like you've been saying forever." I shook my head, pissed off at myself. "I shouldn't have told you this. Of course you'll take his side."

Merilee leaned forward and took one of my hands in both

of hers. "I take your side. You should be whoever you want to be, not what he says you should be."

"True," Tree said. "You shouldn't change just to please some man. Or—sorry, Mom—to please your parents. But Jenna, you do have talents and an engaging personality and lots of energy. If you did find one thing you felt passionate about and devoted yourself to it, think how much you could accomplish."

A compliment, with a hidden *but*. I had lots of potential, but I wasn't making the most of it. Gee, where had I heard that before?

"And you do care about the environment," Merilee said. "You're, like, a nature-lover."

Kat nodded. "You are. But you don't want to devote your life to that cause?"

"I . . . I'm saying, no one gets to tell me what I should do."

"No," she said. "They don't."

We were all silent for a few minutes. Mom got up, went to the cupboard, and came back with a box of chocolate Milano cookies. When she opened it, we all took one. I sipped coffee, ate chocolate, and glanced around at the faces of four women who'd put aside everything else—Mom's job, Merilee's wedding plans—because they cared about me.

Life still sucked, but this, right now, was a pretty amazing moment.

Mom handed me another cookie. "Does he love you?"

"Not any longer. But . . . yeah, he'd said he was falling in love with me, and that's how I feel—felt—too. But I don't want *I love you, but* love!"

"What?" she asked.

I put the cookie down. "This is going to sound rude, especially this morning when you're being so nice to me, but I don't know how else to say it. I mean the kind of thing I've heard all my life. *I love you, but you're not good enough.*"

"Jenna—" Her brow furrowed. "Is that how I've made you feel?"

I swallowed hard. "Yeah. You and Dad." My sisters, too, but then we all picked on each other pretty equally.

"You've made all of us feel that way," Tree said quietly.

"What?" I turned to her.

"Damn," Mom said vehemently.

"Sorry," Tree said. "This is about Jenna and Mark."

"You're right," Mom said. "But what the two of you just said makes me think. Of course your dad and I love you. You're our wonderful, beautiful daughters. It's because we love you so much that we worry about you, want you to be happy, want you to be everything you can be. And so . . ." She sighed. "And so we push. Perhaps we push too hard. Or we do it wrong."

She picked up her coffee mug, gripped it in both hands, then put it down again, and we four sat in silence. Had Mom ever before admitted she and Dad might be wrong?

"For that, I'm sorry," she said.

My mouth fell open. "Mom?"

She focused on me, eyes sharp. "However, loving someone doesn't necessarily mean you think they're perfect just as they are."

"That's true," Kat said.

"Yeah, right," I said. "You only say that because you kept picking those seriously flawed guys. Now you have Nav, and he seems pretty perfect to me. Creative, successful, super nice, gorgeous, he's even got that great accent, and he adores you just the way you are."

She snorted.

"Kat?" I said.

"In Montreal, Nav dressed like a starving student and he had shaggy hair and a beard and mustache that covered half his face. We argued all the time because I said appearance was important, and he said I was obsessed with it. Turns out, he had issues stemming from his parents and a former girlfriend."

When I opened my mouth to ask, she waved a hand. "A story for later. As for him adoring me the way I am, yes, Nav did love me. But he sure didn't think I was perfect. He got me to take a long, hard look inside myself and confront some insecurities. He helped me figure out why I'd chosen the kind of men I did, the ones who were bad for me. So, we both did some changing." She shot me a pointed look. "Some growing up."

"So did Damien and I," Tree said. "Another long story, but we learn from each other and we're better people for having met."

"You're more confident," I said, beginning to understand. "Not about your work—you were always confident about that—but about yourself as a woman." I picked up the cookie Mom had given me and began to nibble.

Tree nodded. "And even with my work, I'm moving in a different direction so I can reach more people and, hopefully, help more people. Damien and I are doing that together."

Theresa Fallon, working with a man again? She'd never done that since her ex betrayed her. Wow, she'd really dealt with some heavy trust issues.

Mom rested her hand on my forearm. "Is that what Mark hopes for with you? Does he have a similar vision, of the two of you as partners doing something worthwhile."

He did. But . . . I wasn't that kind of person. Was I? A person shouldn't have to change their basic nature to be in a relationship. I turned to Merilee. "You haven't said anything, M. How about you and Matt? Have each of you changed, learned from each other?"

"We grew up together, learned everything together. If we changed, it was day by day, in small ways, so we never noticed." She sucked her lips inward and pressed them together, the way she did when she was thinking hard about something. "For all of you, you knew who you were as grown women, then you met these great guys. For me, I have no idea who I'd have been as a woman if I hadn't known Matt."

"You've always been a unit," I said. "That's how it worked for you two, but I don't want that. I'm independent, a free spirit." I glanced around the table. "A flake, if that's what you want to call it. Maybe, just maybe, with Mark I felt a craving to really love a guy and have him love me back, but I don't want to be half of a unit. Especially when he's the leader and I just follow along."

"Each couple finds their own way," Mom said. "Your dad and I have completely different jobs and interests and we're very independent, but we support each other one hundred percent. Kat and Nav have very different jobs, too. Theresa and Damien have built separate careers, but they're going to work on a project as a team. It'll challenge them. They're both intelligent, strong-minded people. They'll fight."

Tree chuckled. "Count on it."

"And the product they come up with," Mom went on, "will be a joint one and better than either of them could have achieved alone."

Tree nodded. "That's how it could be with you and Mark. If that's what you wanted. You don't have to be the follower; you'd bring your own skills and talents and make a team."

It did sound appealing. Two independent people with complementary skills working together as a team. On environmental projects . . . and maybe on raising children. My heart lifted at the thought. Then it dropped again. For Mark and I to be a team, I'd have to become the person he wanted me to be. The person Mom and Dad had always wanted me to be. Gently, I touched the butterflies on my shoulder. No one should have to give up their basic self in order to win love.

"But it has to be what you want," Mom said. "You know what I'd suggest, don't you?"

"Make a pro and con list," Kat said promptly.

Now, there was familiar, if annoying, ground. But this morning, emotionally exhausted and feeling more in tune with my mom and sisters than ever before, it wasn't in me to be annoyed. "I haven't heard that for a while."

"Because every time I started to say it," Mom said dryly, "you stormed off, climbed into Mellow Yellow, and disappeared somewhere. I know. That kind of decision-making process is mine, and you've always preferred a, shall we say, less structured one?"

"I trust in the universe, and it rarely lets me down."

"It sent you Mark," Mom said.

"Now you just have to figure out what you're going to do with him," Kat said.

"If you change your mind and want to make a pro and con list," Tree said, "we'll all help."

"Uh, this is going to sound rude," I aimed for a joking tone, "but why are y'all suddenly being so nice to me?"

Tree and Kat exchanged glances, then Kat spoke. "I guess we've mellowed since we got together with Nav and Damien. We realized some things." She glanced at Mom. "Like, that each of us had some sister-type issues that it was time to outgrow."

"Hallelujah," Mom said. "In your own ways, you were always so competitive." Then she grimaced slightly. "I suppose your Dad and I had something to do with that, putting so much pressure on you."

None of us spoke, then Tree squared her shoulders. "That's true. None of us is perfect, not even the two of you. But we all love each other, and we can be better people. Such as"—she nodded toward Mom—"staying home from the office to help one of your daughters who's hurting."

"I should have done it more," she admitted.

None of us responded. After a moment, she said, "Should I make more coffee?"

"I'm coffeed out," Merilee said, and the rest of us nodded.

Mom gave me a tentative smile. "How are you doing, Jenna?"

"I'm confused. Last night, I told myself I'd been stupid, and I was never going to let myself love a man again."

"That sounds lonely," Merilee said softly.

"I wasn't lonely in the past. I was having fun. Then I met Mark and . . . I barely know him but I've never felt this way before." Now, the prospect of a future without him did feel lonely. I propped my elbows on the table, rested my face in my hands, and sighed. "How do you know if a man's the right one?"

All four of them exchanged glances. Kat said, "For me, it was like a sudden blinding revelation—of something that should have been obvious for a while. Theresa?"

"It grew from the moment I first saw Damien. Really quickly, like it was inevitable. I've never felt anything like it."

I nodded. That was how it had been for me, with Mark. "Merilee? No point asking you, I guess, since you and Matt chose each other when you were seven. You've been like Siamese twins."

"Best friends who grew up together," Mom said. "Right, Merilee?"

"Yes. And how about you, Mom? How did you know Dad was the one?"

"I made a pro and con list," she said promptly.

"Oh God, Mom," I said, then I noticed her eyes were twinkling. "You're teasing, aren't you?"

"A little. Honestly, I did make a list. But only after my heart had spoken. You know me, I'm very practical, so I made a list to make sure I wasn't getting carried away and making a bad choice." She smiled at me. "So I guess, in answer to your question, we each had our own way of knowing. Only you can know for sure if Mark is your special man."

I sighed. He couldn't be. My special man would love me for who I was. Mark had said he was falling for me, but then made it clear he'd only let himself fall the rest of the way if I turned into a different person.

After the last hour of conversation, nothing had really changed in the end. I heaved another sigh.

Mom's lips curved sympathetically. "That doesn't sound encouraging. Have we helped at all, dear?"

I reached for her hand and squeezed it, then forced a smile for her and my sisters. "Yeah, because you showed me you care, and you all shared things. Personal things." Even if I never saw Mark again, I felt so much happier about my family.

And chances were that I wouldn't see him. The way we'd left things last night, he wasn't likely to get in touch with me. And I had no reason in the world for tracking him down. Besides, he'd soon be off to Indonesia.

Cute female scientists and local women would flirt with him and he'd be oblivious, but eventually one of them would break through. They'd become lovers. And yes, damn it, I was jealous.

Movement caught my attention. Merilee was toying with an uneaten cookie, turning it end over end. She'd stayed quiet for most of the conversation, big blue eyes looking from face to face, expression sober. Here we were, discussing my pathetic love life, when she was getting married on Saturday. Time to stop wallowing in self-pity and think about someone else.

I got up and wrapped an arm around her shoulders. "Hey, sis, enough of me hogging the conversation. Rumor has it there's a wedding coming up, and about a million things left to do. You have an army of workers here, and I know General Tree has a plan. Tree, pull it out and give us our marching orders."

Tuesday afternoon at the end of the closing remarks, Adrienne said to Mark, "We're going for a drink."

"We are?" Much as he liked Adrienne, he was depressed and pissed off and not in the mood to socialize. "My grandparents are expecting me for dinner."

"They eat at seven thirty. It's only five o'clock. Something's wrong and you need to talk."

"I do?" He felt more like licking his wounds in private. For the first time in his life, he'd laid his heart on the line and what had Jenna done? Drop-kicked it back.

"You do." Adrienne took him by the arm and pulled him along. They exchanged goodbyes with a few colleagues as she tugged him past the hotel bar where others from the symposium were finding tables. Then she took him out the front door, down the street a couple of blocks, and into another hotel. Its bar was quiet, and she chose a table at the back. When a waitress appeared promptly, she ordered a cranberry and soda. "Mark?"

Though he wasn't much of a drinker, today he'd have gone for a double Scotch. But he was driving, so instead said, "A beer."

The waitress began to list off choices and he broke in. "The first one." Who cared what it was?

As soon as she left, Adrienne said, "You've been upset all day. What happened?"

He sighed. "We broke up."

"Why? I thought everything was going so well." Her jade eyes narrowed in concern behind the lenses of her glasses, and her brow creased below the fringe of short, spiky red hair.

"So did I." He took a nut from the bowl on the table and ate it without tasting it.

"Come on, what did you say? What did she say?"

"I wanted her to go to Indonesia and work on the coral reef project." He shook his head, remembering his own idiocy. "Damn, Adrienne, I told her I was falling for her. I talked about the future. And at first she seemed keen, then she got all pissed off." In the end, he was just another guy—like the Greek sailor, the French chef. He'd only been with her three days. It shouldn't hurt this much.

He took the beer glass the waitress handed him, and had a long swallow.

"Pissed off at what?" Adrienne asked.

"Hell if I know."

"What did you say right before she got mad?"

He drank again, thinking back. "She's been unfocused, working on a lot of different projects. Environment, kids, abused women. I pointed out how much more effective she'd be once she focused on one thing, got the relevant education, and so on."

"Hmm." Her eyes were still narrowed. "Is that what she wants to do?"

"I thought it was what we'd been talking about, but apparently not. You know my communication skills suck," he said bitterly. "She's all about freedom and variety. She doesn't want to focus, doesn't want to be tied down. Doesn't want to make the most of her potential." What it came down to was that she didn't want to be with him.

She winced. "Your words or hers?"

"Both, I guess. We were kind of, uh, slinging words back and forth." His mouth twisted. "It wasn't pretty."

"You were being judgmental."

"Yeah, I guess. So was she, though," he said defensively.

"About my way of life. Anyhow, bottom line, she doesn't want to change."

"And you want her to change." She lifted her glass and sipped. "Which you told her."

"I was being honest. And," he leaned forward, "damn it, Adrienne, I wanted to be with her. Right from the beginning, she was special. It was like she bewitched me and—" He snorted. "Yeah, and I lost my brain. The chemistry, the love-making, the sheer fun of being with her—"

"Fun?" she interrupted. "I'm not sure I've ever heard you use that word."

"My grandparents tried to drum it out of my vocabulary." Then, when she opened her mouth, he held up a hand. "I know. Judgmental again. Sorry. Anyhow, yeah, I was bewitched. I began to see her as a partner I could make a life with. Work, love, kids. She's the only woman I've ever met that I imagined a future with, and it was pure fucking fantasy."

He reached out automatically toward the bowl of nuts, and Adrienne slapped his hand lightly. "Stop it, you'll spoil your appetite for dinner."

"Huh?" He glanced down and realized the bowl was almost empty. "Did I eat those?" He hadn't tasted a single one.

"Yeah." Keeping her hand over the bowl, she said, "You thought you were falling in love with her, and that maybe she felt the same way?"

He sighed. "Yeah. What an idiot. Obviously, she didn't."

She sipped again, her furrowed brow telling him she was thinking. Then she put the glass down and leaned forward. "Mark, you want her to change. How about you? Do you see yourself making any changes?"

"Yeah. Being more flexible and spontaneous, more open to creative input. Trying to be more attuned to people, like she is. Enjoying the moment more." He gave a ragged laugh.

"Enjoying life more. At least that was the plan, when I imagined sharing life with her." Now . . . if he lived that way, it'd only remind him of Jenna and a broken heart. Shit, he was screwed.

"Those are good things. Did she tell you you had to do them?"

"No. Teased me, though. And got me doing things I wouldn't have."

"Hmm." She drummed her fingers on the table for a minute. "How would you have reacted if she said she didn't want you to present your paper yesterday, she wanted the two of you to go on a picnic?"

"What?" What was Adrienne talking about? "She'd never do that."

"Going on a picnic would be being flexible and spontaneous and living in the moment. Why wouldn't she ask you to do that?"

"Because she knows how important my work is to me."

"Everyone who knows you realizes that. What you're saying is, she respects who you are."

"I guess."

Her brows rose.

Was she saying he didn't . . . ? "Oh."

"So the question is," she said, "do you respect who Jenna is? Do you love her for who she is, or will you only love her if she changes? Who's the woman who made you fall in love?"

A good question, and one he'd have to think about. One thing was clear, though. "If she doesn't change, we can't be together."

"Maybe not in the way you envisioned it. But every relationship's different. Remember when you dated that woman who wanted you to work at a university, buy a house, settle down? That was her image of the future, but it didn't work for you. Now you have an image of the future, and it doesn't work for Jenna. You can break up. Or you can consider different images."

"You mean, be partners but she wouldn't always work on projects with me? She'd be doing something else, somewhere else?" Being a butterfly. Insecurity reared its head. "How could I . . . hold onto her if I wasn't with her? She's never been into monogamy. She's beautiful and fun and smart and she'll always have lots of guys after her."

She gave a snort of disgust. "You want to hold onto her by chaining her to the bed? Or maybe locking her into a chastity belt? Get a grip, Mark."

"No, of course not, but . . ." Jenna had accused him of wanting to clip her wings. He picked up his glass, tilted it, and realized it was empty. When had he drunk his beer?

"It's always about trust. Whether you live in the same house or on opposite sides of the world. I'm here in a bar with you. Instead, I could be with some gorgeous woman who's fascinating and brilliant and is totally coming onto me. Maybe I'd feel attracted, even aroused. But if she says, 'Let's go get a room,' am I going with her?"

He shook his head.

"Why not?" She held up her left hand and wiggled her wedding ring. "Because of this?"

"No. Because you love Laura."

Her face crinkled into a smile. "You're not so dumb after all."

He sure as hell didn't feel very smart. "Now I'm really mixed up. What do I do?"

The smile faded to sympathy. "I wish the two of you had more time, like Laura and I did when we got together. If love and trust develop over time, you can be more sure they'll stand the tests. Distance, sexy come-ons from other people, quarrels, whatever."

"In two days I'll be on a plane to Bali."

"You either need time, or you have to take a leap of

faith." She sighed. "And I know you're not the type to leap. I can relate to that because I'm not either." She rose, a little awkward with her pregnant belly, and came around the table to hug his shoulders. "Maybe she isn't the right woman, Mark."

He rested his head on her arm, feeling hollow and achy inside. A leap of faith? No, he couldn't do that. And time had run out for him and Jenna. "I guess she's not."

She squeezed his shoulders, then released him. "I need to get going. Laura and I are having dinner with friends."

"And I need to get back to my grandparents." All he wanted was to be alone. Maybe he'd plead a headache and retreat to his room.

"What would they think of Jenna?"

"They wouldn't approve."

"That's what I figured. But don't let them make your decisions for you. And remember, you're not them. I like the idea of you being more spontaneous and flexible. For what it's worth, I think Jenna's been good for you."

He shook his head. He felt as battered and achy as if he'd been hit by a bus. No, Jenna had not been good for him.

Chapter 14

Wednesday night, I again sat a table with my family—or at least Mom, Tree, and Kat—as well as Matt's mom Adele. It was M's combination bridal shower and stagette, hosted by a friend of M's who'd convinced her parents to close down their cozy Italian bistro for the night.

As we drank fruity martinis and Merilee tore into the pile of gifts, I tried not to let the others see how tired and depressed I was.

Thank God for Tree's project plan because it had kept me busy for the past two days. I'd tried to be upbeat for Merilee's sake, joking to my family that I was busy with that pro and con list. In fact, I had even gone so far as to pull out a piece of paper, draw a line down the middle, and write "Pro" on one side and "Con" on the other.

Then, after staring at it for ten minutes, I'd ripped it up. Though I hadn't written a word, big black letters filled my brain: *He doesn't really love me.* At least with my family, it had always been *I love you, but.* With Mark, it was *I'll love you if.* If I became the person he thought I should be.

God, I felt shitty. I'd been right on Monday night. I needed to banish him from my thoughts, stop dreaming childish dreams, and get on with the amazing life I'd been living before he entered it. For once, the universe had screwed up royally when it sent me that man.

Merilee was laughing and blushing as she opened gifts like edible massage oil and his and her leopard print thongs.

"Damien hates thongs," Tree said, "but he'd look hot in leopard print briefs. Maybe I'll do some shopping, for when he gets back."

Merilee's next gift was vaginal balls. "Ooh," Kat exclaimed, "I wonder how those would combine with tantric sex?"

I forced a smile, genuinely happy that my sisters all had wonderful men who loved them, men they could play fun sex games with and make passionate love with.

I'd thought Mark and I were heading that way. Until I realized he didn't think I was good enough for him.

As I watched Kat, I remembered something she'd said about her and Nav. How they'd argued about things like her choices in men and the importance of appearance. They'd disagreed and they'd pushed and challenged each other. She said they'd both confronted some tough issues. But neither had said they'd only love the other if they changed.

That was how I'd interpreted what Mark had said. But now I wondered if I was being fair. Had he been saying I wasn't good enough or telling me he saw something in me, some deeper potential, that I'd never let myself see? Though I'd called myself a free spirit—a person who didn't do long term—had I subconsciously bought into my family's assessment of me as a flake?

I ran my fingers over my upper arm and shoulder, lingering on the first butterfly, the one I'd gotten when I was fifteen. My proud statement to the world of just who Jenna Fallon was, and how different from the rest of my family. I'd added one after Travis—a statement that a butterfly wouldn't be tied to one man. And more over the years, as the whim struck me, affirming that I was free, independent. I'd always figured I was following my own path, not competing with my near-perfect sisters.

Not competing on their turf. Not Tree's, of academic brilliance and devotion to improving the situation for aboriginal peoples. Not Kat's, of social skill and all-around smarts. Not Merilee's, of love-bonding with one guy. But really, I'd been competing by asserting how different I was.

Except, I was smart and good with people like Kat. And, like Tree, I wanted to make the world a better place. And maybe at heart I was like M in wanting one man, one love.

Of course I was different, too. I loved to travel, loved variety, and didn't want to settle in one spot. In those ways, I was like Mark. But he thought in terms of long term, and I never had.

Because I was afraid I couldn't stick the course?

Matt's mom Adele, sitting beside me, said, "Thank heavens that's over. No mother wants to think of her boy in a thong."

I realized I'd missed the last few gifts, and the cute waiters were bringing out round serving trays of pizza. "Right," I murmured. Hadn't I sworn to stop agonizing over Mark?

And yet, I couldn't. My feelings for him were too deep. I couldn't give up on us—give up on my dreams again—until I was absolutely sure.

Picking up my almost-full martini glass, I took a sip. All this angst and analysis wasn't like me, but I could do it.

What would happen if I took the path Mark had offered and did think long term? Maybe, just maybe, love and children. A stimulating, unconventional life. I could combine my special connection with the environment and my love of people, and I could travel to places I'd dreamed of. I could study, learn, become more and more knowledgeable and skilled. Make a substantial contribution to the world rather than just touch down here and there.

I remembered something I'd been thinking back in Marianne's Diner. You got to decide for yourself who you wanted to be. Had Mark really told me I had to change, or had he meant that it was time to take a close look at myself and decide who I wanted to be? I was turning thirty. Did I still want to be the same girl I'd been at twenty?

Slowly, I put my glass back on the table. I'd thought Mark didn't respect me, but maybe he did. Maybe he respected me more than I respected myself. Deep inside, maybe I was the one who thought I wasn't good enough, who never stuck at anything long enough to really have to prove myself—or to risk failing.

Fear of failing, of not being good enough. Fear of loving and not being loved back. And here I'd thought myself so gutsy, heading out on the open road, alive to all the possibilities. Really, I'd been slamming doors shut, out of fear.

It was time to have the guts to commit myself. To risk failure and loss, but to try my damndest to make things work. To follow dreams that no longer seemed childish, but very adult.

I sprang up. "I have to go."

My family and Adele stared at me, then Kat beamed and said, "Mark. You've decided."

"Mark?" Adele echoed in a puzzled tone.

"She met a guy," Kat explained. "And now she's going after him. Right, Jenna?"

"Yeah." Hope and anxiety skittered through me. Would Mark give me another chance? If he really cared, surely he would. "Will you tell Merilee? Apologize for me?"

"Of course." Kat rose and hugged me. "Good luck, sis."

Mom and Tree startled me by rising too, circling around the end of the table, and also hugging me. "Go get him," Tree said, and Mom said, "I'm proud of you, Jenna."

Proud? My mother was proud of me?

"Take the car," she said, whipping around the table again to grab her purse. She took out her key ring and pulled a fancy black key off it. "We'll get a taxi." She was offering me her precious Mercedes?

"Thanks." Across the table, I took it from her hand. "Wish me luck."

They all did, and I hurried from the restaurant.

If I'd had Mark's grandparents' address, I'd have driven there. If I'd had his cell or home phone number, I'd have called. Without those, I'd have to head home and do some research.

When I arrived, the house was dark. With all of us females going out for the evening, Nav had decided to take sunset photos and Dad had said he'd stay on campus and work. I ran around back, retrieved the key from its hiding spot in the old horse chestnut, and let myself in.

The phone book first. Chambers was a common last name, and I couldn't remember Mark's grandparents' first names, but maybe there'd be a listing for a Dr. Chambers.

There wasn't.

Okay, so I'd google Mark. I ran upstairs, bursting into the first bedroom, which happened to be M's. The computer on her desk was on, so I opened a search engine and typed *Dr. Mark Chambers.*

Oh, man, there were millions of hits. Literally. I tried again, adding *marine biologist, phone,* and *Vancouver* to the search. Okay, that was better. But when I checked the first few, they weren't helpful.

Impatient, I tried a different approach. Maybe it would be easier to find his grandmother. Though she was in her eighties, Mark had said she still consulted and taught as a neurosurgeon. So this time I looked for *Dr. Chambers, neurosurgeon, Vancouver, and phone.* Yes! There was a number. An office number.

I'd try it. At eight o'clock Wednesday night, likely I'd get an answering machine, but Mark had said she consulted so maybe it was a home office.

A brisk female voice answered on the second ring. "Yes?"

"Dr. Chambers?" I asked, sounding breathless.

"Yes. Who is this?"

"You don't know me. I'm sorry to bother you, but I'm a friend of Mark's and I need to get in touch with him."

"He gave you this number?"

"No, but I, uh, lost his cell number."

"Oh." That one syllable carried a weight of disapproval. "Well, he's not here. He left town." She sounded disgruntled about that, too.

My mouth fell open in shock. Though usually I didn't bother keeping track of days, this week, with M&M's wedding coming up, I knew exactly what day of the week it was. This was Wednesday, and Mark had said he was flying to Bali on Thursday. He must have changed his plans. Maybe because he was so pissed off at me.

"Young lady," she said sharply, "was there something else?"

"Could you give me his cell number?"

She rattled off a string of numbers, and I grabbed a pen and hurriedly scribbled them down. "Thank you."

She hung up.

Great. The woman already disapproved of me. Likely, that would only get worse when she met me. If she ever met me.

With shaking fingers, I dialed the number I'd written down.

Three rings, and I got voice mail. Likely, he was on the plane. I hadn't figured out what to say, so stumbled out with, "Mark, it's Jenna. I've been really stupid. Can you call me so we can talk? I . . ." My mouth trembled on the words "love you." Were they true? How would I know? "I'm sorry. Please call." I at least thought to give my cell number, because he'd have had no reason to keep the scrap where I'd written it.

Susan Fox

Then I hung up. All I could do was keep my cell charged and wait. And hope. Once again, I'd put my dreams on the line. Would Mark shatter them or make them come true?

Thursday morning, after a restless night where hope and fear alternated, I was still waiting. I'd googled flights to Bali and discovered Mark had likely flown to Hong Kong and could be fourteen hours in the air. So, maybe he hadn't even received my message.

When I related the story to my family at breakfast, Mom said, "Good for you, dear. Now don't worry or be impatient. It does no good."

Dad hmphed. "And how many times have I told you that, Rebecca, for all the good it does?" Then he turned to me and said gruffly, "The man would be lucky to have you, Jenna."

In my weakened state, that comment almost brought tears to my eyes.

The family was alone for breakfast. Matt, who often stayed over, had decided to spend his last few nights of bachelorhood at his mom's house. And Nav had gone long before we all got up, heading downtown with his camera gear in hopes of getting some dawn light photos. He had his first major exhibit coming up soon in Montreal and was hoping for one or two special shots.

When our parents headed off to work, my sisters filled me in on the rest of the bridal shower stagette.

"These two very hot guys in firefighter costumes rushed in," Kat said. "And Kimberly gave this totally artificial squeal, 'Oh my God, is there a fire?' The guys sauntered up to where she and M were sitting and one of them said, 'You bet there's gonna be, after we get it stoked.' The other set up a boom box, Sean Kingston was singing about fire burning on the dance floor, and the two of them began to strip."

"Oh, fun! Did they actually go all the way?"

"No, only down to boxer briefs," she said, sounding disappointed. "They weren't real strippers, just a couple of university dance students Kimberley knows."

"How did the moms handle it?"

Tree said dryly, "Pretended to be shocked, but definitely watched."

"And how about you, M?" I asked.

She flushed. "It was kind of silly, but yeah, it was fun." She gave a mischievous giggle. "They had some pretty nice . . . moves."

We all chuckled. Then M sobered. "On a completely different subject, I'd like to visit Gran this morning."

"So would I," I said. I'd been looking for an opportunity since I got home, but Tree had kept me too busy.

Now my big sister said, "We have time to do that. You've all been doing such a great job, we're ahead of schedule. But . . . don't expect a lot. She's really failing."

We got ready quickly, and soon arrived at the attractive care facility where Gran was staying. The receptionist asked us to go in one by one, as it would be less confusing for Gran.

We decided Tree would go first, and she spent about ten minutes, then came out shaking her head. "It's not a good day."

Kat went next, and when she came out, she said, "It's so sad. She's just staring out the window. She didn't say a word."

Slowly I walked into the private room and over to the chair by the window. Every time I saw Gran, she looked smaller, more frail. As Kat had said, her gaze was focused out the window, blue eyes faded behind thick-lensed glasses. When I bent over and pressed a kiss to her cheek and said, "Hi, Gran, it's Jenna," something flickered in her eyes, and she pointed outside.

I glanced out to the beautifully landscaped courtyard. Her

shaking finger was aimed at an ornamental cherry tree, the blossoms long gone. "It's a pretty tree."

"Red breast," she said.

A long-ago memory flickered into my mind. "Robin? Little Robin Redbreast?" It was a nursery rhyme she'd once sung. I glanced at the tree again, just as a robin with a worm in its mouth flew into the leafy branches.

"Oh, Gran, there's a nest."

Neatly screened by leaves, I could just see the nest with a robin perched on the edge, poking the worm down a fledgling's throat.

"Red breast," she repeated with satisfaction.

Once, she'd been able to name all the birds. She'd taught me. I sat on the stool beside her and took her hands in mine. "Gran, I've been in California. Counting peregrine falcons. You remember falcons, don't you?" For the next few minutes, I talked to her about the survey, the birds, the remote nesting sites.

Mostly, she gazed out the window as if she wasn't listening, but once or twice she glanced at my face, and I hoped that on some level she knew who I was and knew I loved her.

When my time was up, I said, "I have to go now, Gran. I'll see you Saturday. Merilee's getting married, remember? To Matt? M&M? You're going to come and have a wonderful time."

She gazed at me with seeming incomprehension.

I kissed her cheek. "I love you, Gran."

She peered closer into my face and when I started to ease my hands from hers, her grip tightened. "Unhappy," she said.

"You're unhappy? What's wrong, Gran?"

"Don't be unhappy." Her frail fingers bit into mine. "Trust your heart."

Unsure whether she was talking about me or herself, or

revisiting some old memory, I said, "That's good advice." Advice I'd in fact been trying to follow.

Her hands released their grip and I stood. "Merilee's going to come in and see you."

When I left, I went outside the facility, sat on a bench by the door, and checked my cell, which I'd had turned off. Nothing.

His flight would have landed. He must have picked up my message. Maybe he had a rushed flight connection and no time to call. Or it was even possible his cell's batteries had run down.

I wanted to trust my heart, but all I could think was, *If he won't give me a second chance, it means he doesn't love me.*

Chapter 15

Hours later, after wedding chores, lunch, and more wedding chores, Mark still hadn't called, and I was seriously depressed. I'd done my best not to let it show, but I knew it did from the wordless hugs of sympathy my sisters kept giving me. Miserable as I was, I enjoyed having this time with them and feeling the new sense of warmth and mutual support.

I did feel awful, though, about casting a pall on the final days before Merilee's wedding. The visit to Gran hadn't helped either; after it, M had been almost as withdrawn as I. We could bring Gran to the wedding, but was there any hope she'd actually be "there"?

In the late afternoon, wedding chores done for the day, we sent M to her room to rest then Kat and I helped Tree get steak, potatoes, and onions marinating for what she called "Damien's Aussie barbie." After that, the three of us headed to our rooms for a little freshening up and quiet time.

I sat down at my desk by the window and faced the truth. Mark had written me off. He might have thought he was falling in love, but it had just been lust and he'd come to his senses. Otherwise, if he really cared, he'd have returned my call.

I gazed out the window at the horse chestnut and was half-way tempted to go out, climb it, and perch in my dreaming spot. Maybe there'd be robins nesting there, too.

Gran had said, "Trust your heart." Had she known she was talking to me, Jenna? Had that been advice for me? Did she know that, while I'd dreamed lots of dreams, I hadn't trusted my heart since I was seventeen and it had let me down so badly?

Then I realized something. The message I'd left for Mark had been kind of garbled. I hadn't trusted my heart, I hadn't poured out all my feelings.

I should phone and leave another message.

But that didn't feel right. I wanted the same thing I'd wanted last night: to see Mark, to touch him, to be face to face when I told him how I felt. To read the truth on his face and know whether I had to give up hope.

Outside my door, I heard Nav's voice, then a bedroom door closed. Kat was with her guy. Tree was probably on the phone with Damien. I knew, from what my older sisters had said over the past few days, that their journeys to love hadn't been smooth sailing and that each of them had had fears and insecurities to overcome. But they'd trusted their hearts, and their men's hearts, and look what it had won them.

I squared my shoulders. No, I wouldn't climb my dreaming tree. I glanced at a photo tucked in the frame of my mirror: me in the driver's seat of Mellow Yellow, the top down, a big smile on my face. In the past, I'd loved heading out on the open road and trusting the universe to determine my direction. This time, I had to grow up and chart my own course.

I had to go to Bali. But how? After buying M's shower and wedding gifts, I was broke.

I gazed a moment longer at the picture and found my answer. Damn, I'd had that car since I was eighteen. It had been my companion through so many adventures.

Resolutely I turned away and checked the clock by the bed. Mom might have already left the office, but maybe not. I dialed the number.

It had been a point of pride to never borrow money, but love trumped pride. When she answered, I said, "Mom, can I borrow enough money to fly to Bali? It'll be short-term, I'll—"

"Mark called?" she broke in, sounding young, excited.

"No, I want to fly out and talk to him."

A long pause, then, "That's a brave thing to do. But what about the wedding? Your sister—"

"No, I don't mean right now. I'd never miss M's wedding. But right after. A red-eye Saturday night or first thing Sunday morning. And Mom, I'll pay you back as soon as I can. Tomorrow morning I'll call the mechanic in California and make arrangements to"—I swallowed hard—"sell my car."

"You're selling Mellow Yellow? Oh Jenna, you really want to do that?"

"No, but Mark's more important."

"We'll talk about the car tomorrow. Here, I've looked up my travel agent's number. She works magic. I'll e-mail her so she knows to put it on my bill."

"Thanks, Mom."

As soon as I hung up, I phoned the travel agent. Thank heavens for workaholics, because she, too, was still at her desk. We talked for a few minutes, and she said, "I'll check out all the options and give you a call first thing in the morning."

"Thank you so much."

I hung up, wondering how on earth I'd find out where Mark was in Bali. I'd really rather not phone his grandmother again. If only he'd told me his friend Adrienne's last name . . .

But, wait a minute. Adrienne, a marine biologist at UBC?

There'd be an online list of faculty members. Okay, I'd do that first thing tomorrow, and call her at work. I'd also phone Neal, the mechanic in California, to ask how I could arrange to sell my car. I'd talked to him on Monday, and he'd said Mellow Yellow was all fixed and ready to pick up.

I lifted the photo from the mirror frame, sentimental moisture clouding my vision. Mellow Yellow and my young friend Anna, along with my family, had been the constants in my ever-shifting life. Now, I was trading my car for the chance at a future with a man I barely knew.

I squared my shoulders and put the picture back. Decision made; move on. I'd talk to Tree. She'd make me a project plan for everything I needed to do before I left.

I rose and headed out to the hall to see if her door was open. Nope, shut. Phone sex with Damien.

"Oh my God!" I heard from Merilee's room. I turned as she came flying out the door, face bright with excitement. "Jenna! That's your car, isn't it?"

"What? No, my car's in California. What are you talking about?"

"Look!" She grabbed my hand, pulled me into her room, and pointed out the open window.

I stared out to see Mellow Yellow, top down, with a very windblown Mark in the driver's seat. "What?" I gaped, not trusting my eyes.

"It's Mark, it's Mark." Merilee jumped up and down. "It is, isn't it?"

Hope surged through me in a rush, making me giddy. "It is. It really is!" I sprinted for the door and down the hall, then flew down the stairs.

Mark's entire body ached from driving for so many hours. It had taken all his energy to haul his butt out of the tiny sports car when he'd pulled up at the house down the street where he'd dropped Jenna off Sunday night—where an elderly woman looked at him askance and said no, Jenna Fallon didn't live there.

He'd stuttered out something about delivering her car and how he must have written down the wrong address. Fortunately, she'd been trusting enough to send him to the right house.

Jenna hadn't trusted him that much. Which made what he'd done even more crazy. When they'd parted Monday night, she'd been furious with him. Was there any hope she'd forgive him? Damn, he should've called Adrienne and asked if he was doing the right thing. Instead, for once, he'd trusted instinct and done something utterly impulsive.

Now, he sat in front of Jenna's house and wondered what the hell he was doing.

And then he knew. The front door of the rambling three-story flew open, and Jenna ran out, face bright with excitement, white-gold curls bouncing, crying, "Mark!"

The joy on her face sent relief surging through him, energizing his exhausted body. He jumped out of the car and rushed to meet her. When she leaped into his arms, he grabbed her tightly and spun her around, both of them laughing. This felt so right. Somehow, they'd work things out.

"What are you doing?" she demanded. "I thought you'd gone to Bali? Why didn't you return my call?"

"What call?" He let her down slowly, keeping his arms around her shoulders. "Did you call my cell? I left in such a hurry, I forgot it." He'd forgotten his laptop too, and barely remembered his passport and wallet.

Gazing down into her sparkling ocean eyes, he said, "I postponed the trip. I flew down to California Tuesday night and picked up your car first thing yesterday morning."

Her arms circled his waist. "Mark, that's sweet, but I don't understand."

He realized two women had come up behind her: one

young, with dark honey-blond hair, looking almost as excited as Jenna, the other a few years older with short auburn
hair and a quizzical expression. Coming up behind them
was a third woman, her longer reddish-brown curls tousled,
holding hands with a dark-skinned man who was buttoning
his shirt.

The Mercedes Jenna had driven to the beach the other
night pulled up and stopped, and a middle-aged woman in a
business suit stepped out.

A family audience. But he didn't give a damn.

He gazed into Jenna's face. "Because your car is your freedom. Your open road."

Her brows pulled together. "What do you mean?"

He was aware of the family moving closer, coming up behind Jenna, silently showing their support. If he hurt her,
he'd have all of them to answer to. And that was as it should
be. It proved they really did love her.

They didn't scare him. He'd hurt her once and he had no
intention of doing it again. "I was wrong. I shouldn't have
asked you to change. I fell in love with you just the way you
are. You're a wonderful person."

For once, he must have said the right thing because her
eyes glowed and her lips curved. "Mark, I—"

"No, wait. I want you to be whoever you want to be, to
climb into your car and go wherever you want. If you think
you can love me, then we'll figure the rest out as we go."

Mischief sparked in her eyes. "You mean, be spontaneous
and impulsive?"

"I can learn."

Her eyes softened again. "Yes, you can. And so can I. I
was going to come to Bali to tell you that."

Mark was aware of another car pulling up, but this time
he didn't even glance up. He stared into the depths of her
green-blue eyes. "You were coming to Bali?"

"A travel agent's checking flights for right after the wedding."

He saw the truth in her eyes, and warmth eased through his tired body. "You were coming to me, Jenna?"

"Yes. To tell you I was wrong. I'm not so free. Deep down, I've been afraid I wasn't good enough to commit. I don't want to be like that anymore. The way I feel for you, it's so new for me, so much bigger than anything I've even imagined. I want to work with you in Indonesia, and I want us to find out if we share a love that's strong enough for us to build a future together. Working and loving side by side."

He touched her cheek. Needing to make sure he understood, he said, "You mean you'd give up all the variety for one man, one cause?"

"We'll create our own variety. Side by side, as partners." She grinned up at him. "That'll be all the excitement I can handle."

"And it'll be more excitement and more joy than I'd ever hoped for."

"You and me both."

He cupped her face between his hands and bent down as she rose to meet him. Their lips touched and he lost himself in her. Now he understood this experience, the magic that happened when they kissed. He and Jenna, both strong, independent people, were two halves of something amazing and utterly right.

Dimly, the sounds of clapping and cheering penetrated his consciousness. He eased his lips from hers. "We belong together."

"We do. I've been falling for you since . . . oh, probably since the moment you ordered strawberry pie."

"I've been falling for you since I first looked into your eyes."

A throat cleared, and Mark glanced past Jenna to see the woman who'd been driving the Mercedes and a distinguished man with graying hair and glasses. The man held out his hand. "We're Jenna's parents, Rebecca and James Fallon."

"Mark Chambers." He shook her father's hand.

Her mother eyed him appraisingly as she, too, shook firmly. "You'll stay for dinner," she announced.

"Thanks, I'd like to." Damn, he hadn't thought this through. This wasn't the way he should be meeting her parents. He knew they were hard to impress, and he needed to show them he was the right man for their daughter. "But I've been on the road for the last two days without a shower or change of clothes, and I'm afraid—"

"One of the men will loan you clothes," she said. "Nav?"

"Yes, ma'am," the dark-skinned man said, a note of humor in his voice. "Mark, we look like we're about the same size."

"And I'm sure"—Rebecca Fallon's deep brown eyes actually twinkled—"Jenna will help you find the shower."

"Uh, thank you, that would be . . . good."

Jenna saved him from embarrassing himself further, by grabbing his hand. "The rest of the introductions can wait until dinner," she said firmly. "Come on."

As she started to tug him away, he remembered something, and told her mother, "There's a strawberry-rhubarb pie in the trunk of the car."

"You stopped at Marianne's?" Jenna said.

"I was going to get glazed strawberry pie, but she said a cooked pie would survive the trip better."

"You're a keeper." She towed him away from her family.

The two brown-haired sisters exchanged a laughing comment he didn't catch, but he did hear the young blonde say, with determination, "I have to see Matt."

Then Jenna was leading him through the front door and up the stairs. "I can't believe you made the drive so quickly," she said.

"I drove all night. I wanted to get back to you and say what I needed to say."

"I felt the same. I even phoned your grandmother."

"You did? How did that go?"

"She didn't sound very friendly."

No, she wouldn't be. His grandparents would disapprove. But this was his life. He wasn't them and he didn't want to live the way they did. In time, he hoped they'd understand.

More immediately, he hoped Jenna's family would.

And, even more immediately, she was ushering him into a bathroom and locking the door. "How tired are you, Dr. Chambers?" She reached for the hem of his T-shirt.

"You're waking me up." Just the touch of her fingers against his skin was stirring him to arousal. "But stop, I'm sweaty and disgusting."

"Sweaty, yeah. Disgusting, never." She reached behind the shower curtain and got the water running as he unbuttoned his jeans and shoved them and his boxers down, freeing his growing erection.

He stepped under the warm spray and groaned with pleasure. Now, if she'd just climb in here with him, his world would be perfect. "At the campgrounds, we had those separate male and female showers."

"I remember," she said. "And I suggested sharing, but you pointed out there'd be other people around."

Her family was somewhere out there. But . . . "You locked the bathroom door."

She chuckled. "I did." Through the clear plastic curtain, he saw her begin to unbutton her sleeveless blouse.

Hallelujah.

Except, this was the woman who liked spontaneity, and he'd told her he could learn.

He shoved back the curtain, not caring that water splashed everywhere, grabbed her by the waist, and lifted her into the tub, clothes and all.

Laughing, she gazed up at him as water soaked through her clothing.

He pulled her close, under the pulsing spray, and kissed her, feeling a sense of love, acceptance, and belonging he'd never experienced before.

She undid her shirt buttons as he unzipped her shorts, and still they kissed as if their lips were fused together. When she was naked, she made a soft, moaning sound against his lips and tried to climb his body.

Exhaustion completely gone now, he hooked his hands under her firm butt and lifted her, supporting her as she hooked her legs around his waist.

"Oh, Mark," she sighed happily, "since I met you, it's sure been one wild ride, but I like how it's ended up."

"Ended up? Oh no, we're just getting started."

ACKNOWLEDGMENTS

Writing a series is so much fun and I'd like to thank Audrey LaFehr, my editor at Kensington, for giving me the opportunity to create the four-book Wild Ride to Love series. *His, Unexpectedly* is the third book—the "automobiles" story—in my sexy "planes, trains, automobiles, and a cruise ship" series about the Fallon sisters. I hope readers will check out the first two books, *Sex Drive* (written under the name Susan Lyons) and *Love, Unexpectedly* and be on the lookout for the fourth.

I'd also like to thank my agent, Emily Sylvan Kim, Martin Biro at Kensington, the Kensington art department who always create such wonderful covers, and my fabulous critiquers: Delilah Marvelle, Lacy Danes, Michelle Hancock, Elizabeth Allan, and Nazima Ali. You've all made this book possible.

Last but definitely not least, very special thanks to my readers. I love sharing my stories with you and love hearing from you. You can e-mail me at susan@susanlyons.ca, write c / o PO Box 73523, Downtown Postal Outlet, 1014 Robson Street, Vancouver, BC, Canada V6E 4L9, or contact me through my website at www.susanfox.ca where you'll also find excerpts, behind the scenes notes, a monthly contest, my newsletter, and other goodies.

If you enjoyed *His, Unexpectedly,* you won't want to miss Susan Fox's deliciously sexy and exciting romance, *Love, Unexpectedly.*
Read on for a little taste of this terrific story.
A Brava trade paperback on sale now!

Chapter 1

"What's new with me? Only everything!" Nav Bharani's neighbor Kat widened her chestnut brown eyes theatrically. She dropped her laundry basket in front of one of the half dozen washing machines in the basement laundry room of their apartment building, then hopped up on a dryer, clearly prioritizing gossip over chores.

Nav grinned and leaned back against his own washer, which was already churning his Saturday-morning laundry. "I saw you Wednesday night, Kat." She'd taken him to one of her girlfriends to supply muscle, setting up a new bookcase and rearranging furniture. "*Everything* can't have changed in two days."

Though something major had happened in his own life yesterday. A breakthrough in his photography career. He was eager to tell Kat, but he'd listen to her news first.

She gave an eye roll. "Okay, *almost* everything. My baby sister's suddenly getting married."

Even in the crappy artificial light, with her reddish-brown curls a bed-head mess and pillow marks on one cheek, Kat was so damned pretty she made his heart ache.

"Merilee? I thought she and . . . what's his name? always intended to marry."

"Matt. Yeah, but they were talking next year, when they graduate from university. Now it's, like, *now*." She snapped her fingers.

"When's now?" he asked.

"Two weeks, today. Can you believe it?" She shook her head vigorously. "So now I have to take a couple weeks off and go to Vancouver to help put together a wedding on virtually no notice. The timing sucks. June's a really busy month at work." She was the PR director at Le Cachet, a boutique luxury hotel in Old Montreal—a job that made full use of her creativity, organizational skills, and outgoing personality.

"Too bad they didn't arrange their wedding to suit your workload," he teased.

"Oops. Self-centered bitch?"

"Only a little."

She sighed, her usual animation draining from her face. Lines of strain around her eyes and shadows under them told him she was upset about more than the inconvenience of taking time off work. Nav knew Kat well after two years. As well as she let anyone know her, and in every way but the one he wanted most: as her lover.

He dropped the teasing tone and touched her hand. "How do you feel about the wedding?"

"Thrilled to bits for Merilee. Of course." Her answer was prompt, but she stared down at their hands rather than meeting his eyes.

"Kat?"

Her head lifted, lips twisting. "Okay, I *am* happy for her, honestly, but I'm also green with envy. She's ten years younger. It should be me." She jumped to the floor, feet slapping the concrete like an exclamation mark.

That was what he'd guessed, as he knew she longed for marriage and kids. With someone other than him, unfortunately. But this wasn't the time to dwell on his heartache. His best friend was hurting.

He tried to help her see this rationally. "Your sister's been with this guy a long time, right?" Kat didn't talk much about her family—he knew she had some issues—but he'd heard a few snippets.

"Since grade two. And they always said they wanted to get married."

"So why keep waiting?"

She wrinkled her nose. "So I can do it first? Yeah, okay, that's a sucky reason. But I'm thirty-one and I want marriage and kids as badly as she does." She gave an exaggerated sniffle and then launched herself at him. "Damn, I need a hug."

His arms came up, circling her body, cuddling her close.

This was vintage Kat. She had no patience for what she called "all that angsty, self-analytical, pop-psych crap." If she was feeling crappy, she vented, then moved on.

Or so she said. Nav was dead certain it didn't work that easily. Not that he was a shrink or anything, only a friend who cared.

Cared too much for his own sanity. Now, embracing her, he used every ounce of self-control to resist pulling her tighter. To try not to register the firm, warm curves under the soft fabric of her sweats. To fight the arousal she'd so easily awakened in him since they'd met.

Did she feel the way his heart raced or was she too absorbed in her own misery? Nav wished he was wearing more clothing than thin running shorts and his old Cambridge rugby jersey, but he'd come to the laundry room straight from an early run.

Feeling her warmth, smelling her sleep-tousled scent, he thought back to his first sight of her.

He'd been moving into the building, grubby in his oldest

jeans and a T-shirt with the sleeves ripped out as he wrestled his meager belongings out of the rental truck and into the small apartment. The door beside his had opened and he'd paused, curious to see his neighbor.

A lovely young woman in a figure-hugging sundress stepped into the hall. His photographer's eye had freeze-framed the moment. The tantalizing curves, the way the green of her dress complemented her auburn curls, the sparkle of interest in her brown eyes as they widened and she scanned him up and down.

As for the picture she saw—well, he must've made quite a sight with his bare arms hugging a tall pole lamp and a sandalwood statue of Ganesh, the elephant god. *Nani*, his mum's mother, had given him the figure when he was a kid, saying it would bless his living space.

The woman in the hallway gave him a bright smile. "*Bonjour, mon nouveau voisin,*" she greeted him as her new neighbor. "*Bienvenue. Je m'appelle* Kat Fallon."

Her name and the way she pronounced it told him that, despite her excellent Québécois accent, she was a native English speaker like Nav. He replied in that language. "Pleased to meet you, Kat. I'm Nav Bharani."

"Ooh, nice accent."

"Thanks." He'd grown up in England and had only been in Canada two years, mostly speaking French, so his English accent was pretty much intact.

His neighbor stretched out a hand, seeming not to care that the one he freed up in return was less than clean.

He felt a connection, a warm jolt of recognition that was sexual but way more than just that. A jolt that made him gaze at her face, memorizing every attractive feature and knowing, in his soul, that this woman was going to be important in his life.

He'd felt something similar when he'd unwrapped his first

camera on his tenth birthday. A sense of revelation and certainty.

Already today, Ganesh had brought him luck.

Kat felt something special, too. He could tell by the flush that tinged her cheekbones, the way her hand lingered before separating from his. "Have you just moved from England, Nav?"

"No, I've been studying photography in Quebec City for a couple years, at Université Laval. Just graduated, and I thought I'd find more . . . *opportunities* in Montreal." He put deliberate emphasis on the word "opportunities," wondering if she'd respond to the hint of flirtation.

A grin hovered at the corners of her mouth. "Montreal is full of opportunity."

"When you wake up in the morning, you never know what the day will bring?"

She gave a rich chuckle. "Some days are better than others." Then she glanced at the elephant statue. "Who's your roommate?"

"Ganesh. Among other things, he's the Lord of Beginnings." Nav felt exhilarated, sensing that this light flirtation was the beginning of something special.

"Beginnings. Well, how about that."

"Some people believe that if you stroke his trunk, he'll bring you luck."

"Really?" Her hand lifted, then the elevator dinged and they both glanced toward it.

A man stepped out and strode toward them with a dazzlingly white smile. Tall and striking, he had strong features, highlighted hair that had been styled with a handful of product, and clothes that screamed, "I care way too much about how I look, and I have the money to indulge myself."

"Hey, babe," he said in English. He bent down to press a

quick, hard kiss to Kat's lips, then, arm around her waist, glanced at Nav. "New neighbor?"

Well shit, she had a boyfriend. So, she hadn't been flirting?

Her cheeks flushed lightly. "Yes, Nav Bharani. And this is Jase Jackson." She glanced at the toothpaste commercial guy with an expression that was almost awestruck. "Nav, you've probably heard of Jase—he's one of the stars of *Back Streets*." She named a gritty Canadian TV drama filmed in Ontario and Quebec. Nav had caught an episode or two, but it hadn't hooked him, and he didn't remember the actor.

"Hey, man," Jase said, tightening his hold on Kat. Marking his territory.

"Hey."

"Jase," Kat said, "would you mind getting a bottle of water from my fridge? It's going to be hot out there."

When the other man had gone into the apartment, Nav said, "So, you two are . . . ?"

"A couple." Her dreamy gaze had followed the other man. "I'm crazy about him. He's amazing."

Well, hell. Despite that initial awareness between them, she hadn't been flirting, only being friendly to a new neighbor. So much for his sense of certainty. The woman was in love with someone else.

Nav, who could be a tiger on the rugby field but was pretty easygoing otherwise, had felt a primitive urge to punch out Actor Guy's lights.

Now, in the drab laundry room, hearing Kat sigh against his chest, he almost wished he'd done it. That rash act might have changed the dynamic between him and Kat.

Instead he'd accepted that she would, at most, be a friend and had concentrated on getting settled in his new home.

He'd just returned from a visit to New Delhi and a fight with his parents, who'd moved back to India when his dad's father died last year. In their eyes, he'd been a traitor when he'd rejected the business career they'd groomed him for and moved to Quebec City to study photography. Now that he'd graduated, his parents said it was time their only child got over his foolishness. He should take up a management role in the family company, either in New Delhi or London, and agree to an arranged marriage.

He'd said no on all counts and stuck to his guns about moving to Montreal to build a photography career.

Once there, he had started to check out work opportunities and begun to meet people. But he'd moved too slowly for Kat, at least when it came to making friends. She'd figured he was shy, taken him under her wing, kick-started his social life. Enjoying her company—besides, who could resist the driving force of a determined Kat Fallon?—he'd gone along.

But even as he dated other women, his feelings for Kat grew. He'd known it was futile. Though her relationship with Jase broke up, and she ogled Nav's muscles when he fixed her plumbing or helped her paint her apartment, she went for men like Actor Guy. Larger than life—at least on the surface. Often, they proved to be men who were more flash than substance, whose love affair was with their own ego, not their current girlfriend.

No way was Nav that kind of man. In the past, growing up in England with wealthy, successful, status-oriented parents, he'd had his fill of people like that.

Though Kat fell for other men, she'd become Nav's good buddy. The couple times he'd put the moves on her when she'd been between guys, she'd turned him down flat. She said he was a really good friend and she valued their friendship too much to risk losing it. Even though he sometimes saw the spark of attraction in her eyes, she refused to even acknowledge it, much less give in to it.

Now, standing with every luscious, tempting inch of her wrapped in his arms, he wondered if there was any hope that one day she'd blink those big brown eyes and realize the man she'd been looking for all her life was right next door.

She gave a gusty sigh and then pushed herself away. She stared up at him, but no, there was no moment of blinding revelation. Just a sniffle, a self-deprecating smile. "Okay," she said. "Five minutes is enough self-pity. Thanks for indulging me, Nav."

She turned away and opened two washing machines. Into one she tossed jeans and T-shirts. Into the other went tank tops, silky camisoles, lacy bras, brief panties, and thongs.

A gentleman would never imagine his friend and neighbor in a matching bright pink bra and panties, or a black lace thong. Nor would he fantasize about having hot laundry-room sex with her.

Glad that the loose running shorts and rugby shirt disguised his growing erection, he refocused on Kat's news. "So you're off to Vancouver." That was where she'd grown up, and where her youngest sister lived with their parents. "When are you leaving? Are you taking the train?" She hated to fly.

She flicked both washers on, then turned to him. "I plan to leave Monday. And yes, definitely the train. It's a great trip and I always meet fascinating people. It'll take my mind off my shitty love life."

"No problem getting time off?"

"My boss gave me major flack for leaving in June and not giving notice. Gee, you'd think I was indispensable." She flashed a grin, and this one did sparkle her eyes.

"I'm sure you are." He said it teasingly, but knew she was usually the center of the crowd, be it in her social life or at work.

"We sorted it out. My assistant can handle things. But it's going to be a crazy weekend. There's tons to organize at work, as well as laundry, dry cleaning, packing."

"Anything I can help with?"

"Could you look after the plants while I'm gone?"

"No problem." He'd done it before, along with playing home handyman for her and her friends. She in turn sewed on buttons, made the best Italian food he'd ever tasted— she'd once dated a five-star chef—and shared popcorn and old movies.

"Thanks. You're a doll, Nav."

A *doll*. Also known as a wimp. As one of his friends said, he was stuck in the buddy trap.

Brushing away the depressing thought, he remembered his good news. "Hey, I have exciting news, too."

"Cool. Tell all."

"You know the Galerie Beau Soleil?"

"Yeah. Ritzy. Le Cachet buys art there."

"Well, maybe they can buy some of my photographs." He fought to suppress a smug smile, then let go and beamed.

"Nav!" She hugged him exuberantly, giving him another tantalizing sample of her curves. "You got an exhibit there?"

"Yeah, in three weeks." He scraped out a living doing freelance photography and selling stock photos, but his goal was to build a career as a fine art photographer. He wanted his photos to display his vision and perspective, and eventually to hang on the walls of upscale businesses, private collectors, and galleries.

This would be his first major exhibit of fine art photography. "They called yesterday. Someone had to cancel at the last minute, and they asked if I could fill in."

"That's fabulous." She gave him another squeeze, then stepped back. "This could be your big breakthrough."

"I know."

For a long moment, while washing machines chugged and whirred, they smiled at each other. Then she asked, "Do you have enough pieces for an exhibit?"

"I'll need a few new shots. Everything has to fit the theme."

"You already have a theme?"

"We're calling it 'Perspectives on Perspective.' " His photographs featured interesting lighting and unusual angles, and often incorporated reflections. They were accurate renditions of reality but from perspectives others rarely noticed. He liked shaking people up, making them think differently about things they saw every day.

"Ooh, how arty and highbrow. It's great. I am *so* happy for you. This is going to launch your career, I just know it. You're going to sell to hotels, office buildings, designer shops, private collectors." Her eyes glittered with enthusiasm. "And I'm going to be able to say 'I knew him when.' "

Nav chuckled. "Don't get ahead of yourself."

Kat hopped lithely up on the closest washer, catlike, living up to her nickname. Sitting cross-legged, she was roughly on eye level with him. "You're a fantastic photographer and you deserve this. You've made it happen, so believe in it. Don't dream small, Nav."

If only that would work when it came to winning Kat.

"Believe in how great you are." She frowned, as if an interesting thought had occurred to her, then stared at him with an expression of discovery. "You know, you really are a great guy."

It didn't sound as if she was still talking about his photography, but about him. Nav's heart stopped beating. Was this it? The moment he'd longed for? He gazed into her brown eyes, which were bright, almost excited. "I am?" Normally he had a fairly deep voice, but now it squeaked like an adolescent's.

Her eyes narrowed, with a calculating gleam. "You know how unlucky I've been with my love life. Well, my family blames it on me. They say I have the worst taste in men, that I'm some kind of jinx when it comes to relationships."

"Er . . ." Damn, she'd changed the subject. And this was one he'd best not comment on. Yes, of course she had crappy judgment when it came to dating. The actor, the international financier, the Olympic gold-medal skier, the NASCAR champ? They swept her off her feet but were completely wrong for her. It was no surprise to him when each glittery relationship ended, but Kat always seemed shocked. She hated to hear anyone criticize her taste in men.

"Merilee said I could bring a date to the wedding, then got in this dig about whether I was seeing anyone, or between losers. I'd really hate to show up alone."

He'd learned not to trust that gleam in her eyes, but couldn't figure out where she was heading. "You only just broke up with NASCAR Guy." Usually it took her two or three months before she fell for a new man. In the in-between time she hung out more with him, as she'd been doing recently.

Her lips curved. "I love how you say 'NASCAR Guy' in that posh Brit accent. Yeah, we split two weeks ago. But I think I may have found a great guy to take to the wedding."

Damn. His heart sank. "You've already met someone new? And you're going to take him as your date?"

"If he'll go." The gleam was downright wicked now. "What do you think?"

He figured a man would be crazy not to take any opportunity to spend time with her. But . . . "If you've only started dating, taking him to a wedding could seem like pressure. And what if you caught the bouquet?" If Nav was with her and she caught the damned thing, he'd tackle the minister before he could get away, and tie the knot then and there.

Not that Kat would let him. She'd say he'd gone out of his freaking mind.

"Oh, I don't think this guy would get the wrong idea." There was a laugh in her voice.

"No?"

She sprang off the washer, stepped toward him, and gripped the front of his rugby jersey with both hands, the brush of her knuckles through the worn blue-and-white-striped cotton making his heart race and his groin tighten. "What do you say, Nav?"

"Uh, to what?"

"To being my date for the wedding."

Hot blood surged through his veins. She was asking him to travel across the country and escort her to her sister's wedding?

Had she finally opened her eyes, opened her heart, and really seen him? Seen that he, Naveen Bharani, was the perfect man for her? The one who knew her perhaps better than she knew herself. Who loved her as much for her vulnerabilities and flaws as for her competence and strength, her generosity and sense of fun, those sparkling eyes, and the way her sexy curves filled out her Saturday-morning sweats.

"Me?" He lifted his hands and covered hers. "You want me to go?"

She nodded vigorously. "You're an up-and-coming photographer. Smart, creative." Face close to his, she added, eyes twinkling, "Hot, too. Your taste in clothes sucks, but if you'd let me work on you, you'd look good. And you're nice. Kind, generous, sweet."

Yes, he was all of those things, except sweet—another wimp word, like doll. But he was confused. She thought he was hot, which was definitely good. But something was missing. She wasn't gushing about how *amazing* he was and how *crazy* she was about him, the way she always did when she fell for a man. Her beautiful eyes were sharp and focused, not dreamy. Not filled with passion or new love. So . . . what was she saying?

He tightened his hands on hers. "Kat, I—"

"Will you do it? My family might even *approve* of you."

Suspicion tightened his throat. He forced words out. "So I'd be your token good guy, to prove you don't always date assholes."

"Ouch. But yes, that's the idea. I know it's a lot to ask, but please? Will you do it?"

He lifted his hands from hers and dropped them to his sides, bitter disappointment tightening them into fists.

Oblivious, she clenched his jersey tighter, eyes pleading with him. "It's only one weekend, and I'll pay your airfare and—"

"Oh, no, you won't." He twisted away abruptly, and her hands lost their grip on his shirt. Damn, there was only so much battering a guy's ego could take. "If I go, I'll pay my own way." The words grated out. He turned away and busied himself heaving laundry from his washer to a dryer, trying to calm down and think. What should he do?

Practicalities first. If he agreed, would it affect the exhibit? No, all she was asking for was a day or two. He could escort her, make nice with her family, play the role she'd assigned him. He'd get brownie points with Kat.

"Nav, I couldn't let you pay for the ticket. Not when you'd be doing me such a huge favor. So, will you? You're at least thinking about it?"

Of course he'd already accumulated a thousand brownie points, and where had that got him? Talking about *roles*, she'd cast him as the good bud two years ago and didn't show any signs of ever promoting him to leading man.

He was caught in freaking limbo.

The thing was, he was tired of being single. He wanted to share his life—to get married and start a family. Though he and his parents loved each other, his relationship with them had always been uneasy. As a kid, he'd wondered if he was adopted, he and his parents seemed such a mismatch.

He knew "family" should mean something different: a sense of warmth, belonging, acceptance, support. That's what he wanted to create with his wife and children.

His mum was on his case about an arranged marriage, sending him a photo and bio at least once a month, hoping to hook him. But Nav wanted a love match. He'd had an active dating life for more than ten years, but no matter how great the women were, none had ever made him feel the way he did for Kat. Damn her.

He bent to drag more clothes from the washer and, as he straightened, glanced at her. Had she been checking out his ass?

Cheeks coloring, she shifted her gaze to his face. "Please, Nav? Pretty please?" Her brows pulled together. "You can't imagine how much I *hate* the teasing." Her voice dropped. "The *poor Kat can't find a man* pity."

He understood how tough this wedding would be for her. Kat had tried so hard to find love, wanted it so badly, and always failed. Now she had to help her little sister plan her wedding and be happy for her, even though Kat's heart ached with envy. Having a good friend by her side, pretending to her family that she'd found a nice guy, would make things easier for her.

Yes, he was pissed that she wanted only friendship from him, but that was his problem. He shouldn't take his frustration and hurt out on her.

He clicked the dryer on and turned to face her. "When do you need to know?"

"No great rush, I guess. It's two weeks off. Like I said, I'll probably leave Monday. I'll take the train to Toronto, then on to Vancouver."

"It's a long trip."

"Yeah." Her face brightened. "It really is fun. I've done it every year or so since I moved here when I was eighteen. It's like being on holiday with fascinating people. A train's a special world. Normal rules don't apply."

He always traveled by air, but he'd watched old movies with Kat. *North by Northwest. Silver Streak*. Trains were sexy.

Damn. He could see it now. Kat would meet some guy,

fall for him, have hot sex, end up taking him rather than Nav to the wedding.

Unless . . .

An idea—brilliant? insane?—struck him. What if he was the guy on the train?

What if he showed up out of the blue, took her by surprise? An initial shock, then days together in that special, sexy world where normal rules didn't apply. Might she see him differently?

If he analyzed his idea, he'd decide it was crazy and never do it. So, forget about being rational. He'd hustle upstairs and go online to arrange getting money transferred out of the trust fund he hadn't touched since coming to Canada.

It had been a matter of principle: proving to himself that he wasn't a spoiled rich kid and could make his own way in the world. But now, principles be damned. Train travel wasn't cheap, and this was a chance to win the woman he loved.

Unrequited love was unhealthy. He'd break the good buddy limbo, stop being so fucking pathetic, and go after her.

But first, he had to set things up with Kat so she'd be totally surprised when he showed up on the train. "Yeah, okay." He tried to sound casual. "I'll be your token good guy. I'll fly out for the wedding."

"Oooeeee!!" She flung herself into his arms, a full-body tackle that caught him off guard and almost toppled them both. "Thank you, thank you, thank you." She pressed quick little kisses all over his cheeks.

When what he longed for were soul-rocking, deep and dirty kisses, mouth to mouth, tongue to tongue. Groin to groin.

Enough. He was fed up with her treating him this way. Fed up with himself for taking it. Things between them were damned well going to change.

He grabbed her head between both hands and held her steady, her mouth inches from his.

Her lips opened and he heard a soft gasp as she caught her breath. "Nav?" Was that a quiver in her voice?

Deliberately, he pressed his lips against hers. Soft, so soft her lips were, and warm. Though it took all his willpower, he drew away before she could decide how to respond. "You're welcome," he said casually, as if the kiss had been merely a "between friends" one.

All the same, he knew it had reminded her of the attraction between them.

She would be a tiny bit unsettled.

He had, in a subtle way, served notice.

Token good guy? Screw that.

He was going to be the sexy guy on the train.

Chapter 2

The buzzer on Nav's dryer went off, but he hadn't returned to the laundry room yet.

He'd said yes to coming to M&M's wedding, then just when I'd been gushing thanks all over him, he'd taken off, saying he needed to do something upstairs.

Well, first, he'd given me that look. The one that downright sizzled. Then he'd kissed me and I'd almost expected . . . almost wanted . . . I touched my lips, still burning from that one brief brush of his.

No, that was crazy.

What Nav and I had was perfect just as it was. Though I'd always had lots of friends, I'd never felt as connected to any of them as to him. Other women said boyfriends come and go, but it's your friends you can count on. I'd never understood what they meant because I'd never had that close a friend. Now that I did, I wasn't risking our friendship, not when every romantic relationship in my life had ended in disaster.

Besides, while I was looking for a husband, Nav's dating behavior was pure player. He hadn't got serious with anyone in the two years I'd known him. Every month it was someone new: a female smorgasbord. He gave lip service to believing in marriage, but whenever I commented that his revolving-door policy wasn't the best way of finding a wife, he'd say—wink, wink—he was holding out for the perfect woman. Yeah, right.

He still hadn't returned and his laundry would be getting wrinkled, so I opened the door of his dryer and got to work. I folded sweatpants, jeans, T-shirts. Nary a designer label. Nav's clothes sense was pretty much "starving artist" even though I kept telling him about reasonably priced consignment stores that carried stylish outfits.

Into the hamper went the running shorts that showed off his lean, muscular legs and awesome butt. Faded rugby jerseys with their Cambridge red lion crest. A Cambridge man. How cool was that?

Boxer briefs. Black and navy, plain old Stanfield's. Soft cotton that hugged his private parts. Damn, it would be so much easier if my best friend was a woman.

I shouldn't be thinking about Nav's package, but the thing was, he had an excellent one. In fact, his whole bod was pretty fine, as I'd discovered bit by tempting bit. Like, when I hugged him. Or when he ran down the street for his morning jog, and I just happened to be at the window when he left. Or when he stretched up to hang my new light fixture, or hefted my new desk, or fixed the plumbing under my kitchen sink . . . No, I wasn't creating I *need a man* chores; it was just so much nicer to have his help than to figure things out on my own.

The view didn't hurt one bit, either. He had strong shoulders, firm pecs, and a breathtakingly tight butt, as well as the aforementioned package.

Which I shouldn't be thinking about. None of it. Not that, nor the drop-dead sexy English accent, nor that gorgeous skin the color of cinnamon. I should focus on the unstylish clothes, the shaggy hair that always needed a trim, the beard and mustache that hid half his face.

Even if he hadn't been my best friend, and even if he had been into marriage, Nav wouldn't be my type. I went for the polish of a successful, cosmopolitan man mixed with the edgy excitement and unpredictability of a bad boy. A man who'd grab me and kiss me senseless rather than give me a brotherly peck on the lips.

So, I was glad Nav had only done the peck thing. Of course I was. Because if he'd really kissed me, I might have kissed him back. And if we'd done that, we'd have crossed a line I had no intention of crossing.

Once, a few years ago, I'd fallen for a neighbor. When we broke up, I'd moved out of the building because I couldn't stand seeing him. I wasn't about to repeat the mistake and risk ruining the best relationship in my life.

All of which meant the size of Nav's package was utterly irrelevant to me, and no way was I going to think about it.

"Kat, what are you doing?"

I swung around, boxer briefs in my hands, to see their owner, still clad in those skimpy shorts. Fighting back a flush, I said, "Folding your laundry."

"You didn't have to do that." He tilted his head, studying me. "You're blushing."

Damn. I folded his undies and put them in his hamper. Totally casually. And lied. "I was thinking about the wedding. My family."

"Ah." He turned toward his dryer. "They really get to you." Muscles flexing in his forearms, he heaved the rest of the dry items on top of the ones I'd folded, guaranteeing wrinkles.

Distracted by his muscles, I tried to remember what he'd said. "Yeah. Isn't that what family's for?" I gave him a rueful grin. "In my family, love's unconditional, but it sure isn't nonjudgmental. There's a reason I don't visit more than every year or so."

Home was no longer the family house in Vancouver. It

was my apartment in this renovated brownstone off St. Catherine near the heart of vibrant Montreal, where I lived side by side with my best friend.

"I know exactly what you mean." He leaned against a washer, all casual male strength and grace, albeit with faded running clothes and shaggy hair. Not that I, who hadn't expected to see anyone this early in the morning, looked much better, though at least my sweats were Lululemon.

"Got another e-mail from Mum," he said, "pressuring me to move to New Delhi. Since she and Dad moved back there, they're getting more and more traditional."

"Uh-uh." I shook my head vigorously. "You're not allowed to." We'd repeated this exchange three or four times over the past year, and I knew—almost—that he'd never move. But I also realized that living in Canada was a bone of contention between him and his parents. Nav was continually getting flack for being a disrespectful son.

His face tightened, and I tensed. Surely he wasn't considering moving. My apartment, Montreal, my *life* wouldn't be the same without him.

Slowly he shook his head, his glossy black curls catching the light. "No, I won't move to India. I love my family, but having half a world between us is a good thing."

I let out the breath I'd been holding. "Great. How would I survive without you?"

"You couldn't," he teased back. Then his gaze gentled. "Kat, you'll always survive. You're a strong woman."

"Yeah, that's me. Tough girl," I joked. But he was right. I'd survived growing up in my weird family, moving to a new province, working in French, and I'd survived having my heart broken more than a dozen times. But I didn't want to have to survive being without Nav.

One of my dryers went off, and I turned to deal with my load of delicates. As I was folding things neatly, my second dryer buzzed.

Nav opened the door and hauled out a pair of cotton pants and a tee. When he started to toss them on top of my careful pile, I grabbed them out of his hands. "Thanks, but I believe in folding clothes. Unlike *some people*, I'm not overly fond of wrinkles."

One side of his mouth kinked up. "*Some people* put too much weight on appearance, material goods, all that crap."

"*Some people* like to make a good impression."

We'd long ago established that we were opposites in a lot of ways, and the appearance thing was a running joke.

I took over the folding, then glanced at my watch. "I need to get to the hotel and reorganize timelines, leave instructions for everyone, rearrange some meetings." My job was challenging, but I loved it. Loved having a key role in the team of bright, dynamic people who were determined to make Le Cachet the best hotel in Montreal.

We hefted our laundry baskets and headed for the elevator.

When we reached the third floor, I put my basket down so I could fish in my pocket for my door key. "Got a hot date tonight?" I asked.

I certainly didn't. It was only a couple weeks since I'd been dumped by my last dating mistake, Jean-Pierre. The handsome, dashing NASCAR champ had said he was seriously interested in me, and his flattery and expensive gifts told the same story. But he'd moved on—either because he was a deceptive bastard or because I'd bored him—and my heart still felt battered.

"You're asking about my love life because . . . ?" Nav raised his eyebrows.

"Thought we might get together for a late-ish dinner." After a long, hectic day at Le Cachet, it would be great to unwind with him. Besides, we should celebrate his exhibit.

He studied me for a long moment. "One of our good old

food-and-a-movie nights?" There was a strange edge to his voice.

Was he afraid I wanted another favor? "Yes, that's all. No more favors to ask, honest. If you have a date or whatever, don't cancel it."

He reflected, perhaps mentally reviewing his social calendar. Not only did he date lots of women, his breakups usually seemed to be friendly and he'd as often be grabbing coffee with an ex as dating someone new. As well, he had three or four close guy friends he hung out with.

Finally he said, "Alas, no date. No whatever."

Ridiculous to feel glad. As ridiculous as the fact that, on the mornings when I was leaving for work as he dragged home with the drained glow of a man who'd had sex all night and desperately needed sleep, it'd put me in a foul mood for the rest of the day. This business of being best friends with a cute guy could be damned complicated, but Nav was so worth it.

"I'll have to settle for you," he joked.

"Hey, watch it with the insults. I was going to bring home a bottle of champagne to celebrate your exhibit."

His chocolate eyes sparked with mischief. "In that case, I can't think of a woman in the world I'd rather spend the evening with."

I chuckled. "Oh, I'm *so* flattered. Okay, champagne it is."

"I'll pick up tourtière from Les Deux Chats."

He knew the spicy pie, a Québécois specialty, was my favorite comfort food. "I probably won't make it home until around nine. Is that okay?"

"Sure. I've got a busy day, too. Knock on the door when you get home."

"You're a doll."

Was that a grimace on his face? He'd turned away before I could get a second look.

*　*　*

It was more than twelve hours later when, pump-clad feet dragging with weariness, stomach grumbling about the hours that had passed since my lunchtime salad, I knocked at Nav's door.

He opened it, wearing gray sweatpants and a faded T-shirt with the sleeves ripped out. "Hey, Kat."

"Tired. Hungry." I sagged against his doorframe and tried not to notice his brown, well-muscled shoulders. "Long, *long* day." I held up the bag I carried. "I come bearing champagne."

"Great. Go get changed, and I'll bring the food."

I grinned. How nice it was to not have to be *on*. To relax, be myself.

After going into my apartment, I left the door unlocked for him. His place was smaller than mine and cluttered with photography gear, so we always hung out at mine.

I stripped off my business suit, shoes, and bra, and gave a head-to-toe wriggle of relief. The business day was over; time to unwind.

The June night was warm, so rather than sweats I chose a light cotton salwar kameez—a midthigh-length tunic in blues and yellows over loose, drawstring waist blue pants. Light, floaty, feminine. I'd seen Indian women wearing them in Montreal and commented to Nav.

He'd said that, according to his mother and aunties, they only fit properly if they were custom made. The next time he'd visited his family in India, he'd taken my measurements and brought me back three outfits. The clothes were so comfy and attractive, I'd become addicted.

Knuckles tapped on my bedroom door. "Dinner's ready."

"Coming."

We never ate at the small dining table tucked into the space between galley kitchen and living room. I only used it to serve elaborately prepared dinners to impress dates. In-

stead Nav and I sprawled on the couch, food and feet fighting for space on the coffee table.

I flopped down on my side of the couch, cozy and relaxed
amid the interesting furniture I'd picked up at auctions and
garage sales—woven rugs, Quebec folk art, a half dozen
flowering plants. Although this morning Nav and I had
mentioned a movie, he had put on a CD instead. One he'd
given me. Pleasant and new-agey, with piano, flute, and sitar,
it suited my mood.

As did the scent of the spicy pork pie that sat on the coffee table. Not to mention the sight of Nav carrying plates and
silverware from my kitchen. It was always a pleasure to
watch him move. A rugby player in school, a jogger now, he
had an athlete's strength and grace. Just as much as the
Olympic skier I'd once dated.

As Nav put the plates down, the spicy scent made my
tummy growl. Thank heavens he didn't avoid pork.

He'd found the bottle of champagne I'd put in the fridge.
Moët et Chandon Grand Vintage 2000 Brut. It sat unopened
on the coffee table along with two flute glasses.

"You sure you want to drink this tonight?" he asked. "It's
pretty fancy. I have a Beaujolais in my apartment."

"You deserve fancy. God, Nav, your first major exhibit.
This is big."

A quick smile flashed. "Thanks. Okay, consider my arm
twisted." He peeled off the foil, loosened the wire cage,
then, using a towel and rotating the bottle, eased the cork
out as deftly as any sommelier could have. Golden liquid
foamed into our glasses.

I lifted my glass to him. "To a huge step on your road to
success."

"To steps forward. And success." He clicked his glass to
mine.

There was something in his voice—determination, fire—

that sent a shiver, the good kind, down my spine. A man with that passion and drive would get what he wanted.

We tasted the wine and I sighed with pleasure. This champagne was one of my favorites. Fruit, honey, yeast, a touch of spice. Fresh, rich, elegant. Perfect for a celebration. And speaking of which . . .

I raised my glass once more. "And here's to M&M as well. May they have a long, very happy, life together." I knew they would. They'd been joined at the hip since they were seven and were each other's most loyal supporter.

Nav drank that toast, too. "This is great wine, Kat."

I suspected he'd rarely, if ever, drunk such an expensive one. He refused to discuss finances—and always fought me for the check—yet it was clear he lived on a shoestring budget. "Glad you like it." Hopefully his exhibit would be a huge success, and he'd finally be able to afford some of the better things in life.

"Awfully fancy for a quiet night at home with a buddy and a plate of tourtière, though."

Maybe so, but tonight everything seemed just right. "Nav, this is perfect. Coming home to food, music. You look after me like, oh, a 1950s housewife."

He had leaned over to cut the pie and there was an odd tone to his voice when he said, "That's what friends are for." When he glanced up, however, his face wore its usual quiet smile, half hidden by his mustache and beard.

"I really wish you'd shave," I said for the zillionth time. I was dying to know what his face really looked like under all that curly black hair. With it, he was round faced and youthful, cute more than handsome. Of course, perhaps he was disguising a weak chin or acne scars.

"You're too obsessed with appearance." He came back with his usual response as he handed me a plate with a hearty serving of tourtière.

He dished some out for himself, and we both dug in.

"Have a good day at the office, dear?" he asked in a saccharine-sweet voice.

I looked up to see a twinkle in his eyes. He was playing off my housewife comment.

"Cute." I wrinkled my nose. "My day was stressful. Leaving on short notice is hard."

"And so is thinking about Merilee getting married." Nav's hand brushed my bare forearm. No doubt he meant it as a comforting gesture, but it felt almost like a caress, sending a quick thrill through me, of recognition, of . . . arousal. Damn.

His hand dropped away, reached for his glass, and I shivered, banishing the sensation.

"I know you want the same thing yourself," he said. "Yet you keep dating men who are . . ." He shrugged.

"I know, I know. I have the worst luck."

"You go for, uh, pretty dramatic men."

That was true. "I can't help who I'm attracted to." Attraction of opposites was normal. I was such an average person. Not brilliant like my parents and my one-year-older sister Theresa, not gorgeous like my one-year-younger sister Jenna. It made sense I'd be drawn to men who were amazing. And when one of those men was attracted to me, it blew me away.

A humorless grin quirked Nav's mouth. "Too true."

Said him, who was attracted to someone new each month. "And, unlike you," I said, "I date seriously." To me, it was a waste of time to date casually. I only went out with men I could imagine a future with. "I want a forever guy."

"And you think these men you hook up with are forever guys?"

Obviously none had turned out that way. "When I met them I thought so." Which only proved I was a bad judge of character, or didn't have what it took to hold their interest and keep them faithful.

"Why?"

"Because I'm an optimist." I sounded a bit snappish, but I was sensitive about this. I was used to my family joking about my crappy taste and the jinx thing, but did Nav have to pick on me, too? Usually he was good about offering a shoulder to cry on, sans judgment. Why was he acting different tonight?

"I know, Kat, and that's a great quality. But you also need some common sense. You meet Olympic Guy or NASCAR Guy, and suddenly you're crazy about them and thinking in terms of forever. What is it about them? Or is it less about them and more about you being so desperate to get married?"

"I'm not *desperate*, damn it. Just because I want to be married and you don't—"

"I do. I just don't—"

"Yeah, sure, I know." Maybe in five or ten years. His current revolving-door policy was so *not* aimed at finding a wife.

"I'm sorry I said that," he said gently. "I know you're not desperate. But maybe when you look at those guys, you see what you want to see. A prospective husband. Rather than what's really in front of your eyes."

Was he right? Damn, this was heading into pop psych self-analysis, the kind of stuff that, in my humble opinion, only made people depressed.

When my family trotted out the old stuff about my rotten taste, and me being a relationship jinx, I always tried to brush it aside. It hurt too much to think that my dating life consisted of attracting either losers or dynamite guys who quickly tired of me.

God, I hated this introspective stuff. "Let's watch a movie."

Normally, Nav would comply, but tonight he said, "Don't feel like it."

At least he changed the topic of conversation. "Have you booked the train yet?" he asked, holding the pie plate toward me and offering me the last serving of tourtière.

His muscular arm was even more tempting than the pie. I shook my head firmly. "No, thanks. And yes, I booked this morning."

He dished the pie onto his plate. "What's your plan?"

I rattled off my timetable for the tenth time today. "Work Monday morning, then the three forty train to Toronto. It gets in around eight thirty, and I'll stay at the Royal York across from the train station. Then I'm on the morning train to Vancouver, arriving there first thing Friday."

"I hope you meet one or two fascinating people." There was an odd note in his voice, but he was looking down at his plate, and that shaggy hair made it so hard to read his expression.

Speaking of that hair, and his general appearance . . . Earlier today, I'd e-mailed my sister Theresa and told her I was bringing Nav as a wedding date. Claiming bragging rights, I'd described him as good looking and successful. Which he was, in his way.

His career was taking off, and I was thrilled for him. Now it was time he dressed for success. For being a flauntable wedding date, too.

For us, discussions about appearance had been a running joke, a stalemate. How could I now get him to listen?

I swallowed the last bite and put my empty plate on the coffee table. "By the way," I said casually, "do you own a suit?" I'd never seen him in one, but didn't every guy have a suit?

His lips curved, then smoothed out. "For the wedding? I can manage something."

Given what I'd seen of his taste in clothes, I hated to think what he might *manage*. "Hmm." I chewed my lip. Could I possibly persuade Nav to let me buy him a classy suit? No, not the guy who fought me for pizza bills.

I respected male pride, but damn it, this was about my pride, too. He needed a makeover before he met my family. They were rough on dates. I'd yet to bring a man home they approved of, and Nav's scruffy appearance would be a big strike against him.

Maybe if I bought a suit and had it delivered, and there was no receipt that would let him return it . . . Still trying to act casual, I asked, "What size are you, anyhow?"

GREAT BOOKS,
GREAT SAVINGS!

When You Visit Our Website:
www.kensingtonbooks.com
You Can Save Money Off The Retail Price
Of Any Book You Purchase!

- **All Your Favorite Kensington Authors**
- **New Releases & Timeless Classics**
- **Overnight Shipping Available**
- **eBooks Available For Many Titles**
- **All Major Credit Cards Accepted**

Visit Us Today To Start Saving!
www.kensingtonbooks.com

All Orders Are Subject To Availability.
Shipping and Handling Charges Apply.
Offers and Prices Subject To Change Without Notice.